"... everything we want in an action hero."
—*Booklist*

"... a secret agent who takes you into the danger zone with a ballsy wit that had me hooked."
—Vince Flynn

He's a razor-sharp new thriller hero—
a James Bond for the 21st century!

ACCLAIM FOR THE ALEX HAWKE
THRILLERS BY
NEW YORK TIMES BESTSELLING AUTHOR

TED BELL

PIRATE

"*Pirate* is a heck of a good ride."

—*Houston Chronicle*

"Bell concocts a rollicking tale ripped from the disturbing headlines of our dangerous times. . . . Anyone who has been savvy enough to follow the saga thus far will find in the pages of *Pirate* not only a finer-tuned Hawke but an author who has clearly mastered his trade. The ingenious subplots gel seamlessly."

—NewsMax.com

"The third and best of the Hawke novels . . . contain[s] more action and interesting characters than most books do in three. . . . Bell easily could be considered the rightful heir to the throne of Robert Ludlum. . . . *Pirate* and its predecessors are unbeatable."

—Bookreporter.com

Spy is also available from Simon & Schuster Audio and as an eBook

ASSASSIN

"Intrigue you can sink your teeth into. . . ."

—Vince Flynn

"Fast and furious. . . . Readers will be caught in the whirlwind of action and find themselves having a grand old time."

—*Publishers Weekly*

"Fascinating characters, a hairpin plot, and wonderfully talented writing. *Assassin* is what you get when you pair a great story with a great writer."

—Brian Haig

"Hawke . . . is smart, resourceful, attractive—everything we want in an action hero. . . . Readers will be enthralled."

—*Booklist*

"I love authors like Clancy, Ludlum, and Flynn. Ted Bell is in that league. His research is so amazing you'd swear the events in the book actually took place. And here's the scary part—they could."

—Glenn Beck, host of *CNN Headline Prime* and author of *The Real America*

"*Assassin* is the most highly imaginative thriller to come along in a long while."

—James Patterson

HAWKE

One of Library Journal*'s Best First Novels of 2003*

"A fiery tale of power and privilege, lusty and sinister intrigue, Hawke is a fast-paced adventure . . . truly an exciting read!"

—Nelson DeMille

SPY

A Thriller

TED BELL

POCKET STAR BOOKS

NEW YORK   LONDON   TORONTO   SYDNEY

Pocket Star Books
A Division of Simon & Schuster, Inc.
1230 Avenue of the Americas
New York, NY 10020

This book is a work of fiction. Names, characters, places, and incidents are products of the author's imagination or are used fictitiously. Any resemblance to actual events or locales or persons living or dead is entirely coincidental.

First Pocket Star Books paperback edition August 2007

POCKET STAR and colophon are registered trademarks of Simon & Schuster, Inc.

For information regarding special discounts for bulk purchases, please contact Simon & Schuster Special Sales at 1-800-456-6798 or business@simonandschuster.com.

Jacket design by Shasti O'Leary Soudant
Photo illustration by Jae Song

Manufactured in the United States of America

10 9 8 7 6 5 4 3 2 1

ISBN-13: 978-0-7432-7724-2
ISBN-10:   0-7432-7724-4

With love, for Page Lee

"A border ain't nothin' but a law drawn in the sand."

—*Sheriff Franklin W. Dixon*
Prairie, Texas

Paul J. Pugliese GCI

SPY

PROLOGUE

The human target clawed up the mud-slick walls of the Xingu River; slipping, sliding, desperate. He heaved himself upon the bank, where he collapsed facedown and lay gasping. After a few minutes, his face half-submerged in a puddle of brackish water, he managed to roll over onto his back. The red equatorial sun flamed directly overhead, achingly bright. When he squeezed his eyes shut, it was doubly painful; one burning red orb scorched each eyelid.

The drums began again.

Kill you. Kill you.

The two-note drumbeat was growing louder, he thought. His fevered mind was no longer really sure of anything. Louder meant closer. Yes. His tormenters were still gaining, coming ever nearer. Just across the river now, were they? He pulled his bare and bloody knees up against his chest and wrapped his thin arms round them, trying to curve himself into a ball. His muscles screamed in protest.

He covered his face with his hands, allowing himself

for a moment the childish hope that he might just curl up and disappear.

Kill you. Kill—

Magically, the drums had stopped. The Indians had stopped at the river! Turned back, for some mysterious reason. Retreated into the jungle thicket. Or, perhaps he'd only slept and the drums had ceased while he was unconscious. He was never sure anymore, really. Modes of existence merged seamlessly. Reality had become unreal. Was he running? Or, dreaming of running? Awake? Asleep? Daydreaming of sleep? It was all one and the same blur.

A plaintive howl had startled a dozen or so lime-colored birds chirruping in the trees above him. They instantly flew away. Odd. The wavering cry seemed to have sprung from his own lips. But, had it?

He knew he had at last reached the nadir. His captor had succeeded in turning him into a howling monkey. A low groan escaped him as he dug into the muck with both hands. Scooping up handfuls of the slimy gruel, he slathered a thin paste of cool mud onto his arms, his burning cheeks, eyelids, and forehead. It afforded him some small measure of relief.

After months in captivity, the man's skin was preternaturally pale. His waxy, deathlike appearance was accentuated by chronic dysentery and the resulting loss of blood. The man was naturally fair, and black-haired. Now his hair was long, falling in a wild tangle, and his nearly translucent skin was a delicate alabaster. After long months in the eternal semi-darkness, his once startling blue eyes had faded to a dull, whitish shade.

The present nightmare had begun months ago. Perhaps six months, perhaps more. He might well have lost track at some point. Slipped his moorings, crossing the bar. He no longer had any sense of time. Besides, what did it matter, when every day was a monotony of hunger and pain? He sometimes longed for some fresh hell to lift him out of the current one. The Indian drums had put paid to that foolish desire.

Since the ill-fated morning his "scientific" expedition had first met disaster on the river, and the subsequent personal trials he had endured in the jungle, the tall, gaunt white man had been living in a world of almost continual darkness. He had not been tossed into some underground dungeon where no light filtered through. His prison bars were made not of iron, but of wood.

The terrorists' slave labor camps were deep within the rain forest. He had spent his days and nights beneath trees the likes of which he'd never seen. At their very top, some two hundred feet over his head, these impossibly vibrant organisms formed a nearly solid canopy of green. Even in the brightness of noon, only trickles of watery sunlight ever filtered down into his great green prison. The absolute gloom of the place, at all hours of the day, was nearly unimaginable.

Alone in the pit, his mind would drift to a treasured book from a boyhood long ago, the story of an innocent man likewise imprisoned in a world of darkness for crimes he had not committed.

I am lost, the hero of his book had said, a kindred spirit alone with his shadows. The book's title now slid into his mind. It was so perfect a description of his current circumstances as to be almost laughable.

Darkness at Noon.

The runaway's scruffy, lice-infested black beard reached well below his sternum. His wild black hair, which fell to his waist, was tied with a strip of canvas into a tail at the back of his head. He was, as the old expression had it, skin and bones. He knew he would be unrecognizable should he miraculously chance upon a sliver of broken mirror, or, in his wildest moments of delusion, some familiar soul.

His only clock was an occasional glimpse of the moon. He had seen, he guessed, at least six full ones. He had lived, by this lunar reckoning, for more than half a year in a place where life was sometimes cheap but more often worthless. In the foul hovel where he slept and slaved, the solid canopy of trees kept his entire camp completely hidden from the sky.

He hated every waking hour but most of all he loathed the temperature drop at nightfall. The pitch-black nights were spent in a cold hell that had nothing to do with sleep, peace, or dreams. His home, before he'd managed to escape, had been a shallow pit, a dank hole he'd shared with others of his ilk, men whose names he did not know. At the bottom of his pit, where he slept and ate and defecated, was a foetid pool of water. It was bone-cold in that pit.

At night, a makeshift thatch of palm kept most of the vampire bats away. But not all.

During his captivity, he had managed to close his eyes for only three or perhaps four hours per night.

Mosquitoes stabbed at flesh rather than biting it, and swooping vampire bats seemed to favor a spot just below his right earlobe. It made sleep impossible.

Each new day, which varied only slightly from the night before it, he and his bleak companions were awakened with buckets of cold water dumped into their pit. Then they were hauled up bleary-eyed and shivering with short lengths of hemp. Miserable souls all, they were formed up into rectangular squads for roll call and marched en masse out to the work sites at gunpoint.

There were many pits such as his. And there were probably many more such camps nearby. A vast army of laborers and soldiers was assembling. To what end, he could not say, for he had only the vaguest notions about what went on beyond his immediate perimeter. He was desperate to learn what engine powered this vast machine, but to enquire would be to risk a quick, brutal death.

Curiosity had nearly killed him once already.

During the day, toiling with his machete or his shovel, he heard the constant chatter of automatic weapons. Explosions ripped the jungle floor, sending plumes of dirt and green debris skyward. Gunfire was his perpetual soundtrack. The guns never stopped. At night, when the prisoners had their weekly bath at the river, he saw tracer rounds arc across the sky, and shells bloom and thud, hammering the air. He never knew why. He didn't know who was shooting. Nor who was being shot. Nor, after a while, did he much care.

The cannons shattered the insect hum of nature.

The jungle thrummed with background music of an inspired composer, punctuated by gunfire.

There were guerrilla soldiers everywhere. They trained at jungle warfare day and night. They used huge flaming torches mounted atop bamboo poles to continue firing rounds, into the small hours. He'd once caught a glimpse of a small village of hollow buildings and fake-fronted houses. He saw men firing from empty windows and leaping over walls. The soldiers were training for urban warfare as well.

His work gang was dedicated to road construction. The gang was constructing a simple limestone causeway in the jungle. A road to nowhere. This rough-hewn road had no beginning and no end. It just was. It simply disappeared into the jungle. No one knew where the highway led. And no one except he seemed to care.

The highway meant something. It was part of a plan. He wanted to know. He meant to find out.

He was a natural spy. And, being curious by nature, the man kept his eyes and ears open, day and night. He had no end of material to record. He would have killed, truly, for a pencil stub, a secret journal, even scraps of paper. But of course there were no pencils and no paper available to him. He watched and listened and tried to retain what he could in the faint hope that he might survive.

He had heard it whispered that his section of limestone road eventually led north past the great falls at Diablo Blanco. Before his capture, he had been in Africa. These Amazonian waterfalls, it was said, made the towering Victoria Falls in Zimbabwe look like a spring torrent. The local Indian laborers whom he sometimes worked alongside called White Devil Falls "the smoke that thunders." Sometimes, when the roaring guns went silent, you could hear that thunder.

One talkative prisoner, a young Belizean named Machado, told him of plans to escape upriver to an outpost river town called Barcelos. Machado had a beautiful, open face, with startling green eyes. His strange looks reflected the remarkable ethnic mix of his native country. Machado told him that he was Garifunas, a blend of African slaves and indigenous Caribbean islanders. Also in his family tree, he said, were Spaniards, British, and Asians.

One night in the camp pits, when the guard had left them alone, Machado confided that this outpost was the most dangerous place on earth. But, if you could reach it alive, you could make your way downriver to Manaus. He was naturally curious about such a place and wanted to ask Machado more about it. One day he found himself breaking rock next to the young fellow who planned to escape to Barcelos.

"Why is it so dangerous there?" he whispered in his broken Spanish to the boy, taking a chance while the guards snoozed in the midday heat. Machado proudly wore a ragged T-shirt that said *You Better Belize It!*

"It's the crossroads of evil, señor," the boy whispered. "The Black Jungle."

"Someone stands at this crossroads?" he asked.

"The Devil."

"Who is this devil?"

"The devil himself, I tell you, or his representative."

"Does this devil have a name?"

"Devil. That's all."

"Where can I find this fellow, whoever he is?"

"You desire an intercession with the dead?"

"Something like that."

"You will find the devil standing at the crossroads where the spirits cross over into our world."

The boy would say no more.

He knew, he had learned the hard way, that it was unwise to be caught speaking and he surely didn't care to draw attention to himself. So, after this exchange with Machado, he kept his head down and his mouth shut. He cleared jungle with his machete and he built his bloody road all day and silently planned his own escape. In this, he knew he was by no means unique.

He was but one of numberless hundreds, maybe thousands, of unwilling captives, an enslaved workforce in the service of some unseen and unknown power. All he knew for certain now was that another universe existed here in this green hell, a complex hive of relentless activity, at least a thousand miles inland from the mouth of the Amazon. And all of it lay hidden from civilization's prying eyes.

Roads were being built. Airstrips too. Armies were being trained here and the gunfire was incessant. Everyone lived and worked and died under the canopy. From what little he'd seen, he doubted this was a force for good.

He'd seen horrible things. Slow starvation. Wanton punishment. Men shot on the spot for no reason. A hand or a foot chopped off on a whim. An untouchable, crashing through the jungle, his naked body a mass of blood blisters. He was still screaming when he disappeared into the vast green hills. No one would come near him. The virus, someone said, they were working on a new virus.

The untouchables lived in the white building across the river. The medical compound. He'd never seen it but he heard about it. Patients who checked in never checked out. Terrible things were said to happen across the river. At night, when it was still, you could hear things. Things you didn't want to hear.

All this, he imagined, somehow led directly to the man who stood at the crossroads. The devil the boy had spoken of. It was he who had arranged the ambush of the expedition, killed his companions, and captured him. He knew the monster's true identity. His name was Muhammad Top. Top, who made sure there were many days when the man wished he'd been lucky and gone down with his friends.

That night, it was whispered in the pits that a boy had been shot trying to escape. He asked the name, but he already knew it. The one friend he'd made. Machado.

Many days he felt so alone he dropped to his knees on the jungle floor and prayed to God to let him die.

1

He had never expected to survive the sinking of his boat. The river had been a quiet mirror that morning, meandering through the endless jungle. Just before the explosion, the leafy green walls on either side of the river had fallen silent. Then a lone bird cried a shrill warning and the peace was suddenly shattered. A sea mine blew the bow off his beautiful black-hulled wooden yawl. The powerful explosion rocked the jungle; the sky above the river suddenly went dark with birds taking wing.

He knew his lovely *Pura Vida* was finished before he drew a second breath.

Pura Vida, the pretty yawl he'd fitted with a retractable keel, had shuddered to a stop, down by the head. She instantly began taking water. She had sunk with nearly all hands in minutes. Small-arms fire erupted from the forest. The river was alive with death. Unseen forces began spitting bullets from both banks. A chorus of fear rose from those choking and dying in the water. The machine-gun attack killed everyone clinging to overturned life rafts or desperately scrambling up the muddy banks.

He himself had been fishing off the stern, his legs dangling over the gunwale. When he heard the explosion for'ard, and felt the yawl stagger and founder, he dove for a semi-automatic rifle kept loaded and stowed in the cockpit. Water rising round his legs, he emptied the thirty-round banana clip into the forest. When it was empty, he slammed in another mag and repeated firing off the port side.

He threw life rings, cushions, whatever he could grab. It was useless. He saw his colleagues in the water, many already dead or dying in a rain of lead. The ship was engulfed in flames and listing violently to port. Staying aboard another second was suicide.

He dove off the sharply angled stern and swam hard downriver, until his lungs, too, were afire. He surfaced and heard that the firing had stopped. Many riddled bodies were floating downstream toward him. That was when he heard the drums for the first time.

He saw painted faces atop long brown legs sprinting madly through the tangled undergrowth along the banks. He submerged once more and grabbed someone whose arm he'd seen flailing weakly minutes earlier. He pulled her to him and saw that she was dead. He held on to the corpse for a very long time. He was entering a patch of white water and he had no choice but to let his friend go if he was to swim safely to shore.

Her name was Dana Gibbon.

He grabbed an overhanging branch and watched the beautiful woman's body drift away with the river. Her head was submerged but one arm was still draped around a piece of debris from *Pura Vida*. Dana had been a brilliant young marine biologist from the University of Miami. She'd been doing her thesis on the Rio Negro. At night on deck, they had sipped *mojitos* and played gin rummy. He never won a hand. And he'd kissed her only once.

Dana's body was lost in a tumult of white water and then she disappeared.

Shortly after Dana's loss, a chance river encounter with a water boa, an anaconda nearly thirty feet long, had left him with a crippling wound to his right hip. The untreated injury became infected. He was no longer able to run. Couldn't run, and he couldn't hide. It was this circumstance that finally led to his first capture.

For some reason, the Indians who originally caught him had not killed him on the spot. He was a healthy specimen if you discounted his wound. He stood over six feet and was very fit. He supposed that was his salvation. He looked fit for work. He was blindfolded and dragged through the jungle to be sold to the highest bidder.

He was sold to Wajari, a great chief of the Xucuru who guarded one of the work camps for Muhammad Top. Top learned he'd been captured. The first night he'd been dragged from the camp and nearly interrogated to death by Papa Top. Somehow, he convinced his interrogator that he was a British scientist and not a spy. Shortly thereafter, he was sent back to the camps to do slave work for the guerrilla armies. There, it was assumed, he would die of natural causes.

His role at the camp was one with an extremely low life expectancy. He was not good at following rules. Now, in addition to his road construction, he was part of a doomed brigade used day and night as human targets.

He'd offended a guard by not responding quickly enough to an unintelligible order. The man had struck him on the side of the head with the butt of his gun, knocking him to his knees. He'd gotten to his feet, his blood up, and grabbed the man by the neck. When the man spat in his face, he'd disarmed him and nearly beaten him to death with his bare fists. No one even bothered to watch. It was over in a minute or two.

He stood glaring at them, taunting the guards with their automatic rifles leveled at his heart, waiting for one of them to kill him on the spot. Two of them grabbed him from behind and bound his wrists behind him with hemp. Then they took him away.

Only Machado wished him farewell. "Go with God," the boy said.

"You better Belize it!" he said to the boy as they dragged him away to the camp commandant's tent.

His punishment was swift and typical. After two nights in a hellish device called the Barrel, he had been assigned to what the guards jokingly referred to as the Green Berets. This joke derived from the fact that new initiates had their heads dipped in a vat of green dye. The Green Berets were a group of condemned men sent into the jungle for target practice.

The tactical commanders for guerrilla combat training in the dense jungle had devised this system to pro-

vide a more realistic experience for their young guerrilla
fighters. The need for fresh targets was never ending.
Most were killed by live fire. Mines or sniper bullets
felled others. A few committed suicide to end the
agony, and a tiny fraction escaped.

HE HAD ESCAPED. He had done it by melting away
during a live-fire exercise with many other fleeing targets. He had found his spot, stopped, clutched his gut,
and screamed as if mortally wounded. He then
dropped into the shallow water of a muddy stream. He
waited for five minutes and no one came. He started
crawling, later swimming as the water deepened. He
swam to where the stream joined a wide green river. He
rolled over to his back and let the water take him away.
The sun broke from behind a cloud. His face broke
into a wide grin: go with the flow.

In this environment escape was a relative term. He
had been on the run for five days and nights. He had
even less food than he'd been provided with in the
camp. Beetles and grubs became a staple. He was exhausted, dehydrated, and on the brink of starvation.

On the sixth day, he could not get to his feet. And
the drums were getting louder. Willing panic to sub-
side, he rested quietly on his back for a few moments,
hidden by the thick reeds, his emaciated chest heaving.
His head suddenly jerked spasmodically to one side.
He'd heard something, indistinct, but nevertheless
disturbing.

After survival as a living target, his ears were keenly
attuned to any variation in jungle sound. He gently

placed a hand palm down on a patch of dry ground, a recently acquired method of detecting hostile vibrations.

A tremor, a snapping twig, or a parrot's sudden shriek might herald the approach of a war party.

Indian headhunters, elite centurions of a murderous cannibal tribe called the Xucuru, had been chasing him since his miraculous escape. He was weak, he knew, to the point of utter exhaustion. He'd slept, but only fitfully, and always with his ear to the ground.

Nothing of significant note, however, now reached his ears. An earlier sound, which had resembled the thrum of a small marine motor, must have been just the sound of his own blood thrumming in his skull. No, there was no motor. No tourist boat full of saviors headed upriver to rescue him and deprive the Xucuru warriors of their evening meal. The tourist idea was admittedly laughable. No tourist boat ever ventured this far upriver. Sane men seldom did.

He would die alone, but not wanting for company. The irony of the jungle. There was too much of everything. Too much vibrant existence, too much life, too much death. He felt it in his bones: the cellular activity of jungle life humming at every conceivable level.

Some of the worst life-forms were in the river.

He'd been drifting with the currents. The wide, olive-green river had been his refuge for two long days. He'd tied leafy branches to his head, arms, and upper body, hoping to blend with the half-submerged logs and floating vegetation on the river. The silvery piranha hadn't bothered him, mercifully. Nor had the candiru, an eel-like fish that swims up any available human orifice. That was the one that terrified him most.

A young member of his expedition had been standing in the river, the water just above his knees, urinating. A week later, he died in feverish agony. A candiru had swum up the boy's urine stream and become lodged in his penis. There, feeding on the host's blood, the tiny creature had grown to enormous size. The resulting infection led to the amputation of the organ and the boy's painful death.

He rolled onto one elbow and pushed the reeds aside so he could see the river.

The Xucuru warriors chasing him since his escape from the compound would not let something like a river stop them. In his mind's eye, lying on the bank, he could see the savages racing through the jungle, their naked bodies slathered with streaks of black and red paint, their seven-foot bows and five-foot arrows, their clubs, their blowpipes, and their spears. All would have sworn the blood oath not to return without his head.

It was widely rumored amongst the prisoners in the camps that no one had ever really escaped. The Xucuru warriors hired by the soldiers were relentless in their pursuit of escapees. They would much rather die by each other's hands than return empty-handed.

Keep moving, his urgent mind told his wasted body. Wait, the body replied. Wait!

Five minutes.

Please.

Yes. Do nothing. Surely there was time to lie here on the banks of the Xingu to be warmed by the sun. How sorely he'd missed its warmth. To relax for a time, let the skin and bones dry out. He let his muscles go, digging his fingers into the soft mud beneath him. He felt his mind start to slip, and wondered if the sudden shivering was malarial. If yes, without the malaria pills they'd taken from him, he would surely die. How could one be so cold and yet so hot at the same instant?

The sun was just another brutal enemy. Once he'd regained some strength, he'd have to drag himself back inside the trees, else the harsh rays would soon fry his flesh. He was nearly as naked as the men who chased him. He was dressed only in what remained of the rags he'd escaped in.

He slept.

And awoke some time later to swarms of piums, clouds of invisible microscopic monsters, which attacked him mercilessly. They left smears of blood where they bit, blood that could attract the piranhas when and if he returned to the river. Fully awake now, for a time, he considered the pleasures to be had in simply dying. Cessation of hunger and pain. Peace. It would be so easy to give in.

His reserves were nil. In captivity, the daily battle to survive had taken its toll, left him depleted in body and mind. He was tired and desperately hungry now. He groaned loudly and fought the urge to sleep again. Hadn't he just slept? How long? A minute? An hour? More? He had no idea.

Around him, the animals of the daylight, too, were noisily preparing for sleep. The nocturnal creatures, their omnivorous appetites whetted, were beginning to stir. The air was suddenly cool. The sun fell suddenly in these latitudes and left behind a sky of cobalt blue and vermilion against which the black palms marching along the riverbank were silhouetted.

High above the treetops, a small cloud, lit from within like a Venetian lantern, hovered above the dark sea of trees. It was really all so very beautiful here. This twilight hour was like some faint memory of love; or fading dreams of happier childhood times. He closed his eyes and tried to hold these comforting images, but they skittered away, leaving a vacuum that delirium could slide into unobserved.

He fixed his pale eyes on the waning yellow moon and wondered if he had the strength of soul to survive.

For not the first time in his life, death looked good.

Alexander Hawke, dreaming of peace, finally slipped into the waiting arms of a coldly beckoning Morpheus.

2

Hawke's vivid dreams were filled not with beauty but with looming images of death and horror. During his long months in captivity, he had become a new man. Different, and, he thought, during those periods when he felt rational, not necessarily better. He had seen true evil up close on a daily basis. For most of his life he'd refused to shake hands with the devil. Now, he felt they were on a first-name basis.

The inhumanity he'd witnessed in the terror-training camps was of a different order of magnitude from anything he'd ever experienced before. In the waning days of the first Gulf War, young Royal Navy Flight Lieutenant Alexander Hawke had been flying close air support at low altitude over Baghdad. His airplane had been blown out of the sky by an Iraqi missile battery and both he and his weapons officer had been captured within the hour. It had been a most unpleasant experience. Yet even his brutal Iraqi jailers had shied away from the kind of cruel savagery he'd witnessed in the jungle camps.

He'd always suspected that men with absolute power were capable of absolutely anything. Now he knew that old axiom to be true. He felt weakened by the sureness of this belief, diminished by his new knowledge. Which was strange. Alex Hawke had always lived by the rule that what did not kill him only made him stronger. But Hawke did not feel strengthened by what he'd seen in the jungle.

He only felt colder.

Colder and harder.

The stars and bit players of these past episodes in captivity haunted his nightmares. In his malarial state, they crowded his waking hours as well. He would see a figure standing in a clearing, beckoning him; blink, and they would be gone. The thin line between nightmare and reality was becoming dangerously blurred. What was he really made of? What was he truly capable of? He didn't know anymore.

The drums were silent. Perhaps the Xucuru had moved on. Missed him, somehow. He was conscious of a strange new sensation. Hope.

Now, lying hidden in his bed of reeds beside the river, edging toward consciousness, he was suddenly sure of one thing. There could be no surrender. Not now. Not yet. He must have slept all night, because he felt just a hint of the old vigor as he struggled awake.

No, not quite yet, old fellow, the narrator of dreams was saying in the background. Feverish and shivering, he allowed himself to drift upward, float into the conscious green realm of heat and jungle. The sun was up, fierce, reflecting off the brown surface of the river and the extravaganza of colors that comprised his forest. He rubbed his neck just below the ear, and his hand came away sticky. A vampire bat had nipped him during the night.

Blood, he thought looking at the smear on his palm. He smiled at the bright red oxygenated sight of it. He was probably infected, and probably dying of septicemia, but by God he was still alive. He had one chance, he thought, small as it might be. One last chance to escape.

You better Belize it.

There was a way, he thought now, sitting up in his bed of reeds, that the doomed expedition he'd led could be remembered as a success. If he could just put his current predicament in the correct perspective, he could argue that this one man, the lone survivor of an expedition purportedly launched to find El Dorado, the Lost City of the Amazon, had succeeded beyond his wildest dreams.

What he had discovered could prove to be vastly more valuable than some fabled city of gold. If he could survive to tell the tale.

He stood up, stretched his limbs. He was free. He had work to do. Yes. He was determined to survive long enough to raise an alarm about things he had witnessed. Evil was spawning under the perfect cover of the canopy. Even in his own span of captivity, he had sensed its insidious monstrosity. A force for terror was growing like some cancerous being, its tentacles reaching deep into the vast uncharted Amazon Basin, unseen and unchecked. Somehow, he had to live long enough to tell this story.

A howler monkey screamed just inches above his head and snapped him back to what now passed for reality. He froze. A lone jaguar was circling nearby, his nose in the air. Hawke would easily die right here if he didn't act fast and with something akin to rational thought. One needed to prioritize at times like this; that's what his stint in the military had taught him about survival in hostile environments.

Hawke did just that.

One, keep breathing. Two, fashion some kind of weapon. Three, get to an outpost on the river. Get help.

A telephone. That's what he needed. For that, he had to reach the nearest sizable river village. He had used the stars last night, making a rough calculation as to where he was. He believed the nearest outpost would be Cuiaba, a few days' river travel to the east. It was hardly civilization but it would do for now.

He would need a sharpened bamboo spear. And a canoe. He'd learned their simple construction watching the Indians build them in the camps. He would find and kill a tapir. With their short limbs, the small piglike mammals were easy to catch. Yes, first track and kill a tapir with his spear. Stretch its skin over a bamboo frame and build some kind of small canoe. Yes.

He shaded his eyes, peering over his stand of reeds, scanning the river in both directions for any sign of the Xucuru. Nothing. Only the indolent flow. The glare off the sun-flecked water was paralyzing, making his eyes red and watery. He needed to get out of the sun and find his tapir, build his boat. He felt dizzy and wanted to lie down again but there was no time for that. He must hurry.

His mind raced ahead of his body as he made preparations to move on.

He told himself he would be safe when his canoe reached Cuiaba. They would give him the pills for his fever. They would bandage his seeping wound. He would eat something other than roots and worms. He would dine on roast lamb and sleep once more in a feather bed. He would see friendly faces once more. He needed—damn mosquitoes!—he needed to get out of the blistering heat or he'd soon pass out again and then his goose would be well and truly cooked.

He managed to stagger a few steps through the deep mud and once more he was safely under the green umbrella. Gathering strength from some resource deep inside, he moved quickly through the tall thicket. He could see the bend in the river curving away. He had an eye peeled for a lone dugout, the inevitable Xucuru scout traveling in advance of the war party searching for him.

He made his plans for the possibility of survival. He would hide by day. He would fashion some kind of torch and travel by night. He would track and kill his tapir and eat its flesh. With its skin, he would build his canoe. When the sun fell, he'd return to the river and civilization.

That, at least, was the plan.

BY MIDDAY, with the sweat pouring off him, and the subsequent chills, Alex Hawke had accomplished most of his objectives. He had eaten raw tapir with gusto.

He'd built a respectable canoe, light and easy to portage. He desperately wanted to keep moving while there was still some light but he found he was completely spent and could do no more. The fever had overtaken him again.

The green world was spinning and he feared he might fall, and perhaps slip into unconsciousness in an exposed or unprotected location. He quickly found a spot where he could remain hidden but still see the river. There he made himself as comfortable as he could under the shade of his newly built canoe. He needed rest, now, sleep.

As he drifted off, he imagined, or perhaps heard, the drumbeat mounting steadily in the jungle. It came to him as a repeating two-syllable beat, high-low, high-low. Slipping down to an uneasy slumber, he thought it sounded like *kill you . . . kill you . . . kill you . . .*

HIS REST was cut short by disturbing sounds on the river. His eyes popped open to see the sun still burning high above. He hadn't slept long. Someone was coming. He sat bolt upright, instantly aware of the danger. He groped for his spear but couldn't find it. Had he left it leaning against the base of the tree where he'd collapsed for a moment? No? He must have done so. He must have—

It wasn't a lone scout in a dugout canoe.

It was a sleek black jet boat from one of the camps with a fifty-caliber machine gun mounted atop a squat tower at the stern. The twin jet drives were bubbling beneath the transom, moving the patrol boat forward at little more than idle speed. Besides the skipper at the helm and the gunner on the stern, there were two men in jungle camo on the bow, one sweeping a submachine gun from side to side and the other holding a bullhorn.

The bullhorn was calling his name.

Hawke! Hawke! Hawke!

So. They had somehow learned his name.

He had no time to ponder that. From the jungle upriver, came an even more dreadful sound. It was the sound of fierce wild howling he'd heard late at night in the camps whenever someone tried to escape. It was the sound of the fighting dogs the guards kept for their protection and amusement.

They'd loosed the damned dogs on him, the dogs and the dark hooded ones who came in the middle of the night. Stood like ghosts above your pit.

"Las Medianoches," Hawke said, whispering the name of every Brazilian child's nightmare, and then he climbed to his feet and ran for his life. *Medianoches . . .* the word meant "middle of the night." For that's when the real monsters came out to play.

He ran in wild desperation. He ran well past the frontiers of exhaustion, deep into uncharted territories of pain. He knew he could not run much longer. The howling dogs were on his heels and he drove himself blindly through the dense jungle, tripping, falling, knowing it was useless even as he pumped his knees and tore through the thick undergrowth and looping vines.

Creepers reached out for his bare and bloodied feet, thorny vines lacerated his face and shoulders and arms.

His mouth was a ragged hole from which no sound issued but hoarse breathing and an occasional curse when he stumbled.

Hawke knew he was already a dead man, down to pure instinct alone. He was running now simply to stave off the inevitable; he was running blindly and without hope, running to gain a few more moments of his short precious life before he would trip and fall and the dogs would be upon him, ripping the flesh from his bones.

This was no way for a man with a future to die.

Suddenly drenched in sunshine, he splashed through a clearing bisected by a small stream that meandered toward the river. Slipping on the mossy rocks, he steadied himself, trying desperately to get reoriented. Then, he hurtled forward once more, racing back into the dark world beneath the canopy that towered overhead.

He could hear the Xucuru warriors chanting behind him, ever closer; and yet closer, the vicious snapping and growling wild dogs that were leading them to their quarry. They were gaining, getting closer now. They were well fed, well rested, and strong. They were relentless trackers who knew the ways of the jungle. Hawke was lost, hungry, and afraid.

The Xucuru wanted blood: his blood, the poor diminished feverish stuff now coursing through his veins; he knew they wanted to see it flow almost as desperately as he wanted to keep it flowing.

Running, he burst into yet another patch of sunshine. This sunshine had wings, diaphanous wings, brushing his cheeks ever so lightly, like cobwebs. Another illusion? Light with wings? He imagined the fever had finally sent his mind reeling, that he'd slipped over into spiraling madness. A second later he snapped back. He realized the circular clearing was filled with countless swirling yellow butterflies lit by the sun above.

He raised his hands and cupped a few of the shimmering mariposas, bringing them right up to his eyes. He wanted to inspect these tiny diaphanous creatures more carefully, each one an individual miracle of nature. He looked up. A swarming tower of these yellow beings rose all the way to the sky above. It was a miracle. He waded into dense but yielding clouds, walking as if in a dream. And stumbling into a sinkhole that sucked at his feet.

Cursing and finally freeing himself from the sucking muck of the muddy hole, he again plunged forward through the gossamer yellow insects, batting their delicate bodies and filmy wings away from his eyes, searching for the far side of the clearing.

He could only hope this mirage of yellow and the quicksand underfoot might slow the dogs and he used this hope to keep moving. He ran hard for a few more minutes. And then, he slammed into an immovable wall and all hope vanished from his mind.

It was a canebrake that finally spelt the end.

The towering wall of green bamboo rose sixty feet above his head. The profusion of stalks grew so closely as to appear almost solid. He sprinted along the wall in both directions, looking and feeling for some kind of a crack or narrow opening. Nothing. No prayer of an opening anywhere, no way to shinny upward either. He slammed against the barrier again and again in a rage of frustration but it was useless. The stalks were thick, every bit as thick as a man's wrist and the bamboo curtain would not yield.

There would be no escape.

It was over.

No admittance, Mr. Hawke.

You're dead.

3

Hawke clung to the bamboo stalks, waiting for the inevitable. Letting his arms take his full weight, he hung his head, looking like a beaten man. His lungs were afire, his legs trembling and shaking uncontrollably. He had no idea how long he let himself hang there, but he knew that any second he would feel the sharp punch of an arrow or a spear between his shoulder blades.

Thunk.

The steel tip of a spear embedded itself deeply in the bamboo a few centimeters above his head.

It parted my bloody hair, he thought, with a mixture of dread and admiration for the chucker's skills. He could feel the spear's impact thrumming in his bones, the vibrations traveling down to his forearms to his hands. So this is how it would end.

Like a man before a firing squad disdaining the blindfold, he wanted to see. He lifted his head, craned it round, and saw another spear and then a third flying toward him. He was not prepared to die with a spear in his back and so he completely about-faced to witness the onslaught of whistling shafts, instantly calculating the angles, deciding which spear would strike where and how he must dodge them.

But they all fell short. A quick flurry of spears hit the ground, all striking at a forty-five-degree angle and forming a semicircle around him. The delicate precision of this instant cage, even in his cornered and desperate state, demanded some appreciation. It had to be deliberate, but why trap rather than kill? Then came the dogs. He saw the loopy saliva of the animals flying as they sprung toward him out of the undergrowth, racing toward him with their snapping jaws wide.

Another spear, then more, at first only a few, but then many, arced toward him. To his complete amazement the upright shafts began to form a more complete circle around him. Hawke braced for the dogs. But, upon reaching this strange and newly formed perimeter, they slowed, then stopped. Howling in frustration, they looked back to their masters, the Indians still in hiding.

Hawke saw that the dogs might easily go around the cage of spears and kill him, or, in some cases, even slip between them. But they did not. The dogs stood rock-still, eyes blazing and tongues lolling, and waited. Hawke, finished, released his grip on the canes and fell to the ground.

He heard a man grunt and looked up.

A tall Indian warrior, a Xucuru whom Hawke recognized from the camps, had stepped into the tiny clearing. It was Wajari, the brutal chief who had been assigned to guard Hawke's construction site. The man was wearing an old itip, a ceremonial loincloth with vertical stripes of black and yellow and red, the same regalia he wore every day.

Wajari, who normally carried a rifle on the job, now wore a machete, stuck inside the cinched waist of his loincloth. He approached Hawke, withdrawing the blade. It was almost over. A swift blow from the machete would put an end to his suffering. But there was something very odd about his eyes. Gone was the fierce expression, replaced by something new and terribly strange.

It wasn't fear, exactly. No, it was worry.

Seeing those troubled black eyes, Hawke knew his life had taken a sudden turn for the better. His head might actually remain attached for a few days longer.

"Hawke," Wajari said, making it sound like "Hoke." Then he was gently taking Hawke's arm and helping him get to his feet.

"Wajari," Hawke said, letting himself be taken. The running was truly over. He felt a sense of relief flood through his body.

"Lord Hawke," Wajari said, seeming to like the sound of it.

"So glad you could make it," Hawke murmured as he was led toward the trees. "One doesn't receive an invitation to a beheading every day."

Wajari ignored his ramblings. Hawke collapsed at the feet of a fierce-looking group of savages whose faces were painted in bright yellow and red. All held machetes above their heads.

To his enormous surprise, the blades did not fall.

Not only did these ferocious cannibals not behead him, but they treated him gently, with a strange blend of caution and respect. They gave him a bowl of manioc beer, which he drank in great gulping draughts. Wajari, who seemed to be presiding over this ceremony, ordered him wrapped in a blanket and placed carefully on a grassy mound.

They moved away, leaving him in the care of a single warrior with a spear. It occurred to Hawke that for some strange reason he was now worth more alive than dead.

Hawke lay under the shade of the trees, watching as the Indians hacked at the canebrake with their machetes. For an hour or more, they were busy cutting sections of four-inch-thick green cane, some about ten feet in length, some shorter. A female member of the war party came forward and presented him with a gourd of water followed by a small bowl of manioc bread.

He ate greedily and, after a time, feeling much revived, Hawke understood what it was the Indians were building.

They were using the bamboo poles and lengths of ropy vines to construct a cage. Ten feet long by four feet wide and approximately five feet in height. The bottom of the cage was filled with a bed of fronds.

It was to be home for the next five days, the large green cage borne upon the shoulders of four trotting savages as they raced through the jungle. These Xucuru, whom he now thought of as his saviors, would rest for short periods and when they moved, they moved very quickly. There was a sense of great urgency about his captors he found puzzling. When they slowed their pace, or spent too long at rest, Wajari would chastise them with his stick, prodding them along.

After three days of this they came to the brown swirling waters of another wide river. It was not the swiftly running Xingu, which he would put behind them many miles to the west. Hawke thought that perhaps this water was the great tributary called *Tapajos,* a river basin much ravaged by gold miners for the last few decades.

At the river's edge, Wajari ordered a rest for his weary men. After some hours, after much bathing and drinking of manioc beer, his cage was lifted again and carried to the river. There, it was mounted atop a long dugout catamaran which had the skull of a jaguar mounted on the long snout of each slender prow. This large craft was one of many hidden in a small inlet in the bank. The secret flotilla had been covered with palm fronds.

With great alacrity, Wajari organized their immediate departure, and soon the long prows of the dugout canoes were gliding over the waters, headed upriver, even deeper into the green maze. Wajari, helmsman of the sole catamaran, brought up the rear and Hawke was reminded of an old joke. "If you're not the lead dog, the view is always the same."

The days were spent under an unrelenting sun. To amuse himself, in the midst of such stunning monotony, Hawke had used a needlelike sliver of bamboo to decorate himself. Using the dark juice of the chi-chi root, he tattooed *"HOLD FAST"* on the knuckles of

each hand. It wasn't much comfort, but he'd always believed they were good words to remember in times of
trouble.

DEAD ASLEEP one night following yet another endless day on the river, Hawke was awakened by the crash
of violent thunder. Jagged spears of lightning criss-
crossed the sky and fat raindrops hissed on the water's
surface. A second later, hard rain hammered the river
and everyone on it. Wajari, who manned the stern of
Hawke's flagship, was poling hard for the shore as they
rounded a soft bend in the river.

Hawke sat up and rubbed his eyes, not quite believing
what he was seeing. Through the undulating curtains of
rain, long shafts of artificial light striped the black water
and river bank. Such light on the shore could only mean
one thing. Civilization! Indeed, as they drew nearer to
the shore, a small village of traditional huts stood along
the riverbanks. The settlement was lit by hissing arc
lights mounted on wooden towers.

Artificial light was unheard of this deep in the
wilderness, and Hawke was mystified. Then he heard
the deep thrum of generators as they neared the riverbank. Civilization, or what passed for it, was at hand.

It was some kind of hastily built trading port, an
unlovely facility, but still a welcome sight. The lights
now revealed a long row of brown-thatched buildings
perched along the shore. There was a long steel dock,
perhaps two hundred feet in length, and upon it were
stout wooden crates stacked as high as the rooftops of
the riverfront storehouses. Men worked frantically with

hand dollies, moving the heavy crates inside. It was a recently arrived shipment, Hawke thought, and they were hurriedly getting the crates sheltered before the impending thunderstorm.

No one took much notice of Wajari and the new arrivals from upriver. Not even the heavily armed men who were guarding the crates glanced toward them. Wajari stood on the prow, one hand resting on the polished jaguar skull that decorated and protected his vessel. He raised his hand in greeting to a tall man wearing some kind of ragged uniform as the catamaran bumped up against the dock.

The man uttered an incomprehensible greeting and had one of his dockhands throw the Xucuru chieftain a line.

Hawke's cage was unloaded by the Xucuru and placed at the far end of the dock away from the crates. Except for Wajari, the Indian war party returned immediately to their dugouts. The rain had let up, so Hawke was content to sit in his bamboo cage under the dripping palms, eat from his bowl of manioc bread, and contemplate his fate. He saw Wajari go inside a smaller corrugated tin building, its windows lit from within. An office perhaps.

He understood without being told that he was being turned over to some new authority. Wajari's concern now made sense. The chief had feared his captive might not survive long enough to complete this transaction.

But, nonetheless, Hawke's spirits rose. He felt better than he had in months. He'd slept on the river, the deep sleep of a man no longer on the run. There had been plenty of water and bread. He had begun a program of strenuous exercise, using the bars of the cage to lift himself with his upper arms, pushing at the sides with his legs. Pilates, he believed the ladies of London called this kind of thing.

Even the fevers came less frequently now. Perhaps the malaria was subsiding. Wajari had fed him a foul, whitish herbal concoction every day. It wasn't the milk of human kindness, he knew now. The man was simply trying to keep Hawke healthy long enough to collect the bounty that was surely on his head. He was in that small building even now, getting his thirty pieces of silver.

Hawke used this rare moment of lucidity and made a decision. He was not going back to the camps. No matter what his new captor planned for him, when Wajari returned and opened his cage he would kill him. Take the machete and use his own blade on him. He'd kill anyone who got in his way.

Then he'd see what he could learn in the small dock office. There were sure to be papers there, documents of some kind that he could use to support his story of the camps. And if he was really lucky, maybe even a vehicle parked on the other side of the warehouses. He'd heard the sound of a motor revving and then being silenced.

He waited patiently in his bamboo cage and plotted his escape. He knew in his bones he was still too weak to run far. But, if he could somehow steal a boat, even a dugout and summon the strength to paddle, make his way back upriver, maybe he could get to a wireless radio, or even a telephone. He would only get one chance to survive this ordeal.

Who would he contact first? There was a man he knew, who now lived up in Miami. A true friend of many years. A man who sometimes worked with a Martinique outfit called Thunder and Lightning. They were the best freelance hostage rescue team in the world. He had U.S. Navy connections, too, maybe good enough to get a search and rescue plane in the air.

His friend's name was Stokely Jones.

Somehow, he would contact Stokely. The man was the most reliable soul he knew; the toughest human being Hawke had ever encountered. Stoke had survived and even thrived in the jungles of Vietnam and New York City. He was a true friend, one of Hawke's closest. Over the years, he had helped Hawke out of far worse scrapes than this one. Hell, this rescue would be child's play to the human mountain named Stokely Jones Jr.

Hawke felt tiny sparks of hope-neurons firing somewhere inside his brain. For the first time in months, he began to think he might actually survive this bloody adventure. If he could just hold fast a bit longer, Stoke would think of some way to get him out. That was the ticket. Somehow, he had to live long enough to get to a bloody telephone.

Is that you, Mrs. Crusoe? Hold on a tick, will you, I've got young Robinson on the line.

4

MIANI

"So how much you want for the trade?" the used car guy said to Stokely, eyeing the silver Lincoln Town Car rental. Man had his pink hanky plastered on top of his balding pink head to soak up the sweat pouring off him. His clothes were plastered to the skin, like he'd just come in out of the rain. It wasn't a good look. It was eighty-eight degrees, according to the radio. Which was warm for early December in most places and just a tad hot for the Miami-Dade metropolitan area.

Even the salesman's little ponytail was limp.

Stokely Jones Jr., who had just recently packed up and moved lock, stock, and barrel to South Florida, didn't mind the heat one iota. In fact, he enjoyed it. It was part of the reason he'd moved down here from New York City in the first place. Heat, humidity, and lots of sunshine. Big blue ocean to play in. Palm trees, swaying in the breezes, lift all the girls' dresses above their kneeses. Paradise, man, no doubt about it. He absolutely loved it.

Stoke was keeping John Greevy, the Auto Toy Store salesperson, out in the sun as part of his negotiation technique. Make him sweat. Somewhere on this vast lot full of heavy metal was an automobile he'd give his eye-teeth for. Not one of the fancy Italian F-cars or Lambos John was pushing, they were way out of his league. No, much better. And he was damned if he'd let this slippery pink rascal get the best of him.

South Florida car lots were notoriously dangerous places to begin with. The tricky thing now was, how to handle this negotiation. Stoke wasn't sure all the wiring in the guy's attic had been properly soldered on the day of installation. He had a bad habit of talking down to the customers. And, he wanted to take Stoke's rental in trade on a new car.

"Let me take you through this one more time, John," Stoke said, smiling at the little guy in the purple linen shirt. Johnny took pains to dress native, creamy slacks with no socks, and tiny little tasseled loafers, but the accent, the mannerisms, were unmistakable. Pure Brooklyn. Park Slope, maybe, but Brooklyn for sure.

"Can we do that, little buddy?"

"Please, Mr. Jones," John Greevy said. "Be my guest."

"This Lincoln right here? It's not mine, okay? What I'm trying to tell you. It's a rental. It belongs to Mr. Hertz. You can't trade in a rental car to buy another car."

"There are ways," the guy said, bending over to check the Town Car's left front tire tread. "Believe me, Mr. Jones, there are ways upon ways upon ways."

"I do believe you. But I'm telling you one more time I'm not going to trade it in. Okay? Man, I haven't even seen the eight-second Pontiac yet. So what are we even talking about here, Johnny? Where the hell is that Pontiac?"

The Auto Toy Store guy had moved so he was standing in Stoke's shadow again. Stoke was about six-eight and built like a very large armoire. He tended to create a lot of shade wherever he went.

Johnny mopped his brow. "Jesus, Mary, and Joseph. You'll see the Pontiac, all right? Just as soon as my boy finishes the detail. Like I told you. Look. Tell you what. Let's step into my office over there and talk about it. I got air in there. You can sit down. I can get your information. You got kids? I got a nine-year old. Johnny Jr. He's a pisser. Lemme show you his picture."

Johnny whipped out his wallet and flashed some pictures in a cloudy accordion plastic holder. Stoke glanced at the kid and said, "Cute as a button all right."

"Yeah. Kid just can't keep his mind on his school-work because he—"

"Johnny. Stop. What's that thing over there?"

"Which? The black Ferrari 430 Spider? Gorgeous automobile."

"No."

"That turquoise convertible? You don't want that. No resale. A color only Ray Charles could love."

"How do you know I don't want it?"

"It's a replica."

"It looks real."

"That's why it's called a replica."

"Holy maca-moley."

"What?"

"Is that it? Is that the car? Over there?"

A gleaming dark car had rolled out of the detail shed behind the guy's back. Johnny craned his head around to look at it and wolf-whistled like he'd never laid eyes on it before this very minute.

Stoke was wishing his jaw was wired shut so it wouldn't be hanging down on his collarbone like this. Bad negotiating tactic, see a car your jaw drops involuntarily on you.

Johnny let out another long wolf whistle.

"Oh, yeah, there she is, my friend, in the flesh. The 1965 Pontiac GTO convertible. Piece of friggin' work, I kid you not, Mr. Jones. You're looking at one bad-assed muscle car. Pumping major steroids, I shit you not."

Stoke managed to get his own smile muscles under control before he let the guy see his face. He even managed a frown in reaction to the car's absolutely gorgeous color.

"Black?" Stoke said, holding a hand up to shade his eyes. "Is that black? The ad said black."

"Black? Hell, no it ain't black. Black Raspberry, my man. Metallic. Totally custom job by my guys in Lauderdale. You like, amigo?"

"Yeah. I like. How much?"

Stoke, trying unsuccessfully to be cool about it, *nonchalant* as his friend and employer Alex Hawke might say, walked over to the car. Johnny followed close behind, trying to stay in his shadow.

"How much you ask?" Johnny said. "Well, we gotta

talk about that, don't we? How the hell you put a number on a piece of automotive art like this?"

"No. I mean how much horsepower has it got." Stoke ran his hand over the almost liquid finish of the bulging hood.

"Were you a Marine? You carry yourself like a Marine."

"Navy. SEAL. Three tours in the delta."

Johnny was busy, opening the driver's door and popping the hood.

"Cool. Semper fi, right? I got a lot of respect for you guys. So, what do we have under the hood? Okay. Very cool. Look at this thing, huh? Chrome headers. Everything you see here is street legal. For starters, we got an Alston chassis with Strange struts, spool and rear housing that holds a—"

"Strange struts?"

"Bear with me, sir, please. Strange is the manufacturer of the after-market struts. Okay? So, the transmission is a 1.96 low Powerglide with brake and TCI4500 converter. The engine powering this eight-second ride is an Indian Adventures special displacing 541 cubic inches and has a Moldex billet crank, Ross pistons, Oliver rods, Edelbrock wide port heads with T&D shaft rockers, a custom sheet-metal intake with two methanol toilets, MSD with crank trigger—"

"Toilets?" Stoke asked, sliding behind the wheel and glancing over his shoulder at the rolled and pleated red leather rear seat.

"It's a racing terminology thing, Mr. Jones. Okay? Stop looking. There's no toilet in the vehicle."

"She'll do a quarter mile in eight seconds?"

"She will. NHRA certified."

"And she's street legal?"

"Absofuckinlutely."

"Mercy."

"You want this car, Mr. Jones? I feel that you do."

"I do."

"Let's do it."

"I need a number."

"Ballpark?"

"Yeah."

"Step into my office."

5

An hour later, Stokely Jones was cruising south on I-95. He rumbled over the bridge connecting downtown Miami to where he lived on Brickell Key. He was at the wheel of his brand-new 1965 GTO, top down, wearing a super-sized shit-eating grin on his face. He simply couldn't believe the chick-magnetizing power of a black raspberry GTO convertible. He'd gotten so many admiring glances driving back to Coconut Grove, his left arm and jaw muscles were tired out just from all the waving and smiling back he'd done in acknowledgment.

There'd been a high school car wash going on at the Dixie Crème and a mess of cheerleaders had swarmed over the car when he'd stopped for a light at the intersection. You girls behave, he'd said to them, blipping the throttle and watching them jump back at the throaty roar. Hey, it's just an old GTO, what are all you ladies so excited about? And it hadn't stopped there.

Now, as he came over the rise on the Brickell Island bridge, two blonde babes in a red Mustang convertible were pulling out of the Mandarin Hotel entrance. As he cruised by, surprise, surprise, Mustang Sally and her cute friend too were totally magnetized.

He checked the rear view, almost surprised they hadn't hooked a damn U-ey and followed him home.

He pulled into the underground parking at One Tequesta Point, the tower that was home to his new Miami palazzo in the sky. He blipped the GTO's throttle again as he rumbled past the old security guy, Fast Eddie Falco.

Fast Eddie, cold cigar stub firmly clenched in his teeth, was reading the *Miami Herald* in his customized golf cart. Reading in the cart seemed to take up a lot of Eddie's time. When he finished the sports section around noon, Stoke knew, he'd whip out an old paperback and dive into his afternoon reading program.

Because the two of them shared a liking for mysteries, Stoke and Eddie had recently started a small book club, just the two of them. They called it the "John D. MacDonald Men's Reading Society." Right now they were reading *Dress Her in Indigo,* and it was one of Stoke's personal favorites. Next Sunday, Eddie's day off, the two of them were planning to drive up to Bahia Mar in Lauderdale and see if they couldn't locate slip F-18, where Travis McGee moored his 52-foot houseboat, the *Busted Flush.*

Hey, Stoke suddenly realized, they could take the GTO.

"Eight seconds, Eddie," Stoke said to the security man as he pulled into his reserved parking spot right next to Fast Eddie's reserved parking place. Reluctantly, he turned the key and shut her down. Fast Eddie still had his nose buried in the paper.

"You hear what I said, Ed? Eight seconds! You believe that?"

"Take your time," Eddie said, not bothering to look up and flipping to the Living section. "I got all day."

You had to laugh.

Stoke hit the switch that raised the ragtop, locked it up, gave it one long last look, and headed for the elevator. He punched 35, his floor, and leaned back against the wood-grained elevator wall, trying to imagine the look on Fancha's face tonight when she saw his new baby pull up outside her place over on Key Biscayne.

It was Saturday and he was taking her to dinner tonight, Sly Stallone's new fusion place over on South Beach's main drag. It would be Rollerbladers on parade tonight on Ocean, and all the muscle boys skating outside Sly's would be ogling the heavy iron parked along the strip. He'd slip the valet guy a twenty to leave the GTO out front where he could keep an eye on it.

Sweet.

He'd been whistling an old tune all the way home, couldn't get it out of his head. Ronnie and the Daytonas, if he remembered correctly. What were the words?

A wa-waaaa, wa-wa-wa-wa-waaaaaa—

He stepped off the elevator into the bright sunshine of the open-air thirty-fifth-floor lobby, strolled down the corridor, keyed in his number on the pad, and walked through his front door. Had to stop right there and admire the view, the sun lighting up half of Biscayne Bay beyond his living room windows. It was beautiful and it was all his.

A wa-waaaaa, wa-wa-wa-wa-wa-waaaaaaa—

Man. Life was good: Turn it on, wind it up, and blow it out.

Two bedrooms, two baths, and a wraparound terrace overlooking paradise spread out below. To buy the condo, he'd sold the small house and large apartment building in Bayside, Queens, that his sainted mother had left him. There was still some money left over to decorate the new crib. And now there was a brand-new piece of automotive art in the parking garage downstairs waiting for him.

He walked over to the tall windows to inspect his universe. A huge freighter was being towed out to sea, moving slowly through Government Cut. A new wide-load cruise ship had just arrived at the Port of Miami, probably quarantined because of some weird bacteria. A little farther east, he saw *Blackhawke*.

The two-hundred-forty-foot black-hulled yacht belonged to his longtime friend Alex Hawke, and she'd been in Miami for the last couple of months and was just out of the yard. Some kind of a weapons and engine refit while Hawke was down in Brazil or Argentina on his quasi-scientific expedition. In reality Alex was doing some unspecified government work. This time it was the British government. Usually, the work was unspecified and so was the government. That was the way Hawke operated. He'd gotten himself into some bad shit down there and had ended up in the hospital. Okay now, thank God.

There was work going on over at the big yacht. Day and night. Tom Quick, Hawke's chief of security, had ordered bulletproof windows installed on all three decks after the near-miss incident in the harbor down in Santo Domingo. And they were upgrading the weapons and propulsion systems. The boat was Hawke's floating operations center and he used it all over the world.

Stoke grabbed a Diet Coke from the fridge and walked back out into the living room. The light was blinking on his machine and he plunked down into the deep suede chaise and punched the message play button. Probably Sharkey, he guessed.

"Hey. It's me," the disembodied voice said, not disappointing him.

It was Luis Gonzales-Gonzales, a Cuban guy he'd recently put on his Tactics International payroll. He was the new company's very first employee, he told Luis, so he'd better be good. Luis's nickname, Sharkey, was because as a boy fishing with his father, he'd lost some of his left arm to a big bull shark down in the Keys. All he had now was a stump. He looked like, yeah, a Sharkey, Stoke had decided. Shark was a fairly laid-back individual, maybe just a little nervous for Stoke's taste, but he'd been a mate on a charter out of Key West for a couple of decades and he knew his way around that vicinity.

Not long after he was hired, Shark had told Stoke he liked this espionage gig a whole lot more than fishing. Stoke paid him five hundred a week plus expenses. Sharkey thought he'd died and gone to heaven. Went out and bought himself a sharkskin blazer to wear to work. Pair of secret agent sunglasses pushed back on his forehead, answering the phone in the rented office space in Coconut Grove. Stoke had to laugh.

Gonzales-Gonzales was Stoke's only employee. Hell, it was only a month now since Tactics even had a payroll. But Stoke's newly formed company had recently landed its first client and it was a good one. His clients had their home office in a big five-sided building up in D.C. called the Pentagon.

Hawke had given Stoke the seed money to get his company started. He'd even helped steer a guy they'd both worked with before, a CIA spook named Harry Brock, to him. Brock, who was now a military intelligence advisor to the Joint Chiefs, had met with him and had put Tactics on a retainer. They wanted him to poke around a little bit down in the Caribbean. Five grand a week plus expenses was a good start. It covered the rent and payroll and even kept the lights on.

From what Stoke was allowed to know, it seemed Harry Brock was planning on making some big presentation at an upcoming seminar on Latin American terrorist activities. Harry had hired Stoke to gather information to fill in the holes in a presentation he was planning to make. Harry told Stoke to look into one specific area, namely Cuba and the Florida Straits.

Harry's boss in Washington, JCS chairman General Charley Moore, was getting very worried about a rising tide of anti-Americanism in Latin America. He was especially juned up about the new Cuba-Venezuela connection. It was that connection that had Washington's pantyhose all twisted up at the moment. Harry Brock was calling in a lot of his sources. Every one of them was tasked to gather intel on the Chávez-Castro love-fest for the State Department's Key West powwow.

The State Department was convinced Fidel was buy-ing arms from the Russians with money from Chávez in Venezuela. Then he was shipping out weapons to all his new Latin American buddies. That was the theory anyway. But they needed confirmation and Stoke was one of the guys assigned to do that.

"How's it hanging, Señor?" Sharkey's recorded voice said. "*Que pasa, hombre?* Listen, man, I think I got some-thing for you. This is still very private but we got to move fast or it won't be. Like, we got to fly down first thing in the morning. Does that work? It does if you want to see this thing before the Federales find out about it. So, lemme know, okay, because—"

Stoke hit the save button and speed-dialed Sharkey's cell.

"Fly down where?" he said the second the real-live Sharkey answered his phone.

"Dry Tortugas. Just west of Key West."

"Tell me why, Luis."

"Fortune offers us an opportunity, boss."

"Good answer."

"Oh, yeah. Look, I got us a seaplane out of Dinner Key. She's called the 'Blue Goose.' Seven o'clock a.m. *Mañana*. Don't be late."

"What about the pilot?"

"Name is Mick. Mick Hocking. No worries, mate, like the man says. Dude ain't saying nothing about nothing to nobody, man. I checked him out through a friend of mine at Miami-Dade PD. He's okay. From Australia or New Zealand or some place. I'll give you his number, you want to call him on his 'mi-ble' like I do all the time."

"What's a 'mi-ble'?"

"What this Mick Hocking calls his cell phone."

"Oh. Mobile. Got it. Hey. You know what the shark said to the clown?"

"No."

"You taste funny."

"That is so lame. Man, I can't believe you even tell a handicapped person a joke like that."

"I'm politically incorrect. Hey, listen. What are we looking at down there? It better be good, compadre, I'm telling you, 'cause I got a lot of paperwork and shit to deal with right here on the homefront."

"It's good. You'll see."

"Yeah, I'll see. I'll swing by and pick you up at six-thirty."

"You get the car?"

"You'll see."

6

THE AMAZON BASIN

Would you kill for a cigarette? Commit murder for a single puff of burning weed? Could the sweet scent of Turkish tobacco drive a man insane? These were the questions the wild creature squatting inside the bamboo cage asked himself. The guard, who smoked in a very civilized manner, affected an air of boredom. He was leaning casually against a wooden bollard, gazing at the river.

Inside the small dock office, an argument was raging. Wajari's basso profundo rose and fell.

Hawke, desperate for a smoke, decided to try to communicate with his guard.

The tall, coppery fellow's uniform was torn and faintly recognizable as British. On his head, a filthy white turban splotched with brown patches that appeared to be dried blood. An Arab, certainly, though perhaps of mixed descent. He carried himself with authority and his dark, heavily lidded eyes betrayed an intelligence beyond his station.

"Speak any English?" Hawke asked, with little hope of a response.

"What's that?" the man said, looking over at him with annoyance.

He spoke in a clipped English accent, with the unmistakable air of a chap unaccustomed to being addressed by caged animals.

Surprised, Hawke answered, "Actually, I asked if you spoke a bit of English."

"More than a bit." Afghani, on one side of the coin.

"What's in the crates?" Hawke asked.

"Who wants to know?" the man said, as if the prisoner were a piece of rotted meat even the tigers wouldn't touch.

"The Great Satan, of course," Hawke said.

The man bent over and peered intently through the bars for a few seconds.

"Satan, I'll grant you. But, great? I think not." He rapped the muzzle of his gun on Hawke's cage. "Tell me who you are."

"The fifth richest man in England, at your service. Now give me a cigarette for Christ's sake."

"You're not Hawke?"

"Not me."

"Lord Alexander Hawke? You must be."

"Never heard of him."

"It's you, all right. I was expecting an Englishman, not the wild man of Borneo. Damn it, man! I've been half expecting you to show up around here. You were supposed to surface a week ago."

"Sorry I'm late. I was detained. Cigarette?"

"Why not? I have to wait until they finish your paperwork anyway."

"My paperwork?"

The man didn't answer. Leaning his carbine against the bollard, he lowered himself to the dock, letting his legs dangle over the edge.

"Mind the piranhas," Hawke said cheerfully.

The fellow pulled a crumpled package of black market smokes from his torn khaki shirt and shook one loose.

"Thanks." Hawke bent forward so that he could accept a light. "I am eternally grateful. What's your name?"

"Wellington Hassan," the man said, lighting another.

"Wellington Hassan. Quite a name."

"Saladin's good enough. My middle name."

"Saladin it is, then. Sal-a'ha-Din. Slave of God. You Talib, Saladin? Taliban?"

Saladin Hassan laughed deeply. "Me? Taliban? Hardly. Afghan, though. I bled for your side, Mr. Hawke."

"Where'd you get your English?" Hawke asked, withholding smoke until it burned.

"My mother. An English rose from Devon. Her family name was Wellington. She met my father when she was working as a nurse in Kabul. We always used English in the house. When the shooting started in Afghanistan, I was recruited as a translator for a British regiment advising the Northern Alliance. I had a military engineering background and some experience of artillery and explosives."

"Really? Which regiment, may I ask?"

"Royal Gloucestershire, Berkshire, and Wiltshire Light Infantry."

Hawke nodded and said, "What theatre?"

"Up in the north. Near Mazar-e-Sharif. Helping the Afghan government develop democratic institutions and disarming militias."

"Good work."

"Until an unfortunate incident, yes, it was."

"What happened, Saladin?"

"We came under fire between bases. I'd told my commander the road had been cleared of IEDs. I checked it three times. I thought it had been. It hadn't. We lost three."

Hawke looked away, inhaled the harsh smoke deeply, and felt almost human. Nicotine brought a great clarity to things, so fresh it was startling. This was, he realized, his first real human conversation in over six months.

"Pretty rough," Hawke said, "I'm sorry."

"What are you doing here, Mr. Hawke?"

"I was with a scientific expedition before your friends in there captured me. These people are your employers? *Las Medianoches*?"

"Perhaps. But only temporarily. I'm an independent contractor. Since I retired from the military, I work for anybody. Recently, I've been doing odd jobs for *El Salvador del Mundo*."

"The savior of the world? Big job, saving the world. Is your current employer up to it?"

"My employer believes world salvation starts here in the jungle. This is where it all begins. At any rate, my life story is of no consequence. You, on the other hand,

are quite a celebrity in this part of the jungle. You're
going to the highest bidder."

"Really? Who's bidding?"

"A man named Muhammad Top and an American
who calls himself Harry Brock."

"Harry Brock?" Hawke knew the name well. Harry
was a bit of a piss artist, but also a tough, hard-bitten intelligence operative with a particularly American sense
of humor.

"Yes. He came down here looking for you. Top
found him first, sentenced him to death for spying. He
said he had information for you."

"So Harry's dead."

"Not yet. He's a very smart man, Brock. He played
to Papa Top's ego, gave him a ton of information, most
of it probably false. They sent him to die in the camps.
Somehow, he got away. Top hired me to find Brock and
dispose of him."

"Ah. You're an assassin. You kill him?"

"Got a better offer."

"Doing what?"

"Harry's paying me to keep an eye on Muhammad
Top. And, look for you. So, now that I've found you,
there is a small seaplane moored upriver. We can steal it,
fly to the town of Madre de Deus. From there, I can get
you somehow to Manaus. And, from Manaus, well,
there are many flights to Rio. You look like you could
use a good doctor."

"Let's fly. Now."

"We will fly, m'lord. Give me a few seconds to
straighten things out in the office."

Saladin got to his feet, picked up his carbine, and went inside.

A loud staccato roar of automatic gunfire erupted inside the small office. The lights were instantly extinguished and glass exploded outward, showering fragments on Hawke in his bamboo prison. There were loud screams and curses. Then another burst silenced the cries from inside.

Saladin Hassan stood in the doorway with a smoking carbine in his hand. He pulled a blade from a sheath on his belt and started working on the cage.

"What was that all about?" Hawke asked.

"I had to shred your paperwork."

7

Prairie, Texas

"Come on in, why don't you, it's open."

Daisy hadn't even heard the cruiser pull up in the drive out front. Now she could see the good-looking boy from the kitchen table. Standing out on the front porch, plain as day.

"It's Homer, honey," she said.

"I can see who it is."

Homer Prudhomme was right outside the screen door under the yellow bug light. Reason he wasn't in any big hurry to come inside, Daisy guessed, was the bad news writ all over his face.

"Homer," her husband said to the boy as he swallowed his macaroni and scootched his chair back from the table a few inches. "Come on inside the house, son. You are not interrupting anything special in here. We eat supper every night."

Homer pulled open the flimsy door and stepped inside the parlor, taking off his hat and riffling the dusty brim through his fingers. His big dark eyes were a little puffy and red. He had waves of dark hair and a cowlick that just wouldn't pay any mind to Brylcreem.

"Sheriff," he said, nodding to Franklin. "Evenin', Miz Dixon."

"Hey, Homer," Daisy said to the boy, "you got something in your eye, baby?" It was true she wanted to mother this child. Nothing wrong in that.

Homer wiped the back of his hand across his face. "No, ma'am. Had the windows down driving out here, that's all. Just a gnat or something flew in my eye."

They waited for the boy to say something else, but he didn't. He had been crying, that much was plain to see.

"What brings you out here this time of night, son?" Franklin said.

"Bad news, Sheriff."

Homer was a tall, good-looking kid with the uniform hanging off his bones. The Tuesday Girls down at the Bon Jour beauty parlor all had a crush on him. Hell, every churchgoing one of them, every lady in Prairie had a sneaker for that boy. The general consensus was he looked like Elvis right before he got famous, when he was still living at home with Gladys and Vernon.

Homer was older than that, shoot, he was almost twenty now and a high school graduate. But he had those same sleepy eyes and those long silky eyelashes. Behind his back, all the gals called him *La Hilacha*. The threadbare one. Homer had grown up semi-Anglo in the barrio part of town.

"Speak up, son."

You could see the boy's mind looking for a way to

say it, whatever awful thing it was he'd come out here to tell her husband.

"Let it out, Homer. It's all right, honey," Daisy said.

Those bedroom eyes looked like they were liable to start filling up again. But Homer bravely took a deep breath and got himself under control.

"They've done . . . I'm sorry, Sheriff, seems like they took another one."

"Another girl."

He rubbed his sleeve roughly across his eyes. "Yessir. I reckon I'm not too good at being the bearer of bad news. I just came from telling Mr. and Mrs. Beers about what happened to their daughter. They're pretty shook up."

Daisy wanted to get up and hug the boy.

She would have, too, if not for how embarrassed he'd be in front of Franklin. It had been a tough year for the boy. He lost his American father when they had that explosion out at the fertilizer factory here about a year ago. Family had to move out of their house after that. Staying in some apartment over the hardware store now. And his momma, Rosalinda, who was originally from Juarez, was never any damn good. Drugs or alcohol, everybody said.

His mother just upped and took off with some married John Deere regional sales manager from Wichita here about six months ago. People said she and her lover boy run off together. Went down to Juarez and kept on going. Nothing runs like a Deere, as they say on television. Rosalinda left Homer to take care of his baby sister, graduate high school, and do his part-time court-

house job all at the same time. Last June, after gradua-
tion, that's when he'd come to see Franklin about a job
on the force.

Of course, Franklin had said yes. He always did,
somebody needed something in this town. And now
she saw those damn worry lines around her husband's
pale grey eyes coming back again. Those damn worry
lines never stayed gone too long lately, worries piling up
like they were around here. Illegals, drugs, border
shootings. And now the abductions of four beautiful
young girls.

The shit around here was knee deep and rising.

The boy looked over to the window, watching something out there maybe, trying to compose himself.

"She's just a baby, you know, Sheriff? Not even fourteen."

"I know what you mean, Homer," Franklin said. He
let go of a sigh and shoved his chair all the way back
from the table. Then he reached for his boots.

Daisy knew what Franklin meant, too. She'd felt it
coming as soon as she'd seen Homer at the door.
Everybody for miles around was living in fear until they
were sick with it. They'd finally sent a posse out on
horseback to look for the girls. Now another one had
gone missing. They'd been snatched from their houses
in the middle of the night. Stolen from the roadside in
broad daylight, waiting on the school bus or coming
out of the Piggly-Wiggly. Drugged and trussed up and
hauled across the border to God knows where all or
whatever.

White slavery, that's what her friend and neighbor

June Weaver said it was. Underage prostitution. Steal the little Anglo girls and put them to work in the cathouses south of the border. June worked the switchboard down at the courthouse. Which meant obviously that not much that happened in this county, good or bad, escaped her notice.

"They took one of the Beers girls?" Franklin said in a tired voice. He was getting to his feet, brushing cornbread crumbs from the front of his jeans. He eyed his deputy, who'd managed to pull himself back together.

"Joe Beers's youngest daughter, Sheriff. Name is Charlotte. Didn't come home from the picture show."

"This evenin', then?"

"Yessir."

"What time is it? I mean right now?"

"Just after nine p.m., Sheriff. Charlotte went to the six o'clock with her girl cousins. Supposed to meet up with them at the Rexall after the show. Didn't sit with them at all. Went to sit up in the balcony with her boyfriend."

"Hollis."

"That's him, all right."

"When did you get the call?"

"About an hour ago. I was out past Yancey in the Crown Vic, looking for our posse. It was Junebug on the radio told me. They got the boyfriend in custody already. He says she went to the little girl's room during the show and never came back."

"What about her purse?"

"Pardon me?"

"She take her purse to the ladies' room?"

"I don't know, Sheriff."

"Homer?"

"Yessir?"

"The posse. You say it like they were vigilantes. They aren't. They volunteered to go. And I deputized ever one of them boys."

"Yessir, I reckon that's true enough."

"I know you wanted to ride with them. Your time will come soon enough. Let's saddle up. I'll go with you in the cruiser. Daisy? Listen to me. You lock up these doors please. Front and rear. Leave that shotgun sitting right there on the counter. It's loaded with double-ought buckshot. I'll be back here in a few hours."

The screen door slammed behind him and she watched him walk all the way across the yard. She liked the way he walked.

HIGHWAY 59 over toward Prairie proper was deserted in both directions. The hills and rocks and sage looked golden in the strong white light of the full moon. Franklin Dixon didn't seem to feel much like talking so the deputy left him alone with his thoughts. Prudhomme could imagine where they were running without too much trouble. Four girls taken in the jurisdiction this month alone. Almost thirty people had been abducted along the Tex-Mex border over the past year. Four girls from Prairie alone. Vanished into thin air, every one of them. Make it five, now, most likely, with Charlotte gone.

"Pretty moon," Franklin said after a few miles.

"Yessir, it sure is."

"No word from that posse."

"No, sir. Not a peep. I don't know what in Sam Hill could have happened to 'em. They're supposed to be back here yesterday evening."

"I know that, Homer."

"Sorry."

"Taillights up yonder."

"Semi. Yessir."

"How fast you reckon?"

"Eighty. Eighty-five."

"Accelerator's the one on the right. Use it, son."

"Bells and whistles?"

"Good Lord gave 'em to us for a reason."

"Yessir."

Prudhomme turned on the siren and the blue rotators and accelerated. The old Ford Crown Vic didn't have much juice but what she did have, Homer used up pretty quickly.

"Slow down, son, you 'bout to rear-end him."

"Yessir. He's slowing down pretty quick with those air brakes. You want me to pull him?"

"He's a lawbreaker I believe."

Homer hit the high beam flashers and the big truck slowed way down fast, moving toward the shoulder of the two-lane, brakes hissing.

"Sheriff, what's your twenty?" the radio crackled.

"Hey, June. We're on 59 and headed in. Deputy Prudhomme told me about Charlotte. You know, I just—hold on a sec, June—what the heck is this big fella doing here, Homer?"

"Beats tar out of me, he just wants to play, I guess."

The big truck seemed to have changed its mind. It lurched along the shoulder and all of a sudden roared back up on to the blacktop and started accelerating down the middle of the road. Deputy Prudhomme stayed on his tail for a moment or two and then the gap started widening. You had to wonder what he had under the hood.

"He's doing more'n a hundred, Sheriff. Company puts governors on them rigs, I thought."

"Pull up alongside and move him gently over into his proper lane."

"Yessir," Homer Prudhomme said, and mashed the go pedal. But just as he was about to pull even with the cab, crowding him, the truck's engine emitted a high-pitched whine and the whole rig leapt forward again, going much, much faster. The big red taillights diminished to pinpricks on the horizon in seconds.

"Well, I'll be," Franklin said, moving his head side to side in disbelief. "You hear that whine? Superchargers."

"He has to be doing near a hundred forty miles an hour, Sheriff."

"Trucks can't go that fast."

"Well. I dunno. This one can. We've lost him."

"Ain't lost one yet and don't plan to start. Stay with him, boy. Do the best you can."

"Yessir."

"June? You still on the air?"

"Right here, Sheriff."

"Listen, we got a race-car driver in a souped-up trac-tor rig out here headed south on 59. Bright red, white, and blue Peterbilt cab with a big red baseball bat painted on the trailer's side. Some outfit called 'Yankee Slugger.' Never heard of 'em. Rolling fast toward the border. Get Wyatt to send a couple cars out to the intersection, will you please. Block the road and—now, what's he doing?"

"He stopped up there on the hill," Prudhomme said.

"June, I'm going to have to call you back. We got to go see about this truck."

"I ain't going nowhere but here. You still want Wyatt to order two squad cars out there, Sheriff?"

"No, June, thank you. We're all right."

Of course, as it would turn out, they weren't all right. Nobody was.

Not even a little bit.

8

Dry Tortugas

What's so dry about the Dry Tortugas?" Luis "Sharkey" Gonzales-Gonzales asked nobody in particular. He was staring down at all the clear blue water below. Sharkey, who was tanned a dark nut brown, was sitting two rows back on the other side of the aisle looking like a true citizen of the Conch Republic. A wicked-looking shark's tooth swung from his twenty-four-carat gold neck chain. He wore a faded fishing shirt with blue marlin leaping around, some old khaki shorts, and his trademark white suede loafers, no socks.

Sharkey had his head turned to the window, cheek pressed against the glass. He was gazing down at the glassy blue-green sea a thousand feet below the seaplane as the pilot banked left and lined up for a landing at a giant brick fortification called Fort Jefferson.

Stokely Jones didn't answer Shark's question about the Tortugas being so dry. He was too busy looking for the *Isaac Allerton*'s skeleton. Wrecks, man. For the last ten minutes, he'd been seeing bones in the white sand beneath the turquoise water, the scattered and broken backbones and ribs sticking right up where you could see them. The *Allerton* was down there somewhere. She'd been caught in a blow off Saddlebunch Keys back in 1856. After her anchor lines were cut, she ground over Washerwoman Shoals, lost her rudder, and sank in Hawk's Channel in five fathoms.

Mick Hocking, the young Aussie pilot sitting to his left, said *Allerton*'s remains were coming up. They were flying over the exact area where Mel Fisher had discovered the Spanish galleon *Atocha* and about a billion dollars in gold. Survey boats were moored in the shallow water, fifty feet or so, Stoke thought it looked like. You could tell the treasure hunters by the survey cable reels mounted on the transoms.

Off the Marquesas, and west over to the Dry Tortugas, the typical things you might find, if you stuck with it a few years, were artifacts and emeralds. Emeralds were almost common. Stoke had always had a fondness for buried treasure, a feeling he'd shared with his boss, Alex Hawke. He'd caught the bug the first time they'd worked together. They were down in the Caribbean, looking for the pirate Blackhawke's lost treasure.

Hawke told Stoke something one time they were diving down here in the Keys. Hawke said it was interesting how many decades it took professional wreckers to figure out that the big Spanish galleons, loaded to the gunwales with gold and silver, would not be found in deep water. They would most likely be in shallow water, like you had right here.

The galleons headed back to Spain would have been here in the South Atlantic during the hurricane season, Hawke said. That was June to October. And, if you looked at any map of the trade routes, and saw the storm tracks, many of those galleons obviously have been blown here into the Florida reef line. Some would be lost in open sea, sure. But many of them would fetch up in shallow water before they ran aground. Then, huge rollers would lift them up and split their keels on the reefs. Voilà, they'd spill all their booty on the bottom down there.

Stoke heard a little crackle in his headphones.

"Ponce de Leon called these islands *'Las Tortugas'* because they looked liked turtle shells on the far horizon," Mick said. "The 'dry' part came later when he found out the hard way there was no fresh water to be had down there. Still isn't, so bring that bottle of Fiji along with you."

"Ponce de Leon, huh? Is that right?" Stokely asked the pilot. Stoke was up front in the cockpit, in the right-hand seat of the seaplane.

"Yep."

"Huh. All that time I was down here, I never knew that."

He'd liked the guy, Mick, right away. Mick was a high time bush pilot from Queensland, Australia, who'd spent most of his career up in Alaska, flying wildcatters around. Mick seemed to understand that this flight was of an extremely sensitive nature. That the missing plane might be a matter of national security, Mick said, and this is a quote, "You'd have to be a fairdinkum wanker or a drongo to fly in here at night below the radar, mate."

Stoke liked him on sight. And he'd asked just the right amount of questions when Stoke had first reached him on his mible.

"You spend much time down here in the Keys, Mick?" Stoke asked him now.

"I did. I was in and out of Key West Naval some back in the day. A few years after your lot, I guess. Did some spec ops training with the SEAL blokes just down the road. Pissingly hot, even for an old sandgroper like me. Heat and Skeet we called it, Mr. Jones. Tough outfit, your SEALs are. I was impressed."

Mick had a crinkly smile, and, like that guy in the Crocodile Dundee movies, he always had a grin stuck in his voice. Cheery. That kind of guy.

"Take a gander down there, Stoke," Mick said in the headphones. "That must be your mate's boat coming up now."

A moment later, Stoke saw an old fishing boat below, moored at the island's disintegrating coal station. The thirty-foot boat, which had been painted blue some time early in the last century, was bobbing up and down, tied to the old wharf. A skinny white-haired guy stood on the bow, waving his floppy straw hat at the approaching seaplane.

Little was left of the island's broken, rusted-out black wharf. It was standing in turquoise water on the west side of the fortress island. This was where all the southbound steamers used to refuel before heading across the straits to Cuba and points further south. The battleship *Maine* had made her last pit stop here, before she was mysteriously sunk in Havana harbor.

Some people thought it was a Spanish torpedo that sank the *Maine,* and some thought it was Cuban terrorists. Whatever it was, America went to war with Spain over the sinking and kicked Spain the hell out of Cuba for good. You'd think Fidel would owe us one, right? You'd be wrong. Fidel was someone Stoke happened to know personally. He never talked about it, but he'd actually been awarded the Cuban Medal of Honor by Castro himself. Yeah, he had that medal in a drawer somewhere, but that was another story.

The old blue fishing boat had to belong to the guy Sharkey had arranged for them to meet. Fort Jefferson was a very out-of-the-way place. Nobody ever came out here unless they were very curious about old island fortresses abandoned after the Civil War.

Stoke had forgotten how massive the thing was. How thick those solid brick walls were, heavy black cannons sticking out all over the place. All they did now was sell a few postcards to touristas who ventured out from Key West after a few too many Cuba Libres at Sloppy Joe's booze emporium. Might come a day when America could use a fort down here, Stoke was thinking. In the event of a Gulf War in our own backyard.

Harry Brock believed, as did Stoke, that this neck of the Caribbean was shaping up fast as a place where the shooting could start. Hell, that's why Stoke was poking around down here, wasn't it? Latin America was blowing up in our faces. Stokely hoped to hell Sharkey had found something useful down here. He didn't have a whole lot of time to dick around.

Stoke turned around in his seat and smiled at his sole employee. His trusty gut was talking to him, it was saying maybe Luis was actually on to something worthwhile. Besides, he was starting to feel more comfortable with Luis lately. Yeah, maybe Sharkey was a little hyper. Nervous type. But Stoke's instincts about the wiry Cubano were trending positive.

"Hey, Shark-bait! This guy we're meeting at the Fort. How come he's got the same name as you?"

"His name is not Sharkey."

"No. It's '*Luis*' I'm talking about. Your real name."

"*Si*, Luis! He's my father. Luis Gonzales-Gonzales Senior."

"Why didn't you tell me that? Now I don't have to worry about trusting the fate of the free world to this old guy. He's still fishing, huh, your daddy?"

"Yeah. A lot of these elders here in the Keys, they came down from Miami soon after the Mariel in '81. They were fishermen back in Cuba. A lot of them took one look at Miami and then came down here to the Keys, man. Cheap housing. Lots of fish round here on the flats back then."

"The old man and the sea, huh? That his boat?"

"*El Bandito*, she's called. That old man going to fish her till he dies, man. He's a good spy, man, keeps his eyes open. Once you said I was officially in the program, on the case, whatever, I asked him to do it. He's got a tiny stilt house on a little spit of land in the Marquesas. He can see everything from there. He's out on the water all day and most of the night. The other fishermen, they are happy to help out. Stick together pretty much and they all hate Fidel as much as I do."

"You guys buckled up? We're going for a swim," Mick said. He'd been circling the landing area, looking for any floating debris before he set the *Blue Goose* down. Now that he was on final, he'd reduced his airspeed to about ten knots above stall speed, nose up, with maximum flaps extended. Air was getting choppy.

"Is it always this rough?" Sharkey asked.

"Clear air turbulence," Stoke said. "Relax."

"Man, what if we crash? Look at all the sharks down there. Those are bull sharks, man."

Stoke craned around in his seat and looked down.

"I thought you said you were a fisherman. This is an outgoing tide. Sharks don't feed at this hour. Sharks only feed on an incoming tide. Everybody knows that."

"Yeah? Tell that to the one bit my damn arm off."

9

"Assume you only live once, Mr. Hawke," Alex said to Ambrose Congreve. Hawke leaned back in his chair and smiled at his old friend. He liked the phrase and had been looking forward to sharing it with the celebrated detective. Congreve was fond of quoting Conan Doyle and, for once, Hawke thought he'd lob in one of his own zingers.

"Muhammad Top actually said that to you?"

Hawke downed the balance of his rum. "I was under duress. I may have embellished it."

Congreve returned his pipe to his cherubic bow of a mouth, skepticism plain on his face.

"It's the bloody truth," Hawke said.

"Torture *is* stressful, I suppose," Congreve said airily.

"Ah, well. It only hurts when you scream," Hawke said, a brief smile flitting across his face.

"Ouch," Congreve said, with a grimace only half-mocking.

Hawke nodded, leisurely recrossing his long legs, draped in soft grey flannel, at the knee. Linking his hands behind his curly black head, he leaned back against the indented leather of the deep club chair.

Alex Hawke looked remarkably fit and relaxed, Congreve observed, given what rough sledding he'd endured in months past. Ambrose, like most, had given Hawke up for dead. Reports had reached London, casting a pall over some quadrants of society and the City. It was widely reported that Lord Hawke's expedition into the Amazon had met with disaster when his yawl, *Pura Vida,* had been attacked by Indians and sunk with all hands.

Two months earlier, Ambrose had seen the sole survivor's stretcher being carried off the Royal Navy air transport flight after it arrived at Lakenheath from Rio de Janeiro. It was raining buckets that night, and all assembled had gathered inside an open hangar door, watching Hawke's gurney unloaded and hurried by a team of navy medics across the glistening tarmac. An ambulance was waiting inside the hangar.

A weary and deathly pale Hawke had attempted a cheery greeting, saluting the few naval chaps present. His brave front could do nothing to hide the terrible shape he was in. In addition to a very worried-looking "C," Sir David Trulove, new chief of SIS, there was a small group from both 85 Vauxhall Cross and Whitehall present, and one got the feeling they'd all come expecting to pay last respects to the corpse.

Congreve, like everyone present, had been horrified at Hawke's utterly wasted appearance. After a brief, private moment with C, who bent to whisper something in his ear as he was being loaded into a waiting ambu-

lance, Hawke was whisked off to Lister Hospital in
Chelsea. There, he was diagnosed as suffering from severe malnutrition, malaria, septic infection from a
snakebite, and God knows what else. He'd been in hospital for two months. He'd made a remarkable recovery,
and had only been released three days ago.

ALEX HAWKE and former Chief Inspector Ambrose
Congreve of Scotland Yard had just completed a
lengthy luncheon at Black's. Hawke's club was on
upper St. James' Street, an ancient bastion for gentlemen of property. The two friends had met in the bar at
one o'clock to hoist a glass or two. One, in honor of
Hawke's hospital release, another celebrating Congreve's semi-engagement to the beauteous and very
wealthy Lady Diana Mars.

Congreve's splendid news, delivered just that morning, had taken Hawke completely by surprise. Congreve, getting married? Hawke, like everyone else, had
Congreve down for a lifelong bachelor.

"Semi-engaged?" Hawke asked, not sure what that
meant.

"Hmm. I haven't exactly asked her. I haven't pro-
posed. But we do have an understanding."

"To understanding!" Hawke said, raising his beaker
of Gosling's rum.

Any witness to Congreve's behavior in Diana's presence over the last year should have known what was in
the offing. Smitten was a gross understatement. Love
was oversimplification. The man was besotted with
Diana Mars. They'd been seen out and about London

so frequently, and in such proximity, many people assumed they'd been married or at least involved for decades.

Ambrose had recently whisked Diana off to the Isle of Skye for a week of sightseeing. They'd also managed to visit the odd distillery, this being preparatory research for a new book the famous criminalist was in the midst of writing.

His book would not be some tawdry tell-all about the Scotland Yard detective's famous exploits amongst the criminal classes; in actual fact, it was projected as a slim volume to be titled *Inspector Congreve's Single Malt Cookbook.* Congreve envisioned the thing as a gentleman's companion, something that would be right at home on the shelf below one's first editions of H.R. Haggard or Sir Arthur Conan Doyle.

Now, they'd abandoned the bar for Black's cavernous smoking lounge. Their faces hidden in the shadows of two large leather wing chairs, the two men spoke of serious matters like love. A tall window, spattered with rain, rose above them and the dingy light filtering down from above was watery and grey. It was a perfectly miserable London afternoon in late November.

Ambrose was freshly aglow, a man in love; his companion Hawke was happy simply to be alive.

"Congratulations, Ambrose. I am extremely happy for you both." Hawke raised his glass.

"Cheers," Congreve said, clinking it.

"One thing you must never forget. I may have said this before, but it bears repeating. Great marriages are made in heaven; but so, too, are thunder and lightning."

"I'll drink to that," Ambrose said, smiling. "I say, you don't think I'm being impetuous, do you? I've known her less than two years after all."

"Not at all. I think it's high time you settled down. And Diana will be a brilliant match for you. You two will be very happy. I wonder, Constable, how do you envision the thing?"

"Well, I am mad about her and—"

"No, no. The marriage. How do you see it? If she says 'yes,' I mean."

"I suppose I haven't really thought that much about it. A comfortable marriage, I'd say. Sturdy."

"Good word, *sturdy*."

"Yes. I imagine our marriage will be a sturdy little barque upon which to ride out the tumult. You know, the tides that sweep us along, and all that sort of thing."

"Quite poetic for a flatfoot. Have you set a date yet?"

"Good Lord, no! As I say, I haven't even officially asked her yet. Although I suppose I'll get round to it one day."

"Well, you—"

A somber porter in cutaway and striped trousers appeared out of nowhere and interrupted whatever it was that Hawke had on his mind. He leaned down toward Hawke in what Congreve imagined to be a conspiratorial fashion.

He whispered, "Sorry to disturb your lordship, but there's a gentleman would like to have a word, sir."

"Is he downstairs?"

"No, sir. He'd like you to give him a call, sir."

"Who is it?"

"He said please give you this, sir."

Hawke took the small envelope from the silver tray and extracted a stiff cream-colored card. He glanced briefly at it, with a silent nod to Congreve as he got to his feet. His expression had changed so quickly, it was as if someone had tapped him with a wand. His eyes, a second ago alight with warmth and humor, had instantly turned ice blue.

"Sorry, Constable, I'm afraid you'll have to excuse me. I might be a considerable while. Perhaps I'll ring you in the morning. Something's come up, you see, and—"

"Don't give it a thought, dear boy, I'll just see myself out. Most enjoyable afternoon."

Hawke turned back to the porter.

"I'll use a private booth, please," Hawke said and quickly strode off into the smoky shadows, porter in tow. Something caught Congreve's eye and he turned to see the accidentally dropped card falling to the faded Persian carpet as Hawke disappeared from the room.

Congreve gazed at the spattered window for a moment, following the descent of a single raindrop, then rose and tossed off the balance of his whisky. He stared at the card face down on the floor for some long seconds. He and Alex were lifelong friends and they had few, if any, secrets between them. He bent and picked the thing up, pausing for a moment to give his conscience some operating room, and then opened the folded message.

On it was the single letter, C, written in green ink.

C was the name given to every chief of the British Secret Intelligence Service, sometimes known as MI-6, since 1909. This was, as Ambrose well knew, because the Service's original founder, Sir Mansfield Cumming, had a habit of scrawling a big green C on every SIS document he signed.

Ambrose Congreve certainly knew the implications of a summons from C. He sighed, audibly, and sank down into the soft womb of the nearest chair, still holding the card twixt thumb and forefinger. It was once more time, it seemed, to don the cloak and unsheathe the dagger. Knowing Hawke as he did, his happy fantasies of marriage and a quiet dog-and-stick life of a country scribe would most probably be put on hold.

Yes. Perhaps delayed indefinitely if, as he imagined, Hawke was soon to journey back into the heart of darkness.

"So it begins," the Scotland Yard man said, the merest trace of an anticipatory smile crossing his lips.

10

The big red, white, and blue painted trailer rig was parked on the shoulder at the crest of the hill. Just sitting there. Big red baseball bat on the sides and rear doors. The words *Yankee Slugger* in blue letters circling the bat. Homer Prudhomme slowed the cruiser, approaching the sixteen-wheeler from the rear. Franklin looked over at him. He was still a little wet behind the ears but he was coming along pretty good for a rookie.

"Okay, we got him," the sheriff said. "Tuck in there behind him, son. Keep your brights on. He's not likely to bolt on you again. Some hophead with a sense of humor most likely. Pay attention to what you're doing, however. These road warriors can get overexcited."

"Yessir."

"Go on now, git."

"Sheriff?" June said on the radio. Homer had opened the door but he still had one hand clenched around the steering wheel.

"Hold the phone a second, June—Homer, go have a

word with that gentleman. Inform him we don't speed here in Mesa County. Anything over a hundred entitles you to free bed and breakfast. Write him up and we'll take him on in."

Prudhomme climbed out from behind the wheel and disappeared into the dust cloud still rising around the trailer. Had his hand on his right hip. Franklin had to smile. He might not be a lawman yet, but he had the walk, by God, down.

"Go ahead, June. I'm sorry."

"What I was saying was, I think we maybe caught a break here with the North boy, Sheriff. The boyfriend says he saw somebody. There was a man at the candy counter. Hollis thought he was looking at Charlotte funny. Before the show."

"Hollis get a good look at him?"

"The unsub?"

Franklin looked out his window a second, eyes searching the blue-white mesquite flats, and then said, "Yeah, June, the *unsub* if that's what we're calling 'em on the TV these days. Hollis get a good look at him? This unknown subject."

"Says he did."

"Caucasian?"

"No profiling," June said.

"June!"

"No, sir. Latino."

"Awright, June-bug. I'll be there directly. We'll have an overnight guest most likely, so turn the cot down and leave a light on at the inn."

Franklin sat back and pushed both boots hard against

the floorboard, stretching his long legs. Couldn't remember the last time he'd sat on a horse, he thought, rubbing his eyes. He was at a funny place in his life. Weary all the time, seemed like. Worried when he woke up in the morning. He didn't used to be like that. Used to wake up with a smile on his face. Well, what were you going to do? Third-generation lawman. Maybe law genes could only stand so much law-breaking, is what Daisy had told him one night he couldn't sleep.

It was the border. His granddaddy, back when he was sheriff, had said something to him once and it stuck. He was talking about a rancher shot dead for moving a fence six feet. Laws were fences, he said. That's all they were.

"A border ain't nothin' but a law drawn in the sand."

A minute later, Homer was back. All by himself and shaking his head in disbelief. He put his hands on the roof and leaned down to speak through the driver's side window.

"You won't believe this one, Sheriff."

"Try me."

"Nobody home up front."

"Say again."

"Wasn't anybody up in the darn cab."

"Homer."

"Sheriff, I swear I ain't lying. Nobody there."

"He run?"

"Shoot, I guess. Doors closed, headlights on, transmission in Park. Empty."

"Let's take a look."

Dixon shoved his door open with his boot and

climbed out. He stretched, pulling his shoulders backward, his eyes on the far hills to the south. Smoke was curling up from the chimney of a ranch house. Ben Nevis's place.

He'd allowed a posse to ride south out of there two days ago. A dozen desperate young fellas from town who wanted to go find their sisters and girlfriends. Idea was, they'd ride down to Nuevo Laredo and see what they could find out about all these missing girls. They were due back yesterday evening and so far nobody had heard word one. Worrisome, to say the least.

The Peterbilt was hissing and steaming when he climbed up on the passenger side running board and tried to look through the windshield. Black glass, like it had mirror inside it. He pulled out his flashlight and put it right on the glass. Couldn't see a thing. He looked across the top of the cab and saw Homer's frowning face on the other side.

"Well, well, well," Dixon said.

"That's what I told you, Sheriff."

"You look back there in his bunk compartment? Maybe he's just watching a racy video in there and doesn't want to be disturbed."

"Yessir, I did check."

"And he didn't go out either door."

"We'd have seen him, Sheriff."

Dixon removed his hat and ran his fingers through his thinning brown hair.

"There was a lot of dust when he pulled over."

"I guess he could have run, Sheriff."

Franklin told Homer to have a look in the glove box.

Get his registration. Jot down all the numbers on the VIN plate screwed into the doorjamb.

"Well. He must have run," the sheriff said to Homer and jumped to the ground. "I'll go have a look around."

Dixon did a three-sixty, bending down to look under the trailer a few times, between the axles, and shook his head. Then he walked away from the truck, a few hundred yards into the desert. There was a rocky mound rising to about thirty feet where he could see the plains better. The wind had come up, and there were scattered tumbleweeds blowing across the highway. There was a sound on the wind, too, but it wasn't any speedfreak trucker beating feet through the desert.

No. It was horses. Maybe a dozen of them.

Franklin looked up, squinting his eyes, and saw a cloud of dust rising out on the plain.

His posse?

He moved quickly to the top of the hill.

The riders were tightly bunched about a half-mile away. Headed right at him at full gallop. Ben's ranch, where they'd left from, the stables were just up the road a piece. Well. The boys were a full day late but at least it looked like they'd all come back safely. When he'd sent them off, he hadn't been so sure about the thing at all. It was dangerous down there, real dangerous. All he knew was, he had to do something for those girls.

He'd have ridden down with them if he hadn't been so worried about his town.

There was a full-blown war raging on this border. An invasion. Illegals and drugs both. All hell had broken loose down in the little border town of Nuevo

Laredo. Lots of people on both sides had died in the crossfire. Two Border Patrol agents had been gunned down here in the last six months. Couple of tourists, too, who'd gotten lost after crossing over the International Bridge at Laredo. Pretty bad. He'd heard a rumor they were sending some fellas down from Washington to look into it. Well, it was about time.

Way past time.

Apparently Laredo PD had found a stash of IEDs under the bridge. Improvised explosive devices, just like the ones used in Iraq to kill Marines. Al-Qaeda on the border? He'd heard crazier things in his life.

The Mexican border was flat broken. And nobody had a clue how to fix it. Ranchers and Minutemen wanted to put up a 2,000-mile-long fence. Money was pouring in, people wanting to put fences on their property. Nothing made sense anymore. A border was a border. Any fool knew that. Folks in Washington just looked the other way. Didn't want to upset anybody. Give Texas back to the Mexicans without firing a shot. That's what was happening to his state.

But not to his town. Not if he could help it.

He had no idea if it was Mexican narco-gangbangers or even dirty Federales behind all these abductions. Or, even if the young ladies had been spirited away to Nuevo Laredo bordellos. But Nuevo wasn't a bad place to start looking, he knew that for sure. It was the most lawless town on either side of a lawless border. Not that that was saying much these days.

Something had spooked the horses. Maybe one of the riders had seen him standing up here on a hill. Anyway, they'd changed direction and now the posse was headed right for him.

He couldn't understand why they were riding so bunched up like that. He strained his eyes, trying to see. Even in the cold moonlight they were still just a tight black mass kicking up a single dust cloud behind them.

"Sheriff? I hear horses."

He'd been concentrating so hard on the strange spectacle he hadn't even heard Homer coming up the hill behind him.

"You're not going to believe this," Dixon said, turning back to the horses. Homer looked and a wide grin broke out on his face.

"The posse! Sheriff, if it ain't about time!"

"They look funny to you, Homer?"

"What do you mean, Sheriff?"

"I don't rightly know. They're riding all bunched up."

"I see that. Something else is wrong."

"Something sure is strange, isn't it?"

"No, I got it. They ain't got their hats on, Sheriff."

"I reckon that's it, all right. No hats. I knew something was wrong."

The posse had galloped to within a thousand yards.

"Sheriff, you know—something really ain't right here. I'm gonna tell you that right now. It just ain't natural the way they're riding those horses—"

Homer raced down the hill, fast as he could, and his words were lost in the wind along with his hat. He was running hard on an angle that might bring him a little closer to the oncoming posse. Suddenly, the horses veered left, once again, now directly toward the sheriff up on the hill. Twelve horses galloped right by Homer flying flat out. The deputy turned his head, mouth wide open, watching 'em pass him by.

Franklin's brain processed it before his eyes did. Why it was that his posse looked so strange in the moonlight. He stared after them until he couldn't stand to look at them anymore. He turned away and gazed up at the moon, thinking about what he'd done, sending those boys down there like that.

The boys on those horses were all dead.

Ever last one of them he'd sworn in, all riding straight up in the saddle, deader than doornails.

How'd they stay up in the saddles? Their hands must have been tied to the pommels. Their boots lashed together tight under the girths to keep them all sitting bolt upright like that.

Homer was right. Not one of them was wearing his hat.

Because not one of them was wearing his head.

Homer was coming slowly back up the hill, his eyes on the ground in front of him. When he got to the top he stopped and looked up at Franklin. Tears he couldn't hold back were streaming down his cheeks. Couldn't blame him. Homer had gone to Prairie High with half the kids in that posse. Played football with most of them. Hell, he knew these boys and—

"Sweet Jesus, Sheriff."

"Let's go call this in, son. You come with me. We'll do what we can for them. I don't want anybody else to see 'em like this."

"This is real bad, Sheriff."

"Yes it is."

But they couldn't leave. They stood and watched the headless horsemen disappear. Twelve horses thundered across the highway, the gruesomely dead boys suddenly flashing bright in the brassy yellow beams of the semi.

They started down the hill toward their cruiser.

Both looked up, startled. The big Peterbilt roared again and then the whole rig lurched forward and just took off down the highway. Franklin figured it was doing about a hundred thirty miles an hour when it disappeared down over the ridge.

The sheriff didn't see anybody behind the wheel when it went roaring by, upshifting gears, loud and fast. Like Homer had sworn, there was nobody driving the truck.

11

The seaplane flared up and splashed down on the clear blue water, her silvery floats throwing out foaming white water on either side. She was an ungainly thing, a Grumman G-21 Goose, painted an unusual shade of light blue, not quite turquoise and not quite any other shade Stoke had ever seen.

Mick Hocking called her the *Blue Goose*.

On the *Goose*'s final approach, Stoke had been able to get a closer look at Fort Jefferson. The place hadn't changed much in forty years. A huge octagonal fortress built out of brick and taking up most of a tiny little island out in the middle of nowhere.

The U.S. Army had built it to guard the southern approach to the Gulf of Mexico. The year it was built, it was declared obsolete. Somebody'd invented an artillery round that could go through six feet of solid brick. The Army had abandoned the place and later turned it into a prison. Dr. Mudd, Stoke knew, the guy who'd fixed John Wilkes Booth's leg, had done hard time here. Union soldiers had found his house by asking everyone in town the same question.

"Is your name Mudd?"

It took about twenty minutes to moor the seaplane at Fort Jefferson wharf, throw their gear in the old man's fishing boat, and get under way to the site. Stoke stood up on the flying bridge of the boat with Sharkey and Luis Sr., who was at the helm. It wasn't one of those modern tuna towers that looked like a jungle gym. This was an oversized solid wood structure, part of the whole wheelhouse on which it was sitting, reached by a ladder down to the cockpit.

Luis Sr. was planted at the wheel. He stood with his bare feet wide apart. His gnarled feet and thin brown limbs looked like roots growing into the deck. He was an older, skinnier version of his son. He didn't have a lot to say and what little he had was in Spanish. Old man had a pint of Graves XXX grain alcohol in his sagging back pocket. Took a pull every now and then, a little eye-opener, no harm done, a simple fisherman who liked to tend his own lines. Man had a tan so deep, he looked like he'd been cured in brine. Stoke liked him.

"Doesn't talk much, does he?" Stoke asked Luis.

"Only if he has something to say."

Luis Jr. had a map out and was talking to his father. Suddenly the boat angled hard to port, and began chugging along on a westerly course at about ten knots.

Stoke understood enough *Español* to know an airplane had gone down right around here a couple of nights ago. Went right over Luis's head apparently because when he told Stoke about it, his face screwed up and he made a ducking motion when he got to that part. Had no lights on, Luis had said, none, and it was a dark night.

Sounded pretty druggy to Stoke, but he didn't say anything to the old man.

Anyway, so it sounded like the old man had seen it go into the water. It had sunk quickly, before he could reach it, and no survivors. Stoke had asked what kind of plane. "DC-3," Luis Sr. had said, sounding very sure. It was an airplane he seemed to know, but of course he would, living down here. Air Pharmacy, Stoke figured, flying bricks of cocaine and bales of marijuana, but still he kept his mouth shut. Didn't want to hurt the old guy's feelings.

Stoke had seen some scuba gear below. Sharkey told him the plane was lying too deep to free dive. This was fine with Stoke. It was a good day for diving, not a cloud in the sky. The highly reflective sandy white bottom helped a lot.

Still, Stoke was getting worried. A lot of these damn flyboy druggies ended up as ocean bottom-nappers out here. More than you'd think. Old airplanes, usually chicken-wired DC-3s, flown by shitty bush pilots smoking dope. Finding a planeload of soggy cocaine and a couple of dead Colombians floating inside was not going to make his day. He motioned to Shark and they went back to the stern.

"What you think about this being a DC-3, Sharkey? Drug mule kind of airplane, right? We ain't DEA, we're not in that business, man. You know that. I hope you didn't bring me down here for some damn drug shit or—"

Sharkey looked hurt. Chin down on his chest.

He said, real low, "I wouldn't do that."

"Shark, come on, man, it's a DC-3! You know what that means. You got to tell me again why I'm down here."

"My father told me he saw a plane go down right next to a little island. I was down here, man, in the Marquesas. On a visit. I didn't see it go down, but I dove on this plane myself."

"Yeah? And?"

"I called you, didn't I?"

"I'm not interested in drug runners."

"It's *not* drugs. I don't know what it is, but no drugs."

"You sure about this."

"Stokely, you got to trust me, man, I'm on the team. Come on. Let's get the tanks. I'll show you."

"Over there by those mangroves?"

"That's it." Sharkey made a slashing motion across his throat. Luis Sr. hauled back on the throttles and the old boat slowed and stopped in about sixty feet of water. There was no wind, and the boat settled into a gentle rocking motion.

"*Muchas gracias, señor,*" Stoke said, smiling up at the skipper. The old guy looked down from the helm and smiled back. Nice smile. People spend their whole life on the big blue ocean, it gives them something you just can't find on solid ground. Peace, maybe.

There was a tiny island with nothing on it but thick mangroves and sea grapes. Just a spit sticking up out of the water, maybe a couple of hundred yards long and maybe fifty feet across. Some debris had floated up inside a small cove, a pool of emerald green water washing up on the white sand. Stuff had gotten hung up in the roots inside the cove. It looked recent. Kind of thing you might see after a plane went down. Stoke thought he saw movement over in the mangroves out of the corner of his eye, but when he looked he didn't see anything.

Probably a big heron or an osprey doing a little fishing. Could even have been a cloud of skeets moving around back in there. He'd go check out the debris after he'd seen the plane. See what had washed up.

"I got to saddle up, amigo," Stoke said.

Sharkey grabbed one tank and handed it to Stoke, then picked up a second one.

"Where you think you're going?" Stoke said, looking at the one-armed man.

"Down to the plane," Sharkey said. "You don't think I'd let you go down there alone, do you? The plane is sitting in a very precarious position. Edge of a shoal. You get inside and she shifts a foot or two, you kiss your ass good-bye."

"You want to come, you come on. But don't worry your ass about me, Luis. I was born alone. I'll go out the same way."

STOKE FELT the cold inrush of sea into two layers of wet suit and started down, the twelve pounds of weight on his belt and his tank helping him descend through all the bubbles. The world suddenly turned off-blue and dark. The visibility was okay, though; good enough to see what he saw. Below the thermocline, down around forty feet, it would get a lot colder and a lot darker.

But they'd gotten lucky.

The plane, one wing sheared off, was hung up on a narrow shelf of limestone in about thirty feet of water. The whole shelf was only a few yards wider than the fuselage. One hundred yards farther east and she would have slipped down into a deep trench.

Stoke gave Sharkey the okay signal and saw him return it. He checked his dive watch and then continued his descent toward the airplane, looking back now and then at Sharkey. It was interesting to see how you went about swimming down here with only one arm. Sharkey seemed to do just fine, considering.

It was a DC-3, all right, intact except that the port wing was completely gone and the whole nose and cockpit were pretty smashed up, meaning it had come in at a very steep angle. It was a very old airplane, unpainted, and there were no exterior markings at all. Just some blackened aluminum on the fuselage where the engine must have caught fire.

Stoke checked up and hung in the water a few seconds, just looking down it, surveying it from nose to tail. He hoped Sharkey was right about this thing because to him the damn airplane looked about as narco as you can get.

He motioned for Sharkey to follow and swam down directly to the nose. The windows were all blown out and a school of angelfish was just swimming out of the pilot's portside window. He saw Sharkey pointing at that window, nodding his head. Stoke flipped his fins and swam right up to peek inside.

Boo!

The dead pilot's lolling head floated up right into his damn mask when he peered inside the cockpit. Stoke pulled away instinctively. The guy's grey face was pretty messed up. Things like his nose were gone. You could see where the fishies had been having a picnic, pecking at him for a couple of days. Stoke pushed the head away from the window and stuck his own inside for a better look-see.

Something big had taken a chunk out of the pilot's right thigh, looked like. And his right hand was pretty much gone. Sharks, barracuda, maybe.

But none of that was the real interesting part.

What got Stoke's complete attention was the fact that the dead guy was wearing a military uniform. You had to wonder what a uniformed officer was doing flying around in an unmarked relic like this. Looked like Sharkey had been right about this damn thing, Stoke was beginning to think.

This was definitely not shaping up like any kind of drug lift. Of course, it could just be a rogue air force guy with a freelance weekend gig or—no. This didn't feel like drugs anymore.

He swung around and found Sharkey hovering about six feet behind him. Gave him a big thumbs-up. He could see the Cuban nodding his head in excitement, see his eyes smiling inside his mask.

Stoke, checking the shark-bit flyboy out, could just barely see military insignia, maybe a piece of a patch on the guy's shoulder. Could only see a little bit of it but if he could move the guy in his seat, he might be able to twist him around enough to find out where this dead cat called home. He reached inside across the guy's chest, carefully because there was broken glass and jagged metal, and grabbed the corpse by the upper right shoulder. He pulled the man's shoulder toward him but the guy didn't move. Still strapped in too tight.

He'd have to swim inside and check out the cockpit anyway.

Stoke turned around to look for an entry point and saw Sharkey's bright orange swim fins disappear inside a ragged opening in the fuselage aft of the former port wing. His diving buddy was one step ahead of him. There was also a big ugly mako hanging around, circling just above the fuselage opening and the big fella had that mean and hungry look. Maybe he was the one who'd enjoyed the cockpit entree earlier and was just dropping by for dessert.

Sharkey had probably seen that big mother too, that's why he'd ducked inside. You could hardly blame him.

Once bitten, as the man says.

Something else beside the shark was bothering Stoke.

All these planes flew with a crew of two.

So. Where the hell was the damn copilot?

12

Alex Hawke was half an hour early for his appointment with C at 85 Vauxhall Cross. He parked his fastback R-Type Continental in the underground parking. The old Locomotive, as he called it, had just turned fifty. Battered but unbeaten, he thought, and, keying the lock, he stood back to gaze lovingly at her gorgeous flanks. He drove her hard and got sensual pleasure doing so. He even loved the hideous paint job, a color he referred to as elephant's breath grey.

He'd grabbed his umbrella for a short stroll along the Thames. He went via the riverside walk, which, mercifully, was open. It was bitter cold and still spitting rain, but the air off the river was bracing and, besides, he needed a good chilling to clear the cobwebs from his brain. Damned rum. He'd better steer clear of it.

Twilight was Hawke's cherished time of day on the river, the hour when the plodding river traffic and headlamps streaming across the bridges acquired that misty glow. It was a scene he'd long associated with the watercolor artist he most admired, Mr. J.M.W. Turner. He walked the Embankment for ten minutes, trying to imagine why on earth C had summoned him. A pretty dark-haired passerby asked the time and he told her, realizing he'd have to hurry back.

Having satisfied himself that his city, despite all it had weathered recently, was still the most beautiful place he knew, he mounted the broad steps and strode through the main entrance at #85 Albert Embankment, Vauxhall Cross. Crossing the gleaming lobby to the bank of lifts, one could not help but notice the architecture. The current MI-6 Headquarters was a five-story, exceedingly modern affair, and was variously known in the intelligence community as Babylon-on-Thames or Legoland. It had been home to C and his several thousand colleagues since 1995.

Hawke, no fan of most modern architecture, found that he liked the place despite his predisposition not to. He was especially looking forward to seeing the chief's private and much ballyhooed lair.

"Lord Hawke!" cried a lovely young woman, walking purposefully toward him across the polished granite. He thought he recognized the tall and perfectly tailored auburn-haired beauty, but he couldn't for the life of him remember her name or even place her. She was a type, to be sure, the English Rose with large liquid eyes and exquisite manners.

"How do you do? Has he sent you down for me?" Hawke said, extending his hand and shaking hers. It was surprisingly warm and for some reason triggered his memory, the name popping to the forefront. He smiled at her and turned away, slipping out of his dripping mackintosh.

"Guinevere, isn't it? You were last seen at Number Ten Downing working for the PM."

"Gwendolyn. Kind of you to remember. Yes, I'm the same Miss Guinness. My friends call me Pippa. I was one of the PM's Garden Girls at Number Ten until this thrilling life of derring-do beckoned. I've been working for Sir David now, oh, a year at least, your lordship."

"Call me Alex, won't you, Pippa? Don't use the title, never have."

She looked at him. It was a brief appraisal, no more than three seconds, tops.

She would find him all right looking, he supposed; at least other people seemed to think so, as far as that went.

Alex Hawke was a strikingly handsome man, high-browed, with a sense of powerful self-control—indifference, some of his harshest critics called it. At best, it was an odd combination of latent ferocity and languid, mannered elegance. He stood a few inches north of six feet and had a full head of unruly black hair. He was well proportioned and quite fit for a man without a current exercise regime beyond sit-ups and pull-ups every morning.

Of course, he had lost a bit of weight in the jungle and it was mercifully slow coming back on. He had that strong Hawke jaw line and a slight cleft in the middle of his determined chin. Above his narrow and imperious nose, a pair of pale, arctic blue eyes. Eyes that turned ice cold when he was troubled. Deep within the iris, flecks of dark blue burned like a welder's torch when he was angered. The overall impression one got, however, was of resolution, tempered by boyish good humor.

Having completed her cursory evaluation, Miss Guinness smiled.

"Sorry. Alex it is, then. So, won't you come along with me? We're up on the fourth floor as you probably know."

"I didn't know, actually," Alex said, happily following her into the lift. "First time he's invited me to the sanctum santorum."

"I'll give you the penny tour later if you have time. There's a rather contentious meeting going on in his office right now, so he's slipped out to meet you down the hall in the *Salon Privée*."

"*Salon Privée?* That's new."

"Sorry. Inside joke. We use the language of diplomacy around here sometimes to break the tension. It's what he calls his private study."

"Splendid," Alex said, regretting the word as soon as it came rolling out. She was young and bright and beautiful and here he was sounding like some ancient and pompous toff. He was curious about the appealing Miss Guinness. To rise from a Garden Girl at Number Ten Downing to C's personal assistant at MI-6 Headquarters was a dizzying leap.

Hawke, who dreaded small talk, said, "He keeps you very busy, I imagine."

"Oh, yes. We never close around here."

"You're his personal assistant?"

She looked back at him before getting out of the lift. It suddenly went rather chilly inside.

"You'd think that, wouldn't you? Collecting visitors in the lobby. No, we're very egalitarian around here. I'm fetching you because I was the only one available."

"Ah."

"I hear you were tortured by Indians in the Amazon. Pity, that."

"Les hommes sauvages, n'est-ce pas?" Hawke said, smiling.

She walked out, her heels clicking smartly on the granite floor, and he quickly followed.

"So, Pippa," Hawke said, struggling to keep up with her pace, "what exactly do you do here?"

"I'm Senior Analyst, Latin American Affairs. It was my field of study at Cambridge."

"Ah. Fascinating."

"WELL, HERE we are, then," Pippa said, leading the way. They had left the granite behind and quickly covered the distance down a thickly carpeted hallway. He certainly didn't miss the drab Ministry-of-Works green corridors of the old Headquarters. The darkly paneled walls here were hung with lovely nineteenth-century marine art, Hawke noticed, some older Thomas Butterfields scattered amongst the Samuel Walters and the newer Geoff Hunts. He considered commenting on his own meager collection and then decided against it. Surely he'd inflicted enough damage already.

Pippa opened one of a pair of double doors and gave him an encouraging smile. "Go right in, Mr. Hawke, he'll be with you momentarily. He's on with the PM."

She smiled again, it was a warmish smile, practiced,

and then she left him, pulling the door firmly closed behind her. Only now did it come back to him. Yes. Gwendolyn. He and Congreve had been going up the cantilevered stairs at Number Ten Downing behind her, both of them relishing the sight of Miss Guinness's spectacular ascent. Seamed stockings, as he recalled . . . yes. Quite a girl.

Sir David Trulove, his face half in shadow, was seated at a small crescent desk. A brass reading lamp with a green glass shade created a pool of light on the red leather top. He was on the telephone and waved Hawke into an armchair by the fire. Hawke sat, and used the few found moments to take in the inner sanctum of the Chief of British Intelligence. It was a far cry from the old digs at Century House, a short stroll from the Lambeth North Underground, but still uninspired.

C's small room was finished in gleaming Bermuda cedar panels. All the lamps, paintings, and fixtures were nautical. Above the fire was a not very good portrait of Admiral Lord Nelson wearing the Order of the Nile given him by the Sultan of Turkey. Nelson, Hawke's hero since boyhood, was also clearly a favorite of C's. In the famous picture, Hawke knew, the decoration was worn incorrectly, having been sewn on by Nelson's manservant upside down. Hawke decided he would be ill advised to point out this irregularity to his boss.

There was, atop the mantel, a glass-encased model of Sir David's last command, the HMS *Yarmouth*. Hawke, like everyone in the Navy, knew her history. She'd had a narrow escape, down in the Falkland Islands off the coast of Argentina.

Two days after the British nuclear submarine *Conqueror* sank the Argentine cruiser *General Belgrano,* Sir David's *Yarmouth,* along with another destroyer, the *Sheffield,* had joined the fray in the Falklands. Both destroyers had been ordered forward to provide a "picket" far from the British carriers. A squadron of Argentine Dassault Super Etendards from the ARA attacked the British fleet. The *Sheffield,* mortally wounded by an Exocet missile strike, had sunk while under tow by Admiral Trulove's *Yarmouth.*

Trulove's destroyer had also been fired upon, but *Yarmouth* had deployed chaff and the missile had missed. It was common knowledge that the tragic loss of the *Sheffield,* finally abandoned as an official war grave, still played upon Sir David's mind. He was convinced the Argentine junta's decision to go to war over the Falkland Islands had been capricious and an act of outright political convenience. Nearly a thousand British boys had been killed or wounded because an unpopular regime had found it expedient to start a war.

"Lord Alexander Hawke," Sir David said, replacing the receiver and getting to his feet. "How very good of you to come."

"Not at all," Hawke said, rising to shake the man's hand. "Very good to see you again." He'd forgotten just what an imposing figure Trulove was when he rose to his full height. He was a good inch taller than Alex, very trim, with a full head of white hair and enormous bushy eyebrows sprouting over his shrewd grey-blue eyes and hawkish nose. Most MI-6 chiefs are recognized with a title only upon completing their tour of duty. Trulove had enjoyed enormous success in a private sector career that followed the Navy. This had led to an early knighthood, long before he'd been lured into the spy game.

"You look a bit thin," Trulove said, looking him up and down. "No Pelham to look after you in the jungle, Alex?"

"Jolly mingy rations out there, I must say."

"Sit down, sit down, please, Alex. Will you have anything, dear fellow? Whisky? Rum?"

"Nothing, thank you, sir. I was just filling my daily alcohol quota when you rang."

"Yes, yes. I know. So. Our old friend Chief Inspector Congreve is considering marriage. That's bloody marvelous. About time he settled down with a good woman. How is dear Diana?"

"You knew? But I just found out myself not four hours ago."

"Ah. Well, good news travels fast," C said, and his sharp eyes twinkled. You always had the feeling the man was checking your pulse for irregularities, like a bloody telepathic physician.

"Give Ambrose my warmest congratulations, will you?"

"Indeed, sir," Alex smiled, trying to imagine who on earth could possibly have overheard his luncheon conversation with Ambrose at Black's. Surely there weren't microphones in the salt cellars at the venerable sanctuary?

"Alex, I'm terribly sorry to have interrupted what was no doubt a most convivial occasion," Trulove said, and all traces of jollity had fled from his face.

"How can I help you, sir?"

C pulled an ancient gold timepiece from his waist-coat pocket and glanced at it impatiently.

"I'll get right to it, Alex. We found a hired lorry parked at Heathrow yesterday afternoon. Terminal 4. Abandoned for at least a week at short-term parking. Hidden under a tarp in the back were a thousand pounds of high explosives on a very sophisticated timer. We found the cache less than a quarter of an hour prior to intended detonation."

"Good lord."

"One certainly hopes. We're keeping this from the public for the time being. In the meantime, we're making good progress. There were three men in the truck and we got a fairly good look at them on the security cameras. We'll catch them. Soon I hope."

"Al-Qaeda? Or, another case of local boys?"

"Neither of the above. Certainly not AQ, although they may have their fingers in it. We'll see. Here's the thing. We learned about this only through an amazing sequence of events involving a chap named Zimmermann. Name mean anything to you?"

"Can't say it does, sir."

"German diplomat. He's Germany's ex-ambassador to Brazil. Or, was. He may be dead now."

"Dead?"

"We know where he is. A New Scotland Yard opera-tor received an urgent call yesterday morning. She passed it to my office and we subsequently found the Heathrow fireworks. An anonymous tip. Something made her keep the caller on the line long enough to put a trace on that call. It was made from a hospital bed in Tunbridge Wells. I supposed you'd call it a deathbed confession."

"The man saved countless lives."

"Indeed he did. He is gravely ill. Poisoned, his doctors think. Someone tried to kill him. Perhaps he's someone who they knew had a change of heart and was planning to give up the Heathrow bombing. He's still in hospital, at least he was as of two hours ago. Tunbridge Wells Hospice, a private one in Kent. Do you know it?"

"Indeed. But, sir, if you know where he is—"

"Alex, I'm sure you of all people will understand. I can't be seen as involved in the thing. The Americans, who are at this very moment climbing the walls in my office down the hall, were running this fellow Zimmermann in some Mexico City operation. There's a fresh crisis brewing down Mexico way, and the German is somehow involved. That's all I can tell you. I can't touch this man but I won't give him up to the Americans until you've had a chat with him first. Do you follow?"

"I think so. I just don't—"

"I would very much appreciate it if you would go out and see him first thing in the morning."

"Jolly good."

"There's one more wrinkle. He refuses to speak."

"Makes chatting difficult."

"Indeed. That's why I strongly suggest you take Chief Inspector Ambrose Congreve along for the ride. He was a language scholar at Cambridge, if memory serves?"

"He was."

"Yes, I thought so. Any number of languages, I seem to recall."

"All of them as far as I can make out," Hawke smiled.

"Good, good. This chap refuses to speak anything but German. None of my own valiant charges seem up to the task. Besides, we could use the Chief Inspector's brain on this thing."

"I'll make sure he brings it along."

"But, Alex, please use assumed names when you interview the man. I don't want this coming back to MI-6 under any circumstances. All clear?"

"Perfectly. Sir."

"Good. Well, I'd best be getting back to my Americans. Thanks for dropping by on the spur of the moment, Alex. I'm most appreciative as always for your help."

"Sir David?"

"Yes?"

"One more thing."

13

Hawke remained seated despite C's dismissal. He made a small coughing noise into his fist and said, "I wonder, sir, did you get round to my last report? I marked it 'Most Urgent.' "

"Your report? I did get round to it, yes," C said, looking up as if he were surprised to find that Hawke, having been dismissed, was still sitting in his chair. He returned to rifling through some papers on his lap, obviously looking for something in particular.

Hawke stood to go. C remained seated but now fastened his fierce eyes on Hawke's.

"You'd like a reaction. I was going to save it for another time, but since you've asked for it, here it is. You posit a possible link between Islamist terrorists and criminal elements throughout Latin America. Doesn't wash, I'm afraid."

"I was sent there to observe. I am merely making projections based on firsthand observation."

"Point taken. But we need to know more, Alex, much more, before we can take any action. Especially regarding any potential connections amongst FARC in Colombia, the Shining Path in Peru, and the *Montaneros* in Argentina. And, finally, Alex, I think you indulge in a bit of hyperbole with your fantasies about Islamic radicals and local guerrillas out there in the jungle. It's just not plausible."

"As I say, I saw this operation with my own eyes. This chap I mention in the report, Muhammad Top, is—"

"No relation to Noordin Top, is he? Fellow who's running the terrorist operation in East Timor?"

"His half-brother. At any rate, Top is building a guerrilla operation the likes of which we've never seen. With all due respect, sir, these bloody *jihadistas* are a huge factor out there. Why, he—"

"*Jihadistas?*"

"Yes. Sorry. My word."

"Good one, too; a neologism I believe it's called. Look here, Alex, please don't be cross. And, please don't misread me. The reason I sent you into the jungle in the first place was to confirm my own personal suspicions about Brazil's current political situation. Britain, as you well know, has heavy investments there and we're about to invest a great deal more on that new hydro dam at Diabo Branco Falls. Don't forget, Alex, I'm the chap who dreamed up your 'scientific expedition' to the Amazon. And I am deeply sorry that—"

"Please, sir. This is not necessary."

"I am deeply sorry, in fact, horrified at the tragic outcome. I'm afraid I terribly miscalculated the dangers involved in sending you up that godforsaken river. And, as I said in my official letter to you, the entire Service is in your debt."

"It's my job, sir. You offered me the opportunity to refuse."

"But you didn't, Alex, and the Service as always is deeply grateful. And, don't get me wrong. I'm extremely concerned about what I read in your report. Deeply disturbed, in fact."

"It is a deeply disturbing situation. Perhaps one of the most dangerous the free world faces at the moment."

"Alex?"

"Yes, sir?"

"I do have one final thought if you'll bear with me another minute. Just occurred to me."

"Of course, sir," Hawke said, and slid back into his chair.

"Tell me about your relationship with the American Secretary of State, Consuelo de los Reyes."

"I beg your pardon, sir? I thought that was private."

"Not your personal relationship, Alex. I already know all about that unfortunate business. Your working relationship is the one in question."

"Ah, that one. I would describe it as cordial."

"Hmm. *Une entente cordiale.*"

"Sorry?"

"A secret agreement to avoid hostilities. Well, no matter, Alex. Look, here. After you've had your little chat with the German ambassador I'd like you to give your old friend the American secretary of state a call."

"A call."

"Indeed. She's chairing a secret and very high-level

security conference in Key West, Florida, a fortnight from now. You're aware of this, of course?"

"Yes. My colleague in Miami is involved. Gathering preconference intel for the Pentagon. I believe you've met him. Stokely Jones."

"Large chap? American."

Hawke grinned. "Tear Stokely Jones down, one could erect a rather large sports complex."

C nodded, not bothering to smile. "Quite. Well. All the American regional ambassadors and LATAM State Department officials will be attending a CIA brief by your friend, Director Kelly."

This was Patrick Brickhouse Kelly, a lanky Virginian whom Hawke had befriended in the first Gulf War.

"National Security Agency will be there as well, Alex. Various U.S. border and police personnel. The Americans are one step ahead of us on this. Like you, some of them suddenly seem to believe Latin America is the world's next terrorist mecca."

"It's true."

"Well, at any rate, I'd very much like it if you were invited to Secretary de los Reyes's Latin American pow-wow. In fact, now that you and I have had a chance to discuss your report in more detail, I think it's critical you be there."

Hawke forced a smile.

Despite his convictions about Papa Top's operations in the jungle, he found the very idea of calling Conch appalling. Humiliating, to be exact. She'd refused to take his calls for months. All of his letters had been returned unopened.

"With all due respect, sir, this conference sounds very much an American—"

Sir David Trulove stood and fastened his somber tweed jacket. He had that resolute look of a man headed once more into the breech. His smile to Hawke was brief, his mind already grappling with the howling Americans down the hall.

"Come now, Alex, you've scraped by in far more perilous assignments than this one. It's a simple phone call. I'm sure Conch, that's what you call her isn't it, I'm sure Conch will be delighted to hear from you after all this time. Besides, a bit of tropical sun would do you worlds of good. You look very pale, to be honest."

Hawke searched for words as the man crossed the room and pulled open the heavy wooden door to leave.

"Sir David, with all due respect, what possible explanation could I offer the American secretary of state for simply ringing her up after all these months and inviting myself to her—"

"You'll think of something, dear boy," C said cheerfully before leaving the room. "Send her some flowers, pink roses, that's usually the ticket. I already forwarded her a copy of your report in the morning pouch. Once she's read it, she'll be chomping at the bit to have you give a first-person account at her conference. Nothing to worry about, I assure you."

Hawke sat back down and stared into the fire for a few moments. He was quite sure C had never sent anyone roses in his entire life. When he felt he could safely exit the room without breaking any furniture, he got to his feet.

Nothing to worry about, Hawke muttered to himself. You'll think of something.

After all, he had nothing to fear but the inestimable and incandescent wrath of a woman scorned.

Pink roses? For the second time this evening, C had absolutely no bloody idea what he was talking about.

14

"All the streetlights are out, Sheriff. You notice that?"

"Yep."

"Transformer down somewhere maybe."

"I don't think so."

"Nobody on the streets."

"Nope."

"Kinda early to be so quiet on a Friday night. Spooky."

"Folks rather stay home than get shot at."

"I guess. Can I ask you a question?"

"Shoot."

"Don't say that!"

"Homer."

"Sorry. I know you don't talk about, uh, Cam Ranh Bay."

"Right. I don't."

"But, see, I can't help but ask you, Sheriff. When you guys, I mean, your squad, when you'd go into a village at night, say. After dark. And you knew they were waiting—waiting for you to come around a corner or what-not. Did you—I mean, did you ever worry about—I mean—"

"Homer. Are you scared? Are you afraid?"

"Yessir, to tell you the honest truth, I am."

"Don't feel bad, son. Everybody is."

"I don't believe that for one minute, Sheriff. I don't think you are."

"Not now, maybe. But I have been."

Homer and Dixon had decided it was probably better to go down to Mexico at night. They'd taken Dixon's pickup, mainly because to take a marked American police vehicle south of the border these days was suicide. They'd even switched the plates, hung a banged-up old Mexican plate on the tailgate. He let Homer drive the thing. He was tired.

They'd all been pretty busy going to funerals.

The whole town had.

It had taken a couple of hours to drive down south of the border from Prairie. During that time, Homer had talked a lot. He couldn't seem to stop. It was mostly about the twelve boys who'd been killed in Mexico. Franklin had listened respectfully; he knew Homer cared deeply about those kids and their families. They'd all been friends since grade school, some cases nursery school. Homer'd been bottling a lot of things up inside and it probably helped him to just let some of it come on out.

The death of the town's best and brightest boys, coming like it did in a single night, would take a long time to heal. In one fell swoop, they'd pretty much lost a generation. Lost the future, Franklin's wife Daisy had said.

All those boys had mothers, and it was the most sorrowful time Franklin could remember. You couldn't walk into a store or the diner or the filling station without seeing tears falling down somebody's face. Women spoke in small groups on the street corners. Menfolk gathered at the Wagon Wheel or the other saloons and mostly drank. It would take a long time before this kind of pain subsided and that was assuming it ever did.

There were a lot of old boys in town who didn't want to wait around for any healing process. Fed up and up in arms, somebody called them. They wanted to ride on down there to Mexico and kill every last body they could find. Believed they knew who'd done it, who'd been abducting the girls and who'd killed the whole posse. They wanted to get their vengeance. It was hard to find fault with their emotions. But the law was the law.

And when Franklin tried to remind those fellas that vigilantism was taking the law into their own hands, one of their number, a Mr. J. T. Rawls by name, said, "Yeah. And your point is?"

"Point is, I'm the law. And you lay a hand on me you'll wish you hadn't, J.T," Franklin had said and that was the end of the meeting. Shut him up, but not for long probably. Rawls was what in Houston they'd call a speed freak. And he also had a weakness for tobacco and the many fine corn whisky products of Mr. James Beam, Clermont, Kentucky.

Rawls had himself a big Chevy dealership out south

of town. He'd gotten rich selling big black Suburbans and SUVs to the wealthy cattle ranchers; he was mean as a diamondback, too. J.T. had up and left his wife of thirty years for a young girl he'd met on the plane over to Houston. Once he'd accumulated all the money he could ever need, he'd run for sheriff. Run twice and been defeated twice. Losing didn't set well with him. It had gotten to the point where he was drinking a bottle of Beam a day.

Folks around town had wondered for a long time how J.T. managed to make so darn much money being drunk most of the time. There were rumors he had some side business interests that wouldn't bear a lot of scrutiny, but nothing ever came of it. Some people thought he was using his Chevrolet dealership to fence stolen cars on both sides of the border.

Another curious thing. The Mexican illegals never crossed his ranch property trekking in. Didn't trash it and eat the dogs and livestock like they did to some others. Franklin meant to look into that sometime. A rich Yankee the Mexicans didn't mess with? Pretty strange.

But that was all before he'd lost J.J., his son Jerry Jr., down in Mexico.

Now Franklin knew it was only a matter of time before Rawls did something stupid and got a lot more people killed. That's when Franklin got the idea to just go on down and talk to the Mexicans first.

A low-watt lamp snaked out of the cigarette lighter and illuminated the map on Franklin's left knee. It was a city map of Nuevo Laredo, the outlaw town situated just over the International Bridge from Laredo, Texas. Used to be a pretty nice place, Franklin thought, gazing out the window at the shuttered storefronts and darkened hollow-eyed buildings that lined the main drag. Tourist ladies used to like to make a day of it, drive down, have lunch, and do some shopping and be back home for supper. Not any more.

It was pretty much the murder capital of the world now.

A lot of windows and doors had been blown out and the plasterwork on most of the building fronts was pockmarked or missing entirely. All this had happened in the last year or two. Drug wars had terrorized this town. No law. No order. Period. Somebody'd said over a thousand people had died in the last year alone. Accidentally on purpose. One Border Patrol report Franklin had seen talked about mass graveyards to the south of town. They had to do something with all those bodies.

He saw movement to his left and swung his eyes that way. Nothing but some old dog slinking around the corner. The town was full of such animals. Crossbred, Franklin thought, with coyotes or jackals or some such thing. Ugly as sin no matter what they were, all bones and teeth.

Every now and again he'd see a human shape or a silhouette looking down at them from above. From a rooftop or to this side or the other of a window or doorway. Homer had noticed them too, but so far he hadn't said anything more about his fears. He knew what they were getting into when he offered to come down here. Boy clearly had his mind set on it, so Franklin finally just said fine let's go.

They'd driven down to Nuevo Laredo to have a parlay with a gang-affiliated gentleman by the name of Felix "Tiger" Tejada. Franklin had gotten a message to him via a detective in Laredo PD. Lieutenant Detective Rodriguez maintained a purely mercenary relationship with one of Tejada's honchos. Somewhat to the sheriff's surprise, the man had agreed to meet with him. Tejada had a lot of conditions, of course, and Franklin agreed to every one of them all without any hesitation. What else could he do? Lose his whole town?

Tiger Tejada, now he was one unusual bandito. He wasn't smart enough to do some of the things he did, so you had to assume somebody up the line was whispering in his ear. And he wasn't brave enough to go out and piss in a windstorm so he hired people to do his killing, stealing, and whatnot. But money? Money was not an issue for this gentleman. The DEA in Austin told Franklin that Tejada was an up-and-comer in the Latino gangbanger world.

Tejada, as a relatively high-ranking member of the *Para Salvados,* was already moving a ton of product over the border. As an amusing sideline, he had the biggest string of fancy brothels and claptrap cathouses south of Laredo. But, his real hobby was trucking aliens across the border at five thousand dollars a head. That's where the big money was, illegal immigration. The Border Patrol called guys like Tiger "coyotes" and it was pretty darn accurate. Coyotes, that's just what they were.

"Next right," Franklin told Homer, putting his index finger on an intersection.

"Where's this meeting supposed to be at?"

"I'll show you here in a minute. Okay, left, and then stop."

"That's it? Right there?"

"Right here. The Plaza del Toros."

"A bullring?"

"Let's go."

15

They pulled up as near the entrance as they could. There was a large number of motorcycles parked under the concrete overhang, maybe thirty or forty of them, all painted in bright metallic colors. What they had in common was a large white death's head painted on the fuel tanks. Below the skull, the symbol PS 13 was painted. *Para Salvados.* PS 13 rode well. They were expensive bikes, Franklin saw, Harleys and Ducatis and big Indians.

They stuck the Mossburg under the seat. Tejada had said no guns, but Franklin wasn't walking in there completely unarmed. Homer had a gun. Franklin told Homer to take his hand off his hip as they walked toward the darkened archway marking the entrance to the crumbling building. He didn't want them getting shot by some trigger-happy crackhead on the way inside. The old building had a damp smell of rotting concrete and urine and time passing by.

They walked out into the center of the ring.

They were standing back-to-back in the middle of a

circle of hard-packed sand about fifty-five yards across. All around them the concrete seats rose up into the darkness under the overhanging rooftop. The bad smell was even stronger out here, different. Franklin wondered if it might be a couple of centuries of blood soaked into the sand beneath his boots. Probably a sprinkling of matador blood mixed in with all the bull blood. Bull blood and bullshit, he amended his thought.

The noble *corrida*. He'd gone as a little kid down to Mexico City. There was a festival of some kind and they went to the Plaza del Toros Monumental. That was the biggest ring in the world at that time. His daddy had wanted him to see El Cordobés and the great Mexican matador, Carlos Arruza.

He'd seen them.

The bulls never had a chance, he thought then and now, gazing up at shadowy figures with guns moving around up on the top rows. Lots of them up there, maybe fifty or so. You had to assume they all had automatic weapons. He felt Homer's trembling when they brushed up against each other. Just take it easy, he told him. We're just here to talk to the man. That's all. We'll talk to him. Then we'll go home. Steady.

"Welcome to the *corrida, Señores,*" a voice said from a tinny loudspeaker mounted high above the ring. It was Tiger. Franklin had heard his voice talking on a tape once at Laredo PD. The Feds had a tap on his home wire at that time and they'd had his cell for a while. He'd stopped using it now that he'd become rich and famous and could afford a sat phone.

"Howdy," Franklin said, not bothering to raise his voice. They could all hear him just fine. A minute later, Tiger had some of his guys file inside the ring and fan out in a circle, maybe thirty of them, all standing behind the wooden barrera not twenty yards away. The barrera was a five-foot fence all around the ring to keep the bulls from goring the spectators. The sweet stench of marijuana wafted up from behind the thing. Some small talk and laughing. Friday night gangbangers having a good old time.

"You didn't get my message about the guns?" the amplified voice said.

"I'm not having a conversation with a loudspeaker. You come on down here and talk man to man. We'll put the guns down."

There was a silence while Tiger thought that one over and discussed it with his compadres in the broadcast booth up at the top of the stadium. A blue-white spotlight suddenly came on, shining right down in their eyes. It was blinding and he hadn't counted on that.

There was a loud bark and then the sputtering staccato sound of one of the big choppers outside exploding into life. This was followed shortly by the fairly awesome sound of about thirty more bikes being cranked and revved under the concrete overhang of the stadium.

"They leaving?" Homer asked.

"I don't think so. I think they're coming in."

The wavering beam of a bike headlamp was visible in the tunnel leading to the ring. The first motorcycle to enter the ring came in slowly and took a left just inside the barrera. The rider made a slow circuit of the ring. The next rider took a right, the next a left and so on, left then right, until there were thirty or more inside, executing a slow parade at the perimeter of the ring.

Behind him, Homer said, just loud enough to be heard over the deep rumble of the bikes, "Looks like Hell's Angels wannabes to me."

Franklin spoke to Homer in a low voice over his shoulder. "Listen. Take your weapon out of your holster real slow and lay it on the ground."

"You sure about this, Sheriff?"

"Yeah. Do it now."

Homer did it but he plainly wasn't happy about it. Franklin kicked the gun away with his boot tip.

"You coming down?" Franklin asked, squinting in the bright lights above. "Turn those dang things off if you want to talk to me."

A few seconds later the lights went out, snapping and popping.

Tiger Tejada came out from behind the barrera and started walking. He waited for a break between bikes, then strode across the ring toward them with a whole lot of attitude. Heck, he was just a kid. Franklin was startled to see he was wearing a shiny jacket that seemed to be made out of blue sequins. His long black hair was pulled back from his face and tied into a ponytail. His narrow face was set in a frown, his eyes black under a high forehead with the entwined letters PS tattooed there. He was wearing black jeans and shiny snakeskin kicks on his feet, looked like some kind of gangbanger rock star.

Tiger was a high-ranking Mexican warlord in a gang known as the *Para Salvados,* or PS. The gang originally formed during the civil war in El Salvador during the 1980s, a war that killed a hundred thousand and left millions impoverished and homeless. Many thousands made their way to the United States and settled in Hispanic neighborhoods in cities like Los Angeles. Victimized by black gangs like the Crips or the Bloods, they soon formed their own self-protective society.

Over time, the PS, with a history of violence and business savvy, had grown to be one of the world's preeminent importers of illicit drugs and weapons. By 2005, they had expanded far beyond the California borders. Huge cells of the gang existed from New York to Florida, and throughout the Midwest states of Illinois, Michigan, and into Texas and even Alaska.

"Ola, Tres Ojos," Franklin said to Tiger, using the street moniker he'd picked up on the FBI taps. Franklin saw a sudden flash of strong white teeth. Maybe he wasn't as stupid as everybody thought. He clearly enjoyed the gringo sheriff knowing his secret handle.

"Ola, Señor," he said with a smile of exaggerated politeness. "Thank you for coming down to visit."

"Pleasure's all mine," Franklin said. "Tell me something, how'd you come by that name?"

The smile became a smirk. *"Tres Ojos.* Three eyes. My third eye is my pecker. Always on the lookout for pussy."

Franklin forced a smile. "Yeah."

"It's good we have this little chance to talk, señor. Tell me. What was it you wanted to discuss? You here to arrest me?"

"I'm here to offer you a way out of this."

"You're offering *me* a way out, señor?"

"Correct."

Tiger turned and looked back at his boys lingering behind the barrera. They all had their gun barrels resting on the top of the fence now, pointed toward the center of the bullring. A couple of them racked the slides on their weapons.

Tiger signaled the motorcycles to stop. When they had done so, he spread his arms in a wide arc and pivoted on his bootheels.

"*Muchachos!* The man says he's willing to offer us a way out of here!"

After the irony of that had a chance to jell there was a chorus of raucous laughter. Somebody behind the barrera fired his 9mm automatic into the air and that really brought the house down. Tejada turned back to Franklin with a glittery mescal look in his eyes.

"Apparently, they do not accept your offer, Sheriff."

"Listen. You want to be a grown-up and have a serious talk, tell me now. If not, my deputy and I will leave. Your call, son."

"I admit to curiosity. What is it you could possibly want from me?"

"I want what I can get."

"What you can get."

"Yes. I can't get the boys back, so I'll take the girls."

"*Las putas?* What's the difference? Really. I don't know what the fuck you're talking about. You wasting my time."

"Tiger, listen to me. You see that big black thing up

there, looks like the sky? It ain't. It's a big Yankee hammer about to come down on your head. I'm offering you a chance to get out from under it."

"What is this fucking hammer?"

"Swift justice. It's coming your way shortly."

"You threatening me?"

"Yes."

"What is it you want? Spit it out. I have other appointments."

"I want you to work for me."

"You are truly crazy, you know that, man?"

"Maybe I am."

"Tell me. What you want, man?"

"Let's take a walk."

"*Si.* Whatever."

"It's called flipping," Dixon said when they were out of earshot. "We start at the bottom which is you. We flip folks in your organization, find out who the guy above them is and go after him. We keep flipping until we reach the top of *Para Salvados.* The head honcho who's getting you into so much trouble."

"You lost me way back with flipping, man."

"Whoever it is. At the top. We take him out. And you take early retirement where nobody can touch you. Guaranteed. You understand?"

"I understand. You think I'm crazy as you."

"I did. I don't anymore. I think you're smart enough to follow your survival instincts."

"Yeah?"

"Tiger. You're in over your head and you know it. Take my offer."

"And if I don't? If I just add your Yanqui blood to this sacred ground of el toro?"

"You do that and men far less polite will come down here in sufficient numbers and with sufficient fire-power to put you and everybody in this town underground. I promise you that will happen."

"You serious, man?"

"Right now, I'm the only thing stopping it."

The kid looked away and Franklin could see him coming to a decision. "It wasn't me. That unfortunate thing with your posse. I heard about that, but it wasn't me."

"We'll see, I guess."

"I need to think about this."

"Think fast. As a show of good faith, I want you to release the five women that were stolen from my town over the last six months. Today is Saturday. I'm giving you forty-eight hours."

"You are crazy, man, fucking loco gonzo. What makes you think I have them?"

"If you don't, you know how to find them. If all five are not back with their families by sundown Monday, I'll take that as a decision on your part and act accordingly."

"Shit. I don't know, man."

"Look at me, Tiger. See who I truly am."

"I see pretty good who you are."

"You've got until sundown Monday."

"I make no promises."

"Pleasure doing business with you, son," Dixon said, walking away from the Mexican. "All right, Homer, get your gun. Time to saddle up."

"*Adios, Tres Ojos,*" Homer said, smiling at the narco.

"You know, perhaps some day me and my compadres will return the visit? How about that? We come see you sometime? You would like that?"

Homer and Dixon kept walking.

As they were climbing in the pickup, Homer said, "Were you kidding about all that 'hammer of justice' stuff?"

"Maybe."

"America ain't got a spare hammer right now, Sheriff, that's the whole damn problem."

"I know. I made it up when we were walking out there."

16

Dry Tortugas

The hungry mako was still in the picture. Loitering in the foreground, swimming lazy loops about twenty feet above the fuselage. Acting like he didn't give a good goddamn, but Stoke would swear the fish kept checking him out, fish with that snaggle-toothed grin of his.

Stoke, back in his Navy SEAL days in the Keys, had always thought this particular make and model of shark was the meanest-looking animal on earth. Fish had a very expensive set of curved knives set into his jaw. His pointy snout and dark eyes gave him a look of intense brainpower, even though he was just a damn eating machine. Definitely came with an aggressive attitude; his eyes looking into the back of your eyes, saying, "Hey! I'm the kind of fish who will personally bite your ass in half."

Mako was a fast fish, too. Any Keys fisherman will tell you a mako can reach speeds of almost twenty-five miles an hour and can jump about twenty feet in the air. They've been known to attack small fishing boats, leaping up suddenly and landing on the deck, biting everything in sight. Like a collision at sea, a thing like that can ruin your day.

Stoke kept one eye on the mako, especially because he was pretty busy trying to stop his arm from bleeding. He'd ripped it on the jagged edge of some protruding cockpit glass. Reaching inside again, trying once more to move the dead pilot around, he'd been forced to pull his hand out in a hurry. What happened was, a big-ass barracuda swam right up inside the cockpit, knocked the pilot's head to one side and gave Stoke the evil eye.

Shit! Tore his damn wet suit, yanking his arm out and slicing his forearm deep and now his cut-up hand was bleeding pretty good, too. Nothing like getting a good blood flow going around man-eating sharks to add a sense of heightened drama to any situation.

One swift scissors kick got him to the entrance to the plane. He poked his head inside. Visibility was way down inside the submerged airplane, but he could clearly see his man Luis poking around in the plane to his left. Sharkey saw Stoke and motioned him forward, pointing down at something below his fins. Stoke checked his right flank first, to see if there were any more jaws-of-death types lurking around in the rear of the fuselage.

It was clear so he swam right through and hung a left toward the cockpit.

Sharkey immediately saw all the blood trailing from Stoke's hand and started shaking his head, pointing upward, meaning he thought the wound was bad enough they should surface and get it taken care of. Stoke shook his head "no" and turned on his Beacon halogen dive light to see what all the excitement was about.

Sharkey had already ripped up a small section of the plane's aluminum flooring. Something was down there and Stoke had the feeling it wasn't any damn cocaine. He swam right down to the small opening and peered through it. Too dark to see anything much but they were definitely carrying cargo down there. He poked his hand down there and felt around. A flat surface under some kind of rough covering.

He stuck his light through the hole and directed the bright white beam fore and aft. There was way too much silt and blood in suspension to see anything much and he had to wait a bit for it to settle.

He looked at Sharkey, mouthing the words "good job." Luis nodded his head, but grabbed him by the elbow and pointed up at the surface again.

Stoke held up two bloody fingers. "Two minutes."

He pulled out the dive knife strapped to his thigh and used it to lever up a larger section of flooring. Now he could maybe get his light down inside there and see what the hell he had here. A foot below the floor frame, what looked like two large rectangular containers were lying side by side and covered with heavy burlap.

Stoke felt his heart pump.

Sharkey helped him get the rest of the floor section up. It took about five minutes. Stoke was starting to feel the loss of blood, but this was damn well worth a little dizziness. There were two long cases, each about six feet across and about twenty feet in length. He tried, but he couldn't see how far they stretched back under the remaining floor.

He sliced open the burlap, making a slit about four feet long and then just ripping the material away.

Inside was a large metal container. There was stenciled information on top, printed in red. The writing was Russian, not one of his languages. Still, a word popped out at him and sent a new sensation flooding through his body, a mixture of fear and satisfaction. He'd seen this word buried in the thick briefing documents Harry Brock had given him to study when they'd met for his initial briefing in Washington.

On the JetBlue back home, he'd opened the brief book and dug in. Read a lot of governmental boilerplate about what he could and could not do as an independent contractor. Perused a CIA overview of all of Latin American countries. And, finally, a long list of all the bad shit he should be on the lookout for when he got to the Caribbean. One whole section had been about black market foreign cruise missiles. Brock had told him to read that section very carefully. He didn't need to tell Stoke why. It was one of the things the U.S. was most concerned about in the region.

Hell, you had half the nation's strategic oil supply going up the Gulf of Mexico to New Orleans. If somebody, Fidel or Hugo, say, started taking out tankers or offshore rigs, you were looking at war on your back porch.

The Russian word he had recognized was *Yakhont*. Stoke sucked a lot of oxygen down and held it there, trying to calm himself down.

Yakhont had a familiar ring to it.

Sharkey and his old man had stumbled on the jackpot.

Yakhont, called *Firefox* by U.S. military, was the new Russian anti-ship missile. It scared the hell out of everybody in Washington. Death with wings. Unstoppable ship-killer. And, precisely what the U.S. government did not want was for even one of these damn things to find its way into the hands of somebody who didn't have America's best interests at heart. That's why it was at the top of the list Brock had given him.

Firefox combined all the qualities of future anti-ship missiles. It was designed to fly at supersonic speeds, be invisible to radar, deaf to jamming, and was guided autonomously on a "shot-forgot" principle. Fire a Firefox and *fugheddaboudit,* game over. It had a range of up to 300 kilometers at an altitude of about 15 meters. The missile would drop down to about fifteen feet just seconds before it hit you.

Flying at roughly 750 meters a second, and performing complex tactical maneuvering during flight, the Firefox would reach its target no matter what. Just one of these damn things could sink a supertanker or an aircraft carrier. And, no navy in the world had an effective means of defending against the Russkies' new missile. Not one.

The missile was designed to be carried by Russian Su-27 and Su-35 fighter aircraft. This was the new Sukhoi Flanker, a front-line fighter that was one of the mainstays of Russian airpower. Sophisticated and extremely expensive. Now, who the hell had planes like that down here in the tropics? Castro certainly couldn't afford any damn Su-27s. Cubans could barely afford breakfast in that island utopia.

But his bosom buddy, Latin America's new Daddy Warbucks, Hugo Chávez of Venezuela, sure could.

Two minutes had been used up. Stoke swam up to Sharkey, who was tapping on his watch and staring at Stoke like he was crazy, which was no newsflash. Stoke knew he'd lost a hell of a lot of blood but he wanted to get this done in one dive and get on the horn to Washington as quickly as possible.

Stoke opened his dive bag and pulled out a small digital camera designed to work underwater. He gave it to Luis and then pointed at the two cruise missiles. Sharkey understood and swam down to photograph the things.

The big barracuda, thank you very much, had left the premises when Stoke got up to the cockpit. He'd chewed up *el Capitán* a little more but Stoke wasn't interested in the man anymore, only his uniform.

It was light blue. Military, but if Stoke expected to find insignia identifying the pilot's outfit, he was mistaken. Anything that could have identified rank or national origin had been removed from the corpse's uniform. And it wasn't fishies who'd done it. Someone had used a knife to cut the patches away. Stoke knew that because he saw the knife still lying in the pilot's lap.

Very interesting. The deceased had been stripped of ID. Somebody had survived the crash. Yeah. Some-

body who'd kept his wits about him before he disem-
barked.

Stoke checked his remaining air. Time to go. He
looked at the pilot one last time before he swam out of
the cockpit.

Hasta luego, amigo, he said silently.

Fly below the radar.

Die below the radar.

17

Congreve pushed back from the table and laced his fingers atop the plump pillow of his tightly buttoned yellow waistcoat. Suppressing a sigh of pleasure, he surveyed the sunny scene of domesticity before him. Basking in the morning light, shafts of pure gold streaming through his windows, the famous detective had the look of a man who had finally grabbed life by the lapels and shook it for all it was worth.

Life was worth, he was now convinced, a very great deal. He'd had a near miss a year ago. A would-be killer's bullet had lodged very near his spine. It had all been quite touch and go for a while. To be honest, though he'd never told a soul, there were not a few times, lying there in the dark in his hospital bed, when he'd heard the angels calling. It was sweet and seductive, the music from heaven. But he'd turned a deaf ear, and it had finally stopped.

Yes, yes, Ambrose thought. Life was certainly hurrying by, running away at breakneck speed. Too fast to stop, and too sweet to lose.

May Purvis, his housekeeper, who'd been quietly arranging a dozen dewy peonies in a silver jug, was suddenly up on her toes. She had her hands clasped to her bosom, and seemed on the verge of a pirouette.

"Well, well, Chief Inspector, look who's come to call of a morning," said a beaming Mrs. Purvis. Ambrose looked over his shoulder and saw Alex Hawke framed in the doorway.

"Ah, good morning, Alex," Congreve said, putting down his *Times* crossword. The man was half an hour early. He'd called the night before. Something about visiting some diplomat in hospital. Very tight-lipped about it and wouldn't say more.

Hawke, never one for a lazy entrance, didn't falter now. Before you could blink, he was kissing the back of Mrs. Purvis's fluttering hand.

"Mrs. Purvis's younger daughter, are you not?" Hawke said, bowing slightly from the waist. "We meet at last!"

"Oh, my! Don't be ridiculous! It's only me, of course. It's poor old May, you silly boy!" she said, giving a half-curtsy.

Hawke took a seat.

"Tea?" May asked Alex, pouring.

She was buzzing about his lordship, teapot in hand, like a bee round a stamen. It was a bit much this early in the morning.

"You might put a patch on mine as well, please, Mrs. Purvis," Congreve said, holding up his cup, a trace of peevishness in his voice.

"Did I tell you I bumped into C, of all people," Hawke

said, putting down his cup and passing the linen over his lips. "After our splendid luncheon at Black's yesterday."

"Did you indeed?" Congreve affected his most innocent smile, his baby blue eyes conveying nothing but simple curiosity. For now he'd decided to let the green ink on the dropped note remain where it had fallen.

"Yes. Bumped into him at Harrods, believe it or not. Buying a tie."

"Harrods?"

"Yes, Harrods. Rather large emporium in Knightsbridge. Surely you know it?"

"Alex. Please. Spare me this day your ridiculous sense of humor."

"Anyway, I saw him."

"Hmm. Anything in particular on his mind? Other than neckwear?"

"Nothing in particular, really."

"I don't believe you for a moment. Marching to the colors again, are we? That's my guess. Drawing steel once more. Is that right, Alex?"

"Hmm."

"What was on that formidable mind?"

"This and that."

Hawke looked at his watch. "We're late. Our meeting with this German chap. We'd better shove off."

"German? Who said anything about Germans?"

"I did. Let's take your Morgan, shall we? The Yellow Peril?"

"ZIMMERMANN IS his name?" Ambrose asked above the wind and engine noise. "This chap I'm to interrogate?"

"That's it."

"Why does that name sound so familiar?"

"Just thinking that very thing. Something to do with the Great War, wasn't it?" Hawke replied.

"Hold on, it will come to me. Ah, yes, the Zimmermann Telegram. The cryptographic lads in Room 40 at Whitehall intercepted and decoded it. Dispatched by the German foreign secretary in 1917. Instructing his German Ambassador in Mexico City to approach the Mexicans about forming an alliance against the United States."

"Exactly. To keep the Yanks out of Europe while the dreaded Hun polished us off?"

"Yes. The Kaiser believed the Americans would get so bogged down fighting a war on their southern border they'd leave us in the lurch. The Mexicans were leaping at the chance to recover Texas, Arizona, and California. Might have worked, too, but for the fact that we cut the Germans' suboceanic cables and rerouted all their transmissions to—"

"Ambrose," Hawke said, "the man you're about to meet was somehow involved in a plot to blow up Heathrow. Herr Rudolf Zimmermann is also the former German ambassador to Brazil. C is a clever man. He's read my report and now he's sending us to interview someone who may possess vital information relevant to the region."

"I still need more details before I interrogate this man."

"I'm afraid details are incomplete."

Congreve smiled. "I pray we make them less so."

Hawke swung the Morgan into the car park. Twenty minutes later, the two men were standing at the dying man's door.

A burly SIS type, an ill-concealed weapon bulging beneath his jacket, sat outside chatting up a pretty nurse.

The SIS man stood, opened the door, and waved them inside an ill-lit and ill-smelling room. It was also stifling. Someone had sealed the windows and pushed the thermostat to ninety. The bed was against the far wall, surrounded by more new technology devoted to keeping people around when by all rights they should be gone.

The patient was a sickish shade of grey and breathing rapid, shallow breaths. Tubes and electrodes ran from all parts of his being to the anti-death machinery. Hawke bent forward and peered at the fellow, bending the gooseneck light so that it shone on his face. He was clearly feverish and suffering chills beneath his blankets. There was something else, Hawke saw, lifting the covers back.

The man was covered with the beginnings of blood blisters. Identical to the same awful thing Hawke had seen on the man crashing through the jungle. One of the untouchables from the medical compound.

"He looks like death," Hawke whispered, glad of his gloves and mask.

Zimmermann's eyelids fluttered and he croaked something indecipherable. It was German all right, but not any German Hawke had ever heard before.

"It's *Hochdeutsch,*" Ambrose said, as if that explained

the matter. "Leavened by some strange continental accent. Must be his dementia speaking."

Congreve leaned down close to the man's face and spoke quietly. *"Grüss Gott, Herr Zimmermann. Ich bin Dr. Franz Tobel. Wie geht es Ihnen?"*

The pale face turned away toward the wall.

After a minute or so of this, the man feebly slid his hand under his pillow and withdrew an envelope attached to a small package in gift wrapping of faded roses. His hoarse whisper was full of incomprehensible pleading as he handed these to Congreve.

"What's he saying?" Hawke asked. "What's he given you?"

"He says these are gifts for his wife in Manaus. A book, perhaps, and a farewell poem of some sort. He wants me to make absolutely sure she receives them."

"One has to honor a deathbed wish," Hawke said.

"Hmm," Congreve allowed.

"I think I'll bid you both *auf wiedersehen,*" Hawke said to Ambrose, taking the wrapped gift and letter. Hawke looked around as if searching for an escape hatch.

"Please don't feel the need to stay. I think he's mildly insane with fever, actually. You go. I'll do the interrogation. Go to Reception and read a magazine. Or, that farewell letter if you really want to pry."

"I do want to pry. It's my métier, you know."

Hawke turned and was out the door in an instant, his face flooded with relief at escaping the noxious oven.

Ambrose moved a chair into position beside the bed and sat down. He took the man's skeletal hand and held it under the dim lamp, examining his skin and fingernails. After a few moments, he put the hand down and leaned in toward the face for closer inspection.

The mouth was conveniently agape. Congreve pulled the white linen handkerchief from his breast pocket, wrapped it round his fingers, and grasped the German's tongue twixt thumb and forefinger, drawing it out.

"Good lord," he said, under his breath.

The tongue, in the small pool of light, was horribly furry and spotted white. Malarial, possibly something far more interesting. Hemorrhagic fever perhaps, although it was quite rare, and confined primarily thus far to West Africa.

"Listen to me, Herr Zimmermann," Ambrose said to the man in flawless idiomatic German. "I perceive that you are dying. You seem to have some kind of parasitic infection. Viral, or, possibly microbial."

"Poison," Zimmermann croaked.

"I don't think so. I think you caught something. Tell me, have you recently been traveling in the Amazon Basin, Ambassador Zimmermann?"

"Igapo," the man managed to say. "The Black River. They—tried to kill me—they tried many times. I was thrown overboard. But, I am still here and—"

"Who tried to kill you, Ambassador?"

He closed his eyes and whispered in Spanish, *"Las Medianoches."*

Ambrose had heard the name from Hawke.

"My wife . . . she's in danger . . ."

"Mr. Ambassador, I want to hear your story. But I fear we haven't a good deal of time."

The man lay back upon the pillow and closed his eyes.

And then he began to speak softly but most volubly and Ambrose leaned in to listen, nodding his head periodically as a dead man's tale came rolling off his discolored tongue.

While he sat there, he learned a few terrifying facts about a union of radical Islamists, guerrillas, and narcoterrorists. About the size of their infrastructure, and the power of their influence in Latin politics. Their possible links to Castro and Venezuelan strongman Hugo Chávez.

If this man was to be believed, it seemed the whole of the southern hemisphere was about to blow up in the Americans' faces. And, if Zimmermann's information was correct, ground zero was going to be the Texas-Mexico borderline. It was frighteningly familiar. A third-party plot to use Mexico against the Americans. Just like 1917. Only this time it wasn't Germans doing the plotting. It was Middle Eastern terrorists.

The German's clawlike grip was surprisingly strong. Congreve looked down and saw the man's head had come up off the pillow and was straining toward him, his watery eyes bulging.

"There is a man in the jungle," he said, his voice raw. "He knows I've betrayed him once. You must stop him before he attacks again. Do you hear me?"

"Give us his name."

"Muhammad. Muhammad Top."

"Papa Top?"

"*Ja.*"

Congreve said, "Where will he attack next?"

"It is written."

"I don't have time for biblical references. Tell me where to find him."

"It is written, I tell you! Written in . . . in—"

Zimmermann was gone.

18

A Selva Negra

Muhammad Top ended his morning prayers with a special flourish, three ascending notes flung to the curved bowl of ceiling above his head. He gave a small sigh, allowing himself the brief luxury of repose. Yes. *Allahu Akbar.* Mighty Allah had replenished his soul during the night hours and now prayer chased sleep from every cobwebbed corner of his waking mind. As he sat kneeling on the hard wooden floor, with nothing but his thin prayer rug for comfort, he shivered.

But, it was not the deep jungle cold that had seeped inside his bones during the night that stirred him.

No, this was a frisson of pure excitement. Papa Top, as he was known to his adoring legions, felt the electric promise of the coming day as a sharp, tingling sensation, one that raced up and down his spine and sped along nerve endings to his extremities. Every day now promised to be a great day, even an historic one. The Day when all wrongs would be righted. And all sins punished. *Inshallah.* God willing.

The Hour of Retribution.

The Reckoning.

Hello, there! Is that you?

Yes, this feeling was so delightfully pleasant he looked down, half expecting to see an erection sprouting from his groin. But no, the sleepy serpent had not bestirred himself, had not yet risen from the dead calm of the predawn hours. Alas, there had been no concubine in his bed last night, nor did he feel need or want of having one sent up now. No. There was far too much work to be done this day.

Let sleeping snakes lie.

Dawn was just breaking in the leafy green stillness beyond his opened doors and windows. It would still be an hour or more before any trickle of sunlight managed to penetrate the gloom at the very top of the rain forest. Even though his small room was suspended just beneath the deep green canopy of the treetops, only thin rivulets of watery pink light ever managed to leak down his walls as the sun rose over the jungle.

Upon rising from his pallet, Papa Top lit one of the many iron torches that ringed the wall of his spare circular bedchamber high in the trees. During morning prayers, the light from the single flickering kerosene torch threw stark orange and black shadows upon the thatched walls of his room. Torchlight was both eerie and comforting and he would have it no other way. He had become, after all, primarily a creature of darkness.

Like running water, though, electricity was now readily available throughout this strange village. Early on, Muhammad Top had decided to erect his empire high in the trees. Because of the heavy flooding that swept through this remote area during the rainy season, it was critical to be above ground level. And, as all military commanders know, one wanted the high ground in battle. Not that he ever intended to fight here.

His life's mission was to take the fight to the enemy.

The newly installed high-capacity power stations meant all manner of wonders were possible. There was a new underground communications bunker, the watertight command center, from which he would soon wage his great jihad on the infidels to the north. Electricpowered buggies and troop trams, for instance, now sped across the suspended rope bridges that formed the network of the warlike community. Battery-powered aerial drones patrolled the skies above looking for intruders. And Trolls that spat lead rolled through the jungle looking for invaders.

Still, in his primary bedchamber, he chose not to have power at all. He preferred candles or torches in spaces where he lived his solitary life.

Of all elements, Papa Top vastly preferred fire.

Once, when Muhammad was a child, he had visited his paternal ancestral village on the parched banks of the Euphrates in Syria. One day an old crone came to visit his house. She was a Syrian Hama, a witch, veiled and wearing a black cotton garment, called an ezar. Embroidered with symbols of wind, earth, and fire, the flowing ezar enveloped most of her frail body and head. Little Muhammad Top had seen only the witch's fierce black eyes and, as she had bent and whispered a strange riddle, smelled her sour breath.

"If your house was burning, Muhammad Top," the woman said to the small boy, "and God in his wisdom allowed you to rush in to save only one single thing, what would that one thing be?"

"I know the answer," the boy had said, deep vertical creases of concentration forming above his long, already commanding nose. "Wait, it will come."

"I am patient beyond words," the witch said.

"If I could save only one thing," Muhammad Top said, "it would be the fire."

"Yes," she whispered, placing her hand atop the boy's head. "Guard the fire," she whispered. "You must save the fire."

He had made her words his life's calling.

The big man now stood, rose to his full height, six and a half feet, stretched, yawned, and walked through his opened bedroom door and out onto his circular veranda. A gourd hung from a peg beside the door and he dipped it into a wooden bucket of water. He drank. He placed his hands upon the wooden railing still wet with dew and gazed down with complete satisfaction at the tranquil scene below.

Enraptured by the sight of his sleeping treetop village, he almost missed the black scorpion moving swiftly along the railing toward his left hand. The little beast was feeling aggressive, waving his lobsterlike pincers in the air. The poisonous jointed tail was held aloft, curved over his back, ready to strike. He'd found one of these ferocious and deadly monsters in his boot yesterday. He was ill disposed toward them this morning.

He lifted his hand a few centimeters to allow the

arachnid passage beneath it and then slammed his hand down on the rail and smashed the creature with a satisfying crunch beneath his palm.

Life was short, but good, he sighed to himself, scraping the remains of the insect from his hand.

Swirling spirals of mist rose from the damp jungle floor. The damp air created perfect halos around the bobbing torches, the countless fireflies of light streaming below. These were the servants and guard changes. His men rushed with guttering torches across the suspended ropewalks linking the circular thatched and tin rooftops of varying diameter below. These were called roundhouses. The larger ones, like the mosque, were built nearer the ground.

Wisps of smoke curled from chimneys, mingling with the mist. In two of the larger roundhouses, built only fifty feet in the air, fires were now being stoked for cooking. Fans drew off smoke during working hours, to prevent even a wisp from escaping the canopy above.

The day was beginning.

Around the great blue dome of the central mosque (the only tiled roof he allowed) were the larger circles of the great common roundhouses and storage rooms built in the last few years. They provided barracks for House Guards, food and water storerooms, dining, emergency generators, and, of course, vast stores of weapons and ammunition.

Above these, smaller circular structures housed officers of sufficient rank to warrant private quarters. Near the river, a sick bay was adjacent to a small room for special prisoners to be interrogated.

Viewed from this position high above, the village re-sembled, he had always thought, a bizarre flowering, a profusion of man-made silver mushrooms, growing in the thick fragrant air amongst the towering dark trunks of the Amazonian trees. Poisonous mushrooms, he liked to think, yes, poisonous to be sure. To the core.

In the beginning, when all the magic spread out below him was but a vision, he had chosen a simple Spanish name for his hidden refuge in the rain forest, *A Selva Negra*. It was, he decided, the perfect name for an empire erected in dark hatred.

The Black Jungle.

19

WEST TEXAS

Y ou think that phone will ring if you just stare at
it long enough?"

"No, I don't, Daisy. It was a crazy idea, going
down there and talking to that Mexican boy. I could
have easily gotten us both killed. I don't know what I
was thinking. Plain stupid, I guess."

"Well, stop staring at it then. Listen, why don't you
go on outdoors, honey? Take a nice long walk. Go riding or something. You haven't ridden Rocket in a
month or more now. He could use a little giddy-up and
go and so could you. For Pete's sake, Franklin."

"I don't want to even look at a damn horse."

"Is something wrong, darlin'? You've been acting
funny all week."

"No. Nothing's wrong."

"Listen. Those boys that rode down to Mexico were
volunteers. Every last one of them. They all wanted to
go. Their *families* wanted them to go! Look for their sisters or their girlfriends or whatever. All you did was

swear them in. You thought you were doing the right thing and you did your duty. That's all anyone can ask of a body."

"Yep."

"You think you should have gone with them. Well, you couldn't. You've got an obligation to protect this town. And God knows it needs protecting. You went down there and tried to do something for those girls and it didn't work. You'll think of something else."

"Yep."

"You don't want to talk. Fine. Go do something then. Turn on the television. Read a book. Dance a jig. You'll go flat crazy sitting around here all afternoon staring at a telephone for lord knows what reason. Or, I will."

"I am sorry to be such a bother to you," Franklin said, getting slowly up from his armchair. "I reckon I'll go on into the office now. Got some work to do."

He plucked his short brim off the rack and started for the front door.

"Franklin, it's Sunday afternoon. This is time you should be with your family."

"I was trying."

"I ain't never seen you like this, honey. Don't say hi to anybody at church. Don't smile when you shake hands with the preacher. These are your friends, Franklin. Folks who love and admire you."

"I'll see you later on then, Daisy. I'll take the pickup in case you decide to go on over to your sister's in the good car."

"You planning on being home for supper?"

"I can't rightly say at the moment."

"What can you say?"

"That's *all* I can say."

"I love you."

"I love you too, baby girl."

FRANKLIN DROVE slowly into town. Wasn't any traffic to speak of, it being Sunday. Just a couple of good old boys heading out to the Wagon Wheel to catch the second half of the Cowboys on the wide screen. The sun still had a ways to go before it set down and that gave him a little lift. He'd do some desk work, take his mind off things. Keep his eye off the clock.

He figured he'd try and get that report done, a short version of the one they had asked him to write up here about a month ago. It had been sitting on his desk, staring at him long enough. Just like high school papers, wait till the day before something's due to write it. Most folks never got out of high school their whole lives he thought, but that was just his opinion.

Some time ago, he'd written what they called a white paper. It was on illegal immigration. This he'd done at the request of the Texas Sheriff's Association. He wasn't special, everybody got asked to write the same thing and send it to some bureaucrat in Austin, whether they lived near the border or not. Well, he sent his in. Next thing you knew, somebody or other up in Washington had called up the governor's office about his report.

The lady in Austin who'd called him here back in November had said something about how they were fixing to have a big government terrorism powwow down in Key West, Florida. State Department, CIA, Border Patrol, and who knows who all else was supposed to be there. Part of the program or presentation or whatever you want to call it was going to be about border problems with Mexico apparently.

The woman from the capital said they'd be real interested in a short version of what he'd put in his paper. The part about increased violence along the border and anti-Americanism. Border Patrol officers getting shot at, stoned on a daily basis by kids heaving rocks. Weapons coming across through tunnels. Drugs by the ton, above and below ground. And the outright lawlessness that prevailed in some of this territory just south of the border. How it was spreading this way.

And, if you can believe this one, they wanted him to attend the conference and maybe even present his report if there was time enough on the schedule. He hadn't even told Daisy about it, it was so preposterous.

Somebody at the U.S. State Department had read his paper. If that didn't beat all, he didn't know what did. He hadn't told anybody at all of course, even Homer or June. But, you couldn't help but be a little, not proud of it, but gratified that somebody that high up in government was actually interested in what you had to say about things.

The Prairie County Courthouse stood in the center of the town square. It was a four-story building dating from 1914, still all original right down to the doorknobs. Even the big sash windows. It was made out of yellow brick and had four doors, one set on each side. The parking was on the south side, the main entrance was on the north, facing Main Street. One of his predecessors as sheriff, an old man named Wyatt, was now working three days a week as an unpaid deputy. Wyatt had a thing about landscaping. He'd put in some walnut trees that had grown pretty big now. They gave a nice shade on hot days.

His office, as well as Wyatt's, was up on the second floor overlooking the main drag. There wasn't much to see up there other than a spittoon, a hat rack, and a checkerboard. June and Homer spent a whole lot of time playing checkers most afternoons. When he walked in he was startled to see the place so empty and he realized he'd been so preoccupied he'd plain forgotten Daisy had reminded him it was Sunday. Then he saw June Weaver, who was sitting with her shoes propped up at a desk just outside his door.

There was loud snoring coming from Wyatt's office. He came in on Sundays to get away from the Cowboys game his wife always had cranked up full volume. Wyatt was a good man. He'd taken over as sheriff when Franklin's daddy had been killed in the line of duty. His father and Wyatt had gotten into a shootout with some bank robbers and a stray bullet had nicked Franklin Sr.'s heart.

June was a pretty little brunette gal. About Daisy's age, she was in her early forties but looked younger. Always watching her weight, not that she needed to do that much. She had her nose deep in a movie magazine.

"Hey, Junebug," he said to her, trying not to spook her.

"Hey, Sheriff. What are you doing here?"

"Thought I'd try to finish that dang report."

"Well, it's past due."

"Anything happen I should know about?"

"Phone hasn't rung once."

"Well, we figured on that, right?"

"Yessir, I guess we did. I'm sorry."

"You want any coffee? I'll bring you a cup."

"I 'preciate it, Sheriff."

He'd brought June coffee and then stared out his office window for a while, just watching folks stroll by down below. Then he'd gotten going on his paper pretty good and an hour or more went by before he knew it. He looked up and saw June was standing in the doorway saying Homer was on the radio and needed him quick.

"He say what the trouble was?"

"He said there was a big bunch of 'em out at the Wagon Wheel raising hell. Liquored up and smashing furniture. Somebody's firing his gun in the air out back."

"Cowboys must be losing pretty bad."

"He said they were calling for your head."

"Ain't my fault the 'Boys are losing. All right. Tell him I'm heading on over there. Phone rings, some news about the girls, you let me know."

"I got operators standing by."

"Be good. I'll see you in the morning."

"You take care now."

The Wagon Wheel was five and a half miles south of Prairie. It was just about what you'd expect, the kind of place folks used to call a juke joint or a roadhouse. There was a lot full of dusty pickups when he turned in. A lot more than you'd normally see, unless it was the playoffs or there was live music like they sometimes had whenever the T-birds or some other band was passing through on the way to somewhere else.

Franklin pulled up and parked next to Homer's cruiser. He noticed the front door was open and the motor was still running. Looked like he'd been in a hurry and felt the need of bringing the Mossburg shotgun too. He made his way through a covey of big Harleys parked near the entrance, taking note of a couple of bikes he'd not seen before. New Mexico tags.

His boots crunched on broken glass when he walked through the door. He saw Homer with his back up against the bar, blood on his face. Two men were holding his arms out to the sides while another one worked on his midsection with the butt end of a busted pool cue, shouting at the top of his lungs, his voice full of rage and spittle. The man with the cue stick was Mr. J. T. Rawls. His face was bright red and his eyes were blazing in the miraculously unbroken mirror behind the bar.

"Why didn't you shoot me when you had the chance, you little fuckin' shitbritches?" J.T. asked. "Huh? Answer me! You want some more? Awright, you—"

"That's enough of that," Franklin said, raising his voice just enough to be heard above all the TV football noise and the music and shouting going on inside. Every head swiveled in his direction and he was conscious of how he must look to them. He was wearing what he wore every day of his life including Sundays.

Dress trousers, a starched white shirt, and a necktie representing Old Glory. His badge was clipped to one side of his belt, his sidearm clipped to the other.

"Enough of what?" Rawls said, turning drunkenly toward the doorway on one heel of his boot.

It got quiet fast.

"J.T., put down that stick. You two boys let Homer go."

"Or, what?" Rawls said.

"Yeah!" somebody shouted. "Or, what?"

It became a kind of a liquor chant. "Or, what?" did, everybody focused on him now, saying it over and over, and Homer slumping to the floor. Homer's shotgun, Franklin saw, was lying on top of the bar in a puddle of beer. There was movement now, as the men formed up close on J.T.'s flanks. A couple of men he didn't recognize stepped in, putting themselves between him and the rancher. They were the motorcycle owners, wearing leather chaps and vests. Big fellas with prison tats on their biceps.

"I got to see about my deputy," Franklin said, walking toward them so they had to step aside.

He waded through the mess of angry men toward Rawls and his deputy, resisting the temptation to put his hand on his sidearm. He was just determined to keep moving forward and that's what he did. Suddenly a hand reached out and grabbed his shoulder and hung on.

"Let me go, Davis," he said to the wild-eyed man. There were tears in the man's eyes. Davis Pike's son Tyler had been a member of the posse. After a couple of seconds of staring at each other, the man looked away and let go. He just looked broken and lost.

"I'm sorry for your loss," Franklin said, and kept moving.

Franklin figured there was about fifty of them in the place. Most if not all of them were drunk as skunks and past all caring which way this thing went. And a lot of them had weapons. He saw some .357s stuck in the waistbands of jeans and a couple of rifles here and there.

When he got to J.T., he stopped about two feet in front of the man. Rawls's chest was heaving, shallow-like, and his eyes had a methamphetamine glitter to them. Suddenly Rawls reached around behind him and grabbed Homer's shotgun off the bar.

"Give me that gun, J.T.," Franklin said softly.

"Yeah. Both barrels, killer," he said, too wasted to notice the Mossburg was a single.

"I am not a killer. I never did kill anybody didn't need killing."

"No? What about my son? What about all them poor boys you sent to their deaths? What about them? You got 'em scalped! What about all the daughters of men here? You know? They're gone, ain't they? Might as well be dead! You know what I think? I think we'll have us a trial by jury right here. I think we can find twelve angry men in this room."

"Good one, J.T.!" someone said.

"Who wants to be on the jury? Say 'aye.' "

A chorus of "ayes" rang out. The men pressed forward making a tight circle around Rawls and the sheriff and the downed deputy.

"Put the gun down now," Franklin said, taking a step forward.

Rawls backed off and raised the gun to his shoulder and aimed it square at Franklin's heart. Franklin thought Rawls was going to pull the trigger right then. Then he stepped forward until the muzzle of the gun was pressed against the sheriff's breastbone.

"Guilty," Rawls said, trying to shove Franklin backward with the Mossburg. But suddenly, Rawls was going down hard like he didn't have legs anymore. Homer, still on the ground, had somehow managed to kick J.T.'s feet out from under him.

Franklin knocked the shotgun barrel aside and knelt beside Homer. The boy's eyelids were fluttering and he looked up and smiled.

"I appreciate that, son," the sheriff said to his deputy. "You got a little kick left in you."

"Howdy, Sheriff. Glad you made it."

"Yeah. Come on. We're going to take you over to the emergency at Southwest Medical."

"You ain't going nowhere but Hell," Rawls said from the floor. He fired the weapon about six inches above the sheriff's head and blew a jagged hole in the veneer of the bar about a pie plate wide.

Franklin grabbed the muzzle and swung it away before the man could fire again. He tried to pull it downward so that if J.T. fired again he wouldn't hit anybody and then there was a muzzle flash and he felt a searing pain in his forearm. He ripped the gun from the man's hands and swung on him. Rawls caught it on the side of his head and fell back, blood pouring from the wound.

He tried to stay sitting upright but he went down. Out cold by the look of him.

The sheriff threw the gun behind the bar and turned toward the mob pressing in on him now, all around him, sensing blood.

Dixon stood his ground.

"It's all over, boys. Time for everybody to go home."

"Hell if it's all over," one of the big Harley fellas said, coming right up in Franklin's face. "I'll be damned if it's all over, you sonofabitch. Why, I'm going to kick your—"

"Sheriff, come quick!" a man said above the murmurs and angry cries. He was standing in the doorway, just a silhouette with the blazing sun falling to the ridge behind him. Something about the way he called out made them all stop, freeze in fact, and look at him. It was Joe Beers. He stepped inside a bit, looking at the mess and Homer on the floor and all, taking the whole of it in and immediately understanding what was going on.

He stepped forward, pushing men aside, and took Sheriff Dixon's hand, pumping it up and down. The man was laughing and crying at the same time.

"I seen your car out there on my way into town, Sheriff. Lord, I'm glad to find you here. I was going to the courthouse. Everbody's there, the whole town. They all want to thank you for getting all our little girls back home safe."

"You mean to say they're all back?" one of the semi-drunk fellas nearest the door said.

The bar went dead quiet.

"He's lying," Rawls said. "Don't believe a word of it."

"All of them. Ever last one. Heck, my wife just called my cell and told me. An old moving van pulled up at the courthouse here not ten minutes ago and dropped them off. All five of 'em is what I hear. It's a miracle is what it is. My wife Sherry's there with Charlotte already. I got to go hug my daughter."

"Are they all right?" Franklin said. "Unharmed?"

"Yes, sir. I asked. Sherry says they're all physically unharmed as far as she can tell. She already called the Southwestern EMS and it's on the way. Check everybody out, make sure they're all right."

"They just brought 'em back?" Davis Pike said, crossing over to where Joe Beers was standing. "Just like that? I find that hard to believe, Joe."

"Well, they sure did. Way I understand the thing, what I hear is the sheriff here went on down there to Nuevo Laredo and had a little talk with them Mexicans. He and Homer there, just the two of them. Took a lot of guts, you ask me. You can thank your sheriff and his deputy now, any you people got any damn manners."

Davis Pike knelt and cradled Homer in his arms, wiping off some of the blood running from his nose and mouth.

"Homer?" Franklin said, kneeling also. "Can you walk?"

"I believe I can, yessir."

Franklin and Davis managed to get Homer on his feet. They each got an arm around him, supporting him, and they started for the door. Men were falling all over each other getting out of their way, looking stunned and averting their eyes.

"You killed my boy, you son of a bitch!" Rawls cried out. "I'm going to get you, you hear me?"

"Sometimes I wonder whose side you're on, J.T.," Dixon said, pausing at the door to look at him. "Texas? Or Mexico?"

"What the hell do you mean by that?"

"You know what I mean."

After that, nobody said a damn word.

20

QUARTERDECK

The course of history, as Sir Winston Churchill so presciently remarked, is always being altered by something or other—if not by a horseshoe nail, then by an intercepted telegram. Churchill was referring, of course, to the Zimmermann Telegram intercepted and decoded by our Room 40 chaps back in the year 1917."

"Ah, yes," C said to Ambrose Congreve, "Room 40. Every schoolboy in England knows that stirring spy saga. Isn't that right, Alex?"

"I seem to remember hearing something about it, yes," Hawke said, prying his eyes away from the wintry scene beyond the window to regard his two companions with a faint smile. He was tired all the time since his escape and return to England. He slept a good deal, more than required, but felt unrestored by it. There were demons lurking and they'd have to be dealt with soon.

Ambrose, who had the floor, paused, took a sip of his whisky and smiled at Alex. Hawke, who had seemed distracted if not downright somber since their arrival at Sir David Trulove's home, was perched on a window seat overlooking a dense thicket of woodland. Something was troubling him and Ambrose had no idea what it might be.

C, his sharp eyes bright and alert as always, was in his favorite high-backed chair near the crackling fire. Sir David was suffering some form of bronchial infection and now sat with a black cashmere scarf swaddled round his neck and had his feet encased in woolen slippers. Despite his occasional coughing fits, he was now in the process of lighting one of his poisonous black cheroots.

A sleeting rain was chattering against the high windows in C's library where the three men had earlier sought refuge from the gathering storm.

Half an hour or so earlier, under sunny skies, Hawke had swung the long bonnet of his Bentley off the A30. From there it had been a leisurely ten minutes or so on some twisting back roads through the pine woods. Then the Bentley slipped across the Windsor-Bagshot Road and shortly thereafter they arrived at the unimposing stone gateway that led to the house known as Quarterdeck.

A lone sentry, most likely a plainclothes detective sergeant from the Met working a rotation shift, waved them inside the gate. There was, of course, a good deal more security on these grounds, but this unobtrusively armed man was the only face the public was ever allowed to see. The neighbors, who were distant in every sense of the word, had no inkling about who lived at the end of the lane.

It was not by any stretch a large house, but it was very handsome. Sir David Trulove's Regency manor house was quietly situated on the edge of Windsor Park, and the flinty bachelor had lived there in comfort and privacy for many years. As they left the beautifully maintained gravel drive and pulled into the car park, Hawke realized why he'd always admired the house. Simplicity. Quarterdeck was a plain rectangle of Bath stone that had weathered over the years to a lovely shade of greenish grey. An ancient wisteria climbed above the shallow portico and encircled a small first-floor balcony, onto which the windows of C's bedroom opened.

An invitation to call upon C at home was most unusual. Originally, C had invited Hawke and Congreve to lunch with him outside on his sunny terrace. It was to be a working repast, he said, an informal chat covering a range of topics. But Hawke knew that C especially wanted to hear about the prior day's visit to the Tunbridge Wells hospital. The chief of MI-6 wanted to hear firsthand what had been revealed to Ambrose yesterday by the late Ambassador Zimmermann.

Hands clasped behind his back, the happy detective had been striding back and forth in front of a small fire laid against the afternoon chill. He was dressed in his favorite suit of tweeds and was wearing, like his fashion idol, the late lamented Andrew Devonshire, bright yellow cable-stitched socks. He had now relayed to C some, if not most, of what had spilled from the dying German's lips.

Suddenly, Ambrose stopped in midstride. He stood

in the middle of the faded Persian carpet, a perfect ring of blue smoke wafting above his head, waiting for some reaction from Alex Hawke.

There was none.

A semi-reclining Hawke stared wistfully down at the mist-shrouded forest, the thick trunks and bare limbs etched black against the stormy grey sky. A dense plantation of pine, beech, silver birch, and oak grew on three sides of the house. Forests had been magic for him as a child, and, he realized, they still were. Finally, he looked up and smiled at Congreve.

"Sorry. You were speaking of Room 40," Hawke said from his window perch. "Tell me about those fellows again? Kept a low profile, did they not?"

"Yes, Ambrose," C said, taking a long puff of his cheroot. "You might refresh both our memories. I think we've got a few more minutes until luncheon is served."

"It was the most secret room in all of Whitehall," Congreve said, resuming his brisk pacing before the fire. "Masked under the deliberately guileless name of Room 40, a pair of civilians had been diverted there to do cryptographic work. One morning, at a very low point of the war, they intercepted a German wireless transmission in a code no one had ever seen before. But the two chaps, Montgomery and de Gray were their names, were determined. They ultimately broke the code and, in doing so, discovered the key to the whole thing."

"What, pray, was the whole thing?" Hawke said, his mind elsewhere but his interest piqued. "I remember learning about this in school but I'm afraid it's been a while."

"Why, the stalemate, of course," C said. "The dreadful deadlock that gripped both armies in the trenches along the Western Front."

"And the key?"

C said, "The key to unlocking this stalemate was finding some way of convincing President Woodrow Wilson that the Krauts were coming after the Yanks' neck, too. It was vital to convince Wilson to get the Yanks into the bloody war. This Zimmermann Telegram, sent from Germany to their station in Mexico City, revealed the German duplicity. And, Mexico's desire to get into the war on Germany's side."

"Yes," Congreve added, "it did the trick. Once the contents of the telegram were published in the American newspapers, there was a huge shift in American public opinion against the Germans. There was now no way Wilson could keep the Yanks out of the war.

"The Americans suddenly had the duplicitous German and Mexican treachery laid out for them in black and white, right there at the breakfast table."

"And over they came. Thus this Zimmermann Telegram saved England's bacon at the last hour," Hawke said, his eyes following a ragged squadron of geese skimming the distant treetops.

"Indeed," C said, expelling a grey plume of smoke. "None of us likes to admit it, of course, but there you have it."

"But what's all this ancient history got to do with our present situation?"

"The present situation?" Sir David said, looking carefully at Alex. "I've got one word for you, Alex.

Mexico. Mexican treachery again rears its ugly head. To be more precise, the Mexican border. The Americans have ignored that problem for nearly a century. They can't do it much longer."

"Not all quiet on the Southern Front," Alex said.

"The Southern Front," C repeated, liking the sound of that. It was good shorthand for the direction his mind was taking. "The Mexicans were the key to the Great War," he added, "and they bloody well may be the key to the next."

"And we've got a German ambassador named Zimmermann involved in both."

"Mere coincidence?" Hawke asked.

"Perhaps," C said. "History has a way of repeating itself."

C got to his feet and rubbed his hands together to warm them up. "Well. I'm famished. Feed a cold and starve a fever. I'm sure there is sustenance to be had in the dining room. Let's continue this at the table, shall we? I'll go make sure we've got a good claret to accompany the delicious goose the kitchen has prepared."

C left them, pushing through the double doors and into the adjoining hallway that led to the dining room.

"Are you quite all right?" Congreve asked Hawke.

"I suppose."

21

Clearly, Hawke wasn't all right. Congreve knew Hawke's many moods, including this one, the black fugue. His condition, at least this present distraction, Ambrose believed, was hardly a deficit or even a mild disorder. It was simply the restless curiosity of a hungry mind. If anything, it explained the man's early success in both the military and in the financial markets. And his recent triumphs in the dicey world of international espionage. Hawke's mind was constantly ranging over a wide spectrum of subjects, often touching down only briefly before moving on. Congreve believed it was what the brain so rapidly assimilated during those brief encounters that mattered.

It surely accounted for Hawke's ability to take by surprise those who dismissed him as merely a wealthy aristocrat laboring in the family's financial vineyards; or those who too quickly took the measure of his strength or courage and found him wanting. Congreve hadn't enough fingers on both hands to count the number of villains who had made the deadly mistake of underestimating Alex Hawke in these last years.

"Let's go in, shall we?" Congreve said softly, putting a hand on Alex's shoulder. "He's waiting."

"Of course. I'm sorry to be so distracted. I've been sick with the bloody fever again. Does something to my brain. I've promised C I'd call Consuelo about getting invited to this damn meeting in Key West. Well, I damn well haven't done it, and I'm sure he's going to bring it up."

"Why haven't you called her?"

"The woman hates me, Ambrose. She feels utterly betrayed and not without some justification. I've been rather a shit. I've no idea how I'm going to accommodate C's request. He's right, of course, to want me there in Florida. Conch's gathering is likely to prove vital."

"The professional should override the personal, I should think, Alex. We'll think of something. Just keep him going on about history during lunch. You can ring her as soon as you get home."

"And say what?"

"Tell her you can't live without her, for starters."

"I won't lie to the woman."

"Are you quite sure it would be one?"

"A lie? How should I know?"

Hawke cut his eyes toward him and left without another word. For now, Conch would remain the enigma she had long been.

They found C at the oval dining table, filling their goblets with an '89 Château Batailley. Hawke had long ago learned not to bring up the subject of C's unwavering loyalty to the French vintners if not their wretched government. Any such discussion would prove fruitless and unpleasant.

"Tell us, Ambrose," Hawke said as soon as they were all seated, "exactly how it was that this purloined telegram changed everything."

"With pleasure, assuming this is not too familiar ground, Sir David."

Sir David looked up from his first course. "Well-trod ground, yes, Ambrose. But my appetite for military history far outweighs my desire for this damnable aspic. Please, Ambrose, tell the story."

"Well, you see, Alex, by early 1917, the Germans had us dead to rights. We were fresh out of young men and fresh ideas along the Western Front. We'd gain a foot of muddy ground only to lose it in the next day's slaughter. Half a million had died at Verdun alone. Our allies the French were drained and the Russians dying."

"But it was the bloody U-boats had us in a corner," Sir David said.

"Indeed. The U-boats had effectively cut our small island off from food and all other supplies. We could have held out for another two months. We were desperate for fresh troops in large numbers, men whose reserves of fighting spirit were still untapped."

"The Yanks."

"Correct. President Wilson was determined to keep the Yanks out of the war. But, Whitehall knew that only the entry of the United States into the fray would chase the German wolfpacks from Britain's door. We were stalemated in that bloody abattoir of trenches, and the

German U-boats were circling in for the kill. But then we got very, very lucky and intercepted Herr Zimmermann's telegram."

Hawke said, "The Mexican government was tempted by the notion that they might reconquer their lost territories in the southwest. Correct?"

Congreve piped up, "Precisely, Alex. This is what I was able to gather from the now deceased yesterday. These Latino-Arab terrorists are developing highly creative strategies for attacks based in Mexico. The border is still the soft underbelly of America. America's greatest vulnerability."

"So this modern-day Zimmermann was following in the footsteps of his famous namesake? Stirring up trouble in Mexico?"

C said, "Until, for whatever reason, he apparently had a change of heart and contacted us. I assume you've brought along this deathbed letter I've heard about, Alex?"

"Yes, sir," Hawke said, pulling it out of his inside pocket. "It's in some code neither Ambrose nor I have ever encountered before, sir. Numeric. Apparently random, but obviously not."

Hawke handed Zimmermann's folded letter across the table.

"I'll get this to our signal section immediately."

C must have pressed a hidden button on the floor with his foot because two people suddenly appeared at the doorway. A man and a very pretty young woman.

"Yes, sir?" the man in the dark grey suit said.

C held out the envelope. "Geoff, get this to Signals

right away. With a note from me. Saying Alex Hawke got it from the dying German ambassador."

"Done, sir," the man said, taking it.

"Oh, Pippa," C said to the woman who'd escorted Hawke up to C's office at MI-6. "You remember Alex Hawke. He's the fellow attending that conference in Key West next week. You'll be accompanying him as aide. Make sure he has everything he needs will you?"

"Of course, sir," Gwendolyn Guinness said, glancing over at Alex Hawke before she turned and left the room.

C said with a brief smile, "Brilliant girl. I'm quite sure you two shall get along famously, Alex."

Hawke shifted uncomfortably in his chair. He knew C was deliberately putting him in an awkward position.

"Sir, with apologies, I haven't spoken to the American secretary about my attendance yet. Terribly sorry. I'm planning to call her this very evening."

"That won't be at all necessary, Alex. I've already spoken to her. Just this morning, in fact. She's expecting you on the fifteenth of December. Now, then. Who'd like some more of this perfectly cooked goose? Alex?"

C rose and moved to the sideboard to carve more meat. Hawke seized the opportunity to lean across the table and whisper to Congreve, "His bloody idea of humor. It's my goose that's cooked. And he's signed up Miss Guinness to make sure I'm well done."

"Don't mind him, Alex. You forget, he's not feeling well."

"Yes, of course," Hawke murmured, his eyes flashing. "The spy who came down with a cold."

22

Stoke surfaced in the shadow of *El Bandito*'s hull. He looked around for a dark fin slicing through the water and was suddenly aware of a black shape looming above him. Sun was so bright, you couldn't even make out the face, but it was Sharkey all right. So, Luis had already gotten himself aboard. Stoke's ascent up the line must have taken longer than he thought. He rapped on his mask with his knuckles. How come everything seemed so blurry up here? Must have gotten saltwater inside his mask.

Either that or the whole damn world was on the fritz.

Luis was leaning out over the gunwale, offering Stoke a hand up the ladder. Stokely was mighty glad to see that brown hand. A minute or so ago, when he was coming up the anchor rode, he was thinking he wouldn't have the strength left to get back on the boat without some help. He was wondering if he could even haul himself all the way to the surface. And wondering where that mako was hiding.

Luis shouted to him again. He had a battered bucket of fish guts in his hand and was in the process of flinging its contents over his shoulder, long loopy entrails and assorted other things. Most of the chum was going in the boat but some of it made it over the gunwales and into the water.

"C'mon, man! Get your ass out the water!"

Stoke looked up at him and smiled. "Where's that damn shark?"

"I'm telling you, you're just not hearing me. Why you think I got out of the water so fast? That mako is nosing around up here on the surface now. He just cruised over to the other side of the boat. I threw some chum over there. C'mon, bossman, grab my hand."

"Chum? You threw chum?"

"Grab the hand, man. I'm telling you!"

"Yeah, yeah, I'm coming as fast as I can," Stokely said, reaching up to take the man's hand.

Luis was wiry, but he didn't look like the kind of man who could pull a midsize Buick out of the water single-handedly. Thank God he was stronger than he looked, because Stoke realized he was fading fast. With his last little ounce of reserve he got up the steps and over the toe-rail and staggered forward toward the pilothouse. He needed to get out of the sun and lie down for a while. He almost made it to the door too. The faded green deck rushed up out of nowhere to greet him. As he went down, Luis grabbed his tank and kept him from hitting the deck.

"Take it easy, boss. Lay down a minute."

"Chum?" Stoke said, sinking to his knees. "You got a

hurt diver coming up and you throw chum in the water? Jesus, Luis!"

"I told you I threw it on the other side. Keep him occupied."

"Yeah, but still—"

"Shit, Stokely, man, we got to get you to the hospital. You bleeding bad, man. It's worse now."

"I'll be all right. Get this damn tank off me. And slice off a piece of that hose there and tie it off above my elbow. Tight. Tourniquet one-oh-one."

"Like this?" Luis said, cinching it with his teeth.

"Yeah, you got it. That's good but tighter."

Stoke tried to get to his feet but it didn't work. He was in serious danger of blacking out. He lowered himself to the deck, rolling over onto his back. The sky was blue above and he tried to focus on a single white cloud that hung just above their stern. It was blurry but maybe that was just the cloud. He saw Luis Sr. up on the flying bridge. Papa was just sitting up there with his back to the wheel, staring down into the cockpit with concern on his face. Nothing a skipper hates worse than human blood running in his scuppers.

What was everybody so damn worried about? It was just a scratch. Problem was, the tourniquet wasn't working too good. When you had arms the size of piano legs, normal-sized things didn't fit too well.

Luis sliced another two-foot section and wrapped it tight around Stoke's arm, cinching it in tight above the first tourniquet and tying it off. The blood flow instantly slowed way down.

"There you go, bossman, that's better."

"You got the pictures?" he asked Luis.

"Every angle. I even got the cockpit and the pilot. I told you, man. I told you I had something down here. You see those damn missiles?"

"Yeah. You got something worthwhile all right. Remind me to give you and your daddy a bonus when I get home. Now listen up, Sharkey. I need you to get on the VHF and talk to the Coast Guard. First, get me a GPS location to give to them. Tell them to send a chopper or a cutter out here immediately and—what's your problem?"

"You look inside that pilothouse? The old man doesn't exactly have the latest technology aboard this boat. I tried to give him a handheld GPS for his birthday and he nearly killed me. You crazy? he says, I never been lost a day in my life."

"You got a radio, right? He's got to have a VHF radio."

"Yeah, yeah, we have a radio."

"Good. Go get the chart. Let's figure out exactly where we are. But get the Coast Guard on the radio and tell them what's going on. National security, got that? Let me just lay here a minute and I'll come in there and talk to them."

"I'll check the chart, then call," Luis said, getting to his feet. "You stay right where you are for a few minutes. You don't look good. Hey, you want some rum? I keep a pint in the fish box."

"I don't drink. But I'll make an exception. Yeah, give me a hit of that stuff. Might help if you poured some on my arm."

Sharkey reached inside the box and grabbed the half-empty bottle of Bacardi. Luis was handing it to Stoke when he got shot.

Stoke had heard the muffled crack of a serious gun. At the same time he looked up and saw Luis spin around, blood spraying from his right shoulder. What the hell? Luis kept spinning around, arms spread out like some wounded paraplegic ballet dancer, trying to figure out where the damn bullet had come from.

"Get down before he shoots you both in the head!" he screamed at Luis Sr. on the flying bridge.

Two more rounds thudded into the thick wooden topsides. Harmless, but for sure attention getting.

"Shit, man, I'm hit! My good arm!" Luis said, dropping back down to the deck. "Damn! Where is he? Where'd that shot come from? I didn't see anybody."

He started to raise his head above the gunwale, but Stoke grabbed his belt and yanked him back down, looking at his shoulder. Just a scratch, a little red furrow in his skin.

"Stay down, damn it! And tell your father to do the same!"

"Look at him, man, he's a sitting duck up there on the bridge! If he comes down that ladder, he's dead."

"Yeah, so tell him to stay put and stay down. Maybe the shooter can't see him up there because of the angle. Tell that old man to sit tight up there and keep his head down."

Luis shouted words to that effect in Spanish. His father nodded his understanding and then smiled down at Sharkey.

"Courage, my son," the old man said in English.

"God helps those who trust in him. He can save us if he will. Nothing is impossible to him. But if he thinks it is good to call us to him, do not be afraid. We will not be separated."

Stoke just looked up at the scrawny geezer and shook his head. You never knew.

"Where's the shooter, boss?" Luis asked, the two of them peering over the gunwale.

"Got to be that little island over to port," Stoke said. "See? Where all that debris is washed up. I thought I saw something moving over there just before we splashed. Shit! You got any weapons on this boat?"

"Yeah. We keep a gun up forward, under Papa's berth."

"Pistol or rifle? Say rifle."

"We got a semiautomatic rifle. It's mine. Special stock and grip so I can fire it with one hand. A Ruger mini-14. Mags hold thirty rounds."

"Perfect. I want you to go up there and get it. But you stay down below the gunwales, Luis. I don't want any heroics here. Just go forward and get me that gun."

Sharkey crawled on his belly toward the open door. Stoke hadn't liked the look on his face. The kid was obviously scared shitless.

In case Luis needed any more incentive to keep his head down, the shooter fired two more rounds and took out the portside windows in the pilothouse, showering the two men with bits of glass. The shooter was either a lousy shot or he had a shitload of ammo and didn't care. In any case, he had to be dealt with in a hurry. Stoke did not want to pass out and leave Luis and his father to deal with this alone.

Two minutes later, Luis was coming back with the rifle and a soggy cardboard box full of shells. His hand was shaking so bad, when he handed Stoke the ammo, the whole thing disintegrated and all the cartridges spilled out all over the damn deck. What were you going to do? Luis was his partner and he was getting some high-level on-the-job training, that's all. Call this the live-fire exercise. Stoke checked the chamber and the mag. Loaded.

"Hey, I got it," Luis said. "Don't know why I didn't think of it sooner. This way I don't have to get shot again."

"Think of what?"

"We just split, man!"

"Split?"

"Leave! Papa's up there at the helm! He cranks her up and we split. Leave this bastard out here to rot in the sun. Fuck him, you know?"

"What about the hook?"

"You mean the anchor?"

"Yeah, I mean the anchor. Who gets to go up on the bow and stand there to haul up the anchor? Papa? You?"

"Oh, yeah. That's right, the anchor. Man, I forgot all about that."

"You got to think this stuff through under pressure, Luis. Business you're in now."

"Right. So what do we do?"

"I'm thinking about that. Give me a second, I'll come up with something."

"Just keep me out of it," Sharkey said.

23

A Selva Negra

Sturdy hemp bridges had been built connecting the numerous roundhouses that comprised Muhammad Top's domain. The largest of bridges was the one that spanned a ribbon of black mirror snaking through the middle of A Selva. This bridge spanned the river and was built of steel.

The river was named *Igapó,* Black Water, and it fed into the great Rio Negro. The Igapó divided Top's fortress compound neatly in half. It provided a natural boundary for the two discrete sections of the terrorist village. The river also formed a very necessary lifeline with the outside world. Save an isolated airstrip or two, camouflaged and hidden deep in the jungle, it was the only way in or out of his world. A vicious stretch of rapids protected the approach from the east. And sea mines had been deployed to both east and west.

Top had chosen this site carefully. *A Selva Negra* had to be erected where no man would dare to venture, even if he were able. First, because of the canopy, it was completely invisible from the air by day. At night, strict blackout rules were enforced on the odd chance that an airplane would ever stray over this trackless expanse.

No drones or spy satellites would ever differentiate this green patch from the trackless millions of acres that surrounded it. Because of the great height of the trees, even thermal imaging could not accurately pick up the living creatures below. Yet here below the canopy lay another world entirely. A world of his own making.

A primary village, *Centro,* stood at the center of this hidden universe. Arrayed around it, over a span of many miles, like great orbiting moons, were the various camps. Military camps where his troops lived and worked. And also secret training camps and forced labor camps that sustained his armies and protected the center.

And then the river. Although dark in color, the waters of the Rio Negro and its tributaries, like the Igapó, were pure, in fact very nearly distilled. Because of its extremely low salt content, the river had the softest waters of any large river in the world. But that's not why he chose this exact location. His sensibilities were too refined for that. No, it was just here, at this precise location, where the waters ran deep and cold, here, that the low nutrient content and the high acidity so greatly decreased the number of biting flies and mosquitoes.

Papa Top was a passionate man, but he was also a supremely pragmatic being who happened to loathe bugs.

The Black Water was spanned by a steel bridge strong enough to support the small, unmanned tanks which patrolled continuously. This bridge, a vital link, connected the two halves of his world. One side was about sustaining life and worship, the other death and destruction. This bridge that connected the two sides of his equation he had named *La Qantara* in honor of a mythical bridge connecting his beloved homeland of Syria with its neighbors Lebanon, Jordan, and Palestine. Qantara was the fantastical bridge of unity that one day, God willing, he himself would build between these nations.

This mission of Qantara, the bridge of the holy, was his life's work. But Papa Top had sworn he would only complete it at the end of his life. He would turn to this effort only after he and his armies had rained death and destruction upon his enemies to the north and brought them begging God's mercy to their knees.

Now the wide, flowing river was quiet beneath the nearly invisible leafy camouflage netting strung above it for miles in either direction. Here in *Centro,* the primitive existed side by side with the latest technology. Dugout war canoes, rafted together, were moored at the eastern ends of the docks. Later in the day, Indian war parties who served Papa Top would board them to begin patrolling the vast network of tributaries that fed into the Igapó. Intruders were discouraged or killed if they got too close.

Farther along were wider canoes, riding deep in the water and loaded with vegetables and other supplies. They had arrived some time during the night and were still waiting to be unloaded.

SLOWLY, the sleepy village below came to life. Shaded windows glowed faintly with light from within. The proud House Guards, in their uniforms of forest green, streamed across wide bridges and descended by trams to the jungle floor below. There waiting generals and lesser commanders ordered them massed in formation for the drills.

In a nearby clearing could be seen the headlights of a convoy of armored ATVs forming up. This motorized group would be traveling to the airstrip to receive an important visitor when he arrived at mid-morning. His first business of the day was to prepare to receive his honored guest.

Papa Top took great satisfaction that this supremely powerful being, Mullah Khan, was coming to him. Khan, the brilliant Iranian physician and scientist, was making his way on a long journey from Tehran. He would enter the country with counterfeit passports he himself had issued. He would arrive at Buenos Aires and then be ferried to a small airfield on the outskirts of the city. From there he would be flown at treetop level to the concealed landing strip that served *A Selva Negra*.

"The mountain is coming to Muhammad," Top laughed aloud to himself, his rumbling voice deep and soft. History in the making. He took one last look at the wheels of his teeming clockwork empire and stepped back inside to dress himself. There was still a great deal of personal preparation to be done before the official reception for the visitor in the Great Room of the Blue Mosque.

Surely today, he thought, gazing at his powerful naked body in a full-length mirror flanked by flaming torches, was the beginning of the most important period of his life. As such, it was a kind of birth. And a man must dress accordingly for such triumphant moments.

Top was a man of oversize features. There was the great head from which gazed his deep-set dark eyes, steady and penetrating. His eyes radiated power and intellect and when they rested upon something or someone, it was as if they could possess all of it, devour it. His skin was dark and yellowish, taut and shiny, like something that had just popped to the surface after some weeks in the river. His head was entirely hairless. There were neither eyebrows nor eyelashes. The lips below the long wide nose were mottled and thick.

His lips opened only when he spoke and then they flared wide, revealing strong, feral white teeth and baby-pink gums. When he spoke in anger, his eyes bulged, more animal than human, and they seemed to blaze with some kind of otherworldly fire.

His great head rested upon a wide and thickly corded neck supported by heavy shoulders of epic proportions, the shoulders of a giant. He had no idea how much he weighed and he didn't care. He knew there was not an ounce of fat to be found. He took care of himself. He drank his cup of bull's blood every night before retiring. This had been his habit for the years he'd spent in the jungle. He was soon going into battle after all.

He chose a black burka woven with golden thread. He had seen a drawing of such a one in a dog-eared book on the life of Genghis Khan. He'd had his seamstresses copy it exactly. He saw that it draped perfectly over his bulging shoulders. Yes. It was perfection. Now. He would need a covering for his head. A turban of gold? No. Not today. Something far less obvious. Nothing in his wardrobe would do, he feared, until something caught his eye.

Under one window of Papa Top's spartan room stood a large black wooden cross. A death's head was painted in white near the base of the thing and over the crossbar were pulled the sleeves of a ragged and torn morning coat, its black tails trailing on the simple wooden floor. Adorning the cross was a battered bowler hat, the top of the cross projecting through a tear in the crown. Around the base of the cross, a ring of white and black candles had been burning all night.

This totem, seldom found in the homes of the sons of Islam, was Papa Top's secret weapon. He had carried it with him all his life. The bizarre effigy had been passed down from his all-powerful mother, a powerful Haitian Voodoo priestess named Mama Top. This totem represented the God of the Cemeteries, the Chief of the Legion of the Dead, embodied on earth in the human figure of Papa Top. In this part of the Amazon, Top was a figure paramount in all matters related to the grave. He was the dark Voodoo god who had long ago conquered the indigenous inhabitants of the jungle, and he still held them in his sway.

Muhammad Top was, of course, a true believer in the all-powerful rule of Allah. He depended on Allah's guidance in all things. But, being prudent and practical, Top had always thought a man should have a back-up religion. The fear inspired by Voodoo served his purposes well. After all, he lived surrounded by noble savages who bowed only to Papa Top.

He placed Papa Top's perforated black bowler atop his head and gazed into his mirror. Unsatisfied, he cocked it to a more flattering angle, and saw that it was good. He showed his teeth. Flashed his eyes.

Let kingdom come, he thought, *and be damned.*

Soon, together with powerful brethren from abroad who would be arriving shortly, Papa Top would set in motion the irrevocable doomsday clock of the future.

He would set the clock for January 20 at noon.

High noon, he thought, chuckling to himself, a joke the cowboy in the White House might appreciate.

The Day of Reckoning.

24

Harry Brock woke up in a bed he did not recognize with a girl whose name he could not recall. She had a gun in his mouth. She was starkly naked, sitting astride his chest, her pendulous breasts glistening with sweat in the hot buggy light of morning. He found that none of these things made it any easier to think straight. She was very pretty this girl, and somehow during the night she'd managed to handcuff his wrists to the painted iron bedposts he was now banging against the plaster wall in a valiant effort to free himself.

He vaguely remembered she'd told him she was a nurse in Manaus. That explained a lot. Harry had a thing for nurses.

After a while, he stopped whipping his head from side to side and banging his wrists against the bedframe because (A) it hurt, (B) it wasn't doing him any damn good at all, and (C) it felt so good when you stopped. Harry was so happy about being relatively pain-free he tried to smile but found that it was tough

to do with the muzzle of an oily snub-nosed .357 scraping the roof of your mouth.

Relax, Harry told himself. Be professional about this
for crissakes. It wasn't the end of the world. It was another of life's endless lessons. Today's lesson: stay the
hell out of backstreet bars in towns where life was exceedingly cheap and you had a huge price on your head.
Stay sober and avoid strange women at all costs, even
gorgeous ones.

He took a few deep breaths like he was trained to do,
holding each for a count of six, and tried to stabilize his
heart, slow everything way down.

Get your bearings, Harry. He was going to say get
the lay of the land but he'd already done that. She was
sitting right on top of him. Christ, what a woman. He
would kill to know her name but he felt at this point in-
troductions would be awkward. Even if she removed
the gun from his mouth, what was he going to say?

Focus, Harry. Okay. He had to be somewhere in the
little shitburg town of Madre de Deus. Yeah. He'd wandered into this Brazilian backwater yesterday afternoon
because a hungry, pushing-forty-years-old guy with
back problems just gets tired of not eating and sleeping
out in the rain under a different tree every night. It had
been a week since he'd taken shelter under an actual tin
roof, and the last real bed he'd actually slept in, he had
gotten out of about two minutes before *Las Medianoches*
rapped on his door and knocked it down.

What finally happened was, how he came to be here
in Madre de Deus, about a week ago he'd started seeing
a bad Xerox of his face plastered all over the charming

town of Barcelos on the Rio Negro. Printed under his mug was a rather large round number calculated in both pesos and dollars. He'd been deeply depressed with how little he was worth until he remembered that in this part of Brazil you could buy a Mercedes E55 AMG with a sticker price of $81,000 for less than $10,000. Dom Perignon was three bucks a magnum, and you could snag a fresh pair of Nike Air Jordans (he had) for a dollar.

Hell, that meant his life was only worth about a thousand pairs of Michael Jordan sneakers. Seemed a little on the low side.

This was a tiny spot on the map, but it was the central city in what is known as the Mato Grosso, where about $12 billion, that's billion with a *B*, worth of cocaine passed through every year. Harry had asked around, dropping a few names and discreet amounts of cash here and there, and managed to hook up with a big-time guy named Osvaldo Sanchez.

Osvaldo, who was president of one of fifty-five international bank-slash-laundries operating here in town, liked to siphon off a hundred million or so every now and then to buy bargain-basement surface-to-air missiles for the glorious pan-American *revolucion* Hugo and Fidel were dreaming about. Because Harry was pretty savvy about the illegal arms business and both men knew the names of a lot of heavy hitters, he and Osvaldo had hit it off and actually developed a good working relationship.

Good enough for he and Senhor Sanchez to arrange a confidential meeting where they would talk turkey and Harry would find out who some of the key players were in what was shaping up as the major drama currently unfolding down here south of the border. Rumors were rampant. Massive terrorist armies moving north to invade Central America. Stuff like that.

But, wouldn't you know it, at the last minute Harry had had to cancel due to a prior commitment (staying alive) and instead of talking turkey with Don Osvaldo he was running for his life and hopping into the back of a poultry truck crossing a bridge to nowhere. Once safely across the Paran River, he'd taken to the jungle, sleeping rough for a week until, good luck, the heat died down. Hiding in jungles is hot, thirsty work. Harry finally succumbed to his baser desires and hitched a ride with a busload of poppy growers to his current residence, a less than idyllic village called Madre de Deus.

All he'd really wanted was a couple of cold *cervezas* and a warm bed. Was that too much to ask? Before Saladin Hassan had left to go find the Xucuru tribe that was holding Alex Hawke for ransom, he had given Harry the address of a place (an abandoned mosque) he could use to hole up in, but only, Saladin had emphasized, in a dire emergency. Saladin, reluctantly giving Harry the key to an upstairs room, said, don't use it. As it happened, he had used it, although in hindsight, maybe that wasn't a really good idea.

It was a scruffy little town he'd slipped into. Losing himself in the horde of merchants, peddlers, and smugglers hoofing it at a snail's pace over the Puente de la Amistad (the bridge of friendship) he thought there was something a little incongruous about the sight of golden domes and spindly minarets rising up out of this lush jungle. But what he found out was, back in 1975, after the outbreak of the civil war in Lebanon, the Islamic population of this region had swelled rapidly and was now somewhere in the neighborhood of sixty thousand in this one town alone.

Why were they here and what the hell were they up to, you might well ask yourself. Well, money. The more the United States shut down the terror networks' cash flow, the more these guys had to turn to alternative sources of income. And what better source of income than drugs? Human trafficking and guns? Not too shabby either.

What Harry was picking up on was a whole infrastructure in this part of LATAM, locally known as the Mafia-Araby, who had taken over all the weapons and narcotic sales and distribution channels down here. This was because the badass Arab sin sheikhs made the local toughs look like a bunch of drugstore gauchos.

And the Mafia-Araby was using all this ill-gotten lucre to finance their Latino terrorist operations. In this region alone, the number of guerrilla training camps had to have risen exponentially. And high-tech weaponry was flooding in, some of it experimental technology stolen from the U.S. and Britain.

Now, you had to wonder, as Harry did on a regular basis, how come his bosses at the Pentagon, Langley, and NSA had missed all these interesting developments in Latin America. Just by walking around, looking at faces, you could see there was not a lot of love for the *norteamericanos* down here, no matter what the race, color, or creed of the people on the streets. What there was a lot of, if you asked Harry, was trouble.

Trouble wasn't brewing; like Milwaukee's finest, it was fully brewed. And, some day real soon, somebody around here was going to pop the top on a whole six-pack of shit.

The funny thing was, all this snooping around he was doing wasn't even Harry's assignment. He'd been ordered down here with a couple of other CIA guys for one specific reason: find Alex Hawke and if he was still alive get him the hell out. Harry had gone to his boss, Charley Moore, at the JCS and volunteered for this assignment when he'd heard about it. He owed Alex Hawke a big favor.

He had met Hawke a year or so ago. Hawke had pulled him off a Chinese steamer just before it sailed Harry back to the Chinese prison hellhole where he was scheduled to spend what was left of his life begging to die. He owed Hawke big time and had planned to repay that debt if he ever got a chance. Now, he had it.

This town was busy, busy, busy. Really hopping. In addition to the group of young Shiite Muslims he'd seen outside a mosque (raising money for the imminent jihad, no doubt), there were countless good citizens packed into the narrow streets, hawking every-thing from designer jeans and leather jackets to plasma TVs, computers, and laser tools. There was some other stuff, too, including tons of choice Colombian mari-juana, hashish, and cocaine for the guys who made a living transshipping the stuff to Puerto Paranagua over on Brazil's Atlantic coast.

Harry didn't pick one up, but he'd heard on the street you could buy a counterfeit Brazilian passport from Brazilian officials for a measly $5,000. And that passport, under the current waiver program created by some benevolent genius in Washington, opened the portals to the fabulous Magic Kingdom lying immediately to the north of the Mexican border. The waiver made a valid Brazilian passport all you needed to travel throughout the United States.

Think about that one for a minute and your head will explode.

He was pretty sure the blossoming suicide bombers hanging around the mosque had figured that one out long ago. If you could afford five grand for a passport, you didn't need to worry about sneaking across the Mexican border to blow shit up in Houston or Chicago or wherever. Just hop a flight to Miami. That's pretty much what Harry was thinking about when the girl had showed up on the stool right next to his.

He'd gone into the first bar he'd seen that looked air-conditioned. No windows, so it was dark inside, too, and he'd felt all safe and cozy inside sipping his *cerveza fria* with a whisky back at the bar. Then, at some point, a girl was sitting next to him. A nurse, she said. It was her day off. What was her name? Caparina. Yeah, that was her name, pronounced like that Brazilian drink he liked, the one made with limes and Cachaca, grain alcohol distilled from sugar cane. Lethal.

Caiparinha. Some kind of butterfly, she'd said it meant in English.

So, what the hell, he'd bought her a few beers, not

many, only a hundred or so. She'd asked him if he wanted to get busy and he said, yeah why not?

Why not? Jesus, he knew why not now. She had a torn Wanted Dead or Alive poster in her free hand and Harry immediately understood that he was up creek number two without a paddle. Now that the sun was up she was comparing his face with the Xeroxed one on the wanted poster. There was a small painting of the Holy Virgin stuck on a nail just above Harry's head. Caparina smiled at him, then reached up and slapped the poster over the painting, the nail head sticking right through Harry's forehead.

A warm breast brushed his cheek as she settled back down, kind of squishing herself onto his lap.

"Mmm-pf!" Harry said, and she looked at him for a long minute and then pulled the gun out of his mouth. The oily aftertaste was pretty bad, but at least he could work his jaw. He thought she was being a good girl, but then he saw her reach for the cell phone on the night table.

"Don't do that!" Harry said.

"Por que não?" she replied, looking again at the poster with the big fat number prominently displayed on the bottom. Harry tried hard as he could but he was darned if he could come up with a zippy and compelling answer to that question. Why shouldn't she call the telephone number on the poster and collect the reward? Seriously. Why the hell not? In fact, there were many thousands of reasons why she should do exactly that. Hell, if their roles were reversed he would do exactly the same—

"You're pretty," he decided to say, letting her have

both the pearly whites and the sleepy brown eyes. Harry was an okay-looking guy. He'd been told he looked like Bruce Willis with hair. He didn't see it, but frankly, whatever. Sometimes it worked, sometimes it didn't. This time, thank you Jesus, it did. She hesitated, then put the phone back and looked at him, that cute little smile on her face. Caparina could obviously tell Mr. Happy was back in town and restless; maybe looking for a place to settle in for a spell.

She got busy. You know, one for the road, after all she had nothing to lose and Harry certainly did not. He was reduced to thinking of turning himself in, getting the reward, and then escaping again. Admittedly, it was a plan with a lot of holes.

He meant what he said. She was pretty. She was a drop-dead babe even sober, meaning when he was sober not her. He looked at her face, too, as she started rocking back and forth on top of him, grinding away at him until he was hard as stone. She had what Harry the world-traveler called a pretty version of the U.N. face. Part Chinese, part Indian, part mestizo, part brown-skin gal. She had long purplish black hair, full lips, and amazing breasts that were now swinging dangerously close to his lips.

"Hey," he said. "C'mon on."

"What?"

"You know what."

"Beg me," she said.

"What?"

"Beg."

"I don't beg."

"Oh, yes you do, Mr. Harry Brock."

"All right, I'll beg."

"I don't hear you."

"Please."

"Louder."

"I can't. Somebody will hear us."

"We're in a deserted mosque, Harry. No one can hear us."

"Wait. We're at my place?"

"Of course. You don't remember?"

"No. I mean, yeah. I sort of knew. I guess I forgot. All mosques look pretty much the same to a guy like me."

"You want to kiss my titties, Harry? This one? Or, this one?"

"Yes. Both."

"Beg me, Mr. Brock."

"Please. I beg you. I'm not kidding. I am sincerely begging here. This could be it for me. The swan song of Harry Brock."

"There. Happy?"

"Oh god, yes. Now the other one."

"Be gentle, Harry. That's a good boy."

WHEN HARRY WOKE up for the second time that morning he realized he had a cigarette in his mouth and involuntarily took a puff. Nothing in recent memory had ever tasted so good. The girl reached over and plucked it from his lips so he could expel the smoke. Shit. He was still cuffed to the damn bed. He must have dropped off for a couple of minutes. The girl took a drag herself and then she said, "I know a joke."

"Yeah? What?"

"A man is in bed with a woman. After they make love, the man says, 'Do you smoke after sex?' and the woman smiles at him and says, 'I don't know, I never looked.' "

Harry burst out laughing.

"That's pretty good," he said.

"Thank you."

"Fell asleep, huh?"

"For about twenty minutes."

"Did you call?"

"Mmm."

"You called? Holy shit. Aw, Christ, Caparina."

"Calm down, Harry."

"Calm down?"

"I didn't call who you think I called."

"The number on the poster. For the reward."

"No."

"Ah. Well, okay, who did you call?"

"My ex-husband. He's on his way."

"Your ex-husband is coming here? Now?"

"What are you doing down here in Brazil, Harry? You're obviously an American. You have no identification. No passport. Nothing. Only this gun and a few thousand pesos. You don't speak Portuguese. Or even Spanish."

"I'm a tourist."

"You came all this way to buy those shitty Nikes? Six hundred tourists die every year in this crappy town. And that's only the reported number."

"That's why I've got the gun."

"I've got the gun, Harry. Last night, when you were drunk, you said something about *Las Medianoches*."

"Really? What'd I say about them?"

"That the *jihadistas* had your friend. You came down here to look for your friend, Harry? Who is your friend?"

"Why is this important to you?"

"Hassan can help you I think."

"Hassan? Who the hell is Hassan? Every second guy you meet around here is called Hassan."

"My ex-husband. He's a good guy, speaks perfect English. Very tough. Not everyone in this country is intimidated by the Mafia-Araby."

"How can he help me?"

"You can help him."

"Why the fuck should I do that?"

"The enemy of my enemy is my friend."

"Not necessarily. Anyway, who's your enemy?"

"The enemy of my people. The jihadists in the jungle who call themselves *Las Medianoches*. This bastard Papa Top."

"What are you, Caparina? Some kind of spy or something?"

"I keep my eyes open."

"Good. We've got something in common. Now, let me go. Okay?"

There was noise coming up the steps beyond the door. Caparina hopped off the bed and pulled her flowered blue cotton dress over her head and smoothed it down over that spectacular body. She was one of those women who look almost as good dressed as they do naked. She stepped into her pale blue panties, wiggled her butt as she hiked them up under her dress, and smiled at Harry.

Harry lifted his head and stared at the door. "Shit. They're coming up the steps. Get me out of these cuffs, will you? Hurry up."

"I can't. No key."

"No key? What?"

"We were playing a game. 'Who's the prisoner?' You lost when you swallowed the key, remember?"

"Aw, shit, Caparina, they're at the door. Can you at least throw the damn sheet over me or something? Jesus. This is embarrassing."

"Say please."

"No."

"Harry?"

"Please."

"Good boy, Harry."

She was bent over picking the sheet up off the floor when the wooden door swung open and a man stepped inside, looking at the scene on the bed with a bemused smile.

"Harry?" the man at the door said.

"Saladin?"

"You two know each other?" Caparina said.

"Of course we know each other," Harry said. "Jesus."

It was Wellington Saladin Hassan. Few months ago, he'd paid this man a small fortune for finding Alex Hawke and returning him safely to England.

"Who's got the key?" Saladin asked the two of them, a big smile on his face.

25

Prairie, Texas

Sunday morning just before noontime Franklin was in the cold barn mucking out the stalls. He had just about finished when he heard an automobile driving too fast up the long dirt drive from the highway. He leaned his pitchfork against the wall and moved over to the open window facing the road. It was Homer in the department's new Crown Vic Interceptor, barreling up the deeply rutted road at about fifty, kicking up a big rooster tail of dust behind him.

Franklin looked up at the cloudless blue sky, any prayer of a quiet Sunday afternoon sliding away from his mind. He walked out of the barn just as the deputy skidded to a stop between the barn and the house.

"Easy, Homer, no fire out here, son."

Franklin walked over to the car wondering what was so all-fired important on a Sunday. It had been nine days since the incident at the Wagon Wheel. Homer had been beat up pretty bad. Still and all, Homer had been back on the job for three days now and, mercifully, things had been quiet since all the hoopla of the week preceding. He'd even had a few afternoons to finish correcting all the errors in that Texas border presentation he was set to give down there in Florida in a week's time.

Mostly it was quiet because Rawls and a few bike riders had been locked up down at the courthouse. He'd put them there for a few days until everything cooled down. He'd let most of them go. He'd wanted to hold Rawls longer, based on a tip he'd gotten about six months ago.

A paid informant had told the Laredo PD that Rawls was suspected of involvement with some kind of border smuggling operation. Drugs, guns, and even automobiles coming through tunnels under the border. According to the snitch, Rawls was in bed with corrupt Federales and *narcotrafficantes* and had been for a long time.

But, they couldn't prove it yet. Franklin just didn't have enough to hold him. So he'd released Rawls on his own recognizance, as June called it.

Homer climbed out of the car and put his hat on, shading his eyes from the sun.

"Sorry to bother you, Sheriff, I been calling you on the phone."

"When they get the kinks out of those cell phones, maybe I'll get one. How can I help you, son? I've been out here in the barn all morning. Daisy went to church services and then to her prayer group lunch right after. I was just going inside to make a ham sandwich and some ice tea. You want to join me?"

Franklin started for the house and Homer followed.

He said, "What I've been calling you about? Somebody's fixing to get their selves lynched here later on today."

"Lynched? Who?"

"I don't know their names. Three Mexican boys, is what I hear."

"Come on over here on the porch and set in the shade, Homer."

Franklin was tired. He stepped up on to the porch and went over to the far end and sat in his rocker. There was a tupelo tree at that end of the porch. He and Daisy had planted it as a sapling when they first bought the place. It gave off pretty nice shade this time of day. He pulled out his bandanna and wiped all the sweat off his face. There was a pitcher of lemonade with all the ice melted sitting on the table and he poured two glasses. Then he leaned back against the old rocker and started rocking, scuffing his boot heels across the dusty floorboards.

He said, "Start at the beginning and tell me."

Homer took off his hat, tilted his head back, and drained his glass. "Like I say, it's three Mexican kids."

"Kids?"

"Teenagers, I'm pretty sure. The banditos apparently broke into Sadie Brotherwood's place last night, looking for liquor in the ranch house. She came home and surprised them."

"She lives over there on the river, right? What's it called?"

"The Lazy B. She stayed on the place when Woody died last spring. She didn't call anybody about the break-in. She got the drop on the boys, put a shotgun on them, and locked them up overnight out in the tool shed. This morning, here about an hour ago, she didn't hear any noise coming from the shed and she called her brother-in-law, old Ed Parks. Ed apparently came over with a couple of his boys and told Sadie not to call you, said they'd take care of this themselves."

"These Mexicans are local boys?"

"No, sir. Illegals. Roy Steerman went over there to Brotherwood's with Ed originally, but didn't want anything to do with it after he got there and left. Been out there in the desert a while seems like. Skin is burned black, Roy said. All of them dehydrated and probably dizzy from drinking their own urine out there. He said when they got there one of them was swimming in the dirt like he thought it was a stream. Like his brain was baked in his brain pan, Roy told me."

Dixon looked away. How many times in his life would he have to hear this same sad story? The law was the law. But children locked in a shed and dying of thirst was a painful way to enforce it.

"Maybe they weren't looking for liquor, Homer. Maybe they were just looking for water."

"That's just what I told Roy Steers here not half an hour ago. He said, 'Nobody over at Sadie's cares two hoots in hell about that. These damn kids are here illegally, broke into a woman's house to steal her property, and they're going to string 'em up.' That's a direct quotation."

Franklin got up without a word and went inside the

house. A minute later the screen door opened and he came out with his hat on. "Let's go, Homer," he said.

TWENTY MINUTES LATER they turned off on the state road that led to the Brotherwood ranch. Homer took a right on to an unpaved stretch and they drove another two miles of barbed wire on either side before they came to the Lazy B. There was a heavy aluminum gate at the entrance to the drive and somebody had closed it and locked it with a length of chain. Homer pulled over on the shoulder across from the gate and got out of the car. He looked both ways and then crossed the baking asphalt to open the gate.

Franklin saw he was having trouble with the lock and started to climb out of the car. That's when the two big fellas stepped out from inside a dense stand of pecans just inside the gate.

"Hey," one of them said. Franklin recognized him as one of the boys from the Wagon Wheel he'd locked up. Had the same sleeveless leather vest and the prison tats covering both arms. If he remembered the arrest record correctly, these two gentlemen's names were Hambone and Zorro. William Bonner, Hambone, and Bernie Katz, Zorro, represented a whole lot more trouble than they were worth.

"Howdy, Hambone," Franklin said to Bonner. He saw that the gate was padlocked with a big Master lock.

"Can we help you?" Bonner asked.

"You can open that gate."

"No can do, Sheriff. Private party."

"Homer," Franklin said, "take your sidearm out and shoot that lock off, will you, please?"

"Yes, sir."

Homer removed his weapon and fired two rounds into the heavy padlock. The thing blew apart, wide open, which surprised Franklin because he'd seen an old commercial where a slow-motion bullet goes right through a padlock without any effect. He reached over and pulled the chain out of the gate rungs and dropped it to the ground. Then he started to swing the right gate inward. Hambone stepped into the path of the gate and crossed his lodgepole arms over his chest.

"Like I say, it's private."

"Mr. Bonner, you boys just got out of my jail. If one of those Mexican boys is harmed, you're going back. If one of them dies, you're going back inside the system for twenty years as an accessory to murder. How do you want to handle this?"

"It ain't murder to kill no illegal alien."

"Murder is murder, Mr. Bonner."

Bonner didn't respond. Just looked over his shoulder and spat on the ground.

"C'mon, Billy," the one named Katz said. "Let it go. We don't need any more shit from this particular asshole."

Bonner looked at Dixon and did his best impression of a man staring daggers into somebody's eyes for a couple a seconds and then he kicked the ground and walked away from the gate.

"Where are your bikes located, Bonner?" Franklin said to the man's back.

"Over there in the pecan grove," Katz said, pointing at the trees. You could see pinpoints of chrome back in there among the dark trunks.

"I suggest you fellas mount up and git. I don't want you in my county any longer. You understand what I'm saying? If you're still here when I come back this way, I'm going to impound your motorcycles and lock you up again. We clear?"

The two outlaws didn't say anything, just turned and headed for the pecan trees.

Franklin swung the two aluminum gates inward while Homer went back for the car. After a minute, he heard the deep popping noise of the two Harleys cranking up in the woods as Homer drove through and came to a stop. He climbed inside and they continued up the drive to the ranch house proper.

Homer was staring straight ahead, driving as fast as he could over the uneven ground. He spoke to Franklin without looking at him.

"You recall seeing those fires at Yellowstone on the TV, Sheriff? Burning out of control? Threatening all those little tinderbox towns."

"Yeah. I remember that."

"Sometimes I feel like the border is one long tinderbox. Like Prairie is nothing but a tiny oasis in the middle of a dried-up pine forest. It's baking hot day after day and folks are walking around knee deep in pine needles. Bone dry. And every damn one of them is striking matches."

"Some folks think those big fires are natural remedies, Homer. Just nature taking care of itself."

Homer looked at him. "I have a real hard time believing that, Sheriff."

"Well, you better slow down, son, there's the ranch house right over there."

There were four or five pickups pulled up outside the house. Homer hit the brakes and they got out and knocked on the front door. They waited a minute but nobody came and so they walked around the side of the house and down to the dried-up riverbed about five hundred yards away.

There was a big live oak tree standing at the bend on the other side of what used to be the river. It had been dead for years, but still had a lot of its lower limbs. Even from a distance you could see that somebody had looped three ropes over the lowest and biggest branch and tied a noose at the end of each one.

"Looks like we're just in time," Franklin said to Homer.

The men were standing at the base of the tree and Franklin could make out three small boys on the ground. They were sitting with their backs to each other, probably all tied together at the wrists. The local men, and one woman, were standing in a circle, just looking down at the boys.

"No need for you here, Sheriff," Ed Parks said, stepping forward as the two lawmen crossed the dusty riverbed.

Franklin said, "Good afternoon, Ed. Boys. You, too, Miz Brotherwood. I hear these kids broke into your house last night."

"That's right they did," Sadie Brotherwood said. "I caught 'em red-handed trying to steal my whisky."

"Why didn't you call the police?" Dixon said, brushing past two of the men and squatting in the dirt beside the boys. Their sun-blackened skin was bloody in places and their mouths were crusted with salt. Their black eyes were glazed with fear and exhaustion.

"Police? No need of calling anybody," Parks said. "Waste of taxpayers' money. We call the po-lice every time we catch a bunch of these *pollos,* you wouldn't have time to hand out parking tickets. No, we like to take care of this business ourselves out here. I told these boys we didn't need no grass cut neither. Hell, they're just tonks. I reckon that's why they're here, brought in by coyotes and looking to cut grass up in Houston."

"Goddamn *pollos* ain't hardly human anyhow," Mrs. Brotherwood said. "I don't know what all the fuss is about."

Franklin looked for some sign of grief in the widow's eyes but only saw hard-bitten hatred and the dull gleam of self-righteousness. He unscrewed the cap from the canteen he'd brought and held it to the lips of the first boy. After the boy had drunk some water, he moved to the next one and repeated the process. The last boy, the smallest, was too weak to lift his head and drink.

"He's mighty thirsty, Ed," Franklin said. "You didn't give them any water?"

"Why waste good water?"

"*Que pasa hombre?*" Franklin said to the oldest of the

three after he'd gulped down some water. "Where are you from?"

"Nuevo Laredo," the boy said, his voice a parched whisper.

"How many of you come across?"

"We were fourteen. We walked until we fell. My brothers and I, we are the last ones."

"What is your name?"

"Reymundo."

"And your brothers?"

"Jorge and Manuelito."

Franklin stood up and looked at Parks and Sadie Brotherwood.

"All right, then. Here's what we're going to do. Mrs. Brotherwood, I'd like you to apologize to Mr. Parks here for bringing him all the way out for nothing."

"It wasn't nothing," she said. "It was three more wet-backs needed a good hanging."

"Ed, you and the boys go on home. Homer and I will see these children get medical attention and then we'll turn them over to the Border Patrol."

"I'm gonna tell you something, Sheriff. I'll go. But it's people like you are going to ruin this great country. There are already more of them than us down here in West Texas. Hell, whole towns of 'em without a single white inhabitant. Not one! You want to give them the whole state? Is that your idea of right and wrong? God-damn it, I don't understand you anymore. I thought you were one of us. Hell, I voted for you in the last election. Now I ain't so sure who the hell you are, Franklin."

"I'm the law, Ed. That's all. Now go on home."

"The law. You think these three here give a flying fuck about you and your laws? Hell, they each paid their coyotes five thousand yankee dollars for the privilege of breaking your damn law. That's the problem, ain't it? It's the damn law that's going to ruin everything, you don't start enforcing it for real. Come on, boys, let's get the hell out of here before I puke on somebody's badge."

"Sheriff?" Homer said. He was sitting in the dirt beside the smallest boy, Manuelito, who seemed to have fallen asleep in the deputy's lap.

"What is it?"

"This one here just died."

26

DRY TORTUGAS

I got it!" Luis said.

"Got what?" Stoke asked.

"I finally figured out the whole anchor thing."

"Yeah? Good," Stoke replied, his mind somewhere else, namely his current life expectancy if he didn't get his arm stitched up soon. "Tell me quick."

Luis said, "Wait, yeah, I think this will definitely work."

"Tell me what you got, Luis."

Luis thought about it another second and then his face brightened. "What I'm thinking, hey, we just leave the anchor here. See? I crawl forward through the cabin up into the bow locker and untie the bitter end of the anchor line. Then we just let the line run out of the boat when we back down and get the hell out of here."

Stoke just looked at him.

"You see? Fuck the anchor, man, we come back and get it later. Or, not!"

"That's a very good plan, Luis. Seriously. If we were leaving right now. But we're not, see? We didn't come all the way out here to leave that gunrunner alive over there on that island. Who is he? Where'd he come from? Where was he flying home to? We've got something big down there in the deep and we need to know who's dealing these weapons. And, dead or alive, I need to get a look at that shooter in the bushes, okay? And, in the unlikely event that he survives, have a chat with him about where he got those Russian missiles."

"Cuba."

"Cuba. How do you know that? You find something you forgot to mention? I thought you said the plane was clean."

"I don't know. But it's a good guess, right? So now what?"

"I'm still thinking."

Stoke was still feeling woozy. The tourniquet helped a little. But, and it was a big one, could he really get up on his knees with the Mini-14, mark the guy's location, and shoot him before he passed out from blood loss or the bends or whatever his problem was making him so lightheaded? Possible, but very low probability of a successful outcome. Normally, he'd slip over the side, swim underwater around the little island, and come up behind the guy. But, in his present condition—

He looked at Luis and then he looked at the rifle and then back at Luis.

"Don't look at me, man."

"Who's looking at you?"

"You."

Damn. Luis was right. He just couldn't see Sharkey doing this. In any way taking the guy on the island out.

No possible way you could expect a one-armed man to try to pull this off. Recently wounded in his one remaining good arm, no less.

Stoke knew approximately where the shooter was, had a rough idea based on the muzzle flash and the angles these shots were coming from. The guy was crouching down in the mangroves on the left side of a little cove near a stand of stumpy cabbage palms. Another thing. He was convinced that the shooter was the copilot. Had to be. No other reasonable possibility. Down at the plane, Stoke had seen what looked like the last remains of blood smears on the right-hand windshield. Like somebody's head had hit it real hard. So. Copilot bangs his head but survives the crash, cleans up the cockpit and his dead buddy, and swims ashore. Yeah, that had to be it.

The survivor had to be one hurting gaucho after thirty-some-odd hours out on that little spit of land all by his lonesome. It was hot out here. Lots of skeets to keep him company. Maybe hurt, maybe no food or water. Hungry. Thirsty. And seriously pissed off that the pretty blue fishing boat he'd seen steaming to his rescue had not come to his rescue after all. Hell, anybody would be upset.

Well, one thing was sure, Sharkey was in no condition now to take the guy out. He was curled up in the stern with his one bandaged arm wrapped around his knees. Sitting over in the corner by the bait box forward of the transom. Staring at Stoke and wondering what he was going to have to do next. But there was another way out of this. Stoke had an idea.

"Take the rifle," he said to Luis.

"Me? I'm doing it? I told you! I can't."

"Yes you can. Listen, okay? Relax. I'm not asking you to stand up and shoot anybody, Sharkey. I got a much better idea. Just slide over here and take the damn gun. Now."

"Aw, shit, man. This is so messed up."

"Do it."

He did it.

"Now," Stoke said, in a very soothing way, "I want you to take this gun over to the bridge tower ladder."

"Climb up?"

"No, not climb up. You think I'm crazy? No, what I want you to do is, scoot over there to the foot of the ladder. Okay? Stay down. Then you take the gun by the muzzle, reach it up high enough so your old man can reach down and grab it by the stock end."

Luis lit up one of those lopsided grins that went on and off like a neon light. Relief flooded his face as he took the weapon. "Papa's going to shoot him?"

"That's right. He's got the high ground and the best angle. But he can't afford to miss, tell him, because he's probably only going to get one shot off before the guy starts blasting him. Papa a good shot? Say yes."

"Good? I've seen that old *hombre* put a mako's eye out at one hundred yards. Fish was leaping twenty feet in the air at the time, right off our transom. Blam, he dropped him."

"Well, see what I'm saying, this'll be cake then. Easy-peasy-Japanesy."

"You check is it loaded?"

"Damn! Didn't you see me check it a few minutes ago? Yeah, it's loaded. Now, listen up, this is important. Tell him to stay down. No heroics till I say so. He's not to do anything right now except take the gun. He's got to keep his head down until you're back in the water."

"I'm going back in the water?"

"Damn right. You're going over the transom. Soon as you give Papa the gun. You're going to crawl astern, get your ass up and over that transom on the double, and then you're going to start swimming like a one-armed bandit, get as far away from this boat as possible."

"What about the mako?"

"Screw the mako."

"You're messing with me, man. Right?"

"How else you think we're going to draw his ass out so Papa can shoot him?"

"I'm already hit once. How many times I got to get shot today?"

"That's the whole idea, Sharkey. That's how we're going to draw him out. Get him to reveal his position. It's the only way your old man has a chance of getting a shot off without getting his head blown off."

"Aw, shit, Stokely, man, I dunno about this. Can't you think of another plan?"

"We haven't got a lot of time for tactical discussion here, Luis. You might have noticed I'm slowly bleeding to death. You wanted to get involved in this stuff, now you're involved in it. Welcome to my world. You're tuned in to the Stokely channel now, brother. All shit, all day, all the time. This is not unusual. Shit just exactly like this goes down all the damn time. All the time."

"Jesus, I don't know, Stoke."

"Luis! Pay attention. You can do this. Now snake your one-armed ass over to that ladder and hand your old man the damn rifle. Okay?"

"Yeah. Fuck. I'll do it."

"Gimme your hat first."

"My Yankee cap? For what?"

"Another idea. I'm going to stick it on top of this rod and jiggle it up and down while you're crawling. Help distract him."

"This sucks, man," Luis said, handing him the cap.

"You're going to be good at this shit, Luis, I'm serious. You've got all the right components. Trust me. I've seen 'em come and I've seen 'em go."

"Lots of turnover on your personal life channel? Is that right? Jesus."

Luis muttered the whole way across the deck. He snaked along using the rifle in his good hand and his left arm fin for propulsion. It looked a little weird but it was effective.

Stoke looked up at the flying bridge. Luis Sr. was crouched up there, staring down at him, screwing the cap back on his bottle of Triple X. His eyes were bright and he had a huge smile on his face. He wasn't drunk. He just knew damn well what was going on. And he had faith.

Stoke took heart.

The old man of the sea was into it.

Papa reached down for the butt of the rifle when his son managed to raise it high enough for him to grab hold. Once his father had the gun securely in his grasp,

Shark dropped back to the deck and instantly started crawling aft. Sharkey was scared but Stoke could see he was going to do the thing, go over the stern and swim away from the boat even though it was the last thing on earth he wanted to do.

Stoke had moved himself aft, crouched in the corner of the cockpit on the port side. He had Sharkey's faded Yankee baseball cap on the end of the fishing rod and now, his eyes on Papa up on the bridge, he raised the navy blue cap above the gunwale, jigging it up and down a few times.

Shots rang out instantly and one of them put a neat hole in Sharkey's Yankee cap. The cap spun but stayed on the rod. The guy could shoot. Stoke scrambled forward a few feet, bouncing the hat around and the rounds kept coming. Luis was huddled by the transom, waiting for Stoke's signal.

"Go, Sharkey, go, go, go!" he said to Luis.

Sharkey didn't say anything, he just did it. He pushed up off the deck and over the transom, hitting the water with a big splash, kicking and using his good arm to paddle furiously away from the stern. Stoke kept moving the cap around as best he could, holding the shooter's attention until the guy figured it out, which Stoke knew wouldn't take much longer.

He looked up at Papa on the tower. The old man looked ready and now was as good a time as any. Most of the rounds were aimed at the Yankee cap and a few were zinging off the stern, going into the water aft where Sharkey was once more unfortunately swimming for his life.

"You see the shooter?" Stoke shouted up to the old man. "You know where he is?"

"Si, señor, yo se!" Papa said, a huge smile on his face. "I got this fish in my sights. In the bushes beneath the coconut palm tree."

"You got the angle? You ready?"

"Si. Es muy perfecto."

"Do it."

PAPA SHOWED HIMSELF then, stood right up, bringing the rifle up into firing position and aiming it even as he got to his feet. He swung the barrel to his left and started firing furiously on semiauto into the mangrove bushes. The rounds were aimed at the base of the tiny island's lone coconut palm tree, splintering it and sending debris into the air.

"Aieeee!"

A scream came from the island. A long dying wail. Papa kept firing, expended the whole mag, and then the screaming stopped for good.

"Bueno, amigo!" Stoke said, hauling himself up to the gunwale so that he could see for himself what the hell was going on. Smoke was rising from the badly shot up mangrove.

"You think I did it?" Papa asked, grinning. *"Es muerto?"*

"Yeah," Stoke said, grinning, "I think he's *muerto* all right. We'll know soon enough."

"Luis!" Papa cried out, waving his arms at his son in the water about twenty yards astern. "It's okay! It's okay! Come back!"

He nudged the throttles, backing down slowly toward his son.

"Your boy was very brave, Papa. Help me get him aboard."

"What we do now, señor?" the old fella said coming down the ladder with the rifle.

"We got to reel in your catch over there. Identify what make and model he is. Then we put him on ice in the fishbox and take him back to the dock."

"No catch and release, señor?" Papa said with a smile.

STOKE FELT LIKE he was going to puke or pass out getting to his feet and taking the boathook from its holder underneath the gunwale to help Papa fish Luis out of the water. He stood there a minute, watching Sharkey approach the boat. His head seemed to clear and he thought maybe he was going to be okay here, long as he didn't try to do too much.

"We did it," Luis said, climbing into the boat, smiling his ass off. "Hey, Papa, you are some action hero, man!"

"De nada," the old man said, still holding the rifle tenderly.

"Okay, Luis. Now you get up on the bow and get the hook up. Let's go see what we caught."

Papa went inside to the lower helm station and ran the boat right inside the little cove going ahead dead slow. As soon as the bow touched sand he killed the engines. Stoke figured they were in about four feet of water. Sharkey stood on the bow, swinging the hook, and heaved it into the mangroves where it snagged in some thick roots. He jumped in, started wading ashore, headed for the smoking palm tree.

Ten minutes later Stoke was bending over the copilot. He had a couple of holes in his light blue uniform, flesh wounds. He was still alive. Barely. Stoke leaned in close to see the patch on his shoulder.

It bore the emblem of the FAV.

The Fuerza Aérea Venezolana.

The Venezuelan Air Force. That's who was buying the missiles.

Now why the hell would Venezuela be doing that? If the wounded guy lived, Stoke would just have to ask him that question.

Suddenly, the guy shuddered. His eyelids fluttered and his lips started moving, too, but nothing was coming out. Stoke bent down, but all he could hear was garbled Spanish.

"Luis," Stoke said, "put your ear down here and tell me what this guy is saying."

Luis leaned over and listened for a few seconds, a puzzled look on his face.

"He says 'Thank you.' "

"What?"

"Thank you very much, that's what he's saying."

"That's a first," Stoke said.

27

A SELVA NEGRA

Killing Americans en masse," Dr. Abu Musab al Khan told Muhammad Top, "will be mere child's play. I am assuming, based on endless reports and assertions by you, that all our military assets are firmly in place and that the phalanxes soon to be moving up into the Mexican mountain range have the ability to achieve this objective."

"Yes."

"All is in readiness with the convoy?" he asked, stroking his beard. "Our friend in Caracas is very nervous."

Muhammad Top had been impatiently awaiting this question since Dr. Khan's arrival the day before.

"Yes. The assets are in place north of the border. Mexican units, loyal to our cause, await your orders as to when to release the vehicles. As you will soon see, we are fully prepared to strike on all fronts, Dr. Khan," Top said, locking his eyes on Khan's. "God willing."

"*Inshallah.* I am looking at the clock above the monitor. Some kind of countdown, I presume?"

"Yes, Doctor. The countdown was initiated this morning."

Top made sure his eye contact with the diminutive scientist was solid for good reason. Khan was now the second most powerful man in the global Islamic terrorist movement. He had known this man for many years. He knew that those shrewd black eyes didn't just see you, they penetrated your very soul.

"I bring greetings and prayers for your success from on high."

"Please assure the sheikh I am prepared to do my sacred duty. The aggressors will trouble us no more after the Day of Reckoning."

Top tried desperately to conceal his surprise at Khan's mention of Osama. No one in the terrorist community was sure whether or not the sheikh was even alive. A recent tape had been played on al-Jazeerah, but there were doubts as to its authenticity.

The true leader of the movement, the almost mythical prince Osama, had not been actually seen, publicly or privately, in nearly three years. Not since December of 2004, when he had released his last video. He called for his jihadist warriors to strike Persian Gulf oil supplies and warned the apostate House of Saud that they risked a popular uprising. Then he disappeared. Now, rumor had it, Khan was preparing to succeed the long-silent leader.

The Western media were strangely silent too. The media simply didn't know what had happened to the man who'd ignited the worldwide Islamic jihad. They didn't know if the much-vaunted prince of darkness had simply gone deeper into hiding as the American troops closed in on him; or, perhaps, he had simply died. It was still entirely possible he was only lying low, lulling the West into a false sense of complacency while planning some great Armageddon.

In truth, even so important a figure in the global movement as Muhammad Top did not know the answer to that puzzle. But he knew that it was Abu Musab al Khan who had recently stepped into the media limelight as the "brains" of the organization. If Khan didn't hold the reins of power, surely he was in the business of seizing them. Top knew that his own success in this current initiative would consolidate Khan's position in the Arab world.

And, so did his esteemed guest.

In any case, Khan was not a man to be trifled with. He was clearly capable of running the movement's global terror operations. Besides, it was common knowledge that Dr. Khan had personally eviscerated men on the spot for failing his particular kind of eye test. It was said that Khan secreted a viciously curved scimitar within the folds of his robes for just such a purpose.

For all of Top's judicious planning, his guest had arrived two hours late. He had been delayed by bad weather, a storm front moving over São Paulo. After a good deal of hand-wringing over arrangements to receive them, the man had finally arrived at the jungle compound.

After Khan's arrival at the landing strip, and travel to the central village, Top escorted him to his temporary guest quarters. He enjoyed the man's reaction as they climbed into a sturdy woven basket to be lofted upward to the large two-story guesthouse situated some two hundred feet up in the treetops. Shortly afterward, the new arrival had descended and begun a guided tour of the bustling complex.

Top had decided to start the tour with the subterranean Command and Communication center secreted in the very heart of his compound. Even Dr. Khan could not fail to be impressed by all the stunning long-distance warfare technology he would see this day. Already Top could sense that Khan was secretly delighted with the Swiss-clock workings and precision perfection of the teeming terrorist enclave.

The two men were now standing before an array of surveillance monitors, their upturned faces bathed in incandescent blue. Each of the flat screens carried a live digital satellite feed from the cameras of Muhammad Top's fleet of tiny UAVs now circling above Manhattan and Washington, D.C.

On-site pilots flew the two-foot-long birds by remote control, using joysticks and input from sensor operators seated next to them. Each ground control workstation received feeds via a Ku-Band satellite data link for beyond line-of-sight flight.

Khan smiled his approval. He had designed these UAV systems and it was the first time he'd seen them in a war-footing operation.

The large central monitor was currently dedicated to lower Manhattan. The Staten Island Ferry was just nearing the wharf and lights were coming on in the of-

fice towers near the Battery. A row of smaller monitors
to either side showed aerial views of Washington, the
Chicago lakefront, the port of Miami, and central Los
Angeles. Beneath these screens, a secondary grouping
of monitors showed views of various border towns
along the Texas-Mexico borderline.

"And how go the preparations for the Lone Star
State?" Khan asked Top, his eyes fixed on a view of the
International Bridge connecting Laredo with its sister
city across the border.

"The convoy is assembled, Doctor. It has moved
north of the border."

The two men were certainly a study in contrasts.
Khan was a small, modest-looking intellectual. Save the
keen intensity of the black eyes, the Iranian would be
indistinguishable at any gathering of Muslim elders in
Tehran. Of less than medium height, he had a great
beak of a nose, with tiny eyeglasses perched on the end
of it. He had very small hands and feet that always
seemed to be still. He was surprising only in that he had
changed into jungle fatigues for the tour.

"Listen carefully," Khan said, taking a step backward
and looking up at his giant host. His black eyes flashing
with the reflections of America on the screens above, he
said, "I am bringing you a message from on high.
Killing Americans is secondary to our true mission. It is
only icing on the pudding. Do you understand that?"

"Doctor, with your kind permission, I must argue—"

"Listen! Don't speak! I am talking about attacking
the foundations of the corrupt state these faithless
pawns serve. God willing, I am determined to scrape

America's bucolic soil down to the tainted bedrock it is built upon! If you don't agree, tell me now."

Top silently nodded his understanding. Patience was required. Khan was having trouble assembling a "coalition of the willing" in the Latin American capitals. More and more it looked as if Top's righteous legions might be marching north alone. Top was willing to go it alone. But if Khan's shaky coalition were convinced to step up, it would seal America's fate.

Khan, visibly tired by the long journey, removed his spectacles and pinched the bridge of his nose. He was secretly fighting a crippling headache. He had been anxious to see his military field commander in the flesh. Everything was riding on this one man. As the final hour approached, Castro was waffling. So was Chávez in Venezuela. Both men needed to see if Muhammad Top's brazen attack could succeed before joining the fray.

Venezuela, in Khan's view, could seal the victory over the Americans. Chávez, despite all Khan's assurances, was taking a wait-and-see attitude. If Top and Khan succeeded, and brought down the U.S. command and control, Venezuela might decide to strike in the ensuing chaos. Chávez had been secretly building a powerful air force. He had amassed squadrons of the latest Russian fighter jets, the Sukhoi 27 Flanker. Armed with the unstoppable Yakhont anti-ship missiles, Venezuelan fighter jets could destroy America's vital oil shipments in the Gulf of Mexico.

It wouldn't be the end of America, but it might be the beginning of the end.

Top alone, of all his commanders, had the best

chance of finally bringing the Americans to their knees. Reports reaching his own mountain hideout from his emissaries were uniformly positive. They all indicated that Muhammad Top had at last built the jihadist juggernaut that would humble the world.

Maybe.

Khan also received monthly intelligence reports from leaders of his South American cells. They provided a more balanced approach to developments in the southern hemisphere. He had carefully monitored Top's progress over the last few years from afar. Read reports from their brethren in Havana and Caracas and Lima. Now he was here to see for himself exactly what had been accomplished here at A Selva Negra.

And what kind of man he had created in the person of Top.

Papa Top had risen to power and prominence in the wake of the 1991 bombing of the Israeli embassy in Buenos Aires. Top and Khan had both had a hand in the planning of this deadly attack. But it was Top's brilliant execution that brought him to the notice of the early al-Qaeda leadership.

After the early success of that Argentine mission, Muhammad Top and his followers had moved north. There, they melted into the Mato Grosso jungles surrounding the Falls at Madre de Deus. Once he had surveyed the jungle and picked his ideal location, Top, always with Khan's guiding hand, began the long and exceedingly difficult process of building a great terrorist army. At the same time, work was begun in earnest on Khan's very advanced robotic warfare technology and surveillance drones in complete secrecy.

Khan was the wise and patient mentor, the man who had stolen Western technology and put it into the hands of North Korea, Pakistan, and his secret terrorist operation in the rain forest. Top was the able and willing protégé who worked tirelessly to build a massive fighting force of Holy Warriors. Khan only stole from the best. He studied Japanese work in robotics and applied their learning to military applications. His endless hard cash ensured a flow of information out of top secret U.S. defense-related firms as well.

Early on, the doctor had urged Top, when his army was at strength, to take the war out of the jungles and mountains and bring it directly to the urban population centers of Latin America. Khan had sent this message to his young lieutenant via a courier in 1995. Along with orders from Khan's mountain headquarters, the messenger had hand-delivered a small gift to Muhammad's jungle headquarters, then in Venezuela. It was a very special book by Carlos Marighella.

Until he was ambushed and killed by Brazilian police, Marighella was one of South America's greatest revolutionary heroes. Just before he died, he had written a handbook offering very practical advice for creating a modern guerrilla unit. His slim volume, far ahead of its time, had been written at the dawn of terror. The well-thumbed volume soon became Top's personal bible. He studied it to the point of memorization and often quoted from it to his staff and field commanders. Marighella's book, *Manual for the Modern Guerrilla,* had been Top's Koran.

Papa Top's sphere of influence now included terrorist cells and guerrilla units across the length and breadth
of South America. Each of these was a curious amalgam
of drug dealers, arms dealers, and common street criminals. Each one had undergone rigorous paramilitary
training under Top's commanders. His melting-pot
army consisted of a seething blend of radical leftists,
radical Muslims, and common street criminals whose
loyalty was vouchsafed only to him.

"Our next stop is across the river," Top said. "The
Robotic Weapons Research Center. Is everyone ready to
move on?"

"Yes," Abu Khan said, eyes glittering in the electric
blue light. "Weapons. Let us go and see our glorious
Robot Warriors."

28

"Gin!" exclaimed Ambrose Congreve, splaying the winning hand upon the patch of green baize in a perfect fan: three queens, three jacks, and a royal straight. Ambrose, already looking tropical in a three-piece suit of rumpled seersucker, sat back in his seat, took a small sip of his spicy Bloody Bull, and relished the expression on his vanquished opponent's face.

"Gin?" Hawke said, startled out of his reverie by his opponent's sudden declaration of victory. He stared at the winning cards magically appearing on the table for a moment and then said, "Impossible."

"Improbably swift, perhaps, but hardly impossible. Read them and weep, dear boy, for n'ere shall you see their like again."

"How can you gin? We've hardly begun this bloody hand. You only drew three cards."

"Indeed, I drew three cards. To wit, the third queen, the ace of diamonds, and the jack of spades filling in a lovely straight. Gin is the name of the game, my good fellow, now tote me up. Let's see what you're hiding. Unless I'm very much mistaken, I believe I've caught you with a gross surplus of costly royalty in your hand. Am I correct?"

Hawke sighed in frustration, and reluctantly began showing his cards. Congreve bent forward, smiling eagerly as out they came. He was not disappointed. Two kings, two jacks, pair of nines, pair of sevens, and some other cats and mice. The hand was worth eighty and change. Not bad, Congreve thought.

"Well, well, well," Congreve said, picking up the score pad and gleefully adding up the totals. "That puts me ahead by a comfortable margin. Just time for one more hand. I spy something that looks suspiciously like Florida down there."

Hawke glanced out of his window and experienced a pleasurable shudder of anticipation. The Atlantic far below was shading from a deep blue to a lovely aquamarine near the shoreline as the small jet began its gradual descent toward the eastern coastline of the sprawling peninsula. For the first time since waking, he smiled.

After the recent weeks of damp cold, Alex had been keenly looking forward to leaving gloomy England astern and spending some time in the warm tropical sunshine. According to his crew in the cockpit, they would be landing in time for breakfast on board *Blackhawke*. It had been over a year since he'd set foot on his beloved vessel.

"I suppose one of us should wake Miss Guinness," he said.

"Yes. I have to say C has chosen a most decorous aide-de-camp for this adventure. Don't you agree?"

"She's not an ADC, that I promise you."

"What is she, then?"

"A spy."

Hawke was only half kidding. British SIS had long used female operators. It was not well known, but during the Second World War, women had been involved in not a few nasty, physical operations. And, since they had always acquitted themselves quite well, there had been little resistance to getting them involved in elite commando or espionage operations ever since. There were several generations of lady operators out there now. Somewhere in the world, Hawke knew, was a cherubic grandmother with a license to kill.

Congreve was trying to get his pipe lit. "A spy? You mean for C? Yes, that would make perfect sense. Sent to keep an eye on you."

"What else could she be doing?"

"She's quite brainy, I believe."

"I don't need another brain. I've got you."

"Well, I daresay she's lovely to look at. Remarkable protuberances."

"Dishy. As long as she keeps her protuberances out of my way. I intend to admire her from afar."

"She certainly doesn't have to stay out of mine. I'm quite looking forward to this tropical holiday you know. There's something bracing about near-naked females splashing in the surf, don't you agree? Stiffens one up before the fray, I daresay."

Near naked? Stiffens one up? Hawke looked for a

trace of irony in Congreve's dancing blue eyes, but could find none.

"You ought to be ashamed of yourself, Constable. You're practically a married man. I promised Diana I'd keep an eye on you and I intend to do so."

"You remember what Sherlock Holmes had to say on the subject of marriage, my dear fellow? In the *Adventure of the Noble Bachelor*?"

"No, I do not. And, frankly, I—"

"Gin," Ambrose said, a small smile of satisfaction playing about his crinkly eyes.

"Again?" Hawke said, throwing his cards down in disgust.

Hawke sensed someone stirring behind him and collapsed back into his seat.

"Oh! Good morning, Mr. Congreve," Pippa Guinness said, peeking at Ambrose over the back of her reclined seat. She yawned and wiped the sleep from her eyes with the back of her right hand. Hawke, who was facing aft, had his back to her and chose not to acknowledge this greeting by feigning sleep.

He'd made a troublesome discovery the evening prior at the Connaught Bar. Over drinks with an old colleague who was recently employed at Legoland, he had learned that the lovely Miss Guinness was the source of many of C's misgivings regarding his Amazon reports. According to his chum, Barry Donohue, Pippa had provided C with her own assessment of the current threat level in the Amazon Triangle. Apparently, she found it significantly lower than Hawke's own estimates. Told C that Hawke was overstating his case.

Hawke wouldn't have minded that necessarily, but then he'd learned that the young woman had never set foot in the Amazon Basin. Her summary conclusions, passed along to C, were handwritten in the annotated margins of Hawke's own carefully prepared reports. According to Donohue, all of her conclusions were based on the accounts of various low-ranking embassy staffers notorious for collecting dated and even erroneous intel in the comfort of their plush offices in Buenos Aires, Caracas, Santiago, and Montevideo. Going out into the field would rarely even occur to them.

It was precisely the reason C had sent Hawke up the river on his "expedition."

None of this, however, seemed to have occurred to the lovely Miss G. Or, to be honest, C himself.

Hawke suffered no delusions about C's assigning Pippa Guinness as his "aide" on this trip. The possibility that she was a bona fide field agent was remote. She was tagging along to keep an eye on him and report back to C on all and sundry that she saw and heard in Key West. HM Government had a big stake in Brazil. He was sure the Foreign Secretary had urged C to keep tabs on its erstwhile field agent whilst he was deep inside the American camp.

Miss Guinness was seated just aft of the forward bulkhead on the left. A flat-screen monitor mounted there showed a GPS map of the lower southeastern United States and displayed their current airspeed, estimated time of arrival, and the time and temperature at their destination. The temperature in Miami, Hawke had noted with satisfaction just before they took off from RAF Sedgwick, was a balmy seventy degrees Fahrenheit. The temperature in London had plummeted into the thirties.

After supper aboard, Hawke's steward had offered to run a film, presenting Pippa Guinness a choice from the onboard DVD library. She'd chosen *Bad Boys,* a fairly recent Will Smith comedy shot in Miami. As it happened, the action comedy was one of Hawke's favorites and he'd watched some of it himself before becoming embroiled in a two-inch thick LATAM file marked MOST SECRET. This he'd been given by C for his in-flight entertainment.

He plowed through his files, studying the charts and tables, mentally rehearsing his upcoming remarks at the Key West conference. It was not as dry as he'd feared. Whoever had prepared it knew their stuff. Having digested three-quarters of the file, he'd nevertheless fallen asleep. Having slept for a few hours, he then resumed studying the thing at first light before falling into Congreve's sticky web of aces and deuces, kings and queens.

"Good morning, Miss Guinness," Ambrose said heartily. "How did you sleep?"

"Most comfortably, thank you," she said. "This certainly beats economy on Virgin Atlantic."

"Indeed it does," Ambrose said. "Hawke Air abounds in creature comforts. Would you like some tea, my dear? Coffee? We're having breakfast on the ground, but I'm sure the galley could scrounge up a scone or two if you're so inclined. Eggs and toast?"

"Tea would be lovely, thank you. I'll just pop into the loo and freshen up if I have time."

"You do. We're landing in about half an hour."

"Brilliant," she said, climbing deftly out of her seat considering the length of her skirt. "How was your gin rummy game? Did you win, Chief Inspector?"

"Handily, my dear, thanks very much."

After she'd disappeared from the cabin and closed the door to the head, Hawke, who'd been feigning sleep throughout this conversation, brought his seat upright and looked at Congreve.

"Handily?" Hawke asked. "Is that what you said to her, Constable?"

"Mmm."

"Handily, my arse. Deal the bloody cards."

29

Half an hour later, Hawke was on the ground. He stepped off the plane onto the tarmac at Opa-locka Airport. The small field handled general aviation overflow from Miami-Dade and was located just seven miles from Miami International. Hawke saw a dark blue Suburban with heavily tinted windows parked just outside the FBO building, about twenty yards away. The familiar figure of Sergeant Tom Quick was striding his way.

"Welcome to Miami, Skipper," Quick said, extending his hand. The young blond American fellow, an ex-Army sniper, was Hawke's chief of security and had been overseeing *Blackhawke*'s refit in Miami these last few months.

"It's good to see you, sir," Quick said, taking Hawke's canvas travel case and slinging it over his shoulder.

"Good to be here," Hawke said, and meant it. "Cheated death once again, Tommy," he added, looking back at his gleaming midnight blue airplane. He was always happy to have it on the ground, passengers and airplane all in one piece.

Quick leaned forward and said softly, "A quick update, Skipper. I just got a call from Stokely Jones saying he was on his way to Port of Miami to meet you and wondering if you'd landed. He says he's got someone he'd like you to meet. A Venezuelan he met down in the Keys. He arrived late last night from Key West where he and his new friend had been in the hospital."

"Stokely was hurt? How much damage?"

"Nothing life-threatening, I don't think, but they kept him overnight for observation. According to him, just a scratch. He was badly cut diving on a wreck day before yesterday. Lost a lot of blood. But he sounded upbeat as usual. He says you'll find his new friend extremely interesting."

"You have Stokely's new mobile number here?"

"Yes, sir."

"I'll call him from the car."

Congreve had emerged from the plane and, ever the gentleman, was offering Miss Guinness a hand as she descended the few remaining steps to the ground.

"Mr. Congreve, great to see you again," Tom said, going over to shake hands with Ambrose and relieve him of his carry-on luggage.

"Young Tom, I am delighted to see you as well," Congreve said, giving Quick his bag. He looked around at the grassy palm-fringed field, stretching his arms skyward and rising up jauntily onto his toes. The man hated flying and was always thrilled to find himself returned to terra firma.

He turned to Quick and said, "Sergeant? May I present Miss Pippa Guinness? Miss Guinness, this strapping young lad is Thomas Quick, formerly of the United States Army and now the man primarily responsible for your security while you're aboard *Blackhawke*."

"Tommy Quick, Miss Guinness," he said, shaking her hand. "Welcome to the tropics. I've got transportation waiting just over there. If everyone's ready, the stowed luggage will be transferred from the plane while we clear Customs and Immigration. Then we'll head over to the Port of Miami. We've got a piping hot breakfast waiting for you aboard ship."

"Ship?" she said, eying Hawke. "He owns a ship too?"

"You'll see," Quick replied, relieving her of her carry-on luggage.

ABOARD HIS BELOVED *Blackhawke* at long last, Hawke excused himself shortly after breakfast and made his way forward alone. After an extended journey sealed at high altitude inside an aluminum tube, he was eager for fresh air and solitude. His boat was the only company he needed at present. He wanted to see all of her, feel her, smell her, run his fingers along her varnished rails and gleaming chrome fittings.

Stopping briefly in his aft quarters, he'd gotten quickly out of the grey slacks and black cashmere sweater he'd worn on the flight and slipped eagerly into a familiar old pair of khaki shorts and a faded Royal Navy T-shirt.

The teak decks were warm beneath his bare feet as

he made his way toward the bow. Nothing beat the fragrance of freshly scrubbed teak for making a man feel whole again. It signified another trip over the horizon, a new adventure around the next turning. Smiling a salute at passing members of his crew, old friends all, he could literally feel the tension of the last few weeks and months seeping out of him. He reached the deserted bow and gazed down at the sunlit panorama of the great harbor and the blue Atlantic beyond.

Thank God for the sea and the simple light of morning.

Hawke considered for a time how very fortunate he was to be here in this place at this time. And what blessed moments of consolation there sometimes were for all the dark and dangerous hours, the harsh realities of his chosen profession. He was happy to have at least a few days of sun-drenched respite before the grim black work began again. Grey London, the narrow streets shining with rain, was already beginning to recede into distant memory.

Now, standing alone on the foredeck, some thirty feet or more above the water, it was time to widen his horizons a bit. The sun was warm. The clean air, briny with salt, was fresh and cool on his cheek. A tumble of white clouds hid a morning sun climbing the brilliant blue bowl of the eastern sky. Gulls and terns wheeled and cried, diving and swooping over the wrinkled surface of the blue waters of Government Cut.

He took a deep gulp of the salt air, pulled it down the bottom of his lungs and held it until it burned, feeling a purifying fire deep inside his chest.

The boy stood on the burning deck.

Alex smiled at the games his mind played. He was not a man for deep introspection or any kind of angst-ridden self-analysis. He simply didn't have time or inclination for such stuff. Emotions and feelings were transitory and not to be trusted. Let his actions bloody well define his character, he'd always thought, because, for better or for worse, that's who he was.

It suddenly occurred to him, as he stood there in the brilliant sunshine, that it wasn't until a man reached his stage in life that he was ever fully aware of beauty or nature or even changes in weather. It dawned on him that it was only now, in his early thirties, standing here on the very brink of middle age, that one didn't take such commonplace things for granted. He took little for granted these days. He accepted that, but wondered why.

Perhaps it had been the tragic loss of his wife Victoria on the steps of a small Cotswolds chapel two years earlier. His heart had been shattered into infinitely small pieces when the sniper's bullet pierced his young bride's heart and stole her life while he looked on, helpless. He was quite sure the wound would never heal. God knows it still hurt.

Then, he thought, there was the recent near miss in the Amazon jungle and the death of every one of his dear colleagues on the river.

Or maybe the explanation was far less weighty and solemn. Perhaps Florida was simply working its balmy magic upon him again. Whatever it was, Hawke was suddenly aware of a strong sense of being, not at home, certainly, but of being in precisely the right place at the right time.

"Skipper?"

"Yes?" he turned to see Tom Quick descending the steps curving down from the starboard bridge wing.

"Sorry to bother you, sir, but an old friend heard you were aboard. She demanded to see you."

Hawke's pet parrot, Sniper, was riding on Quick's right shoulder.

Hallo, Hawke! Hallo, Hawke! Sniper squawked, flaring her large wings.

"Good idea, Tommy, let me have her, will you? Hullo, you old buzzard, how the hell have you been? Huh?"

Damnifiknow. Hellificare! Sniper replied.

"My sentiments exactly," Hawke said, stroking her beak with great affection. "I don't know how I've been and I don't much care, either. Pretty sad lot, are we not?"

What a babe! What a bod! Sniper said, apropos of nothing. Probably just repeating what she'd heard one of the crew remark upon seeing Pippa Guinness coming aboard.

Hawke laughed. Sniper's language grew increasingly salty with the passing years, a result of her hanging out with the loose crowd that inhabited this great barge of his. But the old girl was trained in the ancient pirate's ways and often had warned her master of hidden or unseen dangers.

Sniper fluttered her wings and settled easily onto Hawke's shoulder. He'd had the beautiful bird for many years and it was a comfort to feel her resting there again. She'd gotten him out of more than one scrape, sitting on that shoulder.

Quick said, "She hasn't had breakfast, Skipper. I brought along her Cheezbits."

Hawke held up a handful and Sniper eagerly snapped them up.

"All shipshape below, Tommy?" Hawke asked. He'd been on the bridge for a word or two with his captain, but he'd not yet had time to inspect the engine room or the communications and fire control centers.

He'd placed Quick in charge of overseeing some aspects of the yacht's refit and weapons systems upgrade. The yacht *Blackhawke* was in truth more warship than wealthy man's play toy. She had a gleaming black hull and featured an integrated combat system centered on the Aegis weapon system and the SPY-1 multifunction phased-array radar. The whole kit had cost him a bloody fortune, but he took the long view in such matters. *Blackhawke* was both his fortress and his base of operations when on assignment abroad. He could, thankfully, well afford to have a first-rater beneath his feet when he went to sea.

"I can't say everything went like clockwork, these things never do, but she's certainly seaworthy, combat ready, and ready to sail, sir."

"I had a look at the sea trial reports from the chief engineer. Hard to read between the lines but, superficially at least, she seems more fit than I left her."

Quick smiled. "For a two-hundred-forty-foot vessel, she runs like a bat out of hell, I'll tell you that much, Skipper."

"What the hell is that noise, Tom?"

"Sounds like somebody arriving down on the dock, sir."

"An automobile is making that horrendous sound?" Hawke said, moving to the port rail and looking down at the dock. There was a black convertible just pulling up at the foot of the gangplank, an American muscle car with its rear end jacked up at a very severe angle. A loud blat of exhaust wafted up as the monster's throttle was depressed.

The convertible top suddenly lifted up off the windscreen and began folding back. It revealed Stokely Jones sitting behind the wheel of the wild machine, waving up at him, a big smile stretched across his face.

Hawke smiled back and handed Quick the bird.

Stoke was back. Ambrose was aboard.

His team was together again. They were headed into the thick of it once more.

Alex Hawke was finally feeling alive again.

30

Look outside, Sheriff! What the heck's going on out there?" Homer said, slamming down his Pepsi and half getting to his feet to look over the top of the booth.

Franklin looked up from his cream of barley soup and sandwich. He twisted his head around so that he, too, could look out the front windows. He saw a man in dungaree coveralls running past the drugstore windows. He was moving at a pretty good clip for a lazy Saturday afternoon. A second later, he saw an old yellow dog bounding after the man, both of them moving lickety-split up the sidewalk.

"Missed his bus," Franklin drawled and returned to his soup.

"Prairie ain't got any buses," Homer said.

"Well, there's that."

The sheriff took a bite of his grilled cheese and smiled. Nobody made better grilled cheese sandwiches than Virgil Buff at the Rexall drugstore. Nobody even came close.

The two lawmen had knocked off around one and left the courthouse. Out of sheer habit, they'd ambled directly across the street to the drugstore luncheonette for a bite. It was a warm December day and the overhead fans inside were spinning lazily. The smell of fried onions in the air made Franklin hungry coming in the door. There was a stack of newspapers set on the table by the screen door and he took one.

From his station behind the long Formica counter, owner Roy Sewell waved them over to the last available booth, halfway down on the right. By the averted looks he and Homer received entering and sitting down, Franklin wasn't sure he had too many friends left around this town. But, you know, he'd always said, the law wasn't some kind of popularity contest.

People liked it when the law was on their side and didn't like it when it wasn't. No mystery there.

Roy came over and took their order, nodding when both men said, "The usual." They sat for a few moments in silence and then Homer piped up, "How's your paper goin'? You only got a few days left before you go to Key West."

"Almost done."

"You happy with it?"

"I guess so, Homer. I said my piece anyway."

"I hear on the news that pretty woman secretary of state is even going to be there. What's her name? Consuelo something or other. Cuban, I believe. I've seen her on the TV here a lot lately. Say, you nervous about getting up in front of all those fancy Washington folks?"

"I'm nervous about being gone away so long, to tell you the honest truth."

"We'll be all right. Don't worry. We got Wyatt."

"Yep. We got Wyatt."

In truth, the town had been pretty quiet since the afternoon about a week ago here that the little Mexican boy, Manuelito, had gone to his reward out at the Brotherwood place. There had been a sizable outpouring of grief in the town's small but growing Latino community. Even a few demonstrators and more questions raised about the inhumanity of the U.S. immigration laws, and so forth and so on. Some locals, Hispanics and others, blamed the sheriff for the child's death since the boy had been in Dixon's care when he passed on. Nothing you could do about that. People think what they're going to think.

Since the boy apparently had no family left in Mexico, Franklin had arranged for Manuelito to be buried in the small plot behind St. Mary's. It was the only Catholic church in town, and the priest there was an old friend of Franklin's. The sheriff had spoken at the graveside and tried to express his true feelings about the loss of a child in these kinds of circumstances. He wasn't sure he had, but he hoped he'd given some comfort to the folks who mourned. Two families had stepped forward and volunteered to take in Manuelito's surviving brothers.

"Sit down and eat your lunch, Homer," Franklin said. His deputy had popped up again, upsetting his water glass and spilling it directly onto Franklin's plate. Ruined what was left of a perfectly good sandwich.

"Sheriff, something funny's going on out there. Look at all the people going by. They're all running. Like they were scared or something."

Franklin wiped his mouth with the paper napkin and stood up, sliding out of the booth.

"Come on, Homer," he said as soon as he saw the faces of the townspeople rushing past the drugstore windows. Homer was right. Something about their expressions said they weren't running *to* something but rather *away* from something.

"What's going on, Sheriff?" Homer said, adjusting his short brim and sliding out of the booth, "A twister or something?"

"That's what we're about to go find out. Go ahead. I'll settle us up with Roy."

Homer was first out the door and he was almost bowled over by Frank Teague, a big gangly kid who was the all-state center on the high school basketball squad. He had his baby sister in his arms. Right behind Frank were his mother and grandmother. Farther down Main Street was another group of citizens fleeing some unseen danger.

"Miz Teague," Homer was saying as Dixon stepped out into the street, "where are you running to? What the heck's going on?"

She paused a second, all out of breath, and said, "It's some kind of trouble, Sheriff! A whole bunch of outlaw motorcycles. They've got guns!"

"How many?"

"Maybe twenty or thirty, far as I could tell. Bad. Looks like the Hell's Angels or somebody like that. I heard they already shot up some cars. Blew out a store window."

"Anybody hurt?"

"I don't know, Sheriff. Everybody kinda panicked."

"Where are they now?"

"Still down the road a piece, I guess," the widow Teague said, looking fearfully over her shoulder. "I saw them stopped along the two-lane outside of town. You know, just before you get to Gray's Mobil station. They're probably headed into town! Somebody better do something, Sheriff!"

"Yes, ma'am. It'll be all right. Everybody needs to get off the streets. Right now. You go tell everybody you see. Go on, now."

"Para Salvados," Homer whispered to Dixon. "PS 13, right, the same guys we saw down at the bullring?"

"Could be," the sheriff said. He was already thinking that's who it was. In the last forty-eight hours, he'd had a few death threats on the phone and one in the mail postmarked Laredo. Daisy'd gotten some very disturbing email. He'd heard rumors from various Latino members of the department that down in Nuevo Laredo, some people were blaming him for the death of the little Mexican boy. Tiger Tejada was no doubt stirring the pot.

The woman set off at a run up Main to catch up with her fleeing family. Franklin stepped aside to let other people go by. You could hear the beginning of a faint and distant rumble to the south. Pretty soon here, they'd be entering town at the bottom of Main Street. That would be about eight blocks to Franklin's left. A sound like approaching thunder grew perceptibly louder.

"Homer."

"Yessir."

"Is Wyatt asleep? Get Wyatt on the radio and tell him to get some officers out here on the street. Anybody he can find in the office and on the radio. Okay? Tell him to look out the window. We got a potential panic if he doesn't already know that by now. I want everybody off the street, now. Tell him I want everybody wearing Kevlar too."

"Yessir. How 'bout you?"

"I'm going to try and find out what we're looking at here."

"You want this?" Homer asked, pulling out his Smith & Wesson. Franklin looked at it a second. He didn't carry often, for two reasons. He was trying to set a good community example. And he'd once killed a whole lot of people at close range and was trying to live out the balance of his life without repeating that experience.

Times change.

He took the gun.

"We ain't got a whole lot of time here, Homer. Now, go on, git over there and help Wyatt."

FOLKS WERE STREAMING out of Roy's Rexall now, and Dixon had to squeeze through an onrush of frantic people just to get through the door. He found Virgil, the short-order cook, locking up the cash register and the owner, Roy, breaking the breech of a shotgun he kept behind the counter to make sure it was loaded. Franklin knew he kept it loaded with double-ought buckshot. Wasn't ideal, but better than nothing.

"Roy, you got a quick way to get up on your roof?" The drugstore was on the ground floor of an old four-story brick building with unobstructed views south down Main Street.

Roy vaulted over the counter. "Out the back, Sheriff. Fire escape steps leading up there. You want to go up there?"

"No. I'd like you up there with your shotgun, Roy. Just in case. Will you do that?"

"You got it, Sheriff. Heck is going on?"

"Outlaw motorcycle gang."

"We'll go scope it out."

"Don't show yourself unless you see a signal from me. And for Pete's sake hold your fire."

Roy nodded and then he and the short-order man headed to the back and the dark hallway that led to the rear of the old Victorian red brick building. Dixon hurried back out the front door and onto the narrow sidewalk.

The crowd had thinned out completely, only one or two still on the street. To the south, as far as he could tell, Main Street looked empty all the way to the edge of town. Looked like most folks had disappeared indoors or gotten in their vehicles and hightailed it out of town. In only a few minutes, the townspeople had evacuated.

The approaching rumble was louder now. Much louder. They were getting close. And there were a lot of them, too, kicking up dust and sending a chalky cloud up into the blue skies over the little town.

Dixon walked out into the center of the empty street. He looked up at the top of the building and saw Roy and Virgil up there on the roof, looking down over the parapet. Across the street, the courthouse had faces in every window. No officers had appeared yet, which was probably just as well. Let these boys have their big parade and then just keep on going.

Franklin started walking south down the center of the street. The roar of the engines was getting very close. He'd walked half a block when he saw the first of them coming six blocks away. It was a whole lot more than twenty or thirty of them. From the look and sound, it was more like a hundred of them. Big bikes, too.

They were riding four abreast up Main, moving at a slow speed, maybe ten miles an hour. There were at least twenty or thirty rows of four behind the leaders. The chopper noise, now that there were buildings on both sides, was so loud you couldn't hear yourself think.

He did hear a shout to his right and saw Wyatt and Homer emerge from the courthouse entrance with a couple of other officers. He could see a few more bunched up behind them. All three outside the door had riot guns and were wearing Kevlar sport-coats and Franklin had to make a split-second decision about whether or not he wanted uniforms on the street. Their presence could serve to incite what was maybe going to be a peaceful demonstration or show of force or what-ever these boys had in mind.

He turned to Homer and Wyatt and cupped his hands.

"Back inside!" he shouted. "Get everybody to stay out of sight and stay down unless you hear different. Let the riders pass on through!"

"What's that?" Wyatt cried. His hearing wasn't too good.

"Go back inside!" the sheriff shouted as loud as he could. Homer gave a signal that he understood and the men retreated back into the courthouse building. Twenty seconds later, all the faces had just about disappeared from the windows.

The rumbling machines, mostly stripped-down Harleys flashing chrome, were half a block away and showed no signs of slowing or stopping at the sight of a lone man in the middle of the street, standing astride the center line. Franklin scrutinized the outlaws, but they were still too far away for him to make out the faces of the front four.

All wore polished motorcycle chains, skull earrings and nose rings, wraparound shades, bandannas, and greasy Levi's. On their bare torsos, the leather gear of the *Para Salvados*. Each massive-armed and bearded rider wore the white death's head symbol plainly visible on the front of his black helmet. They all maintained a very precise formation, with at least three feet separating the bikes, and they kept to a speed of around ten miles an hour.

When the choppers entered the courthouse block, he could finally make out a few of the riders. Most of them he'd seen that night at the Plaza del Toros. Then he made eye contact with the rider on the far right. It was *Tres Ojos* himself, Tiger Tejada. *El jefe,* the gang leader, riding low in the saddle, reached down with his left hand and pulled out a sawn-off shotgun from a fringed holster below the seat of his bike.

Tejada was maybe a hundred yards away. He aimed his stubby weapon directly at the sheriff's midsection. Out of the corner of his eye, Franklin saw Homer re-emerge from the courthouse doors. He was carrying a pump action riot control shotgun. Franklin couldn't wave him away because any sudden movement at this point was a very bad idea. He looked quickly to the rooftop where Roy waited, found his eyes and shook his head "no." He could only hope the man understood his desire not to provoke a fight. It was then that Tejada suddenly raised his own gun over his head, pointed into the air, and fired twice.

It was a signal for everyone on a motorcycle.

Guns came out. Rifles. Shotguns. Riders in the middle of the pack fired their weapons into the air. Between shots, they shouted *"Viva Mexico! Reconquista! Viva Mexico!"* It seemed like everybody was shooting. The sound of their shouting, even their gunfire, was almost lost in the deep heavy rumble of a hundred or more growling machines. Franklin held his gun in his right hand, hanging loosely by his side.

He left it there as he stared at Tiger Tejada, shaking his head from side to side as the first row of bikes bore down on him.

He never raised his weapon or took his eyes off Tiger. No, he just stood there in the street and prayed that Homer or Roy up on the roof with his shotgun didn't do any damn fool thing to disrupt their protest ride or parade or whatever you want to call it. He wasn't trying to be a hero, a man alone standing his ground or any of that kind of nonsense. He knew he was going to die. He was just pretty sure this wasn't the way he was going to do it.

Anyway, the bikes were on him before he'd had a chance to move out of the way. Suddenly, Tiger's right fist shot into the air and all the bikes braked to a stop in unison, kicking up a choking cloud of dust, but staying in formation.

Tiger had stopped a foot away.

"Ola," he grinned.

"How you doing today?"

"Not bad, man. You know."

"What can we do for you?"

"Nice town you got," he said, looking around, the sun glinting off the silver bangle hanging from his ear.

"You're here illegally."

"You come to my town, I come to yours. I do what you ask, huh? Return the stinking putas. The next thing I know, a little Mexican boy dies of thirst while in your personal hands. You Anglos place so little value on our lives, eh? Well, this will be a warning to you. No place on this border is safe. Never safe for us. Now, not for you, Mr. Tex-Ass Ranger."

"Reconquista!" the riders shouted, fists in the air. *"Reconquista!"*

It was the secret war cry of the millions of illegal aliens crossing the border. Dixon, like a lot of border lawmen, believed the illegals were in fact an invading army, bent on reconquering the American Southwest. Their swelling number included actual armed members of the Mexican Army, mercenaries from North Korea, Russia, and other communist lands. Increasingly brazen, they fired on American Border Patrol officers and terrorized American ranchers. *Reconquista* was the title of the little speech he'd written for Key West.

"The boy's blood is on your hands, Sheriff. Remember that in the days to come."

Tejada twisted the throttle and popped the clutch, roaring away. In seconds the other riders accelerated, and the waves of Harleys roared past the lone man on the centerline.

The first wave brushed him pretty close on both sides, the first few rows of bikers keeping to their tight formation, once again firing into the air. After about five or six rows had passed him by, clipping his arm or his leg, some of the gangbangers started getting cute, swerving their bikes toward him and then avoiding him at the last second. He figured if he moved in any direction, he'd get hit for sure, so he just stood his ground.

It took a long time for the bikes to rumble past him.

Wyatt, Homer, and the rest of the officers stayed put until the last of the big choppers had almost disappeared up Main. Then they came down the brick walkway, weapons at the ready. The deafening roar of the engines was already becoming a distant rumble moving north and out of hearing range.

"You all right, Sheriff?" Homer said, quickly crossing into the street to where he stood.

"Homer, to tell you the God's honest truth, I reckon we're about one funeral away from a border war."

Then he turned and started to walk away, go back inside, and finish his lunch.

"Put that in your Key West report, Sheriff!" Homer called out after him. "I mean it!"

DIXON HEARD TWO more bikes coming toward him, big Harleys moving very slowly up the now empty street, headed the same direction as the departed Mexicans. He recognized the two boys he'd chased off the Brotherwood ranch the day the child died. Hambone and Zorro.

The two bikes rolled to a stop a few feet shy of Dixon. The riders stayed in the saddle, Hambone picking his teeth with his knife, both men grinning at the sheriff.

"Thought I told you two to move on," Dixon said.

"We did," Zorro said, "Just a couple of scouts, passing through. Keeping an eye on things for you, Sheriff. Looking for Mexicans. Seen any?"

Hambone laughed out loud.

Dixon craned his head around and saw the last bit of dust settling up the road. "You two roughriders are keeping a pretty safe distance, I'd say. You don't want them to get away, you get on after them."

Zorro said, "We ain't necessarily looking for trouble, Sheriff."

"Leastways, not yet, we ain't," Hambone added. "Still rounding up recruits. Getting sizable, Sheriff. Two or three hundred riders in this county alone. I hear there's a thousand over to Laredo. You let us know, come time for the last stand."

"Take your gang violence elsewhere. This is a peaceful community. Now git out of it."

"You might want to watch your ass, old man. Shooting war starts with Mexico, which side you want us on?" Zorro said.

"Yeah, Sheriff," Hambone said. "Texans got to stick together in times of war. You need us."

Dixon looked at him.

"Ain't gonna be no Mexican war, son. We did that once already. Remember the Alamo?"

He turned and walked away to the sound of laughter.

"He fucking kidding?" he heard Hambone say to his back.

"Hey, Sheriff!" Zorro called after him.

"Yeah?"

"What the fuck do you think this is, if it ain't *war*?"

31

THE AMAZON

"Could you please land this thing?" Harry pleaded.

"What? I can't hear you!" cried Saladin Hassan, who was bouncing around up front, doing the driving.

No surprise Hassan couldn't hear. Between the bellicose roar of the airborne Toyota's unmuffled engine and the howl of wind and driving rain, you couldn't really have a normal conversation. Harry Brock cupped his hands round his mouth.

"I said, try to stay on the goddamn ground!"

"Okay! Sorry!"

Harry sat back and tried to wipe away the rainwater streaming from both eyes and running like a river into his mouth. Unlike Saladin and Caparina, he had not thought to bring along a pair of swimmer's goggles. He leaned forward and screamed again, this time directly into the driver's ear.

"I. Said. Slow! Down!"

They hit a ditch and launched again and Harry was

once more hurled sideways against the thinly padded rear seat.

"Too slow and we get stuck in the mud!" Saladin Hassan shouted over his shoulder.

"What about the fucking mines?" Harry screamed, trying to hold on. "You said a lot of these unmarked trails are land-mined!"

"I don't think this one is," Caparina shouted over her shoulder.

"Really? You don't think so? That's good, Caparina," Harry shouted back. "Very reassuring!"

Harry was sitting, occasionally, on the narrow bench seat in the back of the mud-spattered Toyota Land Cruiser. This was definitely not your father's Land Cruiser. There were no windows, no doors, and no damn top. About six inches of water was sloshing around his ankles, one foot in each of the rear foot-wells.

Saladin explained he had cut the roof off years ago. Who needs it? he said. For protection there was only a heavily padded roll-bar overhead. Harry was clinging to it now in hopes of remaining more or less inside the vehicle each time it left the ground. Colonel Hassan, Harry had learned the night before, was with an elite Brazilian spec ops group known as Halcon 4. It means Falcon, Saladin had said. Brock had heard of them. A secret government anti-terrorist unit working this region of the Amazon right now.

"You're not on the road!" Harry yelled, palm fronds whipping across his face. "The road is to our fucking left!"

Saladin cranked the wheel hard left and they bounced

back into the rut. Hassan, his beautiful ex-wife Caparina, and the American spy Harry Brock were careening down a twisting muddy trail full of unpleasant surprises. But at least none of them had been lethal so far.

Unlike Harry, Caparina, who was sitting shotgun and clinging to a grab handle on the dash, seemed to find this mad experience life-affirming and fairly amusing.

Brock tried hard to be philosophical. Be in the moment, Harry, as one of his old girlfriends used to tell him. One of the advantages of this rain was the effect it had on Caparina's faded red T-shirt with the word *Jamaica* emblazoned across her lovely breasts in big black letters. He thought Saladin must be crazy. How could a man ever leave a woman like this?

Apart from the distinct possibility that this narrow twisting road was land-mined, you had to take it on faith there was no oncoming traffic from the opposite direction. Every turn was blind, with towering leafy green walls on either side. Every two minutes or so they'd hit another deep rut or streaming gully and go airborne for an eternity, returning to earth with a great splash of mud in all directions.

Caparina had a soggy, disintegrating map of the Mato Grosso region of Brazil in her lap. Periodically, she would try to show it to Harry, looking for some direction as to which way they should go. But, since the twisting gash in the rain forest they were currently following didn't appear on any maps, it was tough. They'd been driving all morning and Harry was more confused now than when they'd started out.

The driving rain and the mud-splashed windshield didn't help your visibility either.

"Does any of this look familiar?" Caparina said, turning in her seat to smile at Harry. She put her finger on the map, "This area here?"

"How can you tell?" Harry said, leaning forward to give the map a cursory glance.

"What?"

"I mean, Caparina, that everything looks familiar here! Everywhere you go looks exactly like this!"

"Good point," she said smiling at him.

The three comrades, who had only recently decided to join forces, had talked into the wee hours over a late supper and many drinks the previous evening. They decided the first thing was to try and relocate the airstrip where Harry's shot-up airplane had put down three weeks earlier. Harry estimated that, after his capture, he'd been transported over about five miles of rough jungle road, then crossed a river. He'd been taken to one of the many "detention centers" located around the perimeters of the terror training camps. Harry, along with a bunch of rural youths, was there for his "political indoctrination." Harry listened politely, but it didn't take. That's why Top had ordered him shot.

Saladin Hassan was convinced that if they successfully located the secret airstrip, as identified by Brock, they'd be that much closer to finding Harry's former detention center; and, thus, that much closer to finding Top. Saladin, in his undercover role as one of Papa Top's henchmen, had never been allowed to visit these sensitive places without first being blindfolded.

"There should be a river around here somewhere," Saladin said, slowing down and peering over the steering wheel.

"I think we're in it," Harry said, kicking his feet and splashing water forward beneath Caparina's seat.

"I like him," Caparina said to her ex. "He's funny."

Saladin said, "Wait, what's that up there?"

Brock leaned forward. He saw a dark mass a hundred yards ahead, moving left to right across their path.

"What the hell is that?" Harry said.

"Water buffalo," Saladin said.

"That's got to be your river," Caparina said. "Stop!"

Hassan stood on the brakes and they fishtailed to a halt just shy of the swollen torrent. He raised the little fish-eyed goggles up on his forehead and smiled at Harry.

"See? We made it!"

"Made what? I don't recognize this. I don't have a fucking clue where we are!"

"Calm down, Harry," Caparina said.

EVERYBODY CLIMBED out of the Toyota into slushy mud that came up to their knees. Saladin led the way forward to check out the river. Harry, bringing up the rear, could barely make out the small herd of water buffalo moving away along the flooded bank.

Ahead, Harry saw, the road plummeted and seemed to disappear, dead-ending in a muddy brown river some two hundred yards wide. The heavy rains of the past few days had caused the thing to overflow its banks. The raging stream was churning with submerged kapok logs, most likely from a logging station upriver. Logs and other debris were flowing by from left to right. The rain, mercifully, had subsided a little. For a few moments they were able to speak more or less normally above the sound of the rushing river.

"Take a look at this, Harry Brock," Caparina said. She had flattened the rain-soaked map onto the hood of the Toyota.

"I think we're here," she said, putting her index finger on a small tributary. The unnamed river ran west to east through an area of floodplain and flooded forest.

"Yes," Saladin said, studying the map. "That makes sense. What's this larger river over here called?"

"*Igapó,*" she said, "Black Water."

Harry looked around and said, "Is there maybe a waterfall nearby?"

"Impossible to say. Certainly not one on the map. There are so many in this part of the jungle. Some big, some small. Some exist only during the rainy season."

"Why do you ask?" Saladin asked Brock.

"I hid in one. After the plane went down."

"Tell us," Caparina said, putting a hand on Harry's shoulder.

"We all survived the plane's landing. I was the last one off. When Top's welcoming committee started shooting at us, I made it into the jungle. I was the only one who got more than a hundred yards from the plane alive. After slogging it for about an hour, I found a waterfall. I hid inside when I heard the dogs coming."

"Inside. You mean, behind the water?"

"Yes. There was a deep indent in the rocks at the base

of this waterfall. A small cave with a tunnel leading deeper inside. Unfortunately, they caught me before I could do too much exploring. But it looked interesting."

Saladin looked at him. "What do you mean, 'interesting'?"

"It looked like the tunnel could have been manmade."

"How far do you think these falls were from the landing strip?" Caparina asked, suddenly much more interested.

"I didn't get very far from the strip," Harry said. "The jungle was so thick and I only ran for about an hour. Probably less than three miles."

"We're probably here," Saladin said, pointing to the map. "And with this flood, we're not going any further right now. Let's track the water buffalo on foot along the river. There's still a lot of light left in the day and it's better than turning back."

"I agree," Caparina said. "Let's follow this river and see what we see."

"Go with the flow," Harry said, smiling at her. Even soaking wet, she was a babe.

"Right," she said. "Let's get the weapons."

A half-hour later, trudging in the rain through kneedeep mud behind a herd of meandering buffalo, Harry was feeling more than a little discouraged. But he began to notice that the current was speeding up dramatically. It was beginning to at least look more like a run of rapids. And, maybe it was leading to a waterfall.

Suddenly, Saladin, in the lead, halted.

"Listen," he said.

"What?" Caparina said, pausing to hear.

"That dull roar. Up there, not too far. Hear it?"

"Yeah," Harry said, his face showing some life. "That sounds like it."

"All waterfalls sound the same, Harry," Caparina said. "Some are a little louder, that's all."

"I know, but this one sounds like the one I found, that's all I can tell you."

Fifteen minutes later they were standing near the top of a very large waterfall, watching it cascade down into an almost circular pool some forty feet below.

"Yeah," Harry said looking down and nodding his head. "I dove in that pool and swam under those falls. Let's go."

"You're sure about all this, Harry?" Caparina asked.

"It's a hell of a difficult climb down there," Saladin said.

"Almost positive," Harry said.

32

T his mystery man you've kidnapped," Hawke
said to Stokely Jones, "tell me more."
"The Mambo King? You're going to be talking
to him yourself in about ten minutes. You want me to
go faster?"

Hawke glanced at the big sixties-style chromium
speedometer centered behind the steering wheel and
said, "Not really."

The two men were rumbling loudly across the
causeway spanning Biscayne Bay, strapped into the red
leather-pleated front seats of Stokely's outrageous new
automobile.

Hawke, who favored more understated forms of
conveyance, was fascinated by the GTO Pontiac. This
street-legal racing machine, he had just learned, was capable of running the standing quarter mile in a shade
under seven seconds. A small miracle. Hawke, for all
his racing automobiles, had never owned anything that
could touch this metallic beast off the line.

Alex Hawke was eagerly anticipating his meeting

with the Venezuelan officer. Stoke had arranged the rendezvous at the Key Biscayne home of his intended, the beauteous Fancha. He had somehow forged an agreement with the Coast Guard honchos in Key West to maintain custody of the man for forty-eight hours. Or, longer if necessary, since, as Stoke told the commander, it was clearly a matter of national security. The man was now parked temporarily in a staff apartment located above Fancha's boathouse.

"What's he like, your Venezuelan colonel?" Hawke asked.

"You know it's funny."

"What is?"

"Well, like I told Tommy Quick this morning, it's weird, but I feel like I've known this guy all my life. Even though we only met two days ago."

"Really? Why is that, do you suppose?"

"To tell you the honest truth, when we were out there in the Tortugas, I encouraged the man to let his hair down. You know, seeing as how I'd saved his life, I said to him, and this is a quote, 'Fernando, if you got any *frijoles,* spill 'em now, *hombre.*' "

Hawke laughed. "So, he's talking, is he? What the hell does he want?"

"Asylum for him and his family up here in the big Magic Kingdom, I think. That's the best card we got to play. Anyway, I told him you were a big-time government guy and would listen to what he had to say."

"You say which government?"

"Hell, I don't even know which government. I can't keep up with you anymore. You ought to wear those little flag pins, so folks know who they're dealing with at the moment."

Hawke smiled, and realized just how much he'd missed Stoke's company. He looked affectionately at the big man out of the corner of his eye. The sixties steering wheel looked small in his big brown hands.

Hawke said, "You say you encouraged the colonel to let his hair down? Is that right?"

"Yes I did."

"You mean you told this poor guy you'd leave him alone to die out there in the Tortugas. If he didn't immediately agree to tell you everything you wanted to know."

Stoke smiled and shook his head, "C'mon, now. You're in America now. We have rules and regulations when it comes to interrogations."

"War is war," Hawke said quietly.

"Tell me about it," Stoke said.

Hawke shifted his eyes to a beautiful old ketch heeled over and beating to windward, a golden blonde lying spread-eagled atop her cabin house. Hawke could make out a tiny triangle of red material below her waist and nothing above it. What a glorious view that skipper had.

Something, perhaps the sight of such a lovely boat under sail, triggered unpleasant thoughts of the anti-ship weapons Stoke had found on the submerged airplane. The fact that they were Russian-built was troublesome enough. Unfriendly Latin American strongmen in possession of these things was a huge problem. Especially in the Gulf of Mexico. Most of the oil America imported traveled up through the Gulf and entered at the Port of New Orleans.

"So, your new best friend has agreed to share his deep dark secrets with me?"

"Said he would. Just before breakfast this morning. I told him I wouldn't make my world famous five-cheese omelet for him again if he didn't."

"What did you get out of him this morning?"

"He likes to mambo."

"That's a joke I hope."

"You'll see."

STOKE SMILED at Hawke, downshifting to pass an old couple tooling along in a green Volvo covered with "Save the Manatee" stickers. Stoke had nothing against Volvos, or the elderly, but he had almost zero tolerance for manatees. All the fat sea-cows did was eat and get fatter. Didn't even eat anything bad like mosquitoes or snakes. Just hung around clogging the waterways and ate grass all day. They were totally useless. But, hey, what did he know? He was just saying.

"Hold on to your hat," Stoke said, blipping the throttle.

Just before the intersection of Crandon and Harbor Drive, Stoke braked and downshifted once more, then took a hard right on a narrow, unmarked road. The street was barely visible amidst the thick foliage of an overgrown hedge. They crossed a small coral bridge, barely wide enough. The road became crushed shell beneath an arch of severely sculptured ficus hedge. Once over the bridge and through the hedge, the feeling was quiet and cool and withdrawn.

"Does this place have a name?" Hawke asked.

"Place called Low Key," Stoke said. "Get it?"

"That's why there's not even a street sign."

"That's it exactly."

They drove slowly past one or two manicured estate entrances with vine-covered gatehouses. On either side of the gently winding lane were walls of mossy ivory and, visible above them, a few rose-colored crenellated rooftops, peaked, all at various elevations. The few mostly hidden homes, some festooned with exploding bougainvillea, were tucked away in riotous gardens of emerald, blue, and mauve. An old gardener they passed removed his floppy straw hat and held it reverently over his heart as Stoke's American icon rumbled by.

Alex Hawke suddenly found himself thinking about Fancha. He had never set eyes on Stokely's lady friend. He understood that Fancha was lovely to behold. And, judging by this brief sample of her neighborhood, he also had to assume the nightclub singer from the Cape Verde Islands had enjoyed an extremely successful musical career.

Glints of sun bounced off wave tops now visible through the thick palm groves as the bay came back into view. The shell road had turned to brick. It was cool and shady and the air was heavily scented with jasmine. This small and very private road, Stokely said, was called *Via Escondida*.

The Hidden Way.

33

Via Escondida led to a small peninsula that jutted into the bay. At the brick road's end, they came to a broad cul de sac bordered with sharply tailored hedgerows and stately palms.

Stokely had slowed almost to a crawl as they approached an apron of mossy brick marking an entrance. Here was a very impressive set of wrought iron gates cloaked with heavy vines and streamers of bougainvillea. The gates were framed on either side by stands of tall coconut palms and a wild profusion of birds-of-paradise in full flower. Hollywood could not have done a better job.

"This is it?" Hawke asked.

"God's little acre," Stoke said. "Actually, she's got about ten of them back in here. Do you have any idea how much a square foot of dirt costs in this neighborhood?"

"One hardly dares ask. How'd she manage it?"

"She was married to the owner back in the late nineties. A serious club owner from Chicago. Bought this place back in the eighties. He died somehow."

"Somehow?"

"Don't ask, don't tell."

"Another American regulation."

Stoke turned into the gravel drive and stopped just outside the gates beside a crumbling stone column with a shiny keypad mounted on top. He reached out and pressed several buttons. The engine was ticking over nicely and Hawke enjoyed the deep burbling note of the muffled exhaust. It was a lovely sound combined with the tinkle and zing of invisible insects.

He'd had just time enough to read the cracked and peeling painted tiles set into the vine-covered wall. A colorful plaque declared that this was *Casa Que Canta*. The name roughly translated into something like "The House That Sings." Appropriate enough, he supposed, considering the current owner's occupation.

A second later, the gates swung slowly and silently inward revealing a twisting crushed stone drive that disappeared into the wild yet perfectly maintained jungle. On the other side of this faux wilderness, a monstrous white palazzo sitting atop a gracefully sloping lawn that ran down to the water's edge. The house was a blend of Spanish, Moorish, and Italianate influences. A three-story-tall tower dominated one end, which Hawke imagined gave spectacular views of the bay and Miami skyline at night.

The large center portion of the house, which included an ornate entrance portico, was a long colonnade of graceful white arches covered with red barrel tiles. Beyond the arches, a large tiled fountain splashed in a tranquil garden courtyard. Tropical birds of various colors and sizes flitted about the garden.

"How many bedrooms?" Hawke asked, knowing it was the required question.

"She stopped counting at eleven," Stoke said.

Stokely eased the rumbling machine to a stop under the porte cochere and switched off the engine. As they climbed out of the Pontiac, a manservant in a white jacket swung open a tall cypress door, carved and studded with hammered bronze nails. The man, who had flaming red hair swept back in a pompadour, saw Stokely coming around the front of the car, stepped outside, and said, "Lovely morning, Mr. Jones."

"Isn't it, Charles?" Stoke said, beaming.

"Indeed, sir."

"Very laird of the manor these days, aren't we, Mr. Jones," Hawke whispered to him as they walked up the flagstone path to the arched entrance.

"Almost as bad as you," Stoke said, laughing. Hawke, shaking his head, followed him through the door.

Inside, it was dark and cool. A salt breeze filled Hawke's nostrils. The central hallway of blue tile and stucco led all the way through the house. At the far end, the brilliant blue bay and silky green lawn were plainly visible. Hawke, unable to contain his curiosity any longer, slipped away to open a very grand door to his left. He stepped inside. It was the living room, a great barrel-shaped affair with a fireplace at the near end that was surely Carrara marble and must have weighed eleven tons or more.

"Alex?" Stoke said from the open door.

"Sorry, just looking."

"We don't want to keep the Mambo King waiting."

"Where's the lady of the house?" Alex asked the butler as their footsteps echoed down the length of the hall. He was now even more curious about this woman who might one day marry one of his closest friends.

"I'm sorry, gentlemen, Madame said to tell you she had an emergency appointment at the studio. Overdubbing, I think was the expression she used."

"Charles calls Fancha Madame," Stoke said. "Says it all the time. He doesn't mean anything derogatory by it."

"Quite normal, I assure you my good man," Hawke said, suppressing a smile. He wouldn't have missed this for the world.

"Well, we won't be here too long anyway," Stoke told Charles.

"This is Mr. Hawke. He and I are going out to the Boat House to check on our houseguest. How's he doing, Charles?"

"The colonel seems much better this morning, sir. I just took him some tea. Would anyone else like a chilled beverage? Mr. Hawke? Mr. Jones?"

"Maybe later, thanks," Stokely said, and led Hawke out into the sunshine on the lawn. The ruffled blue waters of the bay lapped at the grass and a great white heron picked its way along the shore. Hawke caught a glimpse of a large stucco structure just visible through the grove of coconut palms by the water.

"That's the Boat House?" Hawke asked, surprised at

the size of the thing. It would have made a nice *pensione* on the Grand Canal.

It was an old two-story building, clearly built at the same time as the main house. The architecture was more Venetian and a long dock extended out into the bay. On the landward side, a beautifully tiled exterior staircase led to an upstairs apartment, probably used at one time by servants or the owner's dock master.

There was music coming from the apartment. Loud, but with a lot of static, as if from an old wireless set. Tito Puente and his Mambo Kings were singing "Hernando's Hideaway."

Stoke led the way upstairs and used a heavy key to unlock the weathered wooden door. They entered a small sitting room with old varnished bamboo furniture and a leafy green wallpaper that was tired and water-stained. Shafts of smoky sunlight through the many windows provided most of the room's illumination. An open door on the far wall led to a small Pullman kitchen; a second door revealed a slightly larger bedroom containing a single unmade bed.

In the corner, a man in white pajamas was sitting in a sagging armchair reading the *Miami Herald,* tapping his toes to the mambo beat. An old RCA Victor radio set, sun-bleached blond wood cabinet, stood by his chair. He was young for a colonel, Hawke saw, probably not more than thirty years old. Beneath his pajama top, heavy bandages were visible. He had a lean coppery face, bushy black eyebrows, and no moustache above the white teeth.

The man spread his paper across his thighs and

smiled around his cigar as his host and the visitor approached.

"Colonel," Stokely said, "this is Mr. Hawke. I've been telling him all about our exciting meeting in the Tortugas. Mind if I turn this music down a little?"

The man grinned, showing a lot of teeth. "Señor Hawke, it is an honor. I am Colonel Fernando de Monteras, of the Fuerza Aéreo Venezolana. I am honored by your presence. Forgive me for not standing. Won't you please sit down?"

Hawke and Stokely pulled up two bamboo side chairs.

"Pleased to meet you, Colonel," Hawke said amiably. "Sorry to hear about your accident. Where were you flying from when your plane went down?"

"Cuba. The Isle of Pines. A big island off the southern coast. Do you know it?"

"Well enough. I believe El Jefe landed there with his boat *Granma* prior to his glorious revolution in 1959."

"He is a great politician."

Hawke said, "You're an admirer of Fidel, Colonel de Monteras?"

De Monteras shook his head. "No. I said only that he is a great politician, Señor Hawke. Politics is the art of enriching oneself, the art of robbery; that is the very definition of politics for an immense majority of Latin American people."

Hawke leaned forward and spoke carefully. "I would like to help you, Colonel. I understand from Mr. Jones you seek asylum. I may be able to arrange that. In return I want you to tell me why your government is buying Russian anti-ship missiles from the Cubans. And, of course, a great deal more."

"Señor Hawke, please believe me. If you can provide a safe haven for me and my family now living in fear in Caracas, I will tell you everything I know."

"Why do you want to leave Venezuela, Colonel?"

"I believe my government, in league with others in the hemisphere, is stoking a confrontation with the United States. They are fanning the fires even now as Chávez calls for a communist jihad against American influences in the region."

"You don't support this thinking?"

"Señor, I think such confrontation as Chávez imagines would lead to the ruin of my country and the death of many millions of people. I am a warrior who loves his homeland. But I am not a suicidal fool."

Hawke turned to Stokely. "Could you please call Charles and ask him to send some iced tea and sandwiches out to the Boat House? I think the Colonel and I are going to be here awhile."

Stoke rose from his chair and went to the phone.

"Tell me something, Colonel. Are you really a pilot?"

"No, señor. I am a commandant in the secret police. I wear the FAV uniform sometimes for travel on unofficial business."

"Business that takes you to Cuba. How deeply are Fidel or other Latin American leaders involved in this business of yours?" Hawke asked the Colonel.

"Up to here, Señor Hawke," Monteras said, making a slashing motion across his neck. "If not to their eyeballs."

"I saw pictures of the two missiles on your airplane,

Colonel. Unless I'm mistaken, those are EMP warheads. Electro Magnetic Pulse devices. Am I right?"

"They are, señor. New weapons to destroy command and control centers."

"I know what they are. Only two countries have the technology to generate EMP without the concurrent use of nuclear weapons. Britain and America. So those warheads were stolen. I want to know where and by whom. Now."

"I don't know, señor."

"You don't? Then I don't know if I can help you, Colonel. My very best wishes for a safe trip home."

Hawke stood up and looked at Stokely, shaking his head.

"Please! Señor Hawke, please sit back down, I beg you. I am aware of one name. A man now in England who may have been deeply involved in the illegal purchase of these restricted devices. Perhaps he can be of some help to you."

"His name?" Hawke said, remaining on his feet.

"He's German. A former ambassador in Brazil."

"Zimmermann," Hawke said quietly.

"Yes. You know this name? Rudolf Zimmermann. He negotiated the sale of the EMP technology to my country. Something went wrong during the negotiations. A large sum of money disappeared. Chávez wanted his head. He fled to England, leaving his wife behind at Manaus. I don't know where he is now."

"I know where he is now," Hawke said, returning to his seat and looking at the Venezuelan with narrowed eyes.

"Where is that, señor?"

"He's en route to Manaus in a small urn," Hawke said. "No matter. I want you to tell me absolutely everything you know about this Zimmermann transaction."

"You'll get my family out? What do you want to know?"

"Not what I want to know, Colonel. What I *need* to know."

"I understand the distinction, Mr. Hawke."

"Good."

34

Harry Brock slung his gun over his shoulder and started down the nearly vertical gully that descended beside the waterfall. The narrow muddy ditch ran all the way to the pool at the bottom. The footing was nonexistent but he made it safely down, mostly on his butt, by grabbing at low-hanging branches and exposed roots to ease his rapid descent. He wasn't entirely successful in slowing his fall and made it to the bottom in no time.

Caparina and Hassan followed right behind. Harry watched the girl and was amazed at how much more graceful she was coming down. It had started to rain again, hard, and that didn't make things any easier.

When they had all three finally reached the slope's bottom, Harry cupped his hands and screamed at the top of his lungs, "Yeah, I think this is it all right!"

You had to scream, even though the people you were screaming at were standing only a foot away. They were standing on a rocky ledge at the very bottom of the towering waterfall. The heavy mist made it tough to see more than a foot ahead, and the falling water sounded like God's drum solo.

"Let's go inside," Harry said, edging along the outcropping. Then he left them and disappeared into the swirling mist, pushing through the curtains of white water.

A second later, he had entered the sudden wet stillness at the cave mouth. It was the same one, he saw, the place where he'd hidden. He'd stood right here, terrified, waiting for the dogs to find him. A piece of sheared-off bamboo he'd planned to use as a weapon lay just where he'd left it three weeks earlier. He'd never gotten to use it when they'd burst inside and dragged him away.

Caparina and Hassan waded in, stamping their sloshing boots and wiping the water from their eyes.

"This is it?" Caparina said, hope rising in her voice.

"Definitely," Harry said, fingering his bamboo shaft. "See? My trusty spear."

"This way," Hassan said.

Saladin had wandered off, running his hands over the cave walls. He pulled a rubber-coated flashlight from inside his waistband and clicked it on. Caparina did the same with her own flashlight and Harry followed. Their beams disappeared into the darkness of the tunnel, a gentle incline leading away from the mouth.

"The cave is natural," Saladin said, "the tunnel is not. Hurry." Harry got the feeling he'd been looking for this place for a very long time.

"Come on, Harry." Caparina disappeared into the darkness of the tunnel on the heels of her ex-husband.

They were forced to walk single file through the narrow tunnel. Water dripped from above, annoyingly cold when it spattered on your head and ran down your back. They had to stoop, and sometimes crawl, to climb through some sections. Harry guessed they'd ascended a good fifty feet from the entrance, perhaps passing under a river at some point the dripping was so bad.

"A cavern!" he heard Saladin shout from up ahead.

It was the size of a large church. The rock walls soared twenty feet overhead, forming a natural dome. The air was so damp and cold you could see your breath in the flashlight beams. Precariously balanced towers of stone, each as big as small cottages, rose into the darkness. An underground river, swift and silent, bisected the interior. Brock knelt beside it and plunged his hand into the water. It was a few degrees cooler than the air.

Harry straightened up and stretched for a moment, raising his hands above his head, trying to get the kinks out. He played his flashlight beam on the stone formations overhead.

"You think this is man-made?" he asked Saladin, who was inspecting another connecting tunnel on the far side.

"Not this part, no. But a good deal of this tunnel, yes. Look over here. See where the big grinding bit chewed the rock leading inside the tunnel?"

"Bit?" Harry asked. "This was all bored out? Even Mexican drug smugglers can't dig tunnels this big."

Harry knelt and ran his hands over the scarred rock

beneath his sandals. He couldn't really feel any difference in the rock here. But when he shifted his weight to stand, a loose piece of shale six inches long angled up from the cave floor. He bent down again and removed it, uncovering an opening. He stuck his hand down inside without thinking.

"Ow!" Harry said, yanking his right hand out quickly. He felt as if a razor-toothed animal had snapped at him.

Saladin aimed his beam at Harry's hand. Blisters were already forming on all of his fingertips.

"What the hell?" Harry said. "Something burned me! Christ, that thing's hot."

"Thing?" Caparina said, taking a step forward to see. "What thing?"

Hassan now had his flashlight pointed down inside the hole. After a second, he stuck his own hand inside. Then he looked up at Brock and Caparina and smiled. "It's not hot, it's cold."

"What's that?"

"It's a power line," Hassan said, a grin spreading across his face.

"Power line? In a cave? How come it's so cold?"

"It's a new kind of superconducting cable. Cheap, but very high tech because these things carry five times the electricity of aluminum or copper. Made of a ceramic core surrounded by a sleeve of extremely cold gases. The thermal insulation coating was damaged here; that's why we found this repair hole."

"How'd you get so smart?" Harry asked him.

Caparina said, "He's got his master's in engineering."

"That helps. And where in God's name do you suppose this power line runs to? And, what would you do with all this power out here in the jungle anyway?"

"Let's find out, Harry Brock. Come on, the cable runs north."

TWENTY MINUTES later, the threesome emerged from a well-disguised hole in the hillside. They stood for a moment, trying to get their bearings in a small patch of sunlight.

"This is it?" Harry said, looking around and unable to hide his disappointment. There was nothing but jungle replicating itself in every conceivable direction.

"That cable doesn't come all the way out here for nothing," Caparina said, logically enough. "Let's keep looking."

"Get down!" Saladin cried as he dove into the green thicket. "Shit!"

Harry and Caparina instinctively followed him, diving under the thick green foliage.

"What is it?" Harry asked, seeing Hassan's wide-eyed expression. "What did you see?"

"Up there," he whispered. He was pointing skyward at a wide hole in the canopy.

"Holy shit," Harry Brock said. "A drone. What the hell are drones doing out here in the middle of nowhere? There's nothing to spy on."

"Oh yes there is," Saladin said, watching the silent thing approach.

The twelve-foot-long Unmanned Aerial Vehicle, or UAV drone plane, was headed right toward them, skimming the treetops. The fuselage was matte silver, and there were slender red missiles mounted at the wingtips. A single silver bug-eyed camera hung mounted beneath the nose. Harry Brock knew the thing was a late-generation endurance craft. It could probably stay aloft for twenty-four hours or longer.

"Is it looking for us?" Caparina asked, watching the thing approach. "Or, *at* us?"

"Neither," Saladin said, "it's coming in for a landing."

"I think maybe this is it," Harry said, excited. He pushed a leafy frond aside so he could see beyond the vegetation. "The airstrip."

"Right," Saladin said, peering over his shoulder. "Let's get closer."

They moved quickly through the jungle and hid in the thick growth alongside the middle section of the airstrip. The tiny aircraft made its final descent, touching down at the far end of the weed-cracked asphalt runway. The drone sped along right past them, slowed, and then accelerated and lifted off.

"What the hell?" Caparina said.

"Touch-and-go landings," Harry said. "Whoever's flying that thing is getting in a little practice."

"Is the pilot in that little shed?" Caparina asked.

A small corrugated building painted in camo colors was situated at the far end of the runway. Harry borrowed Hassan's binocs and scoped it out. No movement that he could see behind the dirty windows, no sign of anyone at all. But there was a very odd-looking vehicle parked out on the rain-wet tarmac.

"The UAV's not looking our way," Harry said. "Keep

well inside the tree line till we're just opposite the shed. Check weapons."

Harry checked out the weapon Hassan had given him earlier that morning. It was an interesting gun, a PP-19 Bizon submachine gun with a pistol grip and a folding butt. The gun had a high-capacity "helical" mag with 64 rounds. Harry was pretty happy with it. The gun had been made in Russia in the early nineties and was still in use by Spetsnaz and other law enforcement forces. It was comfortable to carry and would provide a lot of firepower.

They checked up opposite the shed, staying low in the undergrowth. There had been no movement and Harry was pretty sure nobody had seen their approach. The UAV was off doing loopy-loops in the wild blue yonder and no current danger to them.

"Okay," Harry said. "Let's go. I'm going over there. Then I'm through that door. You two wait here till I give the all clear. Understood?"

They nodded. Harry thumbed his selector switch to full auto fire and sprinted the few hundred yards across open ground to the shed. As he ran full tilt toward the door, he checked out the strange vehicle. It was a small tank, weighed maybe a ton. It was about a fifth the size of an Abrams M-2. Main Battle Tank. No turret, just a video camera pod atop a center periscope mount and twin 7.62mm machine guns front and rear. The single hooded camera lens was pointed away from him now and it stayed that way.

He flattened himself just to the right of the door, catching his breath and listening for any sign of life inside. He imagined the conditions inside would be near intolerable in this baking heat. The windows on either side of the door were filthy and caked with mud. He considered peeking through but decided it wasn't worth it. His gut told him the shed was empty.

But you never knew. His gut had been wrong a few times.

He stepped back, turned toward the shed, and planted his foot hard in the middle of the door. The force of the kick sent the thin aluminum door flying inward. Harry rushed inside, staying low, gun out front. He saw the door lying on the dirt floor. His eyes were having trouble adjusting to the sudden darkness inside. But he sensed movement.

"Down!" he screamed.

Against the far wall was a long table stacked with electronic equipment. Mounted on brackets above, there were three small monitors displaying black and white aerial views of the canopy. Seated in an old swivel chair, wearing headphones, was a man in fatigues. Harry immediately saw that this one was alone in the dark room. The guy was just starting to swing around. Harry knew he had a gun in his hand before he even saw it.

"Drop the weapon!" Harry barked. *"No pistola!"*

The guy kept coming around.

"Death wish!" Harry said, low menace in his voice. "I mean it, partner!"

Harry saw the guy's shaded face in profile and his stubby black gun coming up and he squeezed the Bizon's trigger. A short deafening burst. The guy, still in his chair, was slammed back into his equipment and then slumped to the floor, sending his empty chair skidding toward Harry. Brock took a few steps forward and stuck his foot under the guy's shoulder, lifting him up a foot or so, then set him gently back down, dead.

He stepped back outside into the blazing sun and made a beckoning motion to Saladin and Caparina. They were already running full speed toward him.

"I thought I told you guys to wait," Harry said, irritated.

Saladin was all over the pint-sized tank, circling it, inspecting the mud-caked tracks.

"Here's my question about the deceased gentleman in there," Harry said, using his bandanna to wipe the sweat from his eyes. "A UAV like the one we saw can stay aloft for about twenty-four hours. He's got three of them up there. So, what the hell? He's sitting in there day after day looking at a million square miles of tree-tops? I don't think so."

"Probably right," Hassan said, over his shoulder. He was kneeling to inspect the tank's treads.

"So what's he doing?" Brock said, bending down to inspect the rear-mounted machine guns.

"He's practicing for flights somewhere else," Hassan said, "that's what he's doing. You can fly these things seven thousand miles away from the target zone."

"The U.S.?" Caparina said.

"Hey!" Harry said, watching Saladin pawing over the tank. "Stay away from that damn thing. It looks dangerous."

"One camera, and it's facing the wrong way," Saladin said. "The UGV can't see us."

"UGV?"

"Unmanned Ground Vehicle. Looks like a new Iranian Zulfiqar UGV," Hassan said. "Liquid fuel. Called a Troll by the Iranian military, a Tomcat by the Israelis. See the angry red Troll face painted on the flanks? Definitely Iranian."

"A robotic tank. You're an engineer. How the hell does it work?"

"This UG's not a true robot by any scientific definition, because it's not autonomous. Battlebots like this are run by wireless controllers sitting inside virtual reality video displays, like the guy in there was doing."

"These autonomous ones," Harry said, "sound bad. They make up their own minds who they want to kill?"

"Right, you just cut them loose. There are rumors about a big one called the Ogre. It's virtually unstoppable. Ogres use pattern recognition technology to kill anything that moves. Fortunately, those are extremely rare at this point," Saladin said.

At that moment the robot tank lurched slightly and began moving forward. As it did so, Harry saw the camera lens begin to turn toward them.

"Another controller somewhere has picked us up!" Saladin said.

"Quick! Jump on the back," Harry shouted to his two companions as he ran toward the vehicle. He leapt aboard the flat section at the rear. There were two grab-rails, one on either side, probably so troops could do what he was doing, hitch a ride.

"Come on, get on," he said. "Just stay flat on the deck below the camera pod and we should be all right."

He reached his free hand out to Caparina and pulled her onboard. The tank was gathering speed now. Saladin Hassan had to sprint the last few yards before he was able to leap on the back and grab Harry's hand. The surveil camera was now cycling through a 360-degree observation rotation. The lens on its stalk was about a foot above their heads. As long as they kept their noggins down, Harry thought, they'd be invisible.

"Where's this damn thing going?" Caparina said.

"Home to Papa, I hope," Saladin answered.

"You mean Papa Top," said Caparina.

"E.T. go home," Harry said.

Harry Brock looked at Caparina and grinned. Then he banged his fist down a few times on the hot metal surface of the robotic tank.

"You heard me, Ugly. Take us to your leader."

35

KEY WEST

Alex Hawke was unexpectedly charmed by Key West. He had arrived in these emerald waters aboard *Blackhawke* late the previous night. Already, he found the place irresistibly alluring. Disembarking on a whim just after his sunrise swim, he had begun an early-morning stroll through the old naval submarine base. Dew still glistened on the well-cut grass and even the early birds were still sleeping in live oak trees draped with Spanish moss.

He had emerged from the base at Olivia Street and then passed though the narrow streets of town. He whistled past the Old City Cemetery and wondered where everyone was. Not the dead, but the living. He assumed Key West stayed up late and slept late and, at this time of morning, the Old City would normally be deserted.

Following his nose, seduced by a powerful aroma, Hawke strolled the shadowy streets until he found the source of the delicious scent. A tiny corner café was dispensing intensely aromatic Cuban café con leche. He found a seat at one of the small tin tables on the sidewalk, chairs and tables still wet with last night's rain. He zipped up his yellow windbreaker and sat down.

A young man with spiky blond hair and wearing a tight black T-shirt studded with rhinestones came outside and took his order of coffee and croissant. A few minutes later, the waiter, who was still wearing exotic eye makeup from the previous evening, returned with Hawke's breakfast and offered him a slim paperback history of the place called *Isle of Bones*.

"First visit to Key West?" the waiter asked Hawke, looking as if he already knew the answer.

"Right. I've been fishing on Islamorada a few times, but never all the way down here. Beautiful place."

"Hurricanes took their toll, but we'll bounce back."

Hawke gave the waiter some money and said, "Town looks great to me."

"Yeah, well, we're pretty much back to abnormal now."

Hawke laughed and picked up the guidebook.

Since he was in no hurry, he decided to delve into the slim volume of Key West lore. *Blackhawke* would provision here before moving south and the conference was scheduled to run two days. He was not looking forward to his first confrontation with Conch; but he was determined to make his case to the Americans and see a bit of Key West. It would help to have a bit of the local color. He began to read.

THE FIRST MAN who ever stepped out of his boat and set his boots upon this island, Hawke read, found himself knee-deep in bones. Early Spanish explorers, who had somehow survived the treacherous reefs guarding this sun-drenched isle, found an island littered with human bones. Grinning skulls decorated the low-lying mangrove branches as they glided toward shore; more were in the gumbo limo trees, swaying and tinkling in the trade winds.

Bones and more bones. The Spanish explorers had named it *Cayo Hueso.*

The Isle of Bones.

The island was of course a notorious pirate enclave for much of its colorful history. It was ideally located for the skullduggery of freebooters and privateers, preying on the galleons sailing out of Havana, loaded to the gunwales with gold. Hawke's ancestor, the infamous pirate Blackhawke, had no doubt sent more than his share of Spaniards to the bottom after relieving them of their booty.

And then there were the reefs.

The razor-sharp spiny coral reefs that surrounded the island offered pirates a prized source of protection, and a source of bounty as the early "wreckers" plundered booty from foundered vessels. By 1835, "wrecking" salvage had made Key West the wealthiest city in America. Treasure still attracts its share of fortune hunters; it seemed no one could escape the tidal pull the island itself exerts on visitors. Even the most casual guest could sense buried riches around this island. Enormous emeralds sleeping deep in the sand, Hawke imagined, or flashing rubies skittering like crabs beneath the turquoise sea.

Heading back, Hawke felt a palpable air of mystery hanging about the place. You could feel it, he had noticed on his walk, lingering back in the shadows, suddenly at your side, then brushing past as you rounded a corner, only to whirl and face you head on, cool upon your cheeks. At night, he imagined, walking along a darkened side street overhung with heavy magnolias and fragrant flowering frangipani, you could feel the steady pull of the past. On every block, softly glowing windows would hint, if not of treachery, then at least of whispered secrets and inhabitants best left undisturbed.

Blackhawke was moored alongside the great arm of a breakwater that enclosed the submarine basin at the Yard. The Navy, in one form or another, had been stationed in these pristine waters since 1823. In the early days, Key West had been the forward base of the Navy's pirate-hunting West India Squadron. Their mission was to root out the bloodthirsty buccaneers from their hideaways deep in the mangrove creeks up and down the Keys.

When Hawke returned to the docks from his morning reconnoiter, he found the big black ship straining and tugging at her mooring lines. Rain fell, spitting fat drops at first, then coming down in buckets. Greeting the armed security guards both the U.S. Navy and Tom Quick had posted along the quay, he hurried along to *Blackhawke*'s covered gangway and saluted the Navy officer posted there. The man would be there for the duration. Security was tight all over the yard. Navy choppers buzzed overhead. There were divers down now in the basin. They would be inspecting his hull along with the Navy's vessels, making sure everything stayed clean of limpet mines.

Hell, half the State Department was down here for Conch's southern hemisphere security meeting. Brick Kelly, the director of the CIA, was speaking on border protection in about three hours. "Good fences make good neighbors," he'd said to Hawke when last they'd met at the White House. The place would be piled to the rafters with American bigwigs plus one reluctant Englishman who'd invited himself.

Heavy purple cumulus clouds had been stacking up along the southern horizon all morning. The predicted blow building up to the south all morning. It was now right on schedule, roaring up out of the Florida Straits, and Alex Hawke turned his collar up as he left the shelter of the gangway and made his way across decks freshly varnished with rain.

Hawke entered an elevator and rode up three decks. Stepping out and into the driving rain, he then made his way forward to the bridge. Pausing out on the bridge wing, he checked his watch before pushing inside. It was just past noon. He was scheduled to arrive at the Truman Complex, where Conch's conference was being held, at three. He had lunch with Ambrose Congreve and Stokely Jones at noon, but he needed to stop by the bridge and have a chat with his captain.

A new boat was scheduled to arrive in Key West this very evening. A sleek Italian powerboat that he'd been having modified for a very special mission. He and Brownlow, her new skipper, needed to go over the ship's roster. They would hand-pick a crew to man her. Fifteen of *Blackhawke*'s best would be sailing south with them.

Hawke pushed inside the bridge and saw Brownlow and the captain deep in conversation. Good timing. His pulse quickened. He was getting close. No matter what the Americans thought after hearing his remarks, Hawke was determined to sail deep into the heart of the Amazon.

He was going to return to the crossroads of evil. He was going to find and kill the mad giant standing at the doorway to hell.

And God help the bloody fool who got in his way.

36

The American secretary of state, Consuelo de los Reyes, sat back from her temporary wooden desk. She brushed a stray wing of thick brown hair from her high forehead and noticed that her hands, for some reason, were trembling slightly. In an hour or so, she had to give her opening remarks in the auditorium three floors below. But that wasn't the problem.

She knew precisely what she had to say. She had no need of notes, teleprompters, or cue cards. In Washington, in Senate hearings, and in other capitals of the world she was justly admired as a brilliant extemporaneous speaker; but now she found herself reading her opening remarks for the tenth time, trying to focus. Trying to keep her mind busy. Trying to stop thinking about *him*.

This was ridiculous. She should be enjoying herself. She was out of Washington for a few days, thank God. Fewer meetings, fewer phone calls, and no mini-crises blowing up in her face at all hours of the day and night. She was in Key West, for heaven's sake. Her favorite place on earth!

She had chosen Key West as the site of her Latin American security conference for any number of good reasons. The Naval Air Field was strategically and conveniently located for regional State Department, CIA, DEA, and other police and government personnel even now flying in from all over both North and South America. Key West Naval Station was a fairly easy location to secure. Navy fighter squadrons had been patrolling the airspace overhead all week and the perimeter of the old naval base and Truman Complex had been swept and secured for the last ten days.

The news media had arrived, of course, but there was little to be done about that. To be honest, she suspected President McAtee of deliberately leaking a few details about this conference. The president desperately needed good news. The White House needed to be seen as doing something about the growing restiveness along the Mexican border, and in the entire southern hemisphere.

The mainstream media were calling the whole thing a publicity sham. Saying that Key West was an easy terrorist target, the worst possible location for an American security confab. Predicting terror attacks on the island had become a nightly news item. NSA had assured her they'd picked up no terrorist Internet chatter about her impending conference. That was a comfort, she supposed.

Another, more subliminal, reason she had chosen Key West, Conch thought, was the notion of coming home. She cherished any time at all here, however brief.

Her family had been one of the oldest sugar families in Cuba. De los Reyes plantations had dotted that beautiful island for centuries. But her father had been a very wise man. He had seen Castro coming, even when he was considered a *Miskito,* fighting his sporadic guerrilla actions up in the mountains. Gustavo de los Reyes had moved everyone to Florida the day before Fidel rolled into Havana. So Conch had been born and raised right here on the tiny Island Republic of Key West, in a yellow Victorian house just across the way from Truman's Little White House.

She'd grown up fishing the flats with her brothers. In her teens, she'd become an accomplished bonefishing guide in these waters. By the time she left for Harvard and a doctorate in political science, she could spot the wily Mr. Bone sliding across the shallows at sixty yards. At twenty, Conch was legendary among the grizzled old charter skippers down at the docks. She still was, she thought, smiling, it was just a different kind of legend.

She was never happier than when she managed to escape down to the Keys, especially when she had a few days to disappear at Conch Shell. This was her small bungalow hidden away on a small bay north of here at Islamorada. Beer, Buffett, and the slippery Mr. Bone. Of course, it was always more fun when *he* was there. But that was not in the cards right now and so she'd best not think of it.

She sighed and sat back in her chair. She was grateful for these few hours to herself before two days of nonstop sessions got under way.

Save the two Marine guards stationed outside her door, she was alone in her makeshift office. Her temporary quarters occupied a corner suite of offices on the top floor of the old Marine Hospital. Built in the mid-nineteenth century, it was a sturdy brick building, recently whitewashed, with a tin roof and freshly painted plantation shutters. It was also surrounded on all sides by tall palms whose fronds whipped and clawed her windowpanes in the stiff wet wind.

She looked up from the blurry words she'd written on a sheet of notepaper, her eyes refusing to focus. Her view, beyond the rain-streaked windows, was of stormy skies to the west. She overlooked the choppy Sub Basin and the remains of Fort Zachary Taylor guarding the entrance to Key West. To her right, she could just see her old Victorian homestead, Harry Truman's Little White House, the Truman Annex, and the myriad red rooftops nestled under the swaying palms and lowering purple skies above the old town.

If she raised herself up an inch or two off her chair, and looked straight out her windows, however, as she did now, all she could see in the foreground was that damned black yacht.

ALEX HAWKE WAS ABOARD that sky-blotting boat. Some time, surely within the next half hour, the man was going to disembark. Then he would walk ever so briskly across the Yard. He would make his way to the former Marine Hospital and present his credentials to the Marine sentries and Diplomatic Security Service guards stationed at the main entrance security post. He would pass through the X-ray and metal detectors, making breezy chat with the guards.

Would he find a phone downstairs and call up to her office? Or would he go straight to the auditorium to practice his remarks? The meeting would begin in one hour's time. Knowing Hawke, he'd get right down to business. He was dead serious about his topic and when he focused on something, it was all consuming. She knew that firsthand.

She also knew that, were she to get up right now and post herself at the window, she might catch him striding across the coquina walkway. He'd be oblivious to the foul weather. She'd never seen him wearing a raincoat, or any kind of topcoat. What was the line he'd used the day they got caught in a downpour at Mt. Vernon? *Rain's only bad if you're made of sugar.* That was Hawke, all right. All man, all the time, rain or shine.

She looked at her watch and collapsed back into her chair. The truth was, at any minute, Alex Hawke could blow through that door like a force of nature. She wouldn't put it past him. Much bowing and scraping, of course. He knew she was royally pissed off and with good reason. The facts of the matter were not obscure. The man had been an absolute shit, and they both knew it.

But.

But, but, but.

Every damned button on his Royal Navy uniform would be gleaming. His curly black hair would be damp with rain. He would be thinner than usual, she guessed, after what had happened to him in the jungle.

Tall and thin and deeply tanned. And, then he would say something beguiling or charming or both.

Bastard.

Oh, he would stand there, smiling, and then he would aim those blue eyes at her, looking down at her upturned face as though he were about to snatch her up and . . .

He was going to walk right through that door and she had no idea how to handle it. Hell, he'd be here any minute now, she was sure of it. What in God's name was she to do? She could smile, offer her hand, and ask about his voyage down from Miami. Pathetic. No. She would say how delighted she was that he could find time to be here. That she and her senior advisors had all read the insightful report of his time in the Amazon and were sure he'd find a receptive and enthusiastic audience when he spoke and—

Damn it!

She sat back and closed her eyes. She willed her breathing to slow, tried to stop an oncoming tide of images that came rolling in anyway. They broke upon her mind one after another, like waves upon a windswept beach.

TWO YEARS AGO, she and Alex Hawke had spent a blissful week down in these islands, fishing and bathing in the warm sea at Conch Shell. The spinning hands of days unwound quickly, whirling into golden afternoons that dissolved into blood-red sunsets and finished with a sparkle of stars over their sleepy heads. They went about naked and found themselves making love whenever and wherever the notion struck them. She had given her heart to Alex Hawke then, thinking that, finally, she was not misplacing it.

But time and Alex Hawke had a way of breaking that heart, no matter how fiercely she tried to protect it.

Shut the damn blinds, Conch.

Suddenly, she rose from her chair and marched across the scrubbed wooden floor to the west-facing windows. There were four of them, tall casement windows, each with its own set of Venetian blinds. She grabbed each set of cords, yanked each of them to one side or the other until she finally got all four of the damn things to bang down on the windowsills. The office was plunged into deeper gloom.

She turned her back on the windows and stared for a moment with her arms crossed under her breasts, staring at the bad painting of a leaping sailfish that hung on the wall behind her desk. A grinning man with a bent rod stood on the heaving decks of the sport-fishing boat reeling in his trophy.

Hooked, goddamnit.

Ah, well, that's better, she thought, looking at the shuttered windows and feeling her pulse slacken. No more distractions. Now, she could go back to her desk and get some work done. Who was he, anyway, to cause such a hellish fuss around here? There was vitally important work at hand. The next few days would be critical to State's rapidly evolving foreign policy in Mexico and the southern hemisphere.

She sat down at the desk and considered her opening. As she'd reminded President McAtee just before leaving Washington, the battlegrounds of the war on terror were constantly shifting. In her view, they were rapidly shifting to the south. Just look at the Mexican border. Cuba. Why, Chávez and the Venezuelan government had only recently—

"Conch?"

She took a breath. Here we go.

She looked up. Commander Alexander Hawke was standing in her doorway, leaning inside the frame and smiling at her.

He raised his hand in mock salute and said, "Reporting for duty, sir!"

She pushed back from her desk and stood, smoothing the pleats of her navy skirt. Finally she met his eyes.

"Oh, Alex. Come on in, please. No one told me you were here."

He looked toward the shuttered blinds. "Conch, my bloody boat is right out—"

"On your way up to my office, I mean. No one told me."

"Ah. Sorry about that. I guess I gave them the slip."

"That's reassuring."

"Hmm."

He stepped inside the door, fingering the scrambled eggs on the white Royal Navy commander's hat in his hand. She was relieved to see he was a bit nervous, too. She moved to him, trying to avoid those eyes, looking at his epaulets, his buttons, his hands, anything. Without any conscious effort she was taking his hand and remembering how warm his skin felt next to hers in bed.

He said, "I didn't give you much advance warning,

did I? Sorry, my dear girl. I should have rung you, shouldn't I? I just thought I'd pop up here and surprise you. You know, say hello before the conference got started properly. Under way. I do apologize for inviting myself to your conference, by the way. But you should know it was hardly my idea."

"Really? That's a comfort. God knows I'd hate to think you actually wanted to be here. So. How are you, Alex? It's been a while, hasn't it? Last time I heard from you, you were headed off into the jungle."

"I did write. Many times."

"You did."

"You never responded."

"I've been busy. There's a war on. Any number of them in fact."

"Look. It has been too long a while, Conch. I know that. That's why I jumped at the chance to come to Key West." If Hawke was aware of his inconsistency, he did his best to conceal it.

"Well—" she began, and then paused, for she thought she'd heard someone tapping lightly at the door.

"Oh, terribly sorry!" a young woman's voice said. The door hadn't fully closed and now it was opened about six inches. Yes, there was someone there, pushing the door open.

She turned away from him to see who it was. It was a tall and very beautiful young blonde with silky tresses falling softly to her shoulders. She carried a thin maroon leather satchel tucked tightly beneath one arm. Visible on the briefcase were the tiny letters *AH* embossed in gold. Her carefully tailored navy blue suit could not disguise a lush, spectacular figure. Somehow she'd made it through the rain with her makeup and wavy coif perfectly intact.

"Awfully sorry," the young woman said, stepping inside, deftly managing to both look at Hawke but speak to her. "Alex, you forgot this. I thought you might need it in the meeting. I've included the newly edited section on the Brazilian economy which went missing earlier."

"How kind of you," Hawke said, quickly taking the satchel. "Won't you say hello to our hostess, the secretary of state?"

Conch extended her hand to the girl and said, "Consuelo de los Reyes. So nice to meet you. And you are?"

"Guinness, Gwendolyn Guinness," the pretty girl said, smiling effusively but offering nothing more by way of information than to add that she was called Pippa.

Conch smiled back at her, but both smiles soon faded in the growing silence.

"Pippa," Conch said.

"She's my aide," Hawke finally said, the pathetic word sounding as if it had been strangled up from the depths of his damnable soul.

No one seemed to have any idea what to say next. Then Conch broke the spell.

"You call him Alex?" Conch said.

37

The robot tank tore through the jungle like a wounded animal. It was all Harry could do just to hold on. Low-hanging creeper vines whipped at his face and shoulders. He was on the vehicle's right rear, one hand on the grab-rail, one leg wrapped around one of the tank's aft-facing machine guns. Caparina was up front on the left. She was bouncing around, looking back at him, plainly terrified. Hassan was holding on to the right front grab-rail with both hands. Every time the speeding tank hit a deep rut, or strayed from the narrow jungle pathway, the three of them were sure they'd be flung off.

The pint-sized Troll was doing about thirty miles an hour. Because of overhanging vegetation on either side, the passengers felt like they were doing a hundred or more. Dangling creepers constantly lashed their up-lifted faces. You had to constantly duck and bob to keep a vine from lassoing you around the neck.

Now they splashed through a shallow brown river and disturbed a number of sleeping caimans. The

South American alligators were not happy at the noisy intrusion and everyone aboard struggled to keep their flailing feet away from the snapping jaws.

Harry was glad of their speed and the fact that submersion in the river had not stalled the engine. The amphibious vehicle slowed, but kept moving forward, throwing off a bow wave of white water on either side. Soon enough they were dry and plunging back into the deep green stuff.

The lens remained pointed straight ahead. The human controller, wherever he was located, only wanted to keep the thing on the path. Harry sensed the robot was returning to home base. Speed increased and you got the feeling of riding a bucking bronco with a bad case of stable fever.

A half-hour later, it was tough on the bones. Harry was beginning to think the tank didn't know where the hell it was going. They were still deep in the jungle but the path was angling upward and had been doing so for some time now. He figured they must have climbed about a thousand feet in the last twenty minutes or so. The air was slightly cooler and very damp at this elevation.

Suddenly, the damn thing slowed to a crawl. The trail had become muddy and deeply rutted.

They were going so slowly Harry was able to get up onto his knees and take a look at the road ahead.

"Big ravine up ahead," Saladin Hassan called back. "More of a deep gorge."

"I see that," Harry yelled. "Are we going to stop, or get off, or what?"

"I don't think I see any bridge!" Caparina cried. The chasm was looming and she looked like she might jump off. "Do we stay on, Harry?"

It was clearly poop or get off the pot time, Harry saw. The ravine was wide and deep. Hundreds of yards across. Mist was rising out of it so there was probably a river at the bottom. Yeah, he could hear it thundering down there. Rapids.

"Bridge directly ahead!" Saladin shouted. "I'm not sure it will take our weight!"

Harry could see it now. There was a suspension bridge stretching across the chasm. The bridge reached five hundred yards across the ravine and was ten feet wide. A metal grating ran right up the middle of the thing. On the far side, a sheer cliff descended a thousand feet to the river. The bridge angled slightly upward. There was some kind of structure over there on the opposite cliff, barely visible at the edge of the forest. For a second, Harry dared to hope that they had discovered an entry point into Top's military compound.

"Harry? Jump, or not? Make the call!"

Tough call to make. The cabled bridge looked wide enough to accommodate their stubby vehicle, but could it hold the weight of the one-ton "Troll" plus three *pasajeros*? That was the sixty-four-thousand-dollar question, and they were rapidly coming up on a drop-dead decision. Think, Harry.

Whoever was driving this thing obviously knew where he was going. If he was taking the bridge route home now, he'd clearly done it before. It had to hold.

Harry said, "We've got a better chance on this damn thing than we do on foot. We stay on."

Both of them looked at him for a second and then turned their attention back to the looming bridge. They were twenty yards away. Harry used the moment to ready his weapon, as did Saladin and Caparina. You could feel the nervous tension aboard. Good nervous, the kind that gave you an edge.

They rolled into a narrow clearing. Clouds of mist were rising from the river gorge, and Harry watched a flock of snowy egrets slowly winging their way across the chasm. A forest of stunted trees grew from the cliff face. The trees were so smothered with the white birds, they gave the appearance of heavy snowfall. His eye picked up movement on the far side. When he looked again, he saw nothing over there but the squat cliff-top structure he'd seen a minute earlier.

"See that building over there?" Saladin asked.

"Yeah. Doesn't look good," Harry warned, keeping his voice low for some strange reason. "Everybody be ready."

"Think we're expected?" Saladin asked.

"Doesn't matter," Harry said. "All we can do is ride the tiger."

"I'm not liking this," Caparina said, when they were but a few yards from the bridge. Harry wished like hell she was on the back and he was up front with Saladin, but it was too late to manage anything like that now.

"It's adventure," Harry said to her. "Think how dull life would be without it."

"Yeah," she said, unconvinced.

They rolled onto the bridge.

It swayed and sagged perceptibly under the weight of the one-ton tank. Harry racked the slide on his PP-19 Bizon, chambering a round. The gun felt good in his hands, and he was certainly glad of it now. So far, the bridge seemed to be holding their weight, no problem. They were already a couple of hundred yards across, nearing the center of the damn thing. The point of no return.

There was some kind of low white building at the far end of the bridge. But no visible human activity so far.

That was the last happy thought Harry had on the bridge.

"Shit, another Troll," Hassan said.

Caparina said, "What the hell do we do now, Harry?"

Harry looked at the tank coming fast from the other bank. It was a good question. He turned the options over rapidly. The oncoming tank could be on routine patrol. No. That wouldn't make sense because this new one was sending back a live feed of them right now. Surely the operator on the other side had seen them? If they jumped and retreated, they'd just have to take their chances on foot later.

"Sit tight," Harry said. Better to stay aboard and try to take out the oncoming enemy vehicle. It was the only prayer they had of ever getting across. Harry needed to find out what was on the other side.

"Go for the camera," Harry said. "Blind it. Give it another twenty seconds to get in range and open up."

"What if it shoots first?" Caparina said, reasonably enough.

"We shoot back."

When the opposing tank was one hundred yards away, the twin barrels of its forward machine guns opened fire.

"Here we go!" Caparina said, loosing a long burst at the tank.

Saladin braced himself and started returning fire. He loosed a long sustained burst and saw rounds ricochet off the Troll. None of this fire seemed to have any effect on the armored tank. Caparina kept firing. She stayed low behind the steel mud-guard which afforded her a little protection. Harry was having a hard time getting a line of sight with Saladin directly in front of him. Then Hassan fell back. He was hit. He'd let go of the grab-rail. A leg wound was spraying blood into Harry's face.

"Grab the rail!" Harry shouted.

Too late, Harry scrambled forward to grab the man. But the tank lurched and Saladin pitched sideways, sliding from the tank. Caparina screamed. Her ex would have fallen into the chasm, too, but he caught the suspension cable and hung on somehow, his feet dangling in air. How long could he hold on like that?

Riding the tank up front was now clearly suicide. "Jump!" Harry yelled at Caparina. "Jump, damn it!" But she didn't. She stayed with it, riding the damn Troll, leveling ferocious fire at the oncoming tank.

"Last chance!" Harry cried, squeezing his Bizon's trigger and trying desperately to blind the damn robot.

"Only chance!" she shouted back. "I'm going to knock out that camera!"

"Suit yourself, I'm going back to get Saladin!" Harry

screamed at her just before he leapt off the tank. What were you going to do with a girl like that?

He landed hard on the metal grating and scrambled to his feet, bringing his gun up as he whirled around. The tank carrying Caparina now seemed to be accelerating toward the oncoming Troll. It was as if the controllers of both vehicles had finally wised up and wanted to bring this firefight to a speedy conclusion.

Harry raced toward Saladin, saw his white-knuckled grip on the bridge cable. A thousand feet below his dangling feet, the thunderous river waited.

"Saladin! Hold on! I'm coming," Harry said, looking back once more at the girl. Shit. She was still aboard the tank.

Harry shouted, "Are you crazy? Get the hell off that thing!"

She turned briefly and shouted something to him but her voice was lost in the loud crack of gunfire. He ran for Saladin.

At that moment, an explosion rocked the bridge. Caparina's fuel tank had blown. Had she jumped? Christ. He'd been concentrating on Saladin and hadn't seen her. Was she blown off the bridge by the explosion? He couldn't see anything, just a fiery wreck dangling half off the bridge with black smoke billowing up. He stared into the smoke with disbelieving eyes, the intense heat burning his cheeks. No scent of roast pig in his nostrils, no visible trace of a girl's charred corpse.

He waded into the black clouds determined to find her or what was left of her. He saw winking muzzles and heard rounds whistle overhead. The second Troll, blinded by smoke, had ridden right up and over the flaming wreck and was bearing down on him.

Harry had no choice in this matter. He turned around and started running back for Hassan. He ran like a madman, which he probably was, dodging this way and that on the swinging bridge; he kept waiting for the stitch of rounds across his back.

Saladin only had one hand on the cable. But he was still clinging for his life when Brock reached down and grabbed Saladin's trembling forearm with both hands. He managed to haul him up onto the bridge, the adrenalin doing most of the work for both of them. He got him up. Saladin took a few deep breaths and managed to get to his knees.

"The tank," Saladin gasped.

"Yeah. We gotta go. Can you walk?" Harry asked, getting an arm around him.

"Why walk when you can run?" Saladin said, ignoring the blood pumping from his torn right thigh.

They ran for the underbrush, back where they'd come from.

Behind them, their wrecked tank was still burning at the center of the bridge. The little one-eyed bastard that had finished them kept coming and they could both feel the lens on them and see the barrels swivel in their direction as they dodged this way and that, summoning one last ounce of energy for the final sprint. Shit. It was going to be close.

"Go left!" Harry said when they reached the end. "I'll go right. And stay the hell down. The camera won't be able to pick us up."

Both men dove into the brush and crabbed away from the bridge. Rounds were splintering the trees above and behind him, but it was pretty clear the robot had lost them and was firing blind. The operator controlling the thing was just trying to get lucky. Harry managed to slither right to the edge of the cliff and peer through the undergrowth at the smoldering tank they'd abandoned.

Somehow, he and Saladin would get through this. If the girl were still alive—doubtful—he and Hassan would somehow manage to get back across that bridge and find her. They had to find this bastard Top. Had to pop this fucking Top.

Harry had always known his strengths and weaknesses. He probably drank too much. Screwed around too much, even now that he wasn't married anymore. And, as he privately admitted to himself, he knew he probably wasn't the brightest bulb on Broadway. But Harry was as tough as they come, goddamnit. Hard, his Marine buddies would call it. His whole life, the crazy American from Los Angeles, California, had known one true and good thing about himself.

Harry Brock could take a licking and keep on ticking.

38

Homer Prudhomme never did quite recover from how shook up he'd been that godawful night they found the lost posse. It had been three weeks since all his friends had come back without their heads attached. God knows how he tried to shake that image. But, you know, how was he supposed to forget those boys riding across the plains in the moonlight? Or the look in the sheriff's eyes when he'd seen them coming toward him, still tied upright in their saddles? He couldn't, and he wouldn't, ever, forget.

Hell, nobody should ever forget.

And he couldn't seem to run away from dreams about that ghost rider either. The man who was (or, wasn't) behind the wheel of that semi they'd pulled. The "Yankee Slugger" going 140 with no driver behind the wheel. The way that big rig had just got itself in gear and took off down the highway all by itself. If that didn't beat all he had no idea what did.

Even if the sheriff was right, and there was a driver, where had he gone? Thin air? Nobody in the cab. No tracks leading off into the sand. Nothing. Didn't make any sense at all.

And don't you know he'd gone over every last inch of that cab. Stuck his nose in the ashtray. Buried his face in the foam-rubber pillow lying back there on the bunk. Felt for gum up under the seats. He would have known it if there'd been anybody, anybody at all, recently riding up in that cab. He would have felt it, smelt it, and he hadn't. It was enough to make you crazy. Nobody believed in the ghost rider except the sheriff, but his opinion was the only one that counted anyway.

He took another bite of his Mr. Krispy doughnut and stared at the black ribbon of highway unwinding through the desert below. He was well hidden, about a hundred yards off the road, parked up among some boulders and scrub at the top of a ridge. He hadn't seen a car in two hours and didn't much expect to see another one before the sun came up.

It was now three something o'clock in the morning. Even the coyotes had stopped complaining and gone to sleep. He was cold and sleepy, and the Crown Vic's heater was acting up. Had to be down in the mid-forties tonight he guessed, looking out at the empty stretch of desert. He popped another couple of Vivarin and cranked up the radio, singing along with his dream girl, Patsy Cline.

Sheriff Dixon had been down in Florida for a few days, one more lawman making the case for stopping the chaos on the southwest Texas borderline. Homer hoped Dixon could show the folks from Washington just how bad things really were on the border. The thousands of illegals trashing the ranches on their way through, the pollos and the coyotes, the gunrunners and the drug smugglers, too many to count, all being chased around by far too few Border Patrol guys flying helicopters and driving dune-buggies. Add to that, now you had corrupt Mexican Army troops threatening to come across the river to protect the damn narcos!

It was starting to feel like a war.

Mercifully, it had been a very quiet few days in town. He looked both ways down the empty road, then put his head back on the seat and closed his eyes. He said a silent prayer for Dixon down in Key West. That he would give a good speech. That the brass would understand the truth of what he was telling them. Texas needed help down here on the border. And they needed it some kind of bad.

Homer had been lucky this week, though. Nothing much going on since that bunch of Mexican terrorists on motorcycles had rolled through, shooting up the town. All he'd had to deal with was a drunken Rawls, weaving all over the highway one night in one of his million-dollar custom Chevy Suburbans. Homer threatened to lock him up again and he'd been on good behavior ever since. He'd had a crazy visit from the bikers Zorro and Hambone, wanting to be deputized. And a lady teacher he knew had a baby at the Laundromat.

He'd decided to spend his free nights out here in the desert. The same stretch of highway where they'd pulled the Yankee Slugger guy the first time. Had his radar aimed at the top of the hill and he'd turned the warning buzz way up in case he dozed off. A truck with no driver didn't make any sense. But it made a whole lot more sense at night on a deserted road than it did in broad daylight on Main Street.

He must have drifted off 'cause the alarm sounded and he sat up so fast he banged his head on the roof. What? Where? He looked at the digital speed bounce back. Well, well, well. He almost couldn't believe his own eyes.

His radar showed a vehicle approaching a mile south doing over 135 miles an hour! Hot damn, he thought, reaching for the ignition key, if this ain't some rich prick from Houston in an Italian sports job, this could be our ghost rider.

He watched the horizon, waiting for the speeder to crest the next hill, silently praying to see a big red, white, and blue semi roar up into view. Once the truck was well past, he'd get on his tail and stay there. He'd planned the whole thing. Stay back, out of sight, follow the ghost rider wherever he went. However long it took, just stay with him and see where the truck took him. Whatever happened, happened was all. It was, he considered, his first case as a full-fledged lawman.

He was disappointed at what came over the hill.

No big eighteen-wheeler like he'd been hoping for these last couple of nights. No, not a trailer rig, just a four-wheeler going like a bat out of Hades. He sat up straight and gripped the steering wheel as the thing roared past him. The vehicle was light-colored. Maybe even red, white, and blue. Hard to tell in the moonlight. Still. Even in that flash of passing by, he had a hunch of what it was, all right. It could be, maybe it was, the "Yankee Slugger"!

The truck cab, anyway, it just didn't have the trailer hooked up behind it tonight.

He automatically reached for the headlights and then caught himself, letting out a low whistle as he put the cruiser in gear and mashed the accelerator. No lights turning up on the rack tonight. He fishtailed crazily onto the highway and put his right foot through the floorboard, standing on it, watching the needle creep over a hundred. One ten. One twenty. Up ahead, he saw red brake lights flash on and off, disappearing over a dip in the road. He was half-mile, maybe less, behind the phantom trucker. Keep his own lights out, keep the phantom's taillights visible. Maintain about this distance and he should be okay.

The phantom took a left off of Route 53 and now he was smoking west. Looked like he might be headed for a little ghost town about thirty miles outside Laredo. It was called Gunbarrel. It was situated at a bend in the Rio Grande about a half-mile or less north of the Mexican border.

Gunbarrel used to be thriving community in Texas oil boom times, round about the early 1900s. Did pretty good until about fifty years ago when they come to find out the oil business had all dried up and took its business elsewhere. Other than the little cemetery, which was full, Gunbarrel now had a population of maybe two, and both of them were prairie dogs.

The police radio was hopping. The chatter he was picking up tonight was nonstop reports of illegal crossings. You get down here on the border, the law speaks with a different tongue. Here they start calling the illegal crossers "bodies." You hear a lot of chitter-chatter and then someone starts saying, "Okay, look alive! I got six bodies moving northwest toward the radio antenna!"

That kind of stuff makes a lawman uneasy on a night like this. 'Cause now the bodies are carrying heavy machine guns and they're not afraid to use them on anybody in their way.

"Base of the tower! Base of the tower!" somebody on the radio shouted. The desert around Gunbarrel is spiderwebbed with irrigation ditches and deeply rutted farm lanes. The only way you can pinpoint any location for another agent is to use some landmark like a water tower or a radio antenna or whatever. Homer didn't see any tower, nor any bodies crossing the highway.

He saw the truck cab slowing down now and he did the same. They were both doing under thirty at this point, and it was a lot easier to keep track of what was under your four tires. He still kept a good halfmile between the Vic and the ghost rider. As far as he could tell, he hadn't been spotted. He hadn't made positive ID yet, either, but he was sure hopeful it was the Slugger.

Couple of minutes later, there was a faded black and white track-side railroad sign, a wooden rectangle with the word GUNBARREL painted on it in block letters. Sure enough, a hundred yards farther on he came to the old brick railway station house, looking pretty decrepit but still standing anyway. He saw some old abandoned oil tanks, overgrown with weeds, and a falling-down building that had once housed something called the Shell Peanut Company. Now he passed a cotton gin, a flour mill, and even a few dilapidated mansions with gingerbread trim. All of them long ago abandoned to the rats and spiders and tumbleweeds.

Up ahead, he saw the phantom's brake lights flash and he hit his own, mashing down on the pedal. There were no side streets so the trucker couldn't be fixing to make a turn. He was going to stop right here in the middle of a ghost town.

Stop? For what? There was nothing here.

But the trucker was pulling up out front of a big old two-story brick building up ahead on the left. An old factory maybe, covering an entire square block. And with black holes upstairs where all the windows used to be and a wide arched entrance of some kind on the far end, like you might see at a fire station.

He swerved the Vic off the road and nipped in behind an abandoned Texaco gas station that was half burned down, almost hitting the one remaining pump with a busted gumball light on top. The Vic rolled silently over to the empty repair bay and came to a stop right under an old Hires Root Beer sign that had made it through the fire.

Homer shut the Vic down and quickly pocketed the keys, thinking: *You can trust your car to the man who wears the star.*

Homer wore a star, and, over his head, a faded red Texaco star was swinging in the breeze, making a creaky noise. It was shot through with rusty bullet holes. Time to go. He checked his sidearm. He checked his mini-flashlight, too, just to make sure the batteries hadn't wore out.

He eased his car door open (even new, it tended to squeak) and climbed out of the Vic. Then he ran quickly toward the street, keeping the crumbling station building between him and the trucker's cab. He stopped short, and peered around the edge of the building.

The Yankee Slugger was parked just outside the building. Blacked-out windows gleaming in the moon-light.

Damn. He'd been right. The Slugger had turned all its exterior lights off and pulled up outside the arched entrance to the building. Homer figured the guy (or the spook anyway) couldn't see him now and he started moving along the deserted road beside the burned-out gas station.

Suddenly, there was a loud hiss of air brakes and then a big diesel engine growled and he saw that the wide factory door was going up. There still was not a single light shining in that building. But clearly some-one was home to open the big old wooden door. Homer couldn't hardly believe it, this was after all, a *ghost* town, but now the red, white, and blue cab was backing inside, was through the door, and now the door was coming down again. In the wink of an eye, the ghost rider was gone. Disappeared off the face of the earth.

Homer ran across the street, right up to the heavy door that had just slammed shut. He reached out and touched it, and it wasn't wood at all. Solid steel. Some-body had painted it to look like old wood. Not only that, made it look like it was fading and the paint was peeling off too. Now, why go to all that trouble? So no one passing through the ghost town would pay it any mind. That was why.

He ran quickly around the far side of the building, sidearm still holstered, but he had the Mossberg. There was a rusted-out fire escape going up to the second floor. Windows up there, open. Maybe the stairs were still strong enough to hold him. No lights showing anywhere in the building. He scanned the building a second and then he saw it.

What looked like a tiny red eye up there in one of the darkened windows.

Somebody was standing up there, having a smoke. You couldn't see anything but the cigarette's burning coal floating in the blackness.

Another damn ghost?

A ghost didn't worry too much about cancer sticks, Homer reckoned.

39

At three o'clock that rainy afternoon, Hawke, Congreve, and Pippa Guinness stood talking quietly. They stood just inside an alcove off the crowded hallway of the old Marine Hospital. The sleepy naval base was now a beehive of activity. At least a hundred other people jammed the hall. All were moving toward a pair of double doors leading to the cavernous base gymnasium. The crowd was restive, and a certain nervous excitement could be felt in the hall. Overnight, Conch's Latin security conference had seen a dramatic increase in size. There was a palpable sense of urgency about the meeting. And, as Ambrose was explaining, there was a very simple reason for it:

Mexico had invaded the United States.

Rumors were swirling on Capitol Hill about a possible armed incursion by uniformed Mexican Army forces. A credible witness had reported uniformed troops moving north across his ranch at the Texas border in broad daylight. When confronted by the rancher and two of his hands, the men jumped back in their Humvees and hurried south, retreating across the border.

Meanwhile, a U.S. Border Patrol chopper, on routine patrol, had surprised a convoy of drug mules attempting to cross the border. Someone, reportedly driving a Mexican Army Humvee, had opened fire on American agents. It was common, now, to hear of Border Patrol agents being gunned down by Mexican Federales with AK-47s.

These startling episodes had naturally generated an immense public outcry in the hinterlands and capitals of every southern border state. As a result, a new sense of national urgency now surrounded the secretary's security conference in Key West.

The voracious radio and TV pundits, and the vast blogger armies, all sensed a huge story. And all were happy to have fresh meat for the insatiable twenty-four-hour media machine. "Let's go live to the border!" this or that anchorman would say, and then you'd see ruggedly handsome and epauletted correspondents riding right alongside the Border Patrol. The media was flocking to the border, in choppers and Humvees; or, more dashing yet, galloping through arroyos on horseback to the site of the latest attack.

The on-scene reporters noted again the woeful lack of security on America's borders. Some, naturally, blamed the president for not securing them. Why hadn't he just ordered a wall erected? How hard could that be? Some blamed government officials in Mexico City. Others blamed the apparent willingness of scattered Mexican field commanders to ignore our borders and accused these officers of being complicit in drug smuggling. A few thoughtful journalists actually understood that a border war with Mexico had been threatening to erupt for more than a century.

And now it seemed imminent.

In a few Washington circles, at Langley and the Bureau, it was an open secret that the vast drug gangs wielded enormous power within some Mexican military units and most certainly the Mexican police. Long simmering resentments, left over from the War of Independence in 1846, were rising to a boil. And the American people, at least it seemed to Hawke, might be waking up at last to the real dangers along the southern flank.

In Alex's view, everybody with an earbug and a microphone seemed to be having just a bit too much fun playing Cowboys and Indians along the Rio Grande. So far, no one had documented any of these "military" incursions on videotape. But that didn't stop Fox News, CNN, and the rest from trying to scoop each other. It was just a question of who would be first to get the story on film.

When the broad auditorium doors at last swung open, Hawke glimpsed a large oval table and rows of chairs inside a cavernous room. This vast, and pungent, location was apparently the only space large enough to accommodate the growing number of attendees. History, it seemed, was going to be played out on the sailors' newly gleaming basketball court.

The room was filling up. Conch, trailing members

of her staff, DSS, and Secret Service agents, had moved inside ten minutes earlier. She had not paused to speak to the aggressive media types pressing in around her. Nor had she even glanced at Hawke as she passed. This was hardly surprising, given recent events upstairs in her office.

Hawke, on a purely personal level, was feeling lifeless and numb, more than ready for the bloody session to get under way. From his own point of view, this pilgrimage, begun at C's insistence, had already gotten off to a rocky start. He had meant to mend fences. Instead, he'd managed to put up a fresh wall.

He was grateful to have gotten out of Conch's darkened office alive. Miss Guinness, who did not know the fiery Consuelo de los Reyes, was an innocent moth with no idea just how close she'd come to the flame. Her ill-timed arrival had dashed any hopes he'd had of reconciliation. He had whisked Pippa away as quickly as possible, all the while trying to placate Conch with his eyes. He had failed miserably.

Alex Hawke and Consuelo de los Reyes had endured, to say the very least, a long and complicated relationship. It had always been, he thought, a love affair of sorts, constantly recurring, but lasting for an indefinite time, like some perennial light switch. It's on. It's off. It's on again.

A year ago, the affair had plunged into darkness. After learning of Hawke's relationship with the beautiful Chinese actress, Jet Moon, Conch had seemingly thrown the switch permanently. His phone calls went unanswered. So did his carefully composed letters. He had finally given up, imagining that he would not see her again. The idea was painful, but he had adjusted to pain before.

And now, thanks to his Chief of the Service, here he was in tropical Key West, in the midst of a brand-new romantic drama. Thanks to the lovely Miss G's sudden appearance on stage, the long-running tragicomedy starring de los Reyes and Hawke looked to have an even unhappier ending than he'd previously thought possible.

The hallway echoed with a heady hubbub of conversation. Jostling attendees began passing through the final security checkpoint and then filing inside the auditorium. Hawke waved a greeting to his old war buddy Brick Kelly, CIA director. Brick appeared to be enjoying having a serious set-to with a couple of Air Force four-stars. A few feet away stood Peter Pell, the president's new defense advisor.

"Let's get started, shall we?" the young State Department aides kept repeating, gathering people together and gently herding everyone toward the door.

"I suppose we should go inside," Hawke said to Ambrose. He was dreading, as always, another interminable meeting, trapped inside someone else's agenda.

"While we're young?" Congreve said, chuckling at Hawke's obvious discomfort.

Ambrose took Pippa's elbow and the two made their way into the gym. Hawke followed a minute later and quickly found his seat at the table. Ambrose sat on his right and Pippa was seated at one of the chairs provided for support staff just behind Hawke. Conch sat directly across the table from him. She wouldn't return his smile.

Suddenly, Pippa was leaning her blonde head right between Hawke and Congreve, whispering in Alex's ear. There was a warm scent of Chanel rising from the depths of her cleavage and it was all Hawke could do to stare straight ahead.

"Yes?" Hawke said quietly.

"So sorry to bother you again. Please don't forget we agreed to soft-pedal the Bogotá station's role in all this. C does insist we're not quite ready to let the Americans have that juicy bit."

"Ah. Didn't know that. Thanks."

Congreve suddenly looked over at the two of them and Pippa jumped.

"Will you two please pipe down? Madame Secretary is about to speak and she's staring directly at you both."

"Oh, God," Hawke said under his breath, "you're right, she is."

40

Conversation died down as the secretary stood. She cast her eyes about the room, gathering everyone in. Consuelo de los Reyes was a tall, elegant, and very beautiful woman. She could command a room full of star-spangled generals with a single sidelong glance, and her fiery eyes could burn or freeze at will. When she spoke, her words had weight. They seemed to hang for moments in the air before others took their place. As was her habit, she swept a wing of dark auburn hair away from her forehead before she spoke.

"First, on behalf of the president, I'd like to welcome the members of the media who've joined us today," she began. The auditorium erupted into sustained laughter. Everyone present knew the secretary had pitched an all-out battle to have the electronic and print press banned from her conference. The White House, sensing a huge media opportunity, had handed Secretary de los Reyes a very public defeat.

She handled that one well, Hawke thought, sitting

forward at the table. She was steaming, but you'd never know it.

"America is at war with Mexico," she said quietly, and the room went dead still.

"I will come to that unfortunate reality shortly. But, I would like to welcome you to the magic island where I was born forty years ago today. My father and mother are Cuban. I am proud to be Hispanic-American. And grateful for this chance to share my hometown with you.

"As the president says, 'The best pages of history are written in courage.' We here stand at history's front line. While Congress spends its days overreacting to yesterday's attacks, the men and women in this room know that we must concentrate on the most likely current threats.

"Although few acknowledge it as such, there is a new front in the War on Terror. I believe the gravest danger our country faces sits right on our doorstep. Mexico is openly waging a new kind of war on America. Not just the recent border incursions and drug smuggling. Not the tunnels or the deliberate shooting of our Border Patrol agents trying to enforce the law. No. Something far more insidious."

She paused a beat, and said, "I believe the Mexican government is using an invading illegal population as the latest weapon of mass destruction.

"I personally believe the Mexican government has encouraged and promoted illegal attacks on our country for decades. In my office, I have copies of comic book brochures, printed by the government, explaining how to violate our sovereignty. Now, the millions of illegal immigrants who cross our borders threaten entire social and economic structures. It grows worse with every passing day. We are under siege.

"Citizens living along the southern border face chaos. Many of you have read the reports from the U.S. Border Patrol. Border state law enforcement officials and agents fear the danger of total breakdown. Lawlessness is already rearing its ugly head on both sides. Borders, once sacrosanct, are under attack even as political concepts. To defend one's borders, one risks being labeled as racist. I am not a racist. I am an American.

"As always, there are two sides to every story. This is especially true along a borderline. Many Americans want a walled fortress. It's understandable. The Mexicans want jobs and to provide for their families. It's understandable. But they have been encouraged by their government to think they have inalienable rights to cross illegally. And so anger and violence erupt daily on both sides of the line.

"Sheriff Franklin W. Dixon of Prairie, Texas, is with us today. I believe I see him. He's the good guy over there in the white hat."

The audience chuckled at the sight of the somewhat embarrassed lawman removing his white Stetson.

"In our first session tomorrow afternoon, Sheriff Dixon, as well as members of California, Arizona, and New Mexico regional law enforcement agencies and local sheriff's departments, will provide firsthand accounts of this tragic story. They will ask for our help in solving this problem. As you know, the president has committed six thousand National Guard troops to the border. He asked me to assure you that other measures are being taken to solve this situation.

"But the broader crisis we face in Latin America is not limited to the Mexican borderline. No, this new threat goes far deeper than that. It reaches into the jungles of Brazil and Argentina and Ecuador. It stretches to Caracas, where yet another Communist dictator joins Fidel Castro in his grand dreams of humbling Uncle Sam. The Venezuelan dictator has the oil reserves, and thus the money, to make his dreams a reality.

"Castro and his kindred spirits are determined to wreak havoc in our hemisphere. Chávez has said so publicly, and we believe him. Our next speaker, Commander Alexander Hawke, will offer dramatic evidence of a Venezuelan scheme to disrupt oil shipments in the Gulf of Mexico.

"Indeed, as you will soon hear from our distinguished guest, Commander Hawke of the Royal Navy, there is a rising tide of anti-Americanism throughout Latin America, fueled only in part by an oil-rich Venezuela. I have read his report carefully. I wish I could tell you this new threat was posed by ragtag guerrilla armies with little training and unsophisticated weaponry.

"But that is far from the truth. Let me summarize briefly Commander Hawke's findings in his own report to British Intelligence. 'Since the early seventies, the Amazonian jungles have been havens for Hezbollah. Radical Islam has made great inroads in Latin America. They have deep connections to groups like the Shining Path in Peru or FARC in Colombia, or the *Montaneros* in Argentina. They have incorporated organized crime families and street gangs within these countries, converting them from mere criminals to fervent revolutionaries.'

"Using literally hundreds of millions of dollars generated by the sale of Number Four Heroin, these Latin Islamist cells are now financing the creation of well-equipped and well-trained terrorist armies. Hard intel recently acquired by Commander Hawke's Service suggests these powerful new Islamo-fascist operations may have purchased dirty nuclear weapons from Iran and in other markets. They are almost certainly developing bio-chemical weaponry in sophisticated jungle laboratories. So, where do they intend to use these awful weapons?

"The new Latin American terror armies are transnational. They are beholden to no single country. But they do have one common enemy. America. They are bringing this war to the very doorstep of our American allies. And I believe they are preparing to move and soon.

"I will conclude my personal remarks by saying that America is challenged on many fronts. We face threats from every point of the compass. But, for the next two days here in Key West at least, we will concern ourselves with only one compass point. A veritable tsunami, boiling up from all points south."

She paused and gazed out at her audience, her eyes finally coming to rest on Alex Hawke. After a moment, she actually smiled.

"Commander Hawke, welcome to Key West."

41

Lights and cameras swung in Hawke's direction as Alex rose to his feet and said, "Thank you, Madame Secretary. It's an honor."

The monitors arrayed around the room instantly displayed maps and satellite imagery of Brazilian rain forest.

Hawke said, "This is the Mato Grosso area of Brazil. I recently had the misfortune to spend a lot of time in this region of the Amazon rain forest. Here is the true epicenter of burgeoning terrorist activity in Latin America. This region is the home of large leftist guerrilla army units that include narcoterrorists, criminal gangs, and international Islamist terrorist operations."

A hand shot up. Hawke saw it belonged to a famous-face CNN reporter, Hardy Porter.

"Why do you say that, Commander Hawke? Since when have Islamic terrorist groups had a foothold in Latin America?"

"Since 1983, when Hezbollah became the first to establish a base here. These were Shiite Muslims funded, armed, and trained by the Iranian Revolutionary

Guards. These dense jungles were rightly seen as an ideal place to both raise money for jihad and train raw recruits from the countryside. The plan was to forcibly recruit, indoctrinate, and train armed teenage thugs to form a large army of ruthless fighters. The plan has succeeded."

"You're saying such camps actually exist? How do you know?"

"I saw work camps with my own eyes. I lived among them for months doing road construction as a slave laborer. These *jihadistas* are comprised of every nationality, made up of every kind of narco-guerrilla and criminal element. The foot soldiers are mere farmboys, recruited with the promise of high pay and cheap narcotics. The officers I saw, however, were Arab and Chinese."

"*Jihadista?* Never heard that expression before."

"I made it up," Hawke said, suppressing a smile at the ensuing chuckles.

"How do you spell that?" the CNN fellow said, pencil to hand.

Hawke told him. Another hand shot up.

"Sheikhs in the jungle?" someone said. There was some more chuckling from the media contingent. "I thought they preferred desert warfare."

"Many fled to the Amazon jungles, on the heels of the Lebanese Civil War in the mid-seventies. During Osama bin Laden's 1999 visit to Brazil, he spent a good deal of time arousing the faithful. He started terror cells and left his officers in charge. The cells have grown exponentially in ensuing years. One of the men Osama left behind is named Muhammad Top. He poses, I've reason to believe, a grave threat to U.S. security."

A good-looking newsreader from Fox raised her hand. "Why the Amazon?"

"It's a vast, ungovernable area. Little or no law at all. You have a lethal combination of poverty, illicit activity, disenfranchised cocoa farmers and guerrillas, and an ill-equipped or nonexistent military. There are countless rural youths, all too ready to enlist. A terrorist's idea of heaven on earth. Bin Laden knew a good thing when he saw it."

"These terrorists you unearthed down there, Commander. Are they planning attacks on Rio? Buenos Aires? Bogotá?"

"Anything's possible. Muhammad Top fancies himself as some modern-day liberator who would free South America from the Yankee chains. To that end, he is massing armies and training them exhaustively with the latest weaponry. Attacks on the capitals you mention are a possibility. So is an attack on the United States."

Then the CNN reporter said, his voice dripping sarcasm, "More weapons of mass destruction, Commander? I'd hate to see a replay of Iraq."

"I can't speak to that. I saw no WMD with my own eyes. I would certainly not be surprised to learn that they did. They have limitless resources to buy what they can't build."

An air force general raised his hand. "How do these armies of yours move around without attracting any attention?"

"Hidden, General. The forest canopy shields them

from prying eyes. A huge labor force is building a strategic military highway. It could stretch as far as central America, and ultimately into Mexico. This highway would allow them to transport men and materiel. And, give them access to the southern borderline of the United States."

"You saw plans for such a highway?"

"I built a portion of such a highway."

A pretty blonde CBS news reporter raised her hand. "Commander Hawke, can you offer us any proof of this supposed collusion between Latin American countries allied against America? It's a fairly preposterous charge."

"As a matter of fact, I can," Alex said. "Slide, please?"

The monitors filled with Stokely's underwater images of the Russian-built Yakhont anti-ship missiles found aboard the sunken airplane.

"These pictures were shot three days ago in the Dry Tortugas. They were shot inside a downed airplane lying in thirty feet of water. This plane is located about twenty-five miles from Key West. These missiles were being transported from Cuba, where they were purchased, to an air force base outside Caracas, Venezuela."

"Chávez is buying these from Fidel?"

"Yes, indeed. Venezuela purchases weapons from Castro, who buys them from the Russians directly."

"How did you learn this, Commander Hawke?"

"The Venezuelan intelligence officer who actually purchased the Russian missiles in Cuba told me so."

"Any idea what Venezuela intends to do with weapons like this?"

"As I said, every crooked strongman in Latin America

sees himself as the new Simon Bolívar. Chávez's stated goal is to reunite all South America. My source indicates he has ties to the Brazilian terror cells. His primary objective, however, is annexing Cuba."

"What? Could you say that again?"

"Cuba is mired in Venezuelan debt. Should Castro prove mortal, I think you'll see Chávez move to annex Cuba shortly after the funeral."

A flurry of hands shot into the air.

"Commander Hawke, do you really think America should feel threatened by a thug like Chávez?"

"Chávez is determined to humble the Yankee imperialists. Venezuela is spending billions on rearmament. President Chávez is buying helicopters, submarines, and high-tech Su-35 fighters from the Russians. Through secret agreements with Castro, he arranges for thousands of Cuban technicians, who know Russian equipment, to relocate to Venezuela and maintain it. Chávez is Castro's rich uncle dream come true."

"So. We got Russian anti-ship missiles built to be carried by Russian fighter jets owned by Venezuela. Who's Chávez going to shoot at?"

"Venezuela and her allies would use the weapons in wartime against U.S. oil shipping in the Gulf of Mexico."

"Wartime."

"Again. That's what my source said. Wartime. The Venezuelan military war games America all the time."

"Sink our tankers. Venezuela, Mexico, all of them lining up against us. The south against the north. That's what you believe?"

"My chief concern now is that Chávez is supporting the *jihadistas*. He'll use them as a test for weakness before challenging America in the Gulf of Mexico. If the jungle armies succeed—next question."

A silence fell over the gymnasium. It was the first time anyone had said out loud what many had perhaps been hearing and thinking privately. That war in the southern hemisphere was a distinct possibility. That the Islamist terrorists could be very willing pawns to an anti-U.S. movement throughout Latin America. Then a fiery old reporter, a former Yank champ at Wimbledon named Clark Graebner, puffed himself up and spoke.

"Commander Hawke, I don't know you from Adam. I'll take the secretary's word you know a little bit about all this. But what you may not know is that the U.S. Navy is stretched pretty thin right now. As is our Army. As are our Marines. Hell, we hardly have enough National Guardsmen left to stop a dogfight and most of them are headed to the Mexican border. Now you waltz in here, stirring up a whole new pot of trouble with this crazy notion of terror cells in the jungle and Brazilian war games. As if we didn't have enough on our goddamn plate with goddamn Iraq. Now, my question is, what do you have to say about that, Commander Hawke?"

Hawke looked at the red-faced man, his own face devoid of any emotion, and gave his answer.

"Well, sir, I'd say America has fetched up somewhere between Iraq and a hard place."

42

Homer reached up with the idea he would test the fire escape ladder. He wrapped his near-frozen fingers around the cold metal of the bottom rung, but hesitated before he yanked down on it. The damn extension ladder, which was supposed to slide easily down to the ground, was crusty with rust and grime. It might squeak like hell when he pulled on it.

He had to do something. He was tired of waiting here with his back pressed up against the brick wall. The smoker in the window up above him had flipped his butt out into the dark ten minutes ago.

Homer exhaled and saw his breath hang a second and crystallize in the air.

So, was the guy still up at the window, or not?

Hadn't lit another one, the smoker, so, maybe he was just taking the night air. Hell, it was cold as a witch's left tit out here. Maybe a little colder. Homer was freezing his butt off, missing the powerful heater in the Vic. Glad he'd thought to wear his rawhide gloves.

He'd crept around the building twice now, looking for another way inside. There was a tall doorway at the rear, but it was sealed up tight with a heavy slab of aluminum. Padlocked. The door was heavily dented and pried open like a piecrust around the edges. He saw something useful lying almost hidden under a lot of trash. A tire iron. Somebody had tried to get in here a bunch of times over the years and failed.

He didn't see any sense in trying to pry the door open now. It would be way too noisy for his purposes, but he picked up the tire iron anyway, just in case he got desperate enough later on.

Hell with it. He'd try the ladder. He pulled down slowly on the bottom rung, trying to be quiet about it.

Screeeek.

Damn!

He let it go like a hot poker. The grinding noise had been brief and not all that loud. Still, he waited, his heart thudding pretty good inside his chest, expecting to hear somebody shout from the window over his head. Or shine a light on him and shoot him. His gloved hand moved down to grip the butt of his sidearm. His heart slowed down to near normal after a couple of minutes of nothing happening.

Maybe nobody inside had heard the screeching ladder.

Hell, maybe there was nobody inside to *hear* anything.

He looked up at the rotted-out fire escape again. Those iron stairs would wake the dead if he yanked that extension ladder down. Hadn't been used in a few decades probably, maybe more. He looked around the empty side lot, overgrown with weeds. He was looking for a barrel or something he could stand on, maybe reach up and grab the permanent staircase without using the extension ladder. He'd need something pretty high. A couple of big wooden crates would do it.

But he didn't see anything like that.

There was a bunch of crap laying around in the overgrown field out back. A kind of junkyard back there, surrounded by a barbed-wire fence that had seen better days thirty years ago. A couple of old Mack truck cabs and trailers from the fifties were parked right where somebody'd left them sixty years ago.

Maybe he could find something useful back there in the yard. Hell, it sure beat standing here freezing to death. He inched along the wall toward the rear of the building. In the pale moonlight, everything looked silver. Especially the rusted trailer rigs on the other side of the barbed-wire fence surrounding the junkyard.

At the rear of the nearest rig, a couple of fifty-gallon steel drums were lying on their sides. Two of those babies stacked up would just be about perfect. Plus, if he ripped some of the old wire fence out, he could roll those drums back around to the fire escape without making any noise at all.

He kept low and made for the fence. He got there quick and knelt in the bushes, looking back at the looming brick building. No sound, no lights in any upstairs windows. No nothing. He grabbed a fistful of wire stands and yanked. The stuff came away nice and easy in his hand and two or three of the rotted posts just broke off at ground level. He stood up and moved at a low crouch into the abandoned junkyard.

It was about twenty feet over to the oil drums by the trailer and he got there without any alarms going off.

He snapped on his mini-light and stuck it in the one upright drum. There was about a foot of black gooey stuff at the bottom, maybe just old oil, maybe worse 'cause it stunk. The two other drums were empty although the bottom of one of them was completely rusted out. But, hell, they'd do in a pinch. He'd stack 'em, and then haul himself up on the fire escape.

What the hell was that?

HE'D HEARD something. He whipped his head around, automatically looking back at the factory. No, it had been closer. Not a human sound. A kind of a snickering noise. Rats, he thought. Rats inside this trailer? That must be it.

He found himself staring up at the doors of the funky old trailer. You could still make out (barely) the faded words *Tequila Mockingbird* over a bottle of cheap Mexican hootch. The rear doors were locked. Not only locked, but there was a heavy chain wrapped through the handles and locked with a large, rusty padlock. Do you padlock an empty truck and leave it in a field for twenty years? No.

So, what the hell was in there was so all-fired important?

He stuck the tire iron through the twin door handles and pulled back hard as he could without making a huge racket. Didn't budge an inch. He looked at the padlock again, yanked on it. Rusty, but it wasn't going anywhere. Now, he was curious. He stuck the sharp end of the tire iron up under the corner of the steel door and tried to pry it upward. The rusted metal peeled up about six inches. He shoved the tire iron in deeper and pulled upwards really hard. It gave another inch or so. He dropped the iron and snapped on his mini-light again.

He bent down to peer inside the trailer.

Couldn't see diddly-squat in there. But there was one thing. He could see blue starlight coming down from above. So, part of the top of the trailer was missing. Rusted out. And there was one of those narrow ladders going up to the roof that looked like it just might hold his weight. He clicked off his light and stuck it back in his Sam Browne belt.

Hell, climb up, see what was in the old truck and then go find what was going on in the building where the Yankee Slugger cab had disappeared.

He was halfway up the ladder when he heard somebody shout, "Who's out there? This is private property! I got a gun and I'll use it, podnuh. I'm comin' out there." The voice was raw, raspy, and vaguely familiar. The smoker upstairs? The red-eye? Most likely.

He was coming through the open field along the side of the building. He had a light too, a powerful beam that was sweeping the ground in front of him in great looping arcs. In about two seconds he was going to figure out somebody must be in the junkyard.

Homer was about to shout, "Police! Drop your weapon!" but he was in an awkward position hanging on the ladder and besides he had the feeling this guy was the type to shoot first and ask questions later. Or, not ask any questions, ever. Just bury the evidence out here in the yard.

He could jump down and confront the guy but something told him that was a really bad idea. No. Homer had nowhere to go but up. He stuck his boot in the bottom rung, reached for the highest rung he could, and quickly pulled himself up. He got to the top of the ladder just before the light caught him.

"Stop! Hold it right there! You move and you're dead."

Homer swiveled his head around but all he could see was the blinding white light.

"I ain't moving. I'm the law. Put your weapon down."

There was a loud pop and a round whistled past Homer's ear.

"The next one doesn't miss," the man's scratchy voice said. "Throw down that gun and we'll have us a little talk about what happens to trespassers here in Gunbarrel."

Homer put his right hand to his sidearm. He wished he could see the man's face. Judge his intent.

The next round caught him in the upper left arm and almost spun him right off the ladder. It felt like somebody had slugged him hard as they could with a two-by-four, but he managed to keep his footing and hold the ladder tight with his right hand as he climbed the last rung. He could remain on the ladder and wait for the next bullet. He could leap to the ground but he couldn't outrun that beam of light.

He knew he had to go up, up and over. Inside the truck. Now, while he still could.

In that split second, up on the top rung, he saw why there had been so much moonlight streaming down inside the trailer. The top had rusted almost completely away. And shoot, the truck bed was halfway full up to the top with something. Kind of whitish blue in the starlight, the stuff looked like a load of dried-out timber and rocks. Sticks and stones, maybe.

Another bullet whistled a hot tune over his head.

He pitched forward and fell inside.

He landed on top of the pile of sticks and tried to scramble to his feet. Except the truck wasn't full of dried timber at all, Homer saw when he picked one up in his hand.

Hell no, it wasn't sticks and stones.

It was skulls and bones.

43

Can it see us?" Saladin said from the bushes. Harry and Hassan were hiding, watching the battle robot's steady approach across the bridge.

"God, I hope not. Stay the fuck down," Harry said, trying to make himself invisible. "Stop moving around! It's looking for movement!"

"I'm looking for Caparina, damn you," Saladin said, reluctantly crouching down.

"Right. If she made it across and is still alive, we'll get her out. How's the leg?"

"Hurts like hell."

"Bullets are painful things."

The approaching Troll was nearing the end of the bridge. Having no targets, it had stopped firing. Harry studied the tall, hooded periscope camera, whipping back and forth, looking for something to kill. Something distinctly alien about this machine, Harry thought. Spooky. It reminded him of the creatures in *War of the Worlds.* The way they chased fleeing humans around the countryside.

"Let the damn tank roll right by us," Harry said. "On the count of three, you run jump up on the rear."

"That tank's going the wrong way, Harry."

"Trust me. Here it comes."

The one-eyed Troll rumbled closer, ten feet away now.

"Wait until it goes by you, goddamnit! Ready? Okay, here we go. One . . . two . . . three! Go, go, go!"

Saladin took three or four long strides, grabbed one of the grab-rails, and scrambled aboard.

"You have a plan, Harry?" Saladin said.

"Let me get out in front of the bastard, okay? Let the evil eye see me. Good peripheral vision on this little shit. As soon as the camera starts to swivel, and lock on me, cup your hand over the lens."

"We're going the wrong way," Saladin reminded Harry as he ran along beside the tank. The thing was still moving at five miles an hour, in search mode, so it was easy for him to keep up the pace. Dodging plant life was the tough part.

"We'll improvise," Harry said, grinning.

"Meaning?"

"I think it'll stop when it can't see," Harry said, not even breathing hard, pulling dead even with Saladin.

"What makes you think that?"

"What else is it going to do?"

"Good point."

"Why are you whispering?"

"What if it can hear us?"

"Little late for that thought, buddy!"

Harry was pretty sure whoever was controlling this thing back at the ranch couldn't hear what was going on aboard the tank or anywhere else. The technology was advanced, but not that advanced. Harry figured, if the thing could hear? They'd be dead.

He gave Saladin the thumbs-up, then sprinted out ahead. On the tank, Saladin got ready. He pulled himself up and forward enough to be able to reach up and cover the lens with his hand.

"Ready?" Harry said, over his shoulder. He was way out in front now, weaving back and forth on the muddy trail.

"Okay," Saladin shouted, hand poised near the lens. "I'm ready to do this if you are."

Harry checked up suddenly on the right side of the trail. Both men waited for the lens to start its slow arc back toward where he waited.

The guns started spitting lead about a half-second before the lens got to him. Good information, Harry thought. It meant the fish-eye lens had even wider peripheral vision than Harry had calculated. Helpful to know.

The firing continued, but Harry had already ducked and started moving in a right-to-left direction as the lens and synchronized guns swept over and past him moving left to right. Bullets were chewing up the thick vegetation on the right, turning it to smoking shreds. Harry dove into the underbrush on the opposite side of the trail just as Saladin wrapped a big hand around the lens, temporarily blinding the robot.

The twin guns ceased fire immediately, just as Harry had anticipated or at least prayed they would. But the tank kept creeping ahead.

"It's not going to stop, Harry," Saladin said as the Troll rumbled past Brock. He was getting to his feet and smiling.

Harry said, "It will."

"I don't think so."

"Should stop any second."

"Yes, well—"

The robot suddenly ground to a halt, forward progress causing it to slip and slide, the treads smothered in thick brown mud.

"What next?" Saladin said.

"Blindman's Bluff. You keep the lens covered till I say 'Ready.' I'm going to start moving slowly back toward the bridge. I'll start a count aloud down from twenty, go about twenty yards and do a face plant. When I get to 'five,' you take your hand off. The camera will do a recon. Probably a full rotation before the tank starts after me. Then I'll say 'ready' again and pop up in the middle of the trail for it to find me again."

"I think this machine is omnidirectional."

"Meaning it goes both ways? Speak for yourself."

"Are all American spies as crazy as you?"

"Who said I was a spy?"

"Christ, Harry. Trolls do go both ways. They simply reverse the tread direction. Ready?"

"Go."

"Twenty . . . nineteen . . . eighteen . . . seventeen . . ." Harry said, picking and groping his way through the vegetation, headed back to the bridge.

"Five!" Harry said. He dropped on his belly and disappeared in the undergrowth.

Saladin took his hand off the lens. The periscope tube started its rotation above his head.

"Ready!" Harry cried, and Saladin saw Brock now standing in the middle of the trail about a hundred yards before the bridge. Without the slightest hesitation, the Troll simply reversed its treads and started moving back toward Harry and the bridge.

"Watch out!" Saladin yelled.

A second later the lens found Harry. The machine guns opened up half a tick later, kicking up clods of black earth. Harry faked left and crouched, then made a hard move right and stood upright again. The lens paused and instantly swung again toward Harry, who repeated his faking maneuver, this time faking right but moving to his left to add confusion. Harry took some pleasure in how crazy he must be driving this guy at the controls.

The idea seemed to be working, much to Saladin's amazement. Harry didn't get hit and the tank kept heading back down the trail ever closer to the bridge.

When Harry got to the foot of the bridge, he stopped and turned around to face the oncoming tank.

"You want me to blind it now?" Saladin cried, watching the camera swing around toward where Harry stood.

"Wait! Not until the instant he locks me up."

"You'll get shot!"

"I have a plan for that," Harry said. He didn't need to shout anymore because the Troll was getting so damn close. The lens was coming around, Harry could see it easily now, another fifteen degrees ought to put him in camera range.

"Say when," Saladin said nervously, his hand hovering over the bug-eye.

The tank was maybe ten feet from Harry, who stood with one foot on the bridge. The Troll's beanstalk camera and the silent guns were swinging toward him. Harry stood stock still, smiling at Saladin. If Brock was nervous, Hassan thought, he was doing a very good job of hiding it.

Five feet to go and Harry was still alive and on his feet. The lens was almost on him. It had to be.

Four feet.

Three.

"Now!" Harry said, and Saladin clamped his hand down over the bug-eye.

"Get out of the bloody way!" Saladin said. The Troll was about to run Harry down.

"Clear the lens!" Harry said.

In the same instant that Saladin removed his hand, Harry smiled into the camera, then dove headfirst to the ground, directly in the path of the oncoming tank.

"Harry!" Saladin shouted. But Harry was gone, disappearing beneath the tank.

Face buried in muck, Harry had no choice but to hold his breath as the Troll rolled over him. He flattened himself, arms clenched at his sides, the clanking treads missing him by less than a foot on either side. The width was okay, but the ground clearance underneath? A low-slung oil sump or protrusions he hadn't counted on? Shit. He closed his eyes and waited. It was only a few seconds. But time is so relative when a tank is passing over your head.

Finally, the tank cleared. The Troll, with Saladin on the rear, rolled across the bridge. It seemed happy to be going home.

"Harry! You okay?"

Saladin saw Brock getting to his feet, wiping the thick mask of brown mud from his eyes, at the same time sprinting in pursuit of the tank. Saladin stuck his hand out.

Harry caught it, grabbed a rail, hauled himself aboard.

"Congratulations, Harry," Saladin said as they both huddled around the base of the periscope, preparing to face the enemy once more. "Credit where it's due."

"Yeah, well," Harry said, "I'm a professional. Do not try this at home."

44

Lucky old sun was hanging in there, low in the evening sky. Franklin W. Dixon walked over to his hotel room's seaward window, put his hands on the sill, and took a bite of cool, wet air. The brine was sharp in his nostrils. He still hadn't grown accustomed to the tang in the air. Not that he minded it. He could see how a man could grow to love living hard by water. One of those little houses on stilts he'd seen back in the mangrove swamps, a rowboat tied to the front porch.

He looked and looked at his view. He could hardly believe it. His hotel was the cheapest Daisy had been able to find for him, but it was smack dab on the water. It would have been quiet and peaceful, too, if not for that big neon sign that hung outside above his window.

The Green Pelican. Every few seconds, the giant bird buzzed and flapped his illuminated wings and flooded his room with watery green light. Snap, crackle, and pop went the neon buzzard, three seconds on, three seconds off, all night long.

If Key West were not some fancy resort town, you'd call his hotel a flophouse. But, from his small corner room on the top floor of the Green Pelican, he could see that picture postcard harbor spread out below. There were some small islands beyond the harbor. They were covered with pine trees and dotted with tall radio antennas, red lights up top blinking against the dark purple clouds, low on the horizon.

Every kind of motorboat and sailboat was criss-crossing the choppy water. There was a tall ship, a schooner maybe, full of party folks, whooping it up. She was heeled over and sailing right by his hotel. Only a hundred yards away! Her sails, like the sea, looked bathed in liquid copper.

The big old schooner sailed by so close he felt like he could reach out and touch her. There was music aboard, Jimmy Buffett, and it rode in through his windows from across the narrow stretch of water. Franklin tapped his boot heel to the tune and said to himself, *Look who wound up in Margaritaville!*

Funny thing was, it was just like he'd always pictured it to be when he heard that song the first few times. Most things, in his experience, were not at all like what you pictured.

From another window, directly beneath the Green Pelican, he could look straight up colorful Duval Street. Swarms of folks were filling the sidewalks, busy buying doodads, gewgaws, and T-shirts; people hitting the bars and burger joints. Sunset was a busy time here in Key West, he figured. Well, it was sure pretty.

Dixon snapped on the television and leaned back in

the wicker rocking chair. He stretched his boots out on a thin, rosy-colored carpet that smelled of tobacco and spilled whisky. He was still stiff from sitting in the folding chair all day at the conference. Long day, but he was glad he'd come. Tomorrow, he'd say what he had to say and then he'd head back home.

There was a lot of stuff about Mexico on the news, nothing he didn't already know. If there was any good news to be had, it was that folks up in Washington were starting to take the border crisis more seriously. Two states had ordered what little National Guard they had left to help the Border Patrol out with skirmishes. The president had ordered 6,000 more Guardsmen down to the border. He just hoped all this wasn't a case of too-little-too-late. The Border Patrol, the agents he knew personally, were plumb wore out. It was a thankless task.

God help them if it got any worse.

He had a bottle of good bourbon over on the bedside table. His eye lit on it, but he didn't even feel like getting up and pouring himself one. Ever since he'd spoken to Daisy on the phone here about ten minutes ago, he'd felt kind of let down. Sad and lonely wasn't a feeling he was all that familiar with.

Sweet dreams till sunbeams find you.

That's what Daisy had said before she hung up the phone. When he was home, that was always the next to the last thing she said before she fell asleep with her long perfumed hair all spread out on the pillow.

Sweet dreams and leave your problems behind you, that was the very last thing she'd say.

He missed her so bad his heart hurt.

He woke with a start and realized he must have dozed off in his rocker. It was dark outside, and rain was blowing in. The window shades were flapping so hard he was afraid they'd bust off the rollers. He got up to shut everything down and realized what woke him wasn't the wind. It was the phone ringing off the hook on the bedside table. He picked up, wondering who in the world would call him here besides Daisy.

"Sheriff Dixon," he said out of habit.

"Sheriff! I'm so glad I got you! Lord, you're not going to believe this one!"

It was June Weaver, who ran the courthouse switchboard. She sounded all out of breath.

"June, after two days in Key West, I'd believe just about anything anybody tells me. What's going on?"

"Well, you know today was my son Travis's big football game? The playoffs for the state championship?"

He'd forgotten, but he said, "Yep."

"I was driving home after the game, just minding my own beeswax, you know, like I do, and I said, I *saw*, I mean, I saw—"

"Junebug, slow down. You sound like you're about to have a heart attack. Where are you?"

"Yes, sir. I'm home. Just ran in the door."

"Sit down and tell me what you saw."

"Well. I was on the highway headed home. I saw something moving on my right. Over where the river makes that lazy loop, you know, where nobody should be that doesn't have a perfect right to be there."

"I know where you mean. No Border Patrol around?"

"No, sir. Well, I slowed down fast just to see. At first I thought it was big trucks coming across the river. But that didn't make sense so I stopped and got out of the car. Luckily, I had my video camera, from taping the football game, laying on the front seat of the Olds. When I got out of the car, I took it with me just in case, it was something, you know, interesting."

"What was it, June?"

"What I think it was?"

"What you think it was."

"I think it was Mexican Army units in military Humvees crossing the Rio Grande, that's what I think."

Dixon took a deep breath and said, "Why do you think that, June?"

"I know what they look like, Sheriff. You know that. I was with you a few years ago, when you got that award citation from Mexico down in Laredo. These men were in Mexican Army uniforms. Real ones. And they were heavily armed. The Humvees were definitely Mexican Army vehicles. That's what I think."

"Did they see you?"

"Are you kidding me? No, sir, they did not! I crept up through the bushes. But, Sheriff, I got them on tape! Filmed the whole thing. I just looked at the cassette on the TV. You can see them plain as day. I swear."

"Who'd you tell about this, June?"

"Sheriff, I drove over a hundred miles an hour to get home and call you on the telephone. Only thing I did before calling you is stick a chicken potpie in the oven. I'm half starved to death after all that excitement."

"All right, June, now listen. Here's what you do.

Eat your supper. Then I want you to go back to town. Go to the FedEx machine and overnight me that cassette. Got a pencil? Send it to the Green Pelican Hotel, 11 Duval Street, Key West. 33040. For a guaranteed ten-thirty a.m. delivery tomorrow morning. You'll need a FedEx envelope. You still keep some at home?"

"Yessir, I do. I got the address. Wrote it down."

"Good. And don't tell anybody word one about anything until you hear from me. Understand me?"

"Yes, sir."

"All right. Go do it now. I'll call you soon as I get that envelope in the morning."

"This is pretty important, isn't it?"

"It could be. I appreciate your vigilance and courage. Good-bye, June."

HE HUNG UP the phone and stared at the floor. Things were happening pretty fast now. He felt like he was at the eye of one of those famous Key West hurricanes. Evidence of a military incursion by uniformed Mexican Army troops, if that's what was on the tape, would turn this conference upside down. Turn everybody upside down. His presentation was right after lunch tomorrow. Hell, he could skip his damn jibber-jabber. He'd just show June's home movies of invading Mexican troops. Couldn't beat pictures like that with a thousand words.

He sat back down and realized he was about starving. Lunch had been some fancy little finger food and some really bad shrimp quesadillas. He wanted a hamburger, rare, and some French fries. Not to mention a cold beer. Maybe two.

He stood up and pulled his brown oilskin duster off the coat rack. He shouldered into it and then he put on his hat, trying to remember where he'd hidden his wallet. He checked under his shirts in the bottom drawer of the dresser and then remembered putting it under his pillow while he was talking to Daisy lying on the bed. She told him you couldn't be too careful of your money in a place like Key West. Of course, she'd never been here, only been out of Texas once in her whole life, but she was probably right. She usually was. He stuck his billfold in the back left pocket of his jeans, locked his door, and headed downstairs to the street.

There was a man sitting in the lobby he thought he recognized from the conference. At least he recognized the suit, a very wrinkled white suit and very shiny black shoes. You couldn't see his face because he had it buried in the local newspaper. On his left hand was a big gold nugget of a ring with a large diamond. The paper he was reading was the *Key West Gazette,* a paper Franklin had read, cover to cover. It featured mostly help wanted ads and real estate. Which was strange, he thought. The stranger didn't seem the type to be buying himself a house or hiring any short order cooks.

"Howdy," Franklin said on his way out, since he was polite, but the man didn't even have the courtesy to look up when he walked by.

He got a funny feeling walking out the front door. He felt like he was in one of those old black-and-white spy movies during the war. *High Noon in Havana,* something like that.

Life was funny what it threw at you sometimes. He'd never pictured himself setting foot in a peculiar place like Key West, Florida. Back home, even around folks he didn't know well, he could at least identify with them to one extent or another. They all pretty much wore the same clothing. Talked about the same things. They were all related somehow, either by blood or by marriage.

Well, what could you do? That was America for you.

Times were strange. People were stranger. Especially the strangers you saw around here.

But, like Daisy always said, strangers were people too. Who was he to argue with that?

45

Margaritaville was chock full of interesting characters. Just walking up Duval, you came across more unique people in one block than you'd stumble across in Prairie in a whole lifetime.

When Dixon arrived at the bustling café at the southeast corner of Duval and Greene streets, there were a couple of Harleys parked out front and he could hear some pretty good music coming from inside. Looked like a place where a man could duck out of the rain and get a decent cheeseburger.

He liked the name, Sloppy Joe's, and he quickly stepped inside. He looked for someplace to hang his wet oilskin but didn't see one. Dusters didn't seem to have caught on down here. Of course, the only horses he'd seen in town were busted-down mares pulling a bright pink surrey with yellow fringe on the top.

It was still pretty early by Key West standards and luckily there was an empty table right over in the corner. It was way in the back so he figured it would be nice and quiet. He caught a pretty waitress's eye and she nodded "okay," so he went on over there and sat down. There was a fella on stage dressed pretty much the same way he was, jeans and boots. He was singing a Jerry Jeff Walker song. The busty red-headed waitress came right over and handed him the menu.

"What'll it be, stranger?" she said, with a cute smile.

Her name tag announced she was Savannah. He ordered something called the Ernie Burger, rare. "Who's Ernie?" he asked Savannah, "The owner?" And she'd looked at him like he was kidding, which of course he wasn't. She suggested something called Conch Fritters as a go-along and he said, sure, that sounded good too. And a cold Corona with a chilled glass would be nice. Savannah winked at him, told him she liked his hat, and disappeared into the crowd.

So there he was, minding his own business, sipping his beer and listening to Jerry Jeff's "Hill Country Rain," when the stranger in the rumpled white suit from the hotel lobby came over and asked could he sit down.

"Don't see why not," he said, and the man sat.

"Sheriff Franklin W. Dixon?"

"Yep."

"Eduardo Zamora," he said, and stuck his hand across the table, thin gold bracelets dangling from his thin wrist. A big pair of black sunglasses stuck out of his breast pocket and a black tie was tied loosely around his neck. His teeth were very white under his black moustache. His smile was big but not very believable. Franklin looked down at his shoes. Black and shiny, all right.

He shook his hand and said, "What can I do for you, Mr. Zamora?"

"Here is my card, señor. I am a stringer for a chain of Mexican newspapers as you can see. *Los Reformos.* I've got my press pass too, if you'd like to see it. My credentials."

"Like to know what you want," Franklin said, turning the card over in his hand, reading it. He somersaulted it through his fingers before he slid it back across the table. He'd noticed a phone number written in pencil on the back. He'd heard of the Mexican newspaper chain. A big one and not particularly partial to American interests. Backed the Communist candidate for president in the last election. Supported Chávez, too.

"What do you want, Mr. Zamora?"

"A story, of course, I'm a reporter. We'll be hearing from you tomorrow, Sheriff? I saw you listed as one of the Texas Border Sheriffs' Coalition members who will speak, I believe?"

"I'll speak my piece if they have time for me."

Zamora got out a thin spiral notebook and held a stubby pencil poised above the page. "What our readers would like to know is, what do you intend to say to attendees at Secretary de los Reyes's Latin American conference?"

"You've got your press pass, Mr. Zamora. You'll find out tomorrow afternoon."

"I'd like to get a scoop, señor."

"You're at the Green Pelican Hotel, aren't you? Saw you in the lobby a while back."

"You have me confused with someone else. I was here when you walked in, Sheriff, remember?"

Franklin decided to let it go.

"Listen, I don't want to take too much of your time," Zamora continued. "But, it will come as no surprise to learn that people in my country are very unhappy about this security public relations meeting. Feelings in my country are running very high. Still, some responsible journalists, like myself, we are trying to present this American conference to our readers in a fair and balanced way. Our readers would be very interested to hear the personal view of the situation from a Texas sheriff who sees it up close."

"Which struggle is that?"

"The struggle against injustice, señor! The struggle for a humane solution to the pain and suffering. An end to our poor honest people risking death just to find a minimum-wage job to support their families."

"I'm not a politician, Mr. Zamora. I'm a lawman. Your citizens are breaking the law. Day in, day out. And your government is encouraging them to do it. Tell your readers to fix their country instead of breaking mine."

"But this is not true! My government would never—"

Dixon stared at the man until he looked away.

"A borderline ain't nothin' but a law drawn in the sand," Dixon said. "I'm sworn to uphold that law, however fragile it may be. Now, if you'll excuse me, I think my supper's about ready."

The man in the white suit made no move to get up.

"Yes, yes, of course. But, Sheriff, there are stories circulating here in Key West that you plan to show a video shot on the Rio Grande. A very explosive video. Any truth to that?"

"What did you say?"

"A video? Shot recently along the border?"

Franklin just looked at him. There were only two possibilities. One, June had told a lot of folks what she'd seen before she'd called him. Or, two, this hombre had a friend working the Green Pelican switchboard. He favored the latter.

"How'd you hear about that?"

"I have a job to do, too, señor."

"Get up bright and early and see for yourself."

"Your speech is not until the afternoon."

"I might move it up some."

"Señor. I am here to offer a very substantial sum of money for this video. My paper has authorized me to offer you fifty thousand U.S. dollars for the film. I have the money. Here. Waiting for you in a safe deposit box at the Key West Bank on Whitehead Street."

"Who do you really work for, Mr. Zamora?"

"I told you this already. *Los Reformos.*"

"You've got the wrong man. Mr. Zamora. I'm sure you fellas are pretty much used to buying whatever it is you want. But attempting to bribe a law enforcement officer is a serious crime in this country. I think you ought to stand up and walk out now and let me eat my supper in peace."

Savannah had arrived with his food. She put it down in front of him and Franklin began to eat immediately.

He was hungry. *"Uno mas Papa Dobles?"* Savannah asked the Mexican.

"He's not staying," Dixon said.

"Si, uno mas," Zamora said, with a big smile at the waitress. Savannah looked at the sheriff and he nodded, okay, bring him another. It'd be nice to end this without a fuss.

"Listen to me, Mr. Zamora," Dixon said, trying to keep his voice low. "My cheeseburger's getting cold. Now, I don't know who you people are or what you think you're doing. But I want you to know one thing. I'm not for sale. At any price."

"Sheriff, there's no need to get excited. We're both businessmen. I can see you were disappointed with my original number. Perhaps it was a bit underwhelming. Let me make my offer more realistic. I am prepared to pay a hundred thousand dollars for this video. Okay? Cash."

"You got something in your ears?"

"I'm sorry. Still no good, huh? Maybe you have decided to sleep on this offer. Good. I have written my mobile number on the back of the card. If you change your mind before the conference, please give me a call. I wish you good night. *Buenas noches, señor.*"

"Mr. Zamora," Franklin said, dismissing him without looking up. He picked up his burger and took a bite. It was good.

The man stood up and pushed his chair back from the table. He tilted his head back and drained his cocktail. Even though there was no one within earshot he leaned forward and put both hands on the table, speaking very softly.

"Sheriff, I must ask you a personal question. It must be hard to go away on business and leave your poor wife all alone in a small house so far from town. Is it not?"

"Say that again?" Franklin leaned forward and put his nose inches from the man's own.

"Sorry. I am just saying it must be difficult. For your wife. She must get frightened sometimes, without her brave husband to protect her."

"My wife."

"Yes. Her name is Daisy, is it not? Such a pretty name. You must tell her to be careful. The desert is full of coyotes, eh? Especially at night. A woman alone."

Franklin's right hand shot out and clamped around the man's left wrist. He didn't break any small bones, but he came close.

"If you people ever get anywhere near my wife . . . if she even hears a voice she doesn't like on the phone . . . if you or any of your kind ever cause any harm to come to my wife, I will take off this badge and hunt you down like the worthless piece of filth that you are. I will kill you, Mr. Zamora. Do I make myself clear?"

He let go of the wrist and the man in the white suit was gone out the door and disappearing into the throng outside.

Franklin threw some money down. He got up and left his uneaten hamburger on the table. Then he, too, disappeared into the crowded carnival that was called Duval Street.

HE PUSHED UPSTREAM, bucking the tide of boisterous humanity. He was six blocks from the hotel. He could already see the big animated bird up ahead, all lit up in the misty night sky.

He looked at his watch. It was an hour earlier in Texas. Daisy would be finished with her supper. She'd be standing at the kitchen window, washing up the dishes. It would be getting dark pretty soon. The coyotes would be fixing to start singing.

At that instant, he would have about killed somebody for a cellular telephone, even though he hated the damn things.

"Excuse me," he said to the large woman. She was standing on the corner with her right hand pressed to her ear, the way people do these days.

"What? Hey, what the hell do you think you're doing, mister? Give me back my cell phone!"

"I'm sorry. Official police business, ma'am. I won't be long."

He flashed his badge and turned away from her.

"How does this thing work?" he asked her, stabbing at buttons with his index finger.

46

Hawke stared into the coal fire still burning merrily in the basket grate. He and Ambrose had retired to the ship's small book-lined library immediately following dinner. Congreve had suggested a brandy. The detective was feeling a bit homesick, Hawke thought. Missing his beloved Diana Mars and snowy walks by her side in the country. He was anxious to be home.

The conference, Hawke's part of it anyway, was over. Next morning, Ambrose and Pippa were scheduled to fly back to Britain. Hawke himself was headed for points south. He'd given Langley and the State Department what information C had allowed him to share. What Conch and Washington chose to do with the intel he had provided was out of his hands. He was now operating on his own. He was mentally clearing his decks, well on the verge of taking the fight to the enemy.

He was sufficiently motivated. Revenge, in Hawke's mind anyway, was a highly underrated and overly maligned emotion. He personally had found it to be vastly energizing.

On this cold and rainy Saturday night in Key West, only Pippa had elected to go ashore. One last night on the town, she'd said. The two men remained aboard to work on the Code, even though it meant forgoing a spot Hawke had chosen for its name, the Hot Tin Roof.

The small ship's clock on the library mantel struck four silvery bells. Hawke, lost in a daydream of drum-beating savages and thick, unyielding jungle, was roused from his reverie. He had been listening to the lovely song now playing softly over the system. It was Andrea Bocelli's haunting version of *Vorrei Morire.* He'd decided not to dwell for too long on why this particular lyric had such morbid appeal.

It was just ten o'clock and through the library's starboard windows, Hawke could see that the rain had finally let up. A rind of yellow moon was visible behind tattered rags of cloud slowly sliding off to the east. The cold front had almost cleared. Tomorrow promised balmy sunshine.

A sleepy sigh was heard above the gentle music and Alex looked from the fire to his friend.

"I'm afraid I'm bloody well stumped," Congreve said, removing his gold pince-nez glasses and pinching the bridge of his nose. He laid aside the Zimmermann letter. He'd been staring at the bloody thing for hours on end. He stood and stretched his arms above his head.

"You? Stumped?" Hawke said, holding his thistle-shaped snifter aloft so that its many facets refracted the firelight. "Where's Miss Guinness? We need her famous Record Book!"

"Very amusing, Alex. But I tell you, if C's Signals section can't crack it, and I can't crack it, it simply cannot be cracked."

They had discussed a variety of approaches to the puzzle at dinner. They kept coming back to the deathbed letter that, for convenience sake, they now referred to simply as the Zimmermann Letter. The numeric code, so promising at first, was now deemed to be a random sequence, computer generated, and thus indecipherable.

"Everything can be cracked," Hawke said, reaching for the damnable thing. He stared at the letter blindly for a few moments and then put it back down with a sigh of frustration. Numbers. The bane of his existence.

"Gibberish," Hawke said, giving up any last hope of discerning some kind of repeat or pattern. "Maybe you're right. We're both bloody well stumped. There has to be another way."

Congreve eyed Hawke carefully, his invisible cerebral wheels spinning so rapidly and obviously Hawke was surprised they weren't audible. Ambrose stood with his back to the fire, lighting his first pipe of the evening. In a second, the familiar fragrance of Peterson's Irish Blend was in the air.

"Before the towel is thrown," Ambrose puffed, "or, at least, whilst the flag of surrender is still paused midflight above the gaping maw of the rubbish bin, bear with me a moment longer."

Hawke sat back in silence, waiting for Ambrose's genius to slip silently into the room.

"Consider. The ambassador wanted a letter delivered to his wife. We both assumed, until we actually saw it, that the thing might be some kind of poetic deathbed farewell to his soon-to-be widow in Brazil. Yes?"

"Yes," Hawke said.

"You subsequently learned from the captured Venezuelan officer, that Zimmermann's widow has fled Rio de Janeiro for the tatty Amazon River town of Manaus, correct? Fearing for her life."

"Correct."

"A problem arose in Mexico City. The ambassador was abducted from his hotel in the *Zona Rosa* by Brazilian agents, whereupon he was quickly disappeared into the jungle."

"Yes. Where Top tried unsuccessfully to kill him. Zimmermann was up to his neck in this thing. But he lost the heart for it, or the nerve, and escaped to England."

"So, we have a German ambassador with links to Brazil, Venezuela, and Mexico City. And all three somehow go back to this Syrian, Muhammad Top."

"Top stands at the crossroads," Hawke said. "He's the link."

"Why Mexico, though? Why are they in bed with a Muslim terrorist?"

"Who stands to benefit most if Top succeeds? Mexico, I'd say. A few successful border skirmishes, America succumbs to the media outrage, and they have a chance to reclaim all the land they lost to the Americans in the war of 1848."

"I suppose you're right. Finally, Alex, one thing I may have overlooked. There was a second gift in addition to the coded letter. A book of poetry, perhaps. At least, it had the heft of a book to me."

"A book, yes, that's exactly what it was."

"So you examined it?"

"Of course. I'm a snoop."

"And?"

"It's a book. Innocuous enough. A popular novel."

"Any good?"

"It's no *War and Peace*. I can hardly imagine giving it as a final farewell gift to a grieving widow. Still, there can be no disputes about taste."

"*De gustibus non est disputandum.* Still, you kept it."

"I can hardly put it down."

"And where is that book now?"

"Brought it along for the voyage. Stuck it in my library desk over there. I thought to finish it tonight."

"Where, exactly?" Congreve asked, moving to the desk.

"Left bottom drawer most likely. That's where I usually stick things I want to keep track of."

Congreve crossed to the small leather-topped desk, sat down, and opened the left-hand drawer.

"I don't see it."

"It's there."

47

H ere we are. Let's take a look, shall we?" Congreve withdrew the book and placed it on the desk before him, staring down at it.

"Careful," Hawke said. "Anything ticking? You'd best shake it a few times and see if it rattles, Constable."

"Very funny. Still, a rather good, although belated, point. It's the *Da Vinci Code*."

"Hmm."

"The special Illustrated Edition."

"The pictures help, actually," Hawke said. "I wouldn't know the Mona Lisa from Lisa Marie."

"Please, Alex. Spare me."

Ambrose held up the book for closer inspection. He said, "An odd choice, I must admit. For a belated gift to the one left behind."

Hawke smiled. "Somewhere in the heart of the Amazon lurks the last literate human being on earth yet to read the bloody thing. Did you ever get round to it yourself?"

"Like a lamb to the slaughter," Ambrose said. "I rather enjoyed it. Anything at all to do with codes hooks me instantly."

He was holding the book by its spine and shaking it over the desktop. Seeing nothing fall from the pages, he set it down and began leafing through the book slowly.

"Are you going to read it again?" Hawke asked. "Now?"

"Quiet," Ambrose said, lost in some vast, shadowed hallways of thought.

"Are you on to something? Twitchy eyebrows. You've all the symptoms."

"Perhaps I am."

"What? Spill it."

"Don't you find it the least bit interesting, Alex, that the last book Zimmermann bequeaths to his wife has the word *Code* in its title?"

"Funny, that, now that you mention it."

"Yes, isn't it? Hand me the letter, will you, Alex? I left it over there on the table somewhere."

Hawke retrieved the ambassador's coded farewell message and handed it to Ambrose.

"We need a positive supposition here," Congreve said, his eyes darting rapidly from letter to book. He was quickly running his finger down the page Zimmermann had filled with scrawled numbers.

"Namely?"

"That the letter and the book are connected."

"Too simple. Too obvious."

"The truth often is. That is, I suspect, why we haven't cracked the bloody code, Alex. Humans naturally look for complexity where none exists. Whilst I, on the other hand, subscribe to William of Occam's point of view."

"Remind me about William of Occam again?"

"A mediaeval philosopher, Alex. His principle, widely known as Occam's Razor, stated that one should not make more assumptions than the minimum needed. Confronted with a puzzle, reduce the entities required to explain it. In other words, Alex, choose the simplest path through the forest."

"Ah, that's it."

"Entia non sunt multiplicanda praeter necessitatem."

"Exactly."

"Yes. Assume for a moment the widow is not a polymath with multiple degrees in higher mathematics, nominism, or cryptography. Assume she's an ordinary woman possessed of ordinary gifts, an average human being, just like you or me. But, also assume this letter and this book are not the loving farewell of a dying husband, but something far more . . . sinister."

"Such as?"

"A program sequence initiator, for instance. You use the numbers to key in some kind of unstoppable electron virus to disable worldwide communications. Or launch a missile at London. Who knows? Doomsday scenarios are your bread and butter, not mine. I'm a simple copper."

While Congreve spoke, he was rapidly flipping the pages of the novel.

"You've solved far more intricate puzzles than this one. Stick to your knitting, Constable," Hawke said, sensing an excitement in Congreve's expression he'd despaired of ever seeing this night. "Do you see anything in it? Any connection?"

Ambrose was studying the letter, repeating numbers under his breath, and then flipping back and forth through the novel.

"I'm looking, I'm looking. Ah. Yes. Here we go, here's something. The book has one hundred and five chapters, plus a prologue and an epilogue."

"And?"

"And, hold on a tick . . . yes . . . the cryptic farewell message has exactly the same, wait, yes, one hundred and five individual lines of numeric code!"

"Brilliant!"

"Thank you. But it doesn't mean anything, yet."

"Is there anything at the end of the book itself that resembles the code's format?" Hawke leapt to his feet and moved to the desk to look over Congreve's shoulder.

"Yes. Two short numerical lines appended at the end like some kind of coda. It's a match."

Hawke squeezed Congreve's left shoulder vigorously. "You've cracked it, old slug! God bless you for a common genius after all. So, how does the bloody thing work?"

"You take the book, I'll do the code. We'll start with something simple. The ambassador's first handwritten line is 001005005. Take a look at the book, Alex. First chapter, fifth paragraph, fifth word? What is it?"

Hawke flipped rapidly through the book, searching for Chapter One, and then quickly running his finger down the page. "Ah, here it is, fifth paragraph, fifth word . . . *Reckoning*. That's a good start . . . and I must say, Constable, that you have a remarkable ability to, when all seems lost, stick to your—"

"Ah! There you are!" a cheery voice called from the doorway.

Hawke and Congreve looked up from their fevered study of the *Da Vinci Code* and the accompanying message.

"Pippa!" Ambrose almost came out of his chair with delight.

Hawke slipped the folded letter inside the novel and snapped it shut. Then he slid the book under some loose papers on his desk.

"We'll finish our literary discussion later in private," he murmured to Ambrose. Congreve nodded his agreement.

"Ah, Pippa," Hawke said, "here you are."

"I was wondering where you two had run off to! My last night in Key West after all. Hullo, Alex."

"Have a good time, did you?"

She giggled, slightly tipsy, and said, "I danced and danced, really."

"Ah, lovely," Ambrose smiled wistfully at the girl, seemingly at a loss for further dialogue.

"At the Hot Tin Roof?" Hawke said.

"No, some little dive called the 'Varoom Room.' "

"Ah," Alex said, instantly running out of conversation as well. Finally, he looked at Congreve and said, "Your fiancée, Diana, loves to dance, does she not?"

"We are not engaged, Alex. We simply have an understanding."

The little minx did look rather fetching posed in the doorway, Alex thought. She had her blond hair up in rhinestone combs and it now fell in a few stray wispy curls about her blushing cheeks. She was wearing red, a sheath of silk under a red satin shawl, and it was, Hawke saw uncomfortably, an inspired choice. Her cups runneth over, he saw, despite making every human effort not to notice.

Hawke dragged his eyes away, looking pointedly at Ambrose. "Well, I'm for bed then."

"So early, Alex?" Congreve said. "A tinge of autumn in the air, is there? Hmm."

Hawke looked at him. "What?"

"No need to get snarky, old sausage," Ambrose said, chuckling into his brandy snifter.

At that moment, Tom Quick entered the room.

"Skipper, you asked to be informed the minute Wally arrived back from Cancun. Pulling up at the dock right now."

"Thanks, Tom, I'll be right down."

"Wally?" Pippa asked, twirling a red satin evening bag by its strap, "Who's he?"

Alex said, "Not a 'he,' Pippa, a 'she.' A new boat. You'll see her in the morning before you leave."

"Can't I see her now?" Pippa asked, smiling at Hawke from under her long lashes.

"You certainly cannot. There's a good deal of preparation to be done before dawn," Hawke said. He was anxious to get his first real look at her and get feedback from the crew just returned from a quick shakedown cruise to Cancun. The first radioed reports from her new skipper, Gerard Brownlow, were encouraging. She was blisteringly fast and very seaworthy. Armed, she'd be lethal in a fight.

"A quick nightcap after all that preparation, Alex?" Pippa asked shyly, her long lashes lowered.

"I think not. Good night, Constable. And I wish you a very good night as well, Miss Guinness. It's been a pleasure having you aboard. Most helpful. A pleasant homeward journey."

"Pity about him," Pippa said as Hawke crossed the room to confer with Tom Quick. "You're not going to bed, too, Mr. Congreve?"

Ambrose said, "Well, I suppose I could be persuaded to have just one more brandy. Just the one, mind you! Don't be naughty."

"We need to crack that code, Constable. Tonight, if possible."

Ambrose said, "I'll read the thing straight through, Alex. Soon as I'm finished, I'll ring you up. First light too early?"

"Not at all."

"Code?" Pippa said, plopping herself into Alex's still warm chair. "What code?"

"The Da Vinci Code," Alex said, pausing at the door, "Read it?"

"Not yet."

"You and Mrs. Zimmermann," Alex said on his way out.

48

GUNBARREL, TEXAS

Homer crouched down on the forlorn pile of bones and waited. He was hiding in a rear corner of the trailer. He was up against the rear door, about four feet below where the top would have been if it hadn't rusted out. He had his gun out and he was breathing hard. His shoulder burned like the devil and was bleeding pretty good now out of the exit wound. Hadn't hit bone, just muscle. He'd stuffed his bandanna in the little hole but what he needed to do was tie it off. He could hear the man outside, maybe a hundred yards away.

He took a chance and put the gun down a second so he could wind a tourniquet around his upper arm. He wound the bandanna tight, clenched the knot in his teeth and pulled. Hurt like a bitch, but he felt the bleeding ease up instantly.

"Shitfire!" the man on the ground said. Must not have seen the tangle of wire fencing Homer had ripped down. Sounded like he'd tripped over it and gone down hard. It was a heavy thud; he was a big man. When he got up, his steps were slow and heavy.

He had a smoker's hack and the sound of his cough was getting closer. Homer couldn't figure out why the sound of the man's gunfire hadn't brought all the outside security lights on and more folks streaming out of the big brick warehouse building. Then he got it. Except for the Yankee Slugger that had pulled inside, the building must be empty. The smoker out there was all she wrote.

The lone night watchman.

Who was watching what, exactly? A junkyard?

No. Something really, really interesting, that was what. Somebody had put serious money into that fancy electric sliding door. And then paid a lot more to make the whole building look old and weathered. And invisible to anyone who happened to take a detour through a forgotten hole in the wall called Gunbarrel, Texas.

"Hey. You in there, asshole?" Smokey said, between hacks. "You still alive and kicking?"

Voice sounded familiar. Homer didn't say anything. He picked up a bone. It was surprisingly heavy, a leg bone, thigh maybe, and threw it hard across at the opposite sidewall of the truck. It made a hollow clang, more of a *thonk*. Two loud shots instantly rang out. Jagged, Magnum-sized holes appeared in the trailer's aluminum siding. This was at the other end of the big open truck, right where the bone had bounced off.

"Throw the gun out," Smokey said. He was standing now near the rear of the truck. Maybe six feet from where Homer was hiding. The voice was starting to sound more and more familiar, but it was so hoarse he still couldn't place it.

"I ain't got any gun," Homer said, his voice sounding like it was on reverb.

"Shit. You said you was a lawman. Toss out your damn gun. I could just set out here, couldn't I, pod-nuh? Jes' let you starve and rot in there, y'know. Ain't nobody ever going to find you in there, Lone Ranger. I promise you that damn much."

"I'm hit."

"I figured you was."

"Need a doctor."

"Where'd I catch you?"

"Arm."

"Bleedin' pretty good?"

"I guess."

"Yeah? So throw out your fuckin' six-shooter and we'll talk about getting you over to the emergency room."

Homer picked up another bone. It was smaller than the first one he'd thrown, only about a foot long. Rotted black cloth had stuck to one end of it, embedded in a knobby joint. Part of the person's shirt, maybe. There were still some pieces of people's clothing mixed in with all the bones. Lots of sandals. He tied more black rags tight around the bone. Didn't look that realistic. Had a good heft to it, though.

"You win. I'm throwing out the gun."

"I'm waitin'."

"Here she comes."

Homer sailed the bone high and long with his pitching arm. He hoped to get it all the way to those tall weeds outside the wire fence. Then he might have a chance. Either the guy would go look for it in the weeds and leave the ladder unguarded. Or, being fat and lazy, he just might take the easy route and believe what he wanted to believe. That he'd seen a gun go flying over his head and now he had an unarmed kid trapped in a forty-foot-long coffin that was half-full already.

Most people, in Homer's limited experience, believed what they wanted to believe.

"Smart kid," Smokey finally said, still huffing and puffing just outside the truck doors. "Okey-dokey, son. I'm coming on up that ladder."

Homer heard a grunt and felt the noticeable dip of the man's weight on the bottom rung of the ladder. Big guy, all right. Heavy. He'd have one hand on the ladder and the gun in the other. Gun in the right hand most likely, if you trusted the law of averages.

Homer pressed his cheek against the cold aluminum siding as the smoker slowly mounted the steel ladder. He was crouched in the shadows. The ladder went up the right side nearest him. He could see the top rung. When they saw each other's faces, hell, there wouldn't be more than six feet between them.

Homer's finger tightened in the curve of the trigger. He blinked a few times, and tried to swallow. He hurt. Cold sweat was stinging his eyes. He'd never killed a man before. Never fired a shot with his service revolver in the line of duty. He wasn't even much of a shot. Smokey was almost to the top, grunting and wheezing. He saw white fingers curl around the top rung.

Homer Prudhomme, looking at his shaking gun hand, thought to himself, *Son, you can't win with a losing hand.*

Eternity passed. His hand suddenly stopped shaking.

"Hey," Smokey said, near the top rung now. "Where the fuck are you at, boy?"

He could see the slotted top of the man's cowboy hat. The top half of his face, his eyes.

"Hey! You hear me? I said. Where. You. At?"

"Waiting for you," Homer said and fired twice at the whole head and shoulders now silhouetted against the dark blue sky.

The man's head exploded and his body fell away, his fingers finally peeling off the top rung. There was a thudding sound like a big sack of potatoes hitting the dirt. Homer got to his feet and began stacking bones in the corner so he could climb out of this death trap.

He dropped to the ground beside the body. It was face down in the weeds, dead still, except for the right leg which was splayed out at a bad angle and twitching.

He got a hand under the shoulder and managed to get the man turned over onto his back. There was just enough of his face left to recognize him.

The man he'd killed? Mr. J. T. Rawls.

He waited to feel something. Fear, he guessed. Didn't happen. Justifiable self-defense during a murder investigation? The man was going to shoot him, no question about that. He shook his head, trying to clear it of anything but the facts of his developing case. Mr. Rawls, big-shot Chevy dealer, had himself a little sideline business, seemed like. Mexican Midnight Auto Supply? No, something a whole lot bigger than that.

But, what?

49

Homer half expected the rear door of the warehouse to be hanging ajar, but it wasn't. Rawls was dead as dirt, but he'd padlocked the door behind him when he'd come out to check out the noise outside. Homer walked around the building again and figured out the only way inside was still the fire escape ladder.

He reached up and pulled the ladder down, not worrying about the screeching noise anymore. You could make all the noise you wanted in a ghost town with a population recently dropped down to one. He went up the steps and climbed through the open window, shining his mini-flashlight inside first and seeing nothing out of the ordinary. It was an empty room, probably used to be an office. An overturned wooden desk was in the center of the floor.

There was single bulb hanging from a wire in the center of the room. Homer turned the switch but it was either burned out or there was no power. He saw a wooden chair facing the window. Scuff marks on the windowsill where J.T. parked his boots. Rawls was a rich man. Yet, this had been his office. His half-full Cowboys coffee mug was sitting on the seat where he'd left it when he'd heard something outside.

Or, maybe Rawls had his fancy office somewhere else in the building. Maybe he'd just been walking around having a smoke and stepped in here. Walked over to the window to get a little air.

On the floor around the upturned desk were some girlie magazines and some porno stuff. He picked one up. It was a calendar with a naked girl in a tire swing. The year 1988. At the bottom were the words, *Courtesy of Rawls Chevrolet.* J.T. had himself a dealership down here a long time ago. Never told anybody about it. Must have been successful though, size this building was.

He dropped the calendar among the paper cups, and other garbage. Some old Burger Boy and Krispy Kreme sacks and wads of dirty paper napkins. The room still reeked of tobacco and the old sweat-stink of the dead man.

Homer thought he heard something beyond the closed door and stood stock still for a second. It was a faint, humming noise, like heavy machinery moving deep inside the warehouse.

He moved quietly over to the door and pulled it open.

He had no idea what he expected on the other side but it certainly wasn't what he saw.

Which was nothing.

The whole building was empty inside. He was looking at a big empty box at least a hundred feet long, fifty feet wide, and four stories high. No floors. No windows. No staircases. No nothing inside. There was a roof up there overhead. Corrugated aluminum. The arched steel beams that supported it seemed to be fairly new. And the featureless brick walls were freshly painted white floor-to-ceiling on all four sides. There was a narrow steel catwalk beyond the door and he stepped out onto it. He was about twenty feet above the ground floor.

He flicked his mini-light on and played it down below. The spacious floor looked to be painted concrete, spotless and shiny. In the center of the floor was a circle. Just a faint line, really, with a diameter about sixty feet, maybe more.

Homer moved left along the yellow-painted catwalk hung from the ceiling and extending all the way around four sides of the building. Across the way were two office doors like the one he'd just come out of. But he wasn't curious about those doors.

What got his full attention was the fact that the Yankee Slugger cab he'd seen pulling inside this very building about an hour ago, had now disappeared. He certainly hadn't heard that big diesel crank up, and he would have, wouldn't he? Even when he was hiding out there in the boneyard, he would have heard that monster cranking up, backing out into the street, and roaring off. He hadn't heard a thing. But the Slugger was gone.

He saw that the catwalk had a single staircase leading down to the ground on the street side of the building.

He moved toward it along the narrow metal walkway carefully, not because there was anybody to hear him, the place was obviously empty, but because if he tripped and went over the rail, well, that would be all she wrote for damn sure.

He went downstairs slowly, keeping his light aimed on the steps all the way to the ground. The big main door, so cracked and peeling on the outside, was a shiny brushed steel on the inside. No handles or locks. It just slid up into the wall above it. He turned away from his inspection of it and looked at the faint outline of the circle in the center of the floor. Had it changed? It looked different than it had when he'd been up on the catwalk. He went over to check it out, kneeling down inside the circle to feel its outline with his fingers.

Now he could see that the big sixty-foot circular section was slightly lower than the rest of the floor. Like a tiny depression. The outline he'd seen from above was due to the fact that this section wasn't flush. There was about an eighth of an inch of dull steel showing all the way around. Something, a sound maybe, made him lean forward and put his ear to the floor.

It was that gear noise he'd heard earlier up in Smokey's office. A deep whirr, and then a soft hiss.

And suddenly the whole center section was moving. He was dropping down through the floor.

He stood up and quickly stepped off the moving platform. He stepped away from the hole, watching wide-eyed as the huge round section of floor descended slowly and steadily. Almost noiselessly. A foot. Two feet. Still dropping. He could hear something down there now. The noise of whatever machinery below supported a huge round section of concrete floor. A massive hydraulic lift of some kind. And now, another noise. A big diesel firing up. Then, a second one started. A third. More.

Wait a minute. Trucks? In the basement?

He lay down flat on his stomach, trying not to hurt his wounded arm any more, and inched forward until he could see just over the edge. There was a faint reddish light down there, swirling with diesel fumes. It was too thick to see anything but shadowy shapes in the red mist. He shoved himself forward a few more inches, lowered his head, and peered down inside.

If there was somebody down there aiming to blow his head off it was going to happen now. He hadn't heard anybody and he thought he would have. But, you never know.

Nobody shot him. But what he saw beneath him took the breath right out of him.

Monster rigs. A whole lot of them, tractor trailer trucks, in fact. Maybe fifteen, or even more, he thought. At least twenty. But that was only all the ones that he could see from this angle. The underground garage was big, he could see now, lowering his head even more, because the great oval section had now descended flush into the lower level floor.

All the way at the back of the lower level was a well-lit tunnel.

So, that was how they did it, got the ghost trucks across the border with nobody catching on. He'd seen all the reports of Mexicans building tunnels under the border. Big ones, with air-conditioning even. To move illegals and drugs into the States. But this tunnel was something else entirely. It was large enough to accommodate eighteen-wheelers. Must have taken years to build this thing. Rawls owned a construction company in addition to everything else. He was in cahoots with the Mexicans somehow. Bringing trucks in for some reason.

Homer's case was starting to add up. J.T. had been a smuggler, a crook. And a traitor. He'd never killed a man before, but if he had to start, it wasn't a bad place.

There was a loud snort of a big diesel engine revving. He watched in wonder as, below him, a truck pulled forward and stopped right in the middle of the circular lift. It wasn't the Yankee Slugger he'd seen pull in earlier. No, this was an ancient road warrior, an old fifties vintage Mack truck with faded green paint on the cab and trailer. Yellow road lights now lit up a row of rusty chrome-plated horns mounted on top of the cab. He couldn't see into the cab. Blacked-out windows, of course. He watched, unable to tear his eyes away, as the whole center section started turning clockwise, turning the rig around so it'd be facing the street.

When the lift platform had rotated one hundred-and-eighty degrees, it stopped.

Then the beat-up old Mack truck started rising on its hydraulic pedestal. It was a truck with a big juicy tomato logo and *Ocala Farms Inc.* painted on the trailer. At the same time, the main door of the building started sliding up inside the wall. All this crap going on, Homer thought, and not a single solitary human being on the property besides himself and the man he'd killed.

The whole thing was, what, automated?

Homer figured it was way past the time to beat feet the hell out of Mr. J. T. Rawls's haunted truck graveyard and that is just what he was fixing to do. He ducked underneath the half-opened street door and took off at a run, darting across the ghost town's main street to the burned-out Texaco where he'd parked the Vic.

He'd get on the radio and call in the dead man's location. Then he'd get off the radio and get to the bottom of whatever the late J. T. Rawls had been up to in this little ghost town.

50

A Selva Negra

Harry Brock slapped in a fresh mag and jacked a round into the chamber of his semiautomatic rifle. Then he said, "How old is Caparina, anyway?"

"Almost thirty," Saladin replied.

"Yeah? Told me she was twenty-five."

Harry and Saladin nervously eyed the low, blunt structure on the opposite rim of the canyon. They were nearing the end of the bridge. So far, they'd seen no movement and no more of the hellish little lead-spitting Trolls. But neither man had any illusions about a champagne reception immediately upon arrival on the other side.

Hassan flicked the selector on his weapon to full auto. He, like Harry, was crouched down behind the flared steel mudguard that covered the tank treads. This was all the protection the little green battlebot afforded the casual rider and, as they had witnessed, it was precious little.

"Don't believe everything Caparina says. You'll find yourself one day wishing you hadn't."

"What's that supposed to mean?"

"I believe you're trying to make me jealous. My ex-wife had many lovers before you, Mr. Brock."

"Doesn't seem to bother you much."

"Maybe that's because I view all of her lovers, such as you, not as a rival, but as a fellow sufferer."

Harry grinned at him and cocked his gun. "Lock and load, Saladin," he said. "We're about to go find that loose woman of yours or die trying, I guess."

As the tank neared the last third of the bridge, both men were relieved not to have seen Caparina's charred corpse lying in the smoking ruins of the tank. And they were mildly shocked that no one had bothered to kill them yet.

"Drone aircraft formation," Saladin said suddenly. "Get low as you can. Hug steel, Harry!"

"Shit," Harry said, flattening himself as best he could in the cramped space between the fore and aft mud-guards. Both of them were wearing jungle fatigues the same shade of camo as the battlebots were painted. Harry hoped that it afforded a small measure of visual protection. It all depended on how alert the operator flying the UAV was at this precise moment.

"No movement!" Harry said. "Don't even blink!"

He watched three sleek silver craft bank and turn as they flew up the ravine directly toward them. He saw the telltale red tips at the ends of the wings and knew the goddamn things were armed with air-to-ground missiles. The drone squadron was now on a collision course headed straight for the bridge. All you could do was wait for a launch and watch one of those little red bastards home in on your dead ass.

Nothing of the kind happened.

The lead drone dipped its inverted-spoon nose at the last possible second. Harry held his breath as it streaked directly beneath the bridge with about six inches of clearance. The two flankers streaked across overhead, where they began a lazy turn, climbing to the south. Probably on a search circuit that would route them along the southern perimeter of Top's compound, Harry thought.

If Top was on his game, which he surely was, he'd be scheduling these drone recon flights at odd hours, eliminating any predictability that would allow intruders inside unnoticed. The two intruders aboard the tank whipped their heads around and watched the lone silver bird dart and twist its way up the deep green ravine, finally disappearing around a rocky promontory and into heavy mist. When Hassan and Brock faced forward once more, the Troll was rumbling off the bridge and onto a wide apron of crushed sandstone.

"That was good," Harry said, his eyes darting back and forth, looking for any movement in or around the seemingly abandoned pillbox fortification.

"Why?"

"Nobody sent that drone squad to take us out, or, believe me, it would have. That last flight was on routine patrol and the operator didn't pick us up."

"Asleep at the wheel."

"We got lucky."

"Better lucky than smart."

The remote operations post had been well guarded. Now, it was pockmarked with bullet holes. It was a squat, ugly, rectangular sandstone building, bristling with damaged video cameras and mast antennas. Camouflaged, it also sat just far enough inside the green wall of jungle to be invisible from the air. Like the suspension bridge it guarded, it was disguised with a mat of leafy vines. This was not the camp's main approach, Harry and Hassan figured, it didn't look sufficiently fortified or important enough. God knew how many of these manned outposts lined this stretch of ravine.

But, in his gut, Harry knew they might have found a backdoor to the heart of darkness.

"The entrance to this pillbox is here at the rear," he heard Hassan call out from behind the structure, and Harry went cautiously around back to check it out.

When he turned the corner, Hassan was sticking his boot under one of the three dead guards on the ground. He flipped him over. Harry checked out the other two. All were dressed in jungle fatigues. Each man had a single bullet hole in his forehead.

"What the hell?" Harry said.

"Caparina."

"She did all this?"

"Yes."

"How?"

"It's what she does best, Harry."

"Holy shit. She's still alive."

"You'll find her hard to kill. Let's have a look inside."

This small command post was a more sophisticated

version of the operations shed they'd first found at the airstrip. The controller, dead no doubt of a bullet to the back of the head, was slumped forward at his monitor station before an array of flickering flat-panel screens.

The center screen still carried a real-time image of the bridge they'd just crossed. Another camera angle, mounted on the underside of the bridge, showed the tumult of the rapidly flowing river far below. The third monitor was broadcasting the view from the nose of a drone plane, probably the one they'd just seen, winding its way up the snaking ravine. The fourth was the interesting one. This camera, mounted on a Troll battlebot, was moving at a high rate of speed through the jungle. You could see it was headed toward some kind of low building at the end of a jungle trail.

That building looked extremely familiar.

Yeah. That robot tank was speeding toward the very building he and Hassan were currently inspecting.

Harry shouldered his Bizon and moved to the door. "Let's get outta here. Go take that little bastard out."

"Harry, wait. It's not a Troll. Look again at the monitor. Bottom right-hand corner of the screen. What do you see?"

Harry squinted his eyes, looking carefully up at the monitor. "A piece of boot? Bouncing around on top of a footrest?"

"Yeah. Look familiar?"

"Hell, yeah. It's Caparina's boot. She's coming back for us?"

"You're a quick study," Hassan said, rushing outside to greet his ex-wife, with Harry on his heels.

When Harry and Saladin stepped outside, they saw Caparina. But it wasn't a Troll she was riding. Not at all. It wasn't even a robot. It was a bizarre vehicle that resembled a lunar lander with four giant rubber wheels. It was driven by two carbon-bladed propellers mounted facing aft at the rear. Amphibious, probably. The thing was long and narrow so it could snake through jungle trails, Harry supposed. In addition to the video camera mounted on top of the heavy tubular roll cage, it had, Harry was surprised to see, a kind of steering wheel.

Caparina slid to a stop and smiled down at them from atop her centrally mounted buggy seat.

"I commandeered it," she said before anyone could ask. "Called a Skeeter. Get up here! There are two seats on the back behind me. C'mon, jump! I'm only about one minute ahead of them!"

"Them?" Harry said, not liking the sound of that.

The two men scrambled aboard the vehicle and began to fasten the safety harnesses that secured them to the twin seats aft. Caparina had shed her rain jacket somewhere along the line. She had the sleeves of her mud-streaked white T-shirt bunched up over her sunburned biceps. The thin cotton shirt did little to hide her figure. Her face, too, had been war-painted with streaks of brown mud. She shoved the hand throttles forward and the buggy lurched forward. She fishtailed around the low building and raced out onto the bridge.

"Wait!" Harry shouted. "Where the hell do you think you're going? We've got to find a way inside the central compound!"

"Not today, we don't," she said over her shoulder as

they raced back across the bridge. "There are at least half a dozen assorted machines on my butt right now. The sun's going down. They've got NV lenses that can see in the dark and we don't."

Harry didn't like the word *assorted,* either, but he decided to keep his mouth shut for the time being. He was having a hard time getting the buckle on his seat harness fastened and there was going to be no way to stay inside this damned buggy without being strapped in.

"Run away to fight another day," Saladin said with a wistful smile, lighting an unfiltered cigarette as if he'd just wandered off a goddamn golf course with a scratch round on his card.

"Fight?" Caparina said, glancing back at them. "You two have no earthly idea. I got a peek behind the curtain."

"Tell me what you saw," Harry said, leaning forward and putting his hand on her shoulder. "I need to check in. I need to know what we're up against before I call Washington."

"Tell them you've seen the future of warfare, Harry Brock."

"Yeah? And what future is that, Caparina?"

"Robots, Harry."

51

I love you, too, Sugarplum," Daisy had said to her
husband, marking her place in the old family Bible
with a sprig of bluebonnet wildflower. She was talking on the phone, sitting on his side of the sagging double bed. She'd come in the bedroom for something
when the phone by the bed had rung. She couldn't remember why, what she'd been looking for in here, but
she'd brought her Bible with her.

She must have been thinking about her husband.
How nervous he must be giving a speech in front of all
those important people tomorrow. Standing at the bedroom window, watching the night fall, but seeing in her
mind all those worry lines around his eyes.

That's right when the phone rang, and sure enough
it was Franklin.

One of those spooky coincidences. Serendipity, they
called it. Not serendipity exactly, but something kin to
that.

She'd leaned back against his soft pillow and listened
to him worrying silently at the other end of the line.

They had a bad connection, almost like he was calling from a cell phone. Which was silly, because he wouldn't own one. Wouldn't have one in the house.

"Franklin? You still there?"

"Yep. I'm here."

"Who's that yelling in the background?"

"Nice lady whose phone I borrowed. I guess I should give it back now."

"All right, but you just stop worrying, okay? Go on back to the hotel and try to get some sleep. Tomorrow's your big day. Especially with those tapes June got on video. I'm sure this Zamora fella is just a whole bunch of hot air. Just like the ones tried to scare us last time. And the time before that. All hat and no gun."

"I'm sure you're right. But please just do like I said, Daisy. Lock all the doors and windows and wait by the phone till the cruiser I called in gets out there. Okay?"

"I wish you hadn't done that. I'm a big girl. I can take care of myself. You know that."

"I normally don't bother you, Daisy."

"I know you don't. I'll go close up the house right now, honey."

"Good."

"Night, darlin'."

"G' night."

Daisy had waited for his click and then reached over to put the receiver back in its cradle on her nightstand. The house was suddenly very empty.

"Shoot," she said, staring up at the ceiling.

This wasn't the first time somebody had threatened to harm her to get to Franklin. The last time this had happened, somebody trying to scare them like this, she'd had to tell Franklin every time the phone rang and nobody was there, every time a car she didn't recognize slowed down going past the dirt road that led to their house, every time a letter or package came with handwriting she didn't recognize, every time somebody looked at her cross-eyed buying aspirin in the drug store.

The phone rang again.

"Hello?" Daisy said, thinking it had to be Franklin again.

Silence. Then they hung up.

Another wrong number.

Third one tonight. She hadn't told him about the first two. Didn't want to get him more upset about nothing than he already was.

She swung her legs off the big empty bed and stuck her feet into her house slippers. She'd finish locking up and then she was ready for bed. Had her nightgown on and everything. She'd already locked up all the doors anyway. Now she went from room to room, checking, locking the windows in the kitchen, the small back bedroom, and Franklin's study.

In the parlor, the two windows on either side of the front door were wide open with the thin curtains blowing in. She spread her hands on the windowsill and peered out into the dark night. Not too many stars out and it had turned cold. She heard the faint hum of tires out on the highway, somebody going past at a pretty good clip, on into the night. Then another car going in the opposite direction. Real slow.

She waited, listening for it to keep going past the little dirt road leading to their house.

It did.

The distant hum of a car going by on a lonely highway at night was a weird thing. She often lay in bed, waiting for sleep, and listened to them passing by out there. On a rainy night, especially, there was that sad hissing sound the tires made on the way to somewhere else. Who was it behind the wheel? Where were they going? What was going on in their minds as they watched that long yellow line disappearing in the rearview mirror? Was someone sitting next to them? Who?

Franklin had spooked her, all right.

No question about it. She pulled the damn front windows down, both of them, locked them, and went back into the bedroom. She got down on her knees beside the bed. Looked like she was fixing to pray, but she wasn't. She was just doing the next best thing, getting her gun. She bent down to fetch the double-barreled Parker. It was a rare Sweet Sixteen shotgun that Franklin had rejiggered to fit her for her twenty-first birthday. Sawed a couple of inches off the stock and gave it to her on the big day itself.

A sawed-off gun for a grown-up girl, the card said. She still had it stuck in the mirror all these years later.

She lifted the worn chenille bedspread and felt around with her right hand until her fingertips brushed the smooth cold barrels. She pulled it out and lifted it to her nose. God help her, she loved how that damn gun smelled, more than was natural in a woman.

Daisy kept half a dozen or so shells locked in the

right-hand drawer of the dresser. Double-ought buck-shot. She unlocked the drawer and fished out a couple. Then she levered the gun open and loaded it. She snapped it shut, made sure the safety was on, and went back into the kitchen. After laying the gun across the table, she lit a wooden kitchen match and turned on the gas, lighting the burner under the teakettle.

Sitting there at the kitchen table, facing the bedroom, she knew she could easily swivel her head and see both the front door and the back door. Looking straight ahead, she'd see anybody who just happened to be peeking in her bedroom window.

She'd deliberately left the porch lights on, front and back. And now she decided she'd best turn all the lights in the house off and sit in the dark. That way she could see them before they saw her.

Not that there was any "them," she had told herself, moving from room to room and extinguishing lights, but she'd heard something catch in Franklin's voice tonight when he told her how much he loved her.

You sit watching them in the dark, a kettle takes an extra long time to whistle. And, a ticking kitchen clock sounds a whole lot slower and louder. She had the Parker in her lap now. Pretty soon the cruiser would show up, park out in front of the house. She'd walk around the house with Homer or Wyatt or whoever was on duty, see that there was nothing to see, and then she could maybe go on to bed and get a little sleep. Even though it was so hard with Franklin gone.

Any damn bed felt ten sizes too big without your man in it. All her friends who'd lost their husbands said so.

The thought, when it first came, hit her so hard she almost fell out of her chair.

A woman alone.

That's what the Mexican guy in the restaurant had said to Franklin. You had to worry about a woman alone, he'd said. She was alone, sure. But so were a few other women here in Prairie.

June Weaver, for instance, was very much alone tonight. June had a son named Travis. Big strong football player. But he lived with his father.

June lived alone.

And it was June, she thought, getting nervous and excited all at once, not her, who had the videotape the man down in Key West wanted badly enough to threaten a man like Franklin over. If they knew about her tapes, they probably knew how to find June's address as easy as they'd find—

She jumped up from the table and ran to the phone mounted on the wall beside the stove. June's home number was among the ones scribbled in pencil just above the phone.

Line was busy.

She called the sheriff's office and got a recording. June's familiar drawl telling you what to do in case of an emergency. Which meant whoever was on duty was on the phone.

She took a deep breath and redialed both numbers. Still busy.

52

Daisy grabbed the shotgun and ran into her bedroom flipping the light switch by the door. To hell with it. She shed her slippers and stuck her feet into her boots. No time to dress, she grabbed her terry robe off the hook on the bathroom door. She grabbed a handful of shells from the dresser and stuffed them in the pocket of her terry. Then she hurried back to the kitchen. The phone was ringing off the hook and she paused just long enough to grab it.

"Hello?"

Nothing.

"Who is this, damn it?"

Hearing only silence, she slammed down the receiver, picked it up again, and redialed June's house.

Busy. So was the sheriff's line. Damnation.

Was that June trying to get through to the courthouse? Is that why Daisy couldn't get through to either number? Had to be it.

She ran out the front door and jumped into the pickup, laying the gun on the seat beside her. She twisted the key in the ignition and for a few horrible seconds thought the damn thing wasn't going to turn over. Then it did. She jammed it into gear and fishtailed onto the long dirt drive that led out to the highway. She didn't hardly slow down when she hit the blacktop, just cranked the wheel over and mashed her foot to the floor.

It was freezing in the cab. She pulled the worn terry robe tight around her but it didn't help much. She could be dead before that leaky heater under the dash started putting out anything significant enough to thaw her out.

June Weaver lived six miles further out from town than the Dixons did, in an old two-story farmhouse set back about a half-mile from the highway. The old house backed up onto a small creek that ran through the Weaver property. June had grown up on the place and then lived there by herself ever since the divorce. Her son was a gridiron star at Prairie High School. Going to college on a scholarship. He lived half the year with his dad and half with his mom. It was his dad's turn, she knew, because it was football season and his dad had him on some kind of training regimen.

Daisy was going fast as she could push it, over a hundred, and still it took forever to reach June's place. Her road wasn't marked very well and she had to slow down real fast to find the wooden sign tacked to a fencepost that said *Weaver* in faded red letters. She saw it, braked hard, and swerved off the highway and onto the road leading to the house. Just because it seemed to make sense, she'd doused her headlights as soon as she'd seen the sign and turned off the highway.

A quarter of a mile from the house she saw a car pulled over to the side, two wheels half in the ditch. June drove a twenty-year-old Olds Cutlass Supreme station wagon. Faded gold color. This was not that. It looked new, a two-door, and black. A Ford or a Chevy, she couldn't tell. All cars looked the same these days. Oklahoma plates. She slowed as she approached it, coming up on it from the rear, one hand on the Parker.

She eased up alongside, keeping her gun barrels just below the windowsill. The car was empty. She put the truck in park and climbed out into the frigid cold, taking her gun with her. She bent and looked into the driver's side window and saw a Hertz map on the front seat and a crushed pack of cigarettes on the floor. She stood up and looked at the big old house, the big dark sky looming over the rooftops. June's room was upstairs on the nearside corner. It was dark, too.

She reached her hand out and touched the hood of the rental car. It was still very warm and the engine was ticking softly.

Daisy decided she'd best walk the rest of the way. The sound of her truck pulling up in front of June's house was not going to help anybody tonight. She yanked the keys out of the ignition, stuck them in her robe pocket, and started walking.

A few minutes later, she was standing at the front door listening and not hearing anything inside. Her hands were shaking, but, hell, her whole body was shivering in the cold night air. She tried the screen door and found it unlocked. Her heart thudding in her chest, she twisted the front door knob. The door swung inward without a sound and she stepped inside. She stood quiet a second and then moved on into the living room, the Parker out front, her finger on the forward trigger and the safety off.

"June?" she whispered in the dark. "It's me—Daisy. Are you home, honey?"

Was she home? Maybe, maybe not. June normally parked the Olds in the garage around the back and she stupidly hadn't checked to see if it was back there. How dumb can one person be?

"June, listen, I'm just here to see if you're all right. Okay? I've got a gun. If you're not all right but you can hear me, say something."

The house was dead quiet.

Not a peep.

Nothing.

Daisy smelled something burnt in the kitchen. Like a pie that had been left in the oven too long. Make that chicken pot pie maybe. Daisy moved carefully toward the rear of the house, wishing she'd been smart enough to remove her damn cowboy boots. The wooden floors were creaky and a deaf man could have heard her coming a mile away.

She also wished she'd brought a flashlight. The house was at least a hundred years old, with heavy drapes covering the windows, and it was black as a crypt inside. Nothing looked the same in the dark anyway. She bumped into a little table with a porcelain lamp on it, grabbing the lamp just before it toppled over and hit the floor in a million tiny pieces.

She went through a wide arched door that led to a

long narrow hall going back to the kitchen. At the kitchen door she paused and peeked inside. She could tell the room was empty and was tempted to go turn the damn oven off.

Knowing that this was a really bad idea, she turned around and crept to the foot of the stairs. There was a door on her right; behind it were the cellar steps if she remembered correctly. She tried the knob. Unlocked. She opened it six inches and got that musty, rotted basement smell up her nose. She felt something sticky on the bottom of her boot. She had no idea what it was but since she feared the worst, she was thinking it might be blood. She raised her right foot and swabbed her index finger across her boot heel. She held it under her nose. It didn't smell like blood. It smelled like mud.

She shut the door quick.

There was a deadbolt on the outside of the basement door and she locked it. Then she headed up the stairs to the second floor, no longer caring that each step made a loud groan as she climbed.

"June? Are you up here?" she said, fingering the safety nervously. She was absolutely ready to squeeze the trigger if somebody suddenly appeared at the top of the steps.

Nobody did, but it didn't help her heart rate.

At the top of the stairs she stopped to get her bearings. June's room was at the far end of the hallway, all the way to the left. All the doors along the hall to the left were shut. Same thing to the right. Except there was a bathroom to her right, just across the hall, and she could see inside a little, shadows and shapes. The door was halfway open and she had to stifle the temptation to rush in and rip back the shower curtain just to see what she'd find there. All the shower rings flying and hiding in there was a—

Boo.

Having scared herself silly, she turned left and started toward the door to June's room.

"June? Junebug, are you up here, honey?"

She'd taken about three more steps along the worn carpeting when she heard a muffled noise behind the door. She raised the Parker to her shoulder, aiming it dead center on the door about four feet from the floor. Her hands were shaking badly again, even though it was a tad warmer in the old house. She was sorely tempted to just blow whoever was waiting for her behind that door to kingdom come and ask questions later.

But she moved toward it instead, dropped her left hand, and placed it on the crystal knob. She twisted it, felt it give a half turn, then stop. It was locked. It was an old door with an old lock. All she had to do was put her shoulder into it, force the damn door open, and put herself out of her misery one way or the other.

Something made her step back away from it. A noise. Movement inside. She took one, two steps back. She mounted the gun to her shoulder again and planted her left foot square in the center of the door. It slammed inward, splintering to jagged pieces.

She saw a figure silhouetted, standing in the center of the room by the big four-poster bed. Big shoulders. Small head.

"I'll shoot," she said. "I swear on a stack of Bibles I will."

Her finger tightened on the trigger.

"Daisy?" the person said, so soft she almost missed it. "June?"

"Jesus wept! It's you, Daisy!" June sobbed and took a few small steps toward her.

Daisy lowered the gun and embraced her friend. She was heaving sobs and shaking worse than Daisy was. June was wearing a thickly insulated stadium jacket, which accounted for the big shoulders she'd seen.

"June, what happened? I tried to call you but—"

"I-I came up here to get my medicine. Not ten minutes ago. I heard somebody downstairs. Heard a window break sure as I'm standing here. Down in the kitchen. I didn't know what to do. I locked the door and called the office but I couldn't get through. I tried to call you, too, but first it was busy and then no answer. I didn't know what else to—"

"June, listen. We don't have time. There may be someone down in the basement."

"What?"

"I saw mud on the floor. He must have tracked it in from the creek bed out back. That's the only mud around here I know of. The mud was tracked through the kitchen and stopped outside that door. He's still down there, I guess. I locked the door from this side."

"What do we do?"

"Is there another way out of the cellar?"

"The old coal chute in the back of the house. Don't use it anymore but it still works."

"We have to move. Now. Where's that videotape you're supposed to send Franklin?"

"Right there on top of the dresser in that FedEx envelope. I was just fixing to take it into town."

"Grab it and let's get out of here."

"What about the basement?"

"He's either already outside and coming around the house to kill us both or he's still locked inside down there and really pissed off."

"Daisy. You must be freezing. Take this coat."

She did. They descended the steps as quietly as they could. The door at the bottom of the steps was still locked shut. They tiptoed past it and then ran for the front door.

"C'mon, let's run. My truck's halfway down the drive."

They left the old house in a hurry.

When they reached the two cars, Daisy went over to the black rental car and peeked inside. Nothing on the seat had been moved. The driver had to be still in the basement. She fired both barrels of the shotgun, blowing out the two front tires.

"I can't shoot and drive at the same time," she told June, holding out the shotgun.

"Give me some ammunition," June said, taking the Sweet Sixteen and a couple of shells. She quickly loaded the shotgun and snapped the barrels shut.

They jumped in her truck and Daisy turned on the headlights and stuck the key in the ignition. Just as she twisted it, three starburst patterns exploded on her windshield, covering the two women with chunks of safety glass.

"He's over there!" Daisy cried, "See him? Coming around that mule stall. He's got a rifle!"

The yellow beams picked up a large man in a dark coat, now racing toward them. He was trying to shoot on the run. Rounds were hitting the truck, but the gunman was too dumb to stop and take a stance before he tried to shoot anybody.

"Okay, okay, take it easy," June said. "I've got this one."

He was less than a hundred yards away. She leaned out the window with the shotgun, aimed, and pulled both triggers.

The gunman staggered a few more steps, went down hard.

"He didn't think I'd shoot," June said, collapsing against the seat. "I didn't either."

"You got him!" Daisy said, "Let's get out of here!"

June leaned her head back on the seat said, "Oh my Lord."

Daisy got the pickup turned around in a hurry, and they tore off down the bumpy dirt road back to the highway.

"What time is it, Daisy?" June said a few minutes later, her eyes fixed on the empty two-lane road ahead. She was doing eighty.

" 'Bout nine-thirty."

"I mean exactly."

"Nine thirty-two. Exactly."

Daisy mashed the accelerator to the floor. "If we hurry, we can still make the FedEx machine in time for the last pickup at ten."

53

Hawke stripped off all his clothes on his way to the head in the aft owner's stateroom. He caught a mirrored glimpse of his naked body stepping into the green glass shower. Six months in the jungle on starvation rations were not an especially good way for a man to lose weight. When he'd been admitted to Lister Hospital, he'd weighed only 143 pounds and his body had been wracked with malaria and other exotic bugs.

Now, two months later, he'd reached his fighting weight of 180 pounds, give or take the odd ounce or two. God knew he was trying. Eating right, lowering his alcohol intake, and maintaining the strict daily exercise regimen in the ship's small gym had started to yield dividends. He was rapidly gaining in upper-body strength and increased muscle mass. The salt air and sunshine had been working wonders on him, body and, perhaps, his battered soul.

He leaned toward the glass and rubbed the stubble on his chin. He hardly recognized himself in the mirror anymore. His black hair was cut short in a military brush cut and he was clean-shaven. Save the stark white band around his middle, the tropical sun had deepened his skin color to a dark and healthy tan.

Physically, at least, he was definitely on the mend. The septicemia and malarial symptoms had diminished considerably, as well as the insomnia. He was sleeping better and the nightmares had ceased altogether. To his surprise and delight, the prior evening he'd successfully completed a six-mile night swim in heavy surf off a deserted Key West beach. He was trying to run at least five miles a day on the sandy beaches. Running in sand got you in shape in a hurry.

For all that, he was not yet nearly as fit as he liked to be before going into the field.

But this assignment wouldn't wait. He wouldn't even have time to wish Conch a proper farewell. He'd gotten a message that she'd called earlier. He hadn't called back. He didn't want to say good-bye over the telephone. An image came to him, unbidden, Conch, her lustrous auburn hair splayed out upon his pillow.

Hawke suddenly realized that he desperately needed a shower.

A cold shower, to be brutally honest, to purge all the thoughts of overwhelming desire that featured so prominently in his recent dreams now that he'd recovered. He was uncomfortably aware that a woman had elbowed the nightmare jungle demons aside, fighting for his nightly attentions. The beauteous and brilliant Consuelo had appeared. The scent of her, the touch of her hand sometimes lingered upon waking.

Instead of cold, he reached for the chromium handle marked HOT.

There was a circular rain-head fixture above his head; a hundred or so tiny apertures created the hot needlelike streams he craved whenever he bathed. The temperature was exactly as advertised and he closed his eyes and let the rain-head hammer the tension out of him. Steaming hot water streamed down on his head and shoulders and he stood under the downpour willing his mind and body to unwind.

Relax, he told himself, leaning his head back against the glass wall and controlling his breathing. There was no time for women in his life. Affairs of state beckoned, far more urgent and demanding than mere affairs of the heart. When it was over, if he were able, he would tend to the latter.

He squirted some of the sharp-smelling *L'Orange Verte* body shampoo into his hands, lathering his hair, face, chest and shoulders. Yes, relax, old sport. Focus on the mission. Prepare for battle. Take up the sword. Why was he so bloody distracted tonight of all nights? Two reasons, obviously. The second reason was a very special boat just delivered for the high-speed run down to Brazil.

The first reason?

He didn't even want to think about the first reason now.

But the boat, yes, he could think about her all right. He'd ordered her especially for this assignment and she was a wonder. She was one hundred and eighteen feet long with a beam of only thirty feet and could accommodate a crew of twenty. She drew only four and a half feet of water, a draught that should suit his purposes perfectly. He was planning a speedy trip up the Amazon, with a quick stop at Manaus to reprovision and pick up some equipment he'd need in the interior of the rain forest.

An Italian design group with the wildly improbable name of "Wally" had created the sleek Italian offshore powerboat to his unique specifications, adding armor and weaponry to what was more typically used as a high-speed *Côte d'Azur* cruiser.

The most avant-garde design team in the world had created a vessel built of advanced composites that could cruise offshore comfortably at sixty knots. Three 5,600-horsepower gas turbine engines drove the boat. People had described the new Wally design as "psycho origami."

To Hawke's naval eye, she was a staggeringly beautiful vessel. Her knifelike hull and fiercely aggressive superstructure resembled nothing so much as a wildly experimental stratospheric airship. Lazzarini-Pickering, the principal naval architects at Wally, had designed a boat all rake and flat planes and sharp angles from stem to stern. Stealth, Hawke thought, had long become a design cliché. But this new boat left any such tired ideas in her wake. Even sitting alongside an old Navy pier in Key West, she seemed to be doing fifty knots.

With his newly appointed crew present on the dock, he had just christened her *Stiletto,* smashing a bottle of Pol Roger Winston Churchill against her razor-edged bow. The crew had cheered wildly, eager to be off next morning. Already a crewman was carefully stenciling the newly christened yacht's name in blood red on her dark flanks. She was completely finished in a very deep gunmetal grey, vaguely metallic in direct moonlight.

Her magnificent bow, with a deeply inset teak deck, swept aft to a prominent knife-edged pilothouse built of carbon fiber and laminated composite glass. The three large rectangular windows of thick, bulletproof Lexan, sharply angled aft, were tinted a shade of dark charcoal. The massive air intakes for her gas turbine engines, mounted amidships on either side of the hull, owed much to intensive wind tunnel testing the Wally design team had done in Italy at the Ferrari racing facility at Maranello.

HAWKE PUT his head back and let the stinging water strike his face.

If it was possible for a man to love a machine, he thought, then this was love. Tomorrow morning, he would light out for the Equator and points south. He and his sleek new girl would go racing across the blue sea at speeds approaching one hundred knots. He would take her far up the Amazon, deep into the jungle, and show her where life and death lived together in such uneasy coexistence. He would find the devil standing at the crossroads and he would kill him.

"Need any help?"

With the noise of the shower, he hadn't heard her come into his bathroom. Now there were two more hands washing him. And her naked body was up against his, moving against his leg, her head nuzzling in the curve of his neck and shoulder. Her mouth was at him too.

Hawke said nothing. What was there to say? No? Yes? Maybe? He simply stood there in the green glass box with his head and shoulders against the wall, feeling her hands moving on his upper body now as she set about scrubbing his face and hair and shoulders.

"I was afraid you'd start without me," she said.

"If you get soap into my eyes, you'll be sorry," Hawke said.

"I'll try to be careful."

Her hands moved down the length of his arms and over his chest to his belly where they paused.

"You'll have to do the rest, I'm afraid," she said, blinking the streaming water from her eyes as she looked up at him, smiling.

"I will not. And be thorough about it, will you?"

"I've never washed a man before."

"Really? Then something tells me you are a woman with abundant natural talents."

She bent to her task.

"Hard work."

"Yes, isn't it."

I am drowning, he thought.

And then the woman was in his arms, the two of them were standing in the steamy mist and drenching downpour, both of their bodies slick with soap and heat and desire. He felt the soft weight of her lovely breasts pressed against his chest. He kissed her mouth for the very first time and was surprised at the violence of that kiss, at the need of it, how hard he kissed her and how hard she kissed back, the fierce tenderness of it all, and how wonderful she tasted on his lips.

Somehow, he managed to turn the shower off. He lifted her in his arms and carried her through into the bedroom where he gently laid her upon his bed. She was smiling up at him through half-closed lashes as he reached for the light.

It had been a long time since he had been with a woman and he took her with a gentle brutality, the sweetness of which surprised them both. When the moment came, she dug her fingernails into his hips to take him with her and then she cried out, blessing or cursing his name, perhaps both, and he drove himself into her harder and faster until at last he buried his face in her hair and urgently whispered her name.

Afterward, he lay still on his back, gazing up into the semi-darkness of his cabin and listening to the sound of their tandem breathing. Eventually, her breath slowed and became rhythmic and quiet. Moonlight was pouring through the half-opened shades on either side of his paneled cabin. He closed his eyes, sleep tugging at him, pulling him down.

At some point, he, too, must have drifted off, for he awoke with a start. There were still puddles of moonlight on the floor at the foot of the bed. He sat up, coming awake instantly. It was three o'clock in the morning. The bedside phone was ringing. The green light was blinking, meaning it was his private line.

He reached across her for it, but she'd already taken it off the hook and was sleepily saying, "Hello? Who's this, please? Yes, he's right here. Hold on a tick."

She rolled over and offered him the phone.

"Who is it?" he whispered, his cold eyes flashing with anger at her impertinence.

"It's your friend," she said, stifling a yawn as she handed him the phone.

"Which friend is that?" he said, covering the mouthpiece and instinctively dreading her reply.

"The American secretary of state, Consuelo de los Reyes."

"Conch?" Hawke mouthed the word.

"Mmm."

"Bloody hell, Pippa!" he whispered fiercely.

54

Hawke put the phone to his ear. The girl in his bed turned her back to him and yanked the bedcovers up over her head like a small child desirous of a private tantrum. Was she actually pouting? Bloody hell, he'd just have to ignore her.

"Good evening, Conch," Hawke said, with a good deal more bravado than he'd intended.

It was a full two minutes before Alex Hawke was allowed to insert a single word edgewise.

"Sorry," he finally managed to wedge in.

"He says he's bloody sorry!" he heard the girl under the covers cry, thankful the exclamation was somewhat muffled.

Pippa rose from the bed without another word, swaddled in trailing bedclothes, and padded silently across the hardwood floor to the head. She pulled the door firmly closed behind her. Thirty seconds later, she emerged once more in one of the white terry robes that hung in all the guest staterooms. Her hair looked different, and Hawke realized she must have used his silver military brushes. The robe, which was obviously what she'd worn when she'd crept below to his stateroom, was belted tightly about her waist.

She crossed his cabin without even a backward glance and, on her way out, banged his stateroom door shut just hard enough to avoid splintering it.

"Conch, this is not at all what it seems," Hawke said, wincing at the sound of the slamming door, easily loud enough to be heard over the phone. "Can we just move on?"

"Alex, relax. Your personal life long ago ceased to have any fascination for me. And I would happily let you go back to whoever you were doing except for one thing. I've just gotten off the phone with the president. He is in full crisis mode. And, he specifically asked me to call you."

"Conch," Hawke said, sitting up in bed, coming full awake. He was vastly relieved to be talking business. "How can I help?"

"In the last six hours, all hell has broken loose along the Mexican border. It's not exactly war, but it's close enough. We've had reports of multiple incursions by Mexican Army units in three different states. Border Patrol agents are being openly attacked, shot at without provocation by illegals with AK-47s. A few small border towns in Texas and New Mexico are under siege by rampaging drug gangs on motorcycles. There has been widespread burning and looting of remote farms and ranches. A few small border towns have reported fires raging out of control. Arson."

"God."

"Now, we're getting reports of American vigilantes raiding Mexican border towns in reprisal. Anti-American demonstrations in Mexico City and the countryside are turning violent. This thing is spiraling out of control, Alex. It's insane. The administration is all caught up in planning for the inauguration and we're on the verge of a full-fledged border war."

"An invasion," Hawke said. "That's just how the American people will see this. That the bloody Mexicans have invaded their country."

"Well, for Christ's sake, how else could they see it? It's what's been happening, Alex. You know the numbers. Ten thousand a day coming across. Twelve to twenty million illegals already over. And now, just what we need, Mexican Army units crossing the border."

"You have any proof of that?"

"No. Unfortunately, we don't."

"Uniformed troops takes this to a new level. Has anyone spoken directly to the president of Mexico about this?"

"Of course. That was the first call the president made. Mexican President Fox disclaims any knowledge of his army moving north across our border. Only he could give that order. He says he has not. But, he also says, if these vigilante reprisals against innocent Mexican civilians continue, he will declare Mexico in a state of war with the United States and move four divisions north. He will also immediately stop all oil flow to the U.S. through Mexico."

"What's the president's response?"

"He's going to pull every single National Guard unit

from the interior of the country and disperse them along that two thousand-mile-long border."

"That sounds a lot like war. How long will that take?"

"To organize and mobilize something like that? A week. Less."

"That may not be enough time."

"To do what, Alex?"

"Conch, the whole time I was in hospital I was thinking about Top. I ordered a new boat to navigate the Amazon and its tributaries. I can have a crew ready to go in less than twelve hours. For reasons I'm not sure you'll understand, I'm going back."

"I understand all right, Alex. It's commonly called revenge."

"THERE'S A powerful political angle to this, Alex. Border state governors and local law enforcement are besieging the president to do something immediately. In the meantime, the Minutemen are raising public funds to erect a border wall and money is flooding in. You saw the demonstration in L.A. last year. People waving Mexican flags, chanting, 'Viva la Reconquista!' The Mexicans are taking back the southwest without a shot being fired."

"With the help of the *jihadistas* I saw in the jungle."

"You think the Mexicans are innocent?"

"Hell, no. Ambrose and I interrogated a German diplomat named Zimmermann. Formerly the liaison between the Mexican government and the Brazilian terror army. He's dead now. I think the Mexicans are in this at some level. Maybe not all the way to the president, but someone."

"Alex, look. Our president was just narrowly re-elected, primarily because those southwestern states supported him. Believed he was going to stand up for this country and that our borders still meant something. If he doesn't put a stop to this borderline wildfire and fast, he's going to be country fried chicken right out of the box."

"Pulling the Guard away from all those major cities is a bad idea right now, Conch. A very dangerous idea."

"Right. We see thousands of Internet threats every day. We must have missed this one."

"I saw this threat with my own eyes, Conch."

"What do you want me to do? Invade Brazil? Argentina? We're stretched so goddamn thin right now—caught between Iraq and a hard place, isn't that what you said? Send what few troops we do have, and they'll only be concentrated and vulnerable along a broken border."

"That's only half of it. Send the balance of the Guard to the border and you leave major cities wide open."

"I know."

"Conch, the president doesn't really think the root of this problem is Mexico, does he? That's his dilemma. He can't say what he really believes publicly. He thinks I might be right. Tell me the truth."

"He's not sure, Alex. Nobody in Washington can figure out what the hell the Mexicans are up to, much less the rest of the LATAM leaders. But, every day, there are more attacks on our border agents. Six were shot in the last week. You've got *el Presidente* down there, somewhat believably disavowing any knowledge of armed troop incursions."

"And that may prove true."

"Privately, he has assured us he means us no harm. But he encourages an invasion of our country by millions of his citizens. And then says he's very pissed off at American reprisals against his people."

"Resulting in the current confusion at the White House and up on the Hill," Hawke said.

"With the Mexicans rubbing our faces in it on CNN. I'm just waiting for the mainstream backlash."

"A situation ripe for any third party trying to foment a U.S. border war, isn't it, Conch? Think about it."

"I see where you're going. But to what end, Alex?"

"The oldest trick in the book. Lure the enemy defenses away from your true military objectives. Spread the enemy along the perimeter. Then, attack at the center with overwhelming force."

"Washington."

"Washington. New York. Chicago. Maybe all three at once. I'm trying to find that out."

"You could be right, of course. And, right now, there isn't anyone in Washington who will at least acknowledge this possibility."

"You just did, Conch. I could talk to the president. Tell him what I know."

"There's no time. McAtee needs action now. That's the political reality. Everything points at the Mexican government."

"But the president is not entirely convinced. So his hands are tied."

"Right. He also believes there's something in what you've been saying, Alex. That the radical Islamist terror cells down in the Amazon are somehow mixed up in this."

"Everybody who hates America has a dog in this fight."

"And they've chosen Mexico as the battleground."

"Wouldn't you?"

"Good point."

"As I said, it's possible these border flare-ups may be diversionary tactics. The enemy wants to lure your troops in, leave the real targets undefended. That's not to say Mexicans reoccupying their old land won't want to hold on to it."

"It's perfect, isn't it, Alex? A perfect terror attack plan?"

"Nothing's perfect. Tell the president one thing for me. That the heightened Mexican border trouble may be just a ploy to draw all American troops south away from the center."

"A ploy. We leave our capital undefended. And we concentrate our troops along a clearly defined perimeter where they can be wiped out in a single blow. A formula for disaster."

There was silence while both of them contemplated the horrific ramifications of what she and Hawke had just said. A moment later, Conch spoke again.

"Alex, there's more. And it supports your argument.

General Charley Moore, JCS chairman at the Pentagon, called me three hours ago. He'd just stepped out of an emergency Oval Office briefing with the president. Moore's got a CIA field agent named Brock down in the Triangle area right now—"

"Harry Brock got me out of the jungle."

"Right. He decided to go native after he got you extracted. We thought he was dead. Anyway, he's just turned up alive in Brazil. He checked in with his boss six hours ago. He's seen something down there, something too big for him to handle alone. But he indicates it's a situation that needs immediate attention."

"Papa Top. Harry must have found him. You've got to order a strike, Conch."

"No. In this political climate, Washington has no intention of sending waves of bombers over the Amazon, Alex. You know that as well as anyone. I'm asking for your help. Off the books."

"I'll find Brock. We'll do what we can."

"Brock is holed up outside of Manaus, at a hotel called the Jungle Palace. He's there now, waiting to hear from you."

"Conch, could you get a signal to him? Tell him to sit tight. I'll pick him up there in forty-eight hours."

"Done. Listen, Alex, I'm afraid our hands are tied. I wish there was some way we could—"

"You don't have to say any more. I understand the difficult position you're in, Conch. Neither you nor the president can afford to have a clandestine U.S. operation blow up in your face right now, especially one in Latin America."

"That pretty much sums it up, Alex. As long as you understand that you'll be on your own as far as we're concerned."

"When have I not been on my own?"

"Right. That's your style, isn't it, Lord Hawke? The lone wolf himself."

"Conch. As soon as I return I will try to explain myself. But right now, I've got to get moving."

"Don't be stupid about this."

"I've got the right equipment. The right men. And I know the theater of operations intimately. I want to go this alone. I wouldn't have it any other way."

"When can you shove off?"

"*Stiletto* can be under way in six hours."

"Alex, I hate to say this to you. Especially given how much I hate you at this moment. But I have a really bad feeling about this thing."

"Well, Conch, you know what, it *is* a really bad thing."

"Don't push it. I thought you'd already died once in Brazil."

"Yeah, well, I wasn't ready. I guess I wanted to keep my hand in a while longer. Although some days I feel like just pissing off and retiring to the bloody Bahamas. Lie in a hammock all day and whistle 'Rule, Britannia.' "

"Good night, Alex."

"Good night, Conch."

"Be careful. *Vaya con Dios.*"

55

Hawke was up and moving early next morning. The rising sun sent brilliant red rays streaking across the wave tops as the day dawned, cool and clear. Beyond the walled perimeter of the old Naval Station, Key West was still sleeping it off.

The only audible sound on *Blackhawke*'s topmost deck was the cry of screeching white gulls and black scimitar shearwaters, diving and swooping off the ship's great stern. That, and the martial tune of the Union Jack on its massive mahogany staff, snapping smartly in a fresh morning breeze.

Hawke found Ambrose Congreve already tucked in to his customary pair of three-minute eggs. Seated all alone on the curved stern banquette, the famous detective was wearing a wide-brimmed Panama and a three-piece suit of pale yellow linen. He was scribbling furiously in the code book.

"Good morning, Alex," Ambrose Congreve said. His voice was near to bursting with hearty cheer. "Sleep well, old pot?"

"Like a babe in arms," Hawke replied with a wry smile.

He had finally given up all hope of sleep and risen at five. After a few more necessary phone calls and packing enough gear and tropical kit for two weeks south of the Equator, he'd subsequently gone for a very long swim outside the harbor. He'd pushed himself to the point of exhaustion and beyond just to see if he could do it. He could, and he felt invigorated by the effort. He was more than ready to shove off.

Stiletto was moored along the breakwater, just aft of *Blackhawke,* and arc lights had been blazing on the dock all night long. She was still taking on provisions for a two-week voyage to the tropics. The crew was also loading additional ammunition for the new weaponry Hawke had added at a yard in the south of England. And racing to finish topping off her tanks. After briefing them, Hawke had ordered everyone assembled on her foredeck to be ready to shove off in two hours.

"Have some breakfast," Congreve said, offering a plate of salted fish. "Kippers?"

"I'm trying to quit kippers. Hated the bloody things all my life."

Hawke pulled up a chair and the steward took his order of fruit, coffee, eggs, and toast with Dundee's orange marmalade.

Ambrose said, "The oddest thing. I saw Pippa hurrying down the gangway at dawn this morning. Had her luggage in tow and there was a taxi waiting on the dock. She looked . . . unhappy."

"I booked her an early flight. She was leaving today anyway."

"Well, you're in a mood."

"I am indeed."

"I won't ask."

"Looks like you're making progress with the Da Zimmermann code, Constable," Hawke asked, eying the opened book beside Congreve's plate. The pages were now much marked up with Congreve's pencil scrawling and tabbed with tiny yellow stickers from front to back.

"I will tell you one thing. There is going to be an attack of some kind. And it's been in the works for quite a long time."

"Where? Washington? New York?"

"America, to be sure. But nothing more specific as to date or location yet."

"Too soon to bring Conch into this?"

"Hmm. What can I tell her at this point, really? It's odd, but I keep stumbling across the phrase, *his hand on the Bible*. Whenever does one put one's hand on the Bible?"

"When you swear to something?"

"Hmm. Anyway, halfway through the novel, the coded message comes to an abrupt halt. Absolute gibberish again after page 230. We've hit a wall, I'm afraid."

"You're joking. It just stops working?"

"Yes. I'll keep at it. By the way, Conch was looking for you last night. She rang my cabin. Apparently all hell is breaking loose."

"Yes. She reached me."

"And?"

"Ambrose, I'm terribly sorry to do things this way. I know you loathe surprises. But, I've canceled your flight for London later this morning."

"Really?" Congreve said, touching his linen napkin to his lips. "I must say the idea of a few more days in the tropics is not without appeal."

"I've booked you another. In fact, I believe that's your flight landing now."

"That thing?"

A few hundred yards away, a large baby blue seaplane was on the downwind leg, about to touch down on a glassy stretch of sea beyond the breakwater. She had her nose up and her floats were just about to splash.

"Yes, that thing," Hawke said. "It's quite beautiful, isn't it? An old Grumman Goose. A G-21. Built just after the war, but newly rebuilt, I assure you. The current owner replaced her old radial engines with new turbocharged ones according to Stokely. Stokely Jones is aboard that plane, by the way. I invited him to breakfast."

"Well, I should be delighted to see him again. But, Alex, you can't expect me to actually fly in a contraption like that? Where the bloody hell are you sending me?"

"Ambrose, our only hope is to crack that bloody code book. I think it's the only way to figure out what these bastards have planned. So I need you to get down to Manaus and find the ambassador's widow. Today. You'll be met on the other end by an American named Harry Brock. CIA, and a good man. A NOC, as it happens."

"Not On Consular. Nonofficial."

"Yes. If he buys it, there's no receipt. He's making all the arrangements at that end. You two have one mission. Find Zimmermann's widow, wherever she is. Take your book. Get to the bottom of that bloody code as quickly as possible. I don't exaggerate when I say deciphering that thing as rapidly as possible may prove to be vital. For all of us."

"I couldn't agree more, Alex."

"Look at you, Ambrose," Stokely said, suddenly appearing on the top step of the starboard staircase. "Got the whole Sydney Greenstreet vibe going on."

"Ah, Stokely!" Ambrose said, rising from the table to embrace the huge man. "Marvelous to see you," he said, pounding his broad back.

"Stoke," Hawke said, hugging him as well, "have some breakfast."

"Is that crate airworthy?" Congreve asked, nervously watching the ungainly *Blue Goose* taxi across the water toward the fuel pier.

"Man, I hope."

"Ambrose, you and Stokely simply must find that widow alive. She's the only one who can possibly help us now."

"I agree. I don't hold out much hope for cracking the balance of the book without her."

"*Stiletto* should arrive in Manaus approximately forty-eight hours from now. God willing, and a calm sea, she'll be safely berthed at the Jungle Palace hotel at 0700 hours day after tomorrow."

"And *Blackhawke*?"

"She stays here."

"I'll see you in Manaus, then, Alex," Congreve said, rising from the table. "Godspeed."

Stoke said, "We take off for Shit Creek at eight, Constable. Don't forget your paddle. And, don't be late."

"*Late* does not appear in my vocabulary."

The resplendent criminalist doffed his tan Panama hat and disappeared down the after staircase.

"So, tell me, boss, how the hell are we supposed to find this bad boy in all that jungle?" Stoke said.

"I'm working on that."

Stoke smiled.

"Bring your laptop, boss. We get lost, we'll just go to Google and punch in 'Amazon.com.' "

56

THE BLACK JUNGLE

Muhammad Top, wearing a custom leopard-skin burka and one of his trademark bowler hats, was seated at the controls of a war machine headed east along M Street. He was nearing the target. The softly flashing blue and yellow lights above the Ogre's control and fire monitors bathed his twisted features with an unpleasant sheen. The massive tank was designed to be autonomous on the battlefield.

But what a thrill it was to be at the controls of such a monster.

The Day was coming. The Hour approached. The Minute. Not quite yet, but soon, very, very soon. His eyes were narrowed in concentration as he spun a cursor, using all the electronic marvels at his disposal to maneuver the great mechanical brute through the snowy streets of Washington, D.C.

In his headset, he could hear the squealing protests of the massive caterpillar tracks as he rounded a tight corner into a broad avenue. He had tamed the beast. He could make it go anywhere he wanted. Over the on-board Bose audio system, in his stereophonic head-phones, he was enjoying one of his many guilty Western pleasures. The Stones.

His left hand hovered over a small toggle switch just now illuminated on a panel just below the monitor. The Ogre's Fire Control System was armed and in READY mode.

In a few moments, he would strike the first blow. He would see the flash and hear the thunderous roar of his anti-personnel cannons. Only then, when those who opposed were all dead and posed no further threat, when he had a clearer picture of his target, would he launch his missiles. They would streak away toward their target, creating glowing orange holes where once proud monuments to a former civilization had stood.

The Day was less than seventy-two hours in the future.

He was in drive-by-wire mode, guiding a giant hulk-ing monster, nicknamed the Ogre, through the middle of the New Year's first massive snowstorm. It weighed slightly in excess of one hundred tons. Despite its heavy composite armor, it was capable of speeds up to sixty miles per hour and could climb steps at angles of thirty degrees.

Ogre would accept commands from either human or non-biological intelligence. There was also a manual override system that allowed the Ogre to act au-tonomously. In that mode the tanks were fully func-tional on their own, receiving real-time data input and making fluid battlefield decisions as conditions warranted. It was this specific function that had so electrified Khan in the early days of the planning.

Top, however, had always envisioned a more personal approach to destruction. He didn't want to be seated deep inside a concrete bunker in the fucking jungle when the glorious Hour came. He wanted to be there in the front row when the devil finally got his due. He hadn't told Khan about his feelings. Khan believed in the perfection of machines. He believed the fewer humans involved in making war, the less chance for plans to go awry. He was right, of course, if you didn't count the victims.

The digital information now being fed to the Ogre's CPU was precisely replicating the official NOAA weather forecast for the following week in the Mid-Atlantic States.

A massive low-pressure system was moving across the Midwest directly toward the nation's capital. The onboard dynamic weather analysis presented the tank "Sensor Command" with an up-to-the-second picture of the developing storm system and alerted the driver to every nuance of temperature, wind speed, barometric pressure, and, most importantly, road and off-road conditions.

The snow was nearly blinding. Only the radar and GPS functions now depicting real-time obstacles on his satnav screen kept him on course. Five minutes earlier, he'd almost found himself careening past the Jefferson Memorial and plunging into the icy Potomac. But a loudly bleeping alarm sensor had alerted him to his course deviation and saved him at the last instant.

The icy Washington roads, barely visible and unfamiliar, presented the human sensor operator with a bewildering challenge. Still, with the well-practiced Top at the controls, the enormous treads had been successfully grinding up the miles since his insertion inside the District of Columbia's theater of operations.

Top had been manning the controls for nearly an hour. With the exception of that one minor mishap, he had successfully navigated a crossing of the Key Bridge. He had then entered the maze of confusing side streets of Georgetown. He was now rounding Washington Circle and preparing to move the beast left onto Pennsylvania. So far, he'd been unopposed by forces of any significance. Two D.C. police cruisers had chased him for a few blocks, but he'd dispatched them with only his 23mm machine guns.

He heard a disconcerting alarm sounding. Out of the corner of his eye, he watched the blinking dot of orange light moving across the computer-generated map of Washington, D.C. It was coming this way. At a disturbingly high rate of speed. The words *Manned Armed Vehicle* flashed at the bottom of the screen. *Jara,* he whispered, shit. A tank.

Top spun his turret toward the location of the glowing dot five kilometers away. He had his electronic jam screen up. He didn't think the thing could get close. He wondered why EMP hadn't knocked the vehicle's guidance systems out. Perhaps it was operating visually. In any event, he had plenty of low-yield missiles yet to expend and he was unafraid. He felt, not without reason, invulnerable.

He spun his fire control cursor, moving a bright red dot across the screen with well-practiced ease. When the red dot and the orange dot merged, he stabbed at a yellow button on his panel.

Both blinking lights disappeared, praise be to Allah!

Then he turned his gaze to the icy road dead ahead. He was nearing one of his primary targets. He could feel the shudder of nervous excitement building inside. It was a feeling very much akin to lust.

Top's right hand, the one gripping the joystick, trembled slightly as he twisted the throttle, shoved the stick forward, and accelerated. It was cramped inside, and though there was artificially cooled air, his face shone with a thin coating of sweat.

He successfully navigated the sweeping left-hand turn at forty miles an hour and slowed the machine as he pulled up abreast of the White House. With darting jabs at his controls, he armed the main fire control systems and reached out for the small joystick that operated the giant tank's turret. A second later, he had the North Portico of the White House squarely in his primary gun sight.

A great lantern hung suspended by chains from the porte-cochere that sheltered the North Portico. The lantern glowed a soft yellow through the sleeting snow. He'd seen countless photographs of this famous scene in his life, harried diplomats coming and going through this storied portal, trying to save the world from people just like him.

A burst from his forward machine guns obliterated the lantern. He moved his hand over the primary weapons control panel. He would fire his first missile right through the Great Satan's door!

"THAT'S ENOUGH," he heard Dr. Khan say in his headset. "Come on out. Playtime is over. We're due at the river for the demonstration."

"I did well?" Top asked his superior, exiting the Ogre Tank Simulator. It was even colder in the underground bunker than it had been inside the simulator. And he didn't have the Stones to keep him company, heat his blood.

"Yes. You did well. Almost perfect, in fact."

"Only machines are capable of perfection, Leader," he responded, knowing the words Khan wanted to hear.

"It's a pity you won't be driving one of these brutes north, Muhammad."

"Yes. I come by these skills naturally, Dr. Khan," Top said, accepting his fleece-lined bomber jacket from one of the technicians. "My father commanded the 192nd Armored Division in the Valley of Tears. Golan Heights. 1973."

"I knew your father well. He was a fierce warrior. But he lost. A mere 150 Israeli tanks stopped 1,400 invading Syrian tanks in the bottleneck. It was a disaster. I vowed that day never to see a repeat of your father's humiliation."

Abu Khan knew whereof he spoke.

In 1973, in the Yom Kippur War, Dr. Abu Musab al-Khan had commanded all the mechanized armor divisions deployed on the Golan Heights. It was a mere two-hour tank ride south to Israeli territory. The Golan

Heights protected Israel's north. Any attack from Syria had to be topographically channeled through one of only two passes in which armored vehicles could cross.

The surprised and vastly outnumbered Israeli troops held off the invaders for a vital 48 hours. In that time, they were able to mobilize and deploy the necessary forces required to beat back and ultimately defeat the Syrians.

Khan had long since redeemed himself. He had been responsible for the Syrian buildup of highly advanced weaponry in response to the Yom Kippur disaster. Now, in order to implement the late Hafez al-Assad's vision of a "Greater Syria," Khan's generals possessed 4,000 manned tanks on the Golan crestline.

The troops had doubled in size and were equipped with Scud-C missiles, twice as powerful and four times more accurate than the Iraqi Scuds that rained down upon Israel during the Gulf War. When war came, his plan was to unleash vast numbers of the new Scuds against Haifa and Tel Aviv, sowing widespread civilian panic and seriously disrupting Israel's emergency reserve mobilization.

But Khan had far grander ideas. At a secret meeting in Damascus, he had seen Top's Latin American battle plan in its infancy. It immediately dawned on him that here was a chance to build, test, and field his dream. A remote-controlled air force. And a mechanized army incapable of human foibles and battlefield stupidity because it would be autonomous once launched.

"You've created an invincible army, Leader."

"Yes, God willing. Because there is no chance of

human error. Keep that in mind when you play your little war games, Muhammad, my brother. The Day approaches. It is out of your hands now. *Inshallah.*"

Top looked Kahn squarely in the eyes. In truth, he had come to believe in the vision. The wizard from Damascus believed that infallible machines should strike the first blows in this jihad. Death would roam the streets of Washington, unseen and unexpected. The Cause would be better served if Abu Khan and Muhammad Top were here in the bunker on the Great Day. Let infallible machines do the work of destroying the enemy's military and political infrastructure.

Then send the armies north to wreak havoc on the civilian population.

"Yes, Leader. It is out of my hands."

"I believe the *Bedouin* is ready for inspection?"

"She is. Let us go at once."

Bedouin was a small, unmanned submarine that would ultimately carry a single but very lethal piece of cargo. The sub could be operated from remote locations up to 7,000 miles away. Inside *Bedouin* was a 150-kiloton nuclear weapon. The warhead was shielded to provide protection from the electronic pulse of any simultaneous nearby nuclear explosions. In two hours, the Volkswagen-sized sub was due to be airlifted to Manaus for further shipment to Mexico. From there, *Bedouin* would be transported by tractor-trailer truck to a predetermined location in America.

The location was a small farm just outside of Lee's Ferry, a tiny town located on the Potomac River in Virginia. It was called Morning Glory Farm. Apple orchards. The farm was owned by an extremely wealthy individual from Rio de Janeiro. He in turn was owned by a large multinational company headquartered in Dubai.

The man, a German, had been a traitor.

But the traitor was dead now.

His name had been Zimmermann.

57

"Won't this truck go any faster?" June asked Daisy.

"Do you want to drive? I'm going as fast as I can without killing us."

"I'm just looking at my watch. Don't get all uppity with me, Daisy Dixon."

"What time is it now?" Daisy said, glancing over.

"Quarter to."

"Damn. And FedEx is always on time, too. I've seen his van. Pulls up next to the automated station right on the button every time."

"Well, step on it then. Take the shortcut to the Courthouse."

"Cut through the filling station? Are you crazy? Ross will have his chains up on both sides. He closes at nine."

"When is the last time you took the shortcut, Daisy?"

"I'm married to Franklin. I don't take short cuts."

At five minutes to ten, they rounded the corner on two wheels and careened onto Main Street six blocks west of the Courthouse Square. Daisy thought the street was strangely empty for a Friday night. Most of the lights were off. Everything looked shut up, dark, like a ghost town. Weird-feeling. Something was seriously wrong with this picture.

Elvis had definitely left the building.

"What the hay is going on around here, girlfriend?" June said, taking the words right out of Daisy's mouth.

"The streetlights are all shot out," Daisy said. "Some windows too."

Daisy slowed to a crawl and doused the headlights. They were still five blocks away from Courthouse Square. The FedEx machine sat on the sidewalk right out front of the old building. She looked at her watch. Five minutes until the FedEx delivery kid showed. Daisy knew him from when she taught art at the Prairie High School. His name was Buddy Shirley. He was never, ever late for class.

Daisy saw something else that was very disturbing. A couple of doors were hanging ajar, like folks had left in a hurry. Somebody had shot up the town.

Daisy rolled to a stop and set the brake. "Something's not right. We better just sit tight till we know what's going on."

"Yeah."

"Wait a second. What's that truck doing up there?" Daisy whispered a few seconds later.

"Hell if I know," June said. "We better stop before they see us."

There were very few cars parked on Main Street. But there was a big truck parked directly across from the courthouse. It looked like an old moving van. It was parked outside Sam Robin's appliance store. Which was fine, except for the fact that the rear doors now opened wide and there was a man inside with a powerful flashlight. He pointed it down the street, the beam pausing on the pickup a second, then moving on.

They'd crouched low on the seat.

"Think he saw us?"

"Hell, I don't know. I hope not. Stay down."

As the women watched from four blocks away, a couple of large boys carried another huge cardboard box right out the front door and hefted it up onto the truck's hydraulic lift. Daisy had seen boxes like that. Not that she'd ever owned one, but she knew what it was all right. A super-sized flat-screen TV that cost three thousand dollars minimum.

"Looters," June said.

"Yeah. We'll set tight right here. Buddy has to pass this way to make his pickup."

"You think those looters have guns, don't you, Daisy?"

"What do you think, Junebug?"

"That old truck does not look the least bit local."

"No, it's not. Those boys look Mexican."

"Well, they've got brazen enough, haven't they?" June said. "Just cross the border and do your Friday night one-stop shopping."

"Something bad is going on," Daisy said, her voice low. "Nothing feels right in this town."

June nodded her head. "So, how are we going to get Buddy the envelope? You can't just drive up there next to the van and put the envelope in the FedEx slot and hope Buddy picks it up. Those hombres up there would just as soon shoot us as look at us, you ask me."

"There are more shells in the pocket of my robe. Here. Load up. Both barrels. Have it ready in your hands."

June reloaded the Parker Sweet Sixteen. She snapped it shut with a satisfying click and thumbed the safe button forward to Fire.

"Do you think they saw us?" June said again through compressed lips, looking out of the corner of her eye.

"I think they're pretty busy taking Sam's inventory," Daisy said, grinning at June.

"Shoot, no wonder folks around here hate—"

"Hush! I'm thinking."

"It's ten o'clock, Daisy, on the button," June whispered fifteen seconds later, her head way down, just peeking over the dash at the looters down the street, keeping the gun low. Then she craned her head around and peered back over the windowsill, looking for headlights coming up Main.

"Where is he? You think he got spooked?"

"Buddy will be here, June. Any second now. I've got an idea."

"What is it?"

"I'll flag Buddy down when he comes and just hand him the envelope as he goes by. You put the sheriff's Key West address with a zip code on the envelope?"

"Sure did. Look here. Just like he asked me to."

Daisy grabbed the envelope, opened her door, and stepped out onto the sidewalk. She glanced down the street at the looters, fervently wishing the pickup's interior dome light was busted like it normally was. She shut the door softly and started around the rear of the truck.

"Here comes Buddy," June said from inside the truck. They both saw the van's single pair of headlights moving very quickly up Main Street toward them. Daisy saw the dome light come on again in her truck as June cracked her door.

"June! Stay there! Don't get out of—"

"You're not leaving me here," June said, swinging her door open and stepping out into the street just as Buddy's white FedEx Home Delivery truck roared by her going about sixty, blurring the purple and green letters on the side. Nearly took her door off. When Buddy was almost abreast of the automated pickup box, he hit the brakes hard and fishtailed to a stop, leaving the engine running. The driver's side door flew open, and she saw Buddy's boot hit the pavement.

"Buddy! No!" Daisy screamed, running down the street toward him as fast as she could, "Stay in the damned truck! They've got guns!"

There was a sudden staccato explosion of heavy automatic weapons fire from the other side of the street. Daisy registered a muzzle flash from the man standing on the lift at the rear of the big van. The FedEx panel truck rocked with the force of the slugs and the passenger side window imploded in a shower of glass. She saw two more men rush out of Sam's, both pulling weapons and shouting.

Daisy saw Buddy start to crumple to the street. He

caught hold of the driver's side door, though, and pulled himself back inside behind the wheel. She watched him still trying to pull his door closed and then the panel truck lurched forward, swerving crazily as Buddy floored it, yanking his boot inside. The two looters who'd come out into the street chased him half a block, firing at the back end of the van.

"Go, Buddy!" she screamed as she turned away. "Get out of here!"

58

Daisy ran as fast as she could to her pickup truck without looking back at the Mexicans. She was waiting for one of them to shoot her in the back but nobody did. Back in the truck, June was sitting straight up in the seat and she had the shotgun poking out her window. "They shot Buddy, didn't they?" June said, and there wasn't a trace of fear in her voice now. It was as if the woman had suddenly been rendered nerveless. "Let's go see if we can help him."

Daisy jumped in and floored the accelerator before she popped the emergency brake handle. It was a technique her older brother Rance had taught her. It still worked.

"Whoa!" June said, as they shot forward, the rear tires burning rubber.

"What are you doing?" Daisy cried. June was half-in, half-out the passenger window and they were coming up fast on the old moving van.

"Shooting back," June said. She was sighting down the barrel at the hombre standing on the lift watching

Buddy's escape. The big man turned toward them at the sound of their oncoming truck, raising his gun.

June aimed the shotgun at him, leading him, and pulled both triggers almost simultaneously. The noise inside the truck was deafening.

"Don't mess with Texas, asshole!" June had screamed over the blast.

Daisy was going way too fast now to concentrate on anything other than the road in front of her. The two remaining Mexicans leapt out of the road just in time to avoid being hit by the pickup. The moving van blurred by on her right. She no longer could see the one who'd been standing on the lift.

"Did you get him?" she asked June.

"Yeah," she said, looking back. "Uh-oh. Keep going. The other two are climbing up into the cab."

She saw the lights come on in her rearview mirror. "Here they come."

The moving van was pulling quickly away from the curb in pursuit. It probably wasn't all that speedy, but then neither were they. She mashed down the accelerator, firewalling it.

"Take some more shells, Junebug," Daisy said, eyes straight ahead and both hands on the wheel. "Take 'em all."

"All my life I've been wondering what 'riding shotgun' meant," June said, digging once more in Daisy's robe for the cartridges.

Daisy smiled at her.

"There's Buddy," she said. "I think we're gaining on him."

They could see Buddy's taillights now, disappearing around a bend in the highway and starting up a hill. They were outside the town limits, heading east into the desert over toward Kingsville. The headlights of the big van were still in her rear view, but the Mexicans were having a hard time catching up.

"Can you catch him?"

"He's faster. I'm going to try."

"Can't you signal him to stop? With the lights, I mean?"

"We can't stop, June. The two amigos are still on our butts."

Daisy hit the gas and just stayed off the brakes. About three miles out of town she finally managed to get right up on Buddy's tail and started flashing her high beams at him. He must have recognized her green Ford truck because he slowed down just enough for her to pull alongside. June pulled the shotgun back inside the cab and stuck her head out.

"Buddy, it's us! It's me, June!" she shouted and she saw his pale face at the window looking over at them. There was blood on Buddy's face and down his front. A lot of it.

"What do you want?" he screamed above the wind. "I'm running a little late!"

"We got a FedEx package to go out!" June yelled. "Needs to be in tonight's shipment. Extremely urgent!"

"Tell him it's a matter of national security," Daisy said.

"A matter of national security, Buddy!"

He nodded that he understood.

"Hand her on over," Buddy cried back. "I'll slow up."

"Hold on a second," June said, and turning to Daisy, "Slow down a little, will you please? And don't swerve so much."

Buddy decelerated to about fifty. Daisy matched his speed and eased her truck over till they were just neck and neck about three feet apart. She tried to maintain that exact separation but they were on a winding road and it was a whole lot harder than it looked in the movies.

"How's this?" Daisy said.

"Pony Express?" June grinned at her, putting the gun between her knees and grabbing the FedEx envelope off the seat.

"Exactly."

"Here you go, Buddy!" June said, extending her arm to the FedEx driver.

Buddy reached out and grabbed hold of the envelope in June's hand.

"Got it?" June asked him before she let go.

"Got it!" Buddy yelled, pulling it inside. "Yessum, I'll make sure she goes out tonight! Guaranteed."

"Good! Are you hurt too bad?"

"No, ma'am. Just a scratch I believe."

"Buddy, you get yourself over to Southwest Medical and have somebody stitch you up, okay?"

"Yessum, soon as I get my mail here delivered. Y'all have a good evening now!"

"G'night!"

June sat back and pushed her hair out of her eyes

and they watched the little FedEx truck roar away and disappear over a hill.

"Well, that was fun," June said, smiling over at Daisy. "Are the Mexicans still on our tail?"

"We lost 'em. They couldn't keep up on the steep hills."

"Roll your window up for starters. It's cold as snow in here," Daisy said.

"Whoopee," June said, cranking her window up, "Hey. Look at the sky over there. To the south."

"What is that?"

"Something's burning, I reckon."

"Looks like a lot of 'somethings' burning to me. Over toward Dolores."

"Let's go see."

"I guess that's where what's left of our police force went. I was wondering who gave the looters the key to the city."

Daisy took the first right she could. It was old state road 59 heading south. The sky on the horizon was aglow with a red haze as she crested a hill. A big eighteen-wheeler passed her headed the other way, smoke pouring from its twin stacks as it chugged uphill. Then, a bunch more trucks evenly spaced behind it. One after another, until she thought the line would never end. She counted: twelve trucks in all.

Before she could even digest that fact, she saw something else. Right behind the very last truck in the convoy, one of the two brand spanking new Crown Victorias newly acquired by the Prairie PD.

"That was Homer Prudhomme, I do believe," June said, craning her head around to look. "Wonder where the heck he's going. Following that big convoy?"

"Off on another wild goose chase, I reckon," Daisy said. "It is his night off, I guess."

"Prairie, Texas's, very own Ghostbuster," June said, shaking her head, and Daisy laughed until she cried.

59

Homer had just passed a battered pickup headed in the opposite direction on SR-59. Just a blur, the vehicle was going pretty fast, but it sure had looked an awful lot like Mrs. Dixon's truck. He was too busy trying to stay on the semi convoys' tail to look around and be sure. It had been an old pea-green Ford pickup. Out the corner of his eye, he'd seen a couple of ladies up front, laughing about something maybe.

He remembered it was Friday night. He hoped whoever was in that truck wasn't counting on whooping it up over in the border town of Dolores tonight.

Dolores, at least some of it, was on fire. In his rearview mirror he could still see the reddish glow above the town. Arson, he suspected, because it sure looked from here like it was more than one building. Time was, arson was an occasional thing. A destitute rancher burning his barn down hoping to collect the insurance. But that was then. Now, it seemed like the whole county was going crazy.

All of Texas, if you wanted to be honest with yourself. It was certainly not a good night for a couple of nice ladies to be running around out in the desert that was for sure. It was a bad night, Homer felt, and it was going to get worse before it got better.

Well, he thought, the sheriff was still down in Key West. Supposed to be coming home some time after his talk at the conference, whenever that was. So, maybe that had been Miz Dixon after all, going out to party with a friend, maybe. Like they say, while the cat's away the mice will play.

He smiled and shook his head. It was a side of Mrs. Daisy Dixon that he'd never imagined. She was such a quiet, churchgoing lady from what he'd seen. When she didn't have her nose buried in some Nora Roberts novel, she was fixing supper, tending her knitting, mending Franklin's shirts, or mucking out the barn. He'd never seen her at a single solitary Saturday night square dance, and he'd pretty much decided she had to be one of those foot-washing Baptists who frowned on dancing.

To be truthful, Homer had been a little worried about Mrs. Dixon ever since the boss had left town. All alone out there, and, things being as unpredictable as they'd been lately, it scared him some. She'd always been good to him, the problems he'd had, and he appreciated it maybe more than she knew. It was time to give something back.

But, when he'd mentioned it at work, his idea of just dropping by to check on the missus occasionally, June Weaver had told him in no uncertain terms to leave her be. "You do that, she'll bless you out from here to next

Sunday, Homer Prudhomme," June had said. "She's settler stock, Homer. Texas women can take care of their selves. You'll just make her mad you show up out there looking worried."

So Homer had left well enough alone. If things got worse in Prairie though, he'd make sure to look in on her or just make up an excuse to call and check. Drop off a new mystery book, maybe.

Homer felt right guilty about sticking with his ghost truck convoy while there was a big fire going in Dolores. But he'd convinced himself it was okay. He'd heard some police radio chatter here about twenty minutes ago, and he knew the other two Prairie PD cruisers and a couple of PFD fire trucks and EMS vans were en route to the scene to render assistance. He'd taken a deep breath, shut his radio off, and concentrated on minding his own beeswax.

He knew it was against regs, strictly against regs, but he just couldn't stand all the police chatter right now. He had to think. Had to concentrate on this trucker mystery he'd stumbled on to. He didn't know what it was all about yet, but he could guarantee dollars to donuts it wasn't good. When he got to the bottom of it, and he would, he was pretty sure he wouldn't have been wasting anyone's time.

The big rig hit the brakes for a sweeping curve and Homer slowed it up a bit, too. He was staying five hundred yards back. Just above the rear doors, he'd seen a little camera doohickey. Some of the big trucks were fitted with them these days, so they could see behind them when backing up. He guessed you could turn it on anytime, see who was behind you. Pretty good system.

He was on to something big. He could just feel it.

Homer knew the expression for someone in his position. He was what you called a man on a mission. He'd been following the convoy of eighteen-wheelers for pretty near an hour now. He knew they were headed north, that was for dang sure. North, and by the looks of things, east maybe. Twelve trucks, all headed northeast, carrying God knows what all in those fifty-foot-long trailers. Wherever they were going, they'd have to stop for gas at some point. He checked his gauge. Luckily, he'd filled her up just before spotting the convoy.

One by one they'd put their blinkers on; the big rigs had peeled off as they came to different highways. Like it was all prearranged, he thought. He had his map spread out on the seat beside him. He'd looked at all the possible routes and decided that all of them were basically headed in a northeasterly direction.

Not one truck had taken a turn that would indicate it was headed west, or circling back to the south. Homer could have picked any one of the trucks to follow. They were all basically the same rigs. Up front, Mack, Freightliner, Kenworth, and Peterbilts. All heavy-duty trucks, standard forty-eight-foot aluminum vans, all weighing in at around 26,000 pounds. But they had different logos on the trailers. Even though the cabs were all the same. Funny, he thought, trying to study his map and drive at the same time.

Headed north on 59 out of Laredo, he'd watched them gradually peel off, trying to decide which one would be best to follow. There was no method to it. The big citrus hauler, Big Orange, had turned right off of 59 at Freer. She was headed east over to Alice, Texas, maybe. He stayed with the main convoy headed north, biding his time.

At Beeville, Texas, and again at the little one-horse town of Victoria, another truck turned north, heading up Route 181 or 183 to the I-10, most likely. That was the interstate that ran due east to Houston and points north. He stayed with the main body of trucks, taking 59 all the way to the Houston Tollway.

The trucks all must have had E-ZPass, because they all got in that lane and blew right through. He stayed right with them around Houston, then followed the convoy when it got right back on 59 again headed for the Louisiana border and Shreveport.

But then he got lucky, if you could call it that. At Shreveport, all the trucks got on the I-20, which headed east to Jackson, Mississippi, then northeast up to Birmingham, Alabama, and up to Chattanooga, Tennessee, where you could pick up I-75 headed north. All the trucks but one, that is. What happened was, the last truck separating him, it was owned by the Valley Spring Electronics Company, took a right on a two-lane going due east.

Bingorama, as the saying goes.

The truck now in front of him was very familiar. The cab was the one he'd followed into Gunbarrel. The one that had disappeared inside the garage. The very same one that he and Sheriff Dixon had stopped that terrible night the posse came home without their hats.

It was the same cab, all right, the big Yankee Slugger. When it had braked for a moment on Route 59 just outside of Nacogdoches, Homer had pulled up alongside and tried to look inside the cab.

One thing they'd done to all the Gunbarrel Garage trucks, they tinted all their cab windows dark. Illegally dark, if you wanted to get picky about it. Tinted to almost what he called full limo black. He could pull the truck just for that alone if he wanted to. In his experience, pulling low riders and hot rods, people tinted their windows that dark for only one reason.

So you couldn't see what they were doing in there. Or, who was in there.

It wasn't a ghost driving that rig, haunted garage or no.

He was pretty sure of that much, at least.

Homer didn't believe in ghosts. But, one thing he did know for sure. This truck didn't run on air. Sooner or later, whoever or whatever was driving that thing was going to have to stop for a pee or diesel. And when it did, watch out. Katy bar the door, as his grandma used to say. He was going to follow this truck until it ran out of diesel fuel and then he was going to climb all over that thing, tear that big rig apart and see what the heck made it tick. He was going to get to the bottom of this case.

Because that's just what this was. A case. And by God, Homer was on it.

The truck, if you discounted the illegally tinted windows, was acting like a solid, sober, law-abiding citizen.

Very conscientious driver, Homer, Sheriff Dixon would say. Never speeding. Signaling every lane change or turn. And, for some reason or other, taking the scenic route. They'd mostly been sticking to the secondary roads instead of the freeways or the Interstate, which raised a question in his mind. Why do that? It was slower. Wherever these trucks were headed, they didn't seem in much of a hurry to get there.

Never more than a few miles over the posted limit. Stopping completely for every single stop sign (not a "low-rider drive-by," which meant slowing and then cruising right through) and never, ever crossing the double lines. Of course not, he thought. The truckers, or, whoever, didn't want to give law enforcement any excuse to pull them.

Homer sat back against the seat and relaxed his grip on the wheel. He was in this for the long haul. He'd follow this truck to the North Pole if he had to.

He picked up the radio, thinking he'd call it in.

The sheriff was out of town for a few days. If he radioed in, who would he tell? Wyatt? June would just tell him he was acting crazy again. Behind his back, Homer knew, she called him the Ghostbuster. They all did. Heck with it.

He put the radio down. He'd fly this mission solo.

60

After they crossed the border into Louisiana, the Slugger started easing off the throttle. He dropped down to forty for a bit, then thirty. Homer couldn't figure out what he was slowing up for. The road was cut through heavily wooded country, more like a swamp, and he hadn't seen civilization for almost half an hour. Not even a roadside jelly stand or a lean-to shack.

He slowed way down, opening up the distance. He had his lights off ever since they'd entered the Great Boggy or whatever it was called. There was plenty of moonlight and his quarry wasn't going anywhere without him.

The truck had slowed to about five miles per hour, the right turn indicator flashing now. He was pulling over, all right and now Homer saw why.

There was a small, old-fashioned filling station coming up. Nothing more than a falling down shack with a couple of pumps out front. Homer made a decision. He slowed way down and pulled off on the shoulder into a stand of live oaks with a view down the road. The station was about a thousand yards away. He was low on gas too, the needle hovering just above E. But he wanted to see what the heck would happen at the pump. His blood was pumping. He was on the damned case now, all right. And he wasn't scared, either. Not at all.

He sat behind the wheel of the Vic and waited, drumming his fingers on the steering wheel. He wasn't expecting anyone to get out of the Slugger and he wasn't disappointed. No one did.

A minute later, though, a guy came out of the little office. He paused a second on the doorstep, looking at the big rig parked at his little pump. He raised his right hand to his ear for about fifteen seconds. Talking on his cell phone, Homer guessed. Then he shoved the phone in the back pocket of his jeans and shambled down the steps. He was big, maybe two-fifty, and walked slowly out to see what he could do his customer for.

Unusual for a pump jockey, he was smoking a cigarette. Other funny thing was, the guy didn't go around to the driver's window and say, "What'll it be?" Didn't ask anything, he just did it. Went right to the diesel pump and pulled the nozzle out and started pumping fuel into the silent rig. Which told you something, too.

It took a while to fill that big polished aluminum hundred-gallon tank. Homer, still behind the wheel of the Vic, was in no hurry, except he did have to whizz like a racehorse. Just as he was getting out of his car to answer that important call, the station guy yanked the nozzle out of the Slugger's tank and stuck it back in the pump. Then he waddled back up the steps and into the office. Never even looked at the truck again.

Never said word one to his customer, which told Homer the fat man already knew there was no one behind the wheel of the truck at his pump. Knew it all along. Homer's brain was ticking now and he knew he was beginning to understand. Maybe not all of it. But some of it.

This pit stop was arranged way ahead of time. A little gas station on a deserted road in the middle of the night. Made a lot of sense if you didn't want anybody messing into your business. Whoever was behind all this knew what they were doing. Organized crime, had to be. With very deep pockets. He'd thought drugs all along, and now he was sure of it. Somebody was moving huge amounts of Number Four heroin around the country, running on back roads at night.

He looked at his watch. 0200 hours. He wondered if all the trucks in the convoy were stopping now. At little out-of-the-way stations just like this one. The whole thing was getting curiouser and curiouser.

Homer jumped back behind the wheel and pulled back out of the trees and back onto the highway. He accelerated smoothly the short distance up to the station, tucking in behind the Slugger.

He got out, and removed his service weapon. Then he walked forward to the driver's window and rapped on the black glass with his left hand. Once. Twice. Nothing.

There was a sudden flat blatting sound from the engine, puffs of smoke from the tall chrome stacks, and the Yankee Slugger, in no hurry at all, slowly pulled ahead and out of the station. Her right-hand turn signal went on and then she rumbled back onto the highway. Homer had a funny thought, watching the truck head north still, and taking her easy as always: if he ever did meet up with one of these drivers, he was going to try to get them to teach a driver's ed course! They were good!

Homer turned and looked at the small office building. He needed gas and he knew he wasn't taking too much of a chance if he let the Slugger get a few miles down the road. He'd catch up quickly and they'd continue their cat and mouse game just like before.

"Hello?" he shouted. "You got another customer!"

Nobody came out so he walked between the pumps and across the cracked tarmac to the front steps. There was a neon sign buzzing on and off over the door. It said CITGO. He pushed the screen door open and stepped inside, his gun out in front of him. There wasn't much to see. There was a single lightbulb hanging on a wire over a counter. It had a green metal shade and was swaying slightly as if someone had just touched it.

There was nobody at all behind the counter.

"Anybody home? Hello? I could use some gas anybody cares."

No response.

Not taking it personally, Homer walked around the plywood counter. There was door behind it, presumably leading to the back office itself. The door was cracked and he opened it the rest of the way.

A coppery smell, blood, instantly assaulted his nostrils.

The old man who had owned the station was

slumped forward over his cheap wooden desk. He was missing the top half of his head. His brains were leaking out on to an AAA map of Louisiana, the blood already soaking the paper and spreading across the desktop.

Homer pressed his fingers behind the man's ear, feeling like he had to check for a pulse. There was of course no pulse but—

A powerful motorcycle started up just outside the rear door to the station. Big chopper with straight pipes. Damn, he hadn't even looked out there! Before he could even replace the man's arm, the big bike roared around the side of the office and headed toward the highway. Homer, in his excitement, almost slipped in the blood puddle on the floor around the desk. He raced out the door he'd entered by, vaulted over the counter and down the front steps.

He was just in time to see the blinking red lights of the fishtailing chopper disappear up the black road headed south for God knows where.

He had to get moving. Call this in. Right. Fill up the Vic's tank, get on his radio and call local law enforcement with the crime scene location, a description of the victim, the perpetrator, and his motorcycle. With any luck, they'd have the biker in custody within half an hour. He couldn't wait around. He had to go catch the Yankee Slugger. Then he was going to bust him wide open.

61

It was pitch black outside, nothing but the dripping leaves of the overgrown banana trees in the lush hotel garden. Steady rain was hammering the canvas roof above his head and hissing on the river running beside the deeply rutted hotel drive. Of course it was raining, Ambrose thought. He was in the bloody rain forest.

Ambrose and Stokely were en route to some kind of hospital, moldering away out in the countryside. It was called the St. James Infirmary, which he found a charming name, but apparently the institution itself was not. It was said to be a wretched place, formerly a home for indigent children.

Harry Brock and another man, a local chap named Saladin, had been standing on the hotel dock to help with the luggage and mooring lines when the *Blue Goose* first arrived from Key West. Harry Brock and this other chap had arrived in Manaus four days ago. At Hawke's request, they had been doing all the preliminary legwork on the widow. It had not been easy, Harry said. He'd been shown a badly decomposed corpse with a death certificate attached. The name on it was Hilde-gard Zimmermann.

Saladin wasn't buying it. He had zero confidence in the local police; they'd kept looking.

Harry had told Ambrose, as they stood on the dock under an umbrella, he and Saladin now felt there was a reasonable chance they might find Hildegard Zimmer-mann still alive in a secret hospital currently used by the military. Congreve had thanked him for all his hard work and then asked for a car. He and Stokely would leave for the hospital immediately after checking in and having a bite to eat.

"How long do you think it will take us to get there?" he asked Stokely. They had reached the end of the long hotel drive and were about to turn right onto the pri-mary road along the Rio Negro.

"About an hour upriver. Then we go into the jungle. If the road isn't too washed out, we'll be all right. That's what Brock said."

"You know this Harry Brock quite well, I take it?"

"I do. He helped Alex and me in Oman last year."

"Bit full of it, for my taste."

Stokely looked over at him. It had been a long day in a small airplane and Ambrose was finally beginning to get on his nerves. "If I knew what Harry Brock was full of, I'd order a case of the stuff and split it with you."

"Bollocks."

Stokely was driving, thank God; the roads were ridiculous. The car, some sort of official four-wheel-drive vehicle this Brock character had borrowed. Very official looking, taken from the local constabulary car pool via the CIA station chief in Manaus. It was beastly uncomfortable. Not that he'd ever mention it or complain, of course.

They were all such rugged outdoorsy fellows, every last one of them. Stokely, the Aussie pilot, Mick, this serious Arab fellow named Saladin, and, of course, the American spy, Harry Brock. Wearing their bloody bush shorts, shirts with epaulets, naff kit from the Indiana Jones Collection. Even the very attractive woman he'd met at the front desk, Caparina, he thought her name was, had a machete hanging from her belt.

He'd looked at his luggage waiting to go up on the trolley. All he had in his trunks were three-piece linen suits and gabardine trousers. And the pith helmet he'd found in his aunt's attic which currently adorned his head.

"So, how do you like the Jungle Palace?" Stokely asked, trying to lighten the mood.

Congreve craned around and looked back at their hotel. Three stories high, a wide veranda on each floor, and surrounded by overwhelming vegetation. The shuttered windows, some open to the elements, were aglow through the misty rain.

"The Jungle Palace, I would say, only lives up to half its billing," Congreve said with a grin.

"The Jungle part, you mean?" Stoke said, laughing.

"Precisely."

Harry Brock certainly had exotic tastes in hotels. The Palace was on the extreme fringes of Manaus. Brock had chosen this remote hostelry for one reason. Because it was perched on the banks of the Rio Negro;

and there was a dock where Mick could moor the Grumman Goose seaplane.

Ambrose, bone tired from the flight down, sat back and tried to think positive thoughts. The hotel's bar food was edible, at least. And the barman had Johnnie Black and was generous with his whisky. After flying by seaplane all day from Key West, it had been pleasant to taxi up to one's private dock and heave out the luggage.

The *Blue Goose,* which had this day proved her airworthiness beyond question, certainly looked right at home in this tropical environment. She was moored on the river, just off the hotel dock. And, should it come time to get out of here in a hurry, Ambrose could think of no better man to do the job than the Goose's pilot, a former bush pilot from Queensland, Mick Hocking.

All in all, there were some positives. There was a complimentary bottle of gin in one's room. A vast fourposter with clean linen sheets stiff as boards, and acres of mosquito netting. A veranda outside his room where he could smoke his pipe in peace. And, Ambrose had learned upon checking in, there were eighteen species of bats in the garden.

How perfectly charming. All of this grandeur and luxe living, and only a scant thousand miles up the Amazon River.

Well, no matter, the game was afoot. He and Stokely Jones were wasting no time, already off on their mission to find the Widow Zimmermann and unlock the code. He had the thriller, the book he and Alex Hawke now fondly called the Da Zimmermann Code, resting in his lap. He had sweated bullets over the damn thing, reading and re-re-reading the book until his eyes glazed over.

Finding Hildegard Zimmermann was vital. There was simply nothing more he could do, no possible arrangement or rearrangement of words or ciphers, that would budge it forward past the midpoint. Where were those brainy chaps in Room 40 when one really needed them?

He closed his eyes, exhausted, in the vain hope of a catnap before they arrived at their destination.

"We're here," Stoke said seconds later, and he sat bolt upright just as they drove through the iron gates. There was a dimly lit guardhouse and uniformed sentries on either side of it. Seeing the police shields on their doors, the guards snapped to a salute as the speeding buggy passed through. Ambrose noticed high stone walls with nasty concertina wire atop them. They soon passed under an arch, including an ancient portcullis, and now were on the hospital grounds proper.

St. James Infirmary suddenly loomed in the head-lights. It looked more like a large prison reformatory than a hospital for destitute children. Pretty ghastly, but there you had it. They slowed, and Stokely waved some kind of credential at a lone sentry posted at the entrance to the bricked forecourt. He waved them in, and Stoke parked next to a decades-old ambulance standing just outside the main entrance.

"I speak fluent Portuguese," Congreve reminded Stokely, opening his door. "Just in case."

"Don't say anything unless you have to," Stoke said as they climbed out of the car. "Anybody wants to know, you're an English doctor who's here to examine the patient for scientific reasons."

"And who are you?"

"A friend of the guy who slipped the chief of state security in Manaus ten grand so you could see her tonight, Doc."

"Ah. Why is she here?"

"This is where you go before you disappear."

At the end of a long dark hall, an elderly woman in a starched nurse's uniform sat at a reception desk in a pool of white light.

"May I help you?" the old woman said, her Portuguese sounding very neutral, if not downright unfriendly. She was tapping her pencil on a clipboard: a sign-in sheet upside down.

"Good evening, I'm here to see a patient," Congreve replied cordially in the nurse's native tongue.

"Name?"

"Mine? Or, the patient's?"

"Yours," she said, rather impatiently.

"Dr. Congreve. Dr. Ambrose Congreve."

She checked the clipboard and looked up at Stokely. "Who is he?"

"My driver."

Stokely offered her his best credential, a broad white smile.

She hesitated, then wrote something on a thin slip of note paper. She folded the paper and shoved it across the desk. In return, Stoke slid a sealed envelope across to her. She pocketed the envelope and nodded her head, indicating the stairwell.

"The Latin way," Stoke said, opening the note the nurse had given him.

"It works," Congreve replied, following him to the stairs.

"Your driver? You have to say that?"

"Whom would have me say you were?"

"Psychiatrist would be more like it. I've been trying to cure your fear of flying all damn day."

"Where are we going, Dr. Jones?"

"Room 313," Stoke said, "top floor."

If the hospital was grim, the top floor was grimmer. It was a long, poorly lit corridor. Filthy. There was a nurse's station situated beneath a skylight at the center of the wide hall. The periodic lightning flashes gave the elderly nurse on duty a distinctly netherworld appearance. She wore steel-rimmed spectacles that glinted with each strobe as she silently watched their approach.

They paused at her desk and another envelope was delivered and pocketed. The nurse said a few words in Portuguese and Congreve nodded.

"What did she say?" Stoke asked.

"We're allowed ten minutes, max. No gifts. No items can enter or leave the room."

"You've got the lady's book?"

"Of course. Underneath my mackintosh."

Room 313 was at the end of the long hall, on the right. The door was closed and Ambrose tapped lightly upon it before entering. The patient was in a bed on the far side of the room, beneath a dormer window overlooking the hospital grounds. Heat lightning flickered in the heavy cumulus clouds moving rapidly over the treetops.

A candle was burning on the woman's bedside table, and it nearly guttered out when the door swung open. Ambrose fingered a switch on the wall but nothing happened. A jagged arc of lightning flashed across the sky as the two men crossed to the bed.

There was a sagging shelf of books and a crucifix mounted on the wall above her head. Asleep, she was lovely. White hair framed her pale face, and her thin chest rose and fell slowly under the white muslin gown. There was only a whisper of breath from her lips. She appeared so peaceful propped up against her pillow, Congreve was loath to disturb her.

"Hand me that chair, will you?" he whispered to Stokely.

"Thank you." He pulled the wooden chair right up to the bed. He placed his gift on the nightstand beside the candle. Then he reached out and gently took the old woman's hand.

"*Frau Zimmermann?*"

Her eyes fluttered open.

"*Ja?*" She responded automatically in German, asking Congreve if it was time for her medicine.

"*Nein, nein,*" Congreve said in a perfect mimicry of her dialogue, "I'm a friend of your late husband, come to ask you a favor."

"*Was ist los?* What's going on?" she asked, raising her head from the pillow and searching Congreve's face. Stokely hung back in the shadows, invisible in this light.

"Do you speak English, Madam Zimmermann? It would be simpler."

"Of course I speak English. I am a diplomat's wife."

Her voice was remarkably strong given her feeble appearance.

"I saw the ambassador in England. Shortly before he died."

"You knew my husband?"

"Not well. We met once, but we spoke of many things. He . . . he asked me to give you this. It was his last request."

"Gifts are not allowed in here," she said, a flicker of fear in her eyes, but then she saw the book in Congreve's hand.

"Please take it. There is a letter for you. Inside."

She took the book and it fell open to reveal the letter. She pulled the single page from the envelope. Congreve watched her eyes scan the rows of numerals as easily as if she were reading a child's poem.

She folded the book across her chest and closed her eyes. For a moment, Congreve thought she'd gone back to sleep.

"Whose side are you on, Doctor?" she said, her eyes remaining shut.

"Your husband's," Congreve said, silently praying it was the right answer.

"Why have you come?"

"Before he died, your husband saved the lives of many hundreds of people at Heathrow Airport. I believe that, knowing the end was near for him, he had . . . he had a change of heart. About whatever it was he'd been involved with."

"He was a broken man, Doctor Congreve. These people in Brasilia, these Arabs, they tricked him into doing things he should never have involved himself in. The bombing at the synagogue in Rio. What could he do? He protected his family. He was a good man, Doctor. A statesman. He had a brilliant career."

"Why did he do it?"

"Money, of course. Why does one do anything? Money or power. He had plenty of the latter. He knew I was dying. We had spent all our money. We lived too well for too long. Sold everything. He still needed money for my treatment. Sadly, it only prolonged the agony. Look at me."

"I'm very sorry."

"Have you broken our code?"

"Some of it. There is a break, right in the middle and—"

"I know, I—forgive me. I'm very tired."

"I've come because I think you can help me, Frau Zimmermann. You, too, might save a lot of lives."

"Help you?"

"With the balance of the code. Help me break it. Please. It's another attack, isn't it? Against the Americans this time?"

The nurse cracked the door and said, "Five more minutes."

After she'd gone, the woman said, "I don't want to die in this horrid place, Doctor. I want to go home."

Congreve looked quickly over at Stokely, who nodded his head in the affirmative.

"Perhaps I can arrange that. I will try. I know someone who may be able to help you. You have to tell me who is responsible for your being here."

She suddenly opened her blue eyes and looked up at him.

"Do you promise? You'll help?"

"I promise. But you have to help me first. Now. There isn't much time, I'm afraid. A matter of a week or less, if what I've deciphered thus far is accurate. Tell me who is holding you against your will. And why."

"The answer lies above."

"Above?"

"With Jesus."

Congreve's eyes went immediately to the crucifix. His mind racing, he looked at the peeling paint on Christ's robe, the faded gold leaf of the cross. The feet, he noticed, and the hands, had nails driven through them directly into the plaster wall. The wood and porcelain figure would be difficult to remove and examine. There was no time.

"Jesus? I'm afraid I don't understand you."

"No, no, not the crucifix. The books! The books beneath the cross!"

"Ah. Of course."

Ambrose stood and examined the drooping shelf of books, scanning the titles on the spines. They were mostly works of European history and politics. A book of poems by Longfellow. However, in the exact middle was a single novel. He pulled it from the shelf and examined the dust jacket of the hardcover book.

O Codigo Da Vinci.

"If you know enough to bring me this book, you'll understand that one. You'll find the answers to your questions in that volume, Doctor."

"The second half of the Zimmermann Code is in the Portuguese edition of the Da Vinci book," Congreve said, more to himself than anyone in the room. It was not really a question.

"Yes. You'll find the second half of my husband's letter can easily be decoded with the Portuguese translation. It's the way he liked to do things."

The nurse was at the door again. Before she'd finished clearing her throat, Ambrose whirled and looked at her.

"One minute! Please!" Ambrose said it so sharply and with such authority that the nurse instantly withdrew, pulling the door softly shut behind her.

The poor woman looked up at him with pleading eyes.

"Exchange the dust jackets, I beg you, Doctor. Then replace the Portuguese edition on the shelf with the English one you brought. They check all my possessions. Every night. If one book is missing, I'll go hungry. Or, worse."

"One more question. Who is doing this to you? Who poisoned your husband?"

"The ones who come in the night. *Las Medianoches.*"

"Thank you," Ambrose said, quickly slipping her book inside his yellow mac. "Thank you very, very much indeed. May I have your husband's letter back, Madame Zimmermann? I promise to mail it along with the book to you when I've finished my work here."

"Of course. The book is worthless without the letter. Good-bye, Doctor Congreve. I do pray I shall go home soon. I want to die in my own bed."

"I shall do all that I can. I promise you. Good-bye."

"Papa Top is an animal," she whispered as he and Stokely moved toward the door. "He cannot be understood any other way. He cannot be treated in a civilized way, Doctor. Never forget that."

"What is it?" Stokely whispered as they hurried down the hallway and into the stairwell. "What's with the book?"

"It's so simple!" Congreve said under his breath. "I can't imagine why I didn't think of it myself."

"What?" Stokely said as they reached the bottom of the steps and walked quickly past Reception.

"The Portuguese edition of the thriller. The one sold here in Brazil. The second half of the coded letter is in Portuguese."

"Yeah. Tell me again why you can't believe you didn't think of that before?"

"Because it was a *possibility,* my dear Stokely."

Stoke was going to say that possibilities were endless, but decided not to get into that philosophical argument. He said, "So, we've got it now? What you and Alex needed to go after the bad guys?"

"Yes, we've got it all right. I pray that we do. And we've got to get that poor woman out of here. Did you see her tongue? Her skin? The same river-borne bacterial infection they used to kill her husband. We need to get your Mr. Brock on this issue immediately. Get her out of this charnel house."

They climbed inside the car and Stokely turned the ignition key.

"Don't worry," Stokely said, "Brock and I will take care of it in the morning."

"The Latin way," Ambrose said, feverishly turning the pages of the new book. "I certainly hope you're right."

As they reversed out of the courtyard, tires squealing, the matronly figure of the Reception nurse appeared at the doorway. She raised her hand and appeared to be calling to them but they ignored her. A moment later, they'd cleared the sentry booth without a problem and were back on the river road, speeding through the pink dawn to the Jungle Palace.

Unseen by the two men, another car had pulled out of the jungle in their wake and was following at a discreet distance, its headlamps extinguished. It was an armored vehicle belonging to the Military Police, a car bristling with gun barrels called a *Cavelrao* by the terrified citizens living in abject poverty in the worst of the slums, the *favelas* of Manaus.

62

O RIO NEGRO

Stiletto knifed through the mist and ghosted toward the dock. The only lights visible on the vessel were a reddish glow from inside the wheelhouse and the red and green LED running lights inset forward on the sharp prow, small haloes of mist encircling each one. As she steamed up river, coming around the wide river bend out of the dark, she looked more like a Jules Verne fantasy submarine than the twenty-first-century monster offshore powerboat she was.

Stokely said, "Damn thing looks like an assault knife with a rudder. Doesn't it?"

The hotel's dock master was standing on the dock beside Stokely watching Hawke's boat slide through the water. The wiry little guy, whose name was Candido, was nodding his head in serious agreement. He let out a long, low wolf-whistle.

"Scary-looking thing, Señor Jones," he said in pretty good English. "I'm telling you the truth, man. Those fuckin' Indians they got up the river? Most of 'em never seen a white man. They see this boat, they're already half toasted."

Candido had been helping Stokely and Harry load miscellaneous supplies, extra ammo, and fresh vegetables on the dock for the last couple of hours or so. He was Stoke's new best friend. How that happened, Mr. Jones had come out to the dock and handed him a thick envelope earlier in the day. Since then, Candido had been filling his guest in on recent activities of *Las Medianoches* in this neck of the jungle. If Hollywood was doing these bad boys it would be al-Qaeda meets the Gangbangers meets the Hell's Angels. As far as Stoke could tell, they were a law unto themselves around here. And there was nobody, including the Military Police, that they did not own.

Nobody.

"Carpet tacks?" Stoke said, eyeing the big canvas sacks of the things. "I still don't know why we need carpet tacks."

"You will understand, Mr. Jones, once you're on the river. That, I promise you," Candido said, this wise grin on his face.

Stoke shrugged and stared at the oncoming craft, trying to imagine such a beautiful thing in the heat of battle. He could just make out Hawke. He was the man in the black turtleneck sweater, standing on the starboard bow, talking quietly to the crewmen. Crew had on their jungle camo, Stokely noticed, olive drab tiger stripes. The deck hands were preparing to throw mooring lines to a couple of hotel dockhands waiting for the big vessel's arrival.

It was getting late. Without traffic, the river looked wide, deep, and black. Tendrils of night fog lay scattered on the mirrored surface of the Rio Negro like strings of thin grey wool. The dark jungle crowding the river banks on either side was dead quiet. Stoke shivered just a bit when a howler monkey screamed, shattering the peaceful silence.

Midnight. Hawke was right on time.

Stiletto, her engines ahead dead slow, eased alongside the old wooden pier and lines were heaved ashore. The still air was now filled with the low rumble of her engines and the sounds of her exhaust burbling at the stern. No one on deck said a word now, even Hawke, who had waved briefly when he recognized Stoke among the men lining the hotel dock.

Guns were out onboard Hawke's boat. Every man not handling lines cradled a semiautomatic weapon. Stoke saw some familiar faces. A lot of these men were old friends of his from the Thunder and Lightning spec ops group based in Martinique. He scanned the faces, looking for his little pal Froggy, the Foreign Legionnaire. Didn't see him yet.

During *Stiletto*'s last hours in Key West and rapid transit south, certain modifications had been made. Mods included the addition of four sleek carbon fiber canoes mounted at the stern for when and if they ran out of navigable water. Deck guns had been mounted, fore and aft in rotating turrets armored with bubbles of clear, two-inch thick bulletproof Lexan. In addition, twin .50-caliber machine guns had been mounted atop the wheelhouse with an access from a ladder inside.

There was an armored surround on the mounts so gunners would have reasonably good protection from shore fire.

Also on the stern, two mysterious black boxes. Something Hawke had requested from unnamed sources in Washington after his debriefing with Harry Brock. Stoke thought they looked like oversized dishwashers but they probably weren't.

Stoke knew the two things Hawke feared most on the river were mines and rocket-propelled grenades. RPGs, launched from the banks, could take out the deck guns despite the armor. There was only one antidote to RPGs and that was speed. For speed, though, you needed a whole lot of water. So what was in the boxes?

"Welcome to the jungle, Commander," Stoke said, extending a hand as Hawke stepped easily across the two feet of open water that remained between boat and dock.

"Good to be back," Hawke said, looking back at *Stiletto* in the steamy moonlight. "Under more advantageous circumstances."

"Trip didn't take long."

"Flat seas and light wind all the way, except for the rough bits off eastern Cuba. Upriver, we were mostly flat out all the way from the coast. Brownie, her new skipper, says we set a Key West–Manaus record. This thing is seriously fast, Stoke. Despite all the composite armor and weapons."

"I think we're going to need every bit of it," Stoke said, casting his eyes downriver.

"I'm afraid we will indeed. Everybody ready here? I want to shove off immediately after the tanks are topped off."

"I got my stuff right here. The *Blue Goose* is gone. She took off two hours ago. The pilot, Mick, and Harry Brock, plus a couple of local people Harry's been working with down here."

"Any good?"

"Yeah. I think so. Ones who helped him locate this Papa Top character. And found that Zimmermann lady for Ambrose. They don't exactly admit to it, but I think they're both with some Brazilian spec ops unit called Falcon Five. A man and a seriously good-looking woman."

"You trust them?"

"Down here? I don't trust anybody."

Hawke nodded, thinking through the next steps. Time was dwindling rapidly and he had to use every hour as best he could. "Let's go aboard and attack the maps while they fuel this beast. Where's the world's most ingenious detective?"

"See that light burning in the upstairs corner window? That's him. Working away."

"God love him," Hawke said, "I just hope he can crack this bloody thing. We're running out of time."

63

Hawke and Stokely faced each other across a map-strewn table in the small cabin that would serve as *Stiletto*'s war room. Stoke told Hawke all about the visit he and Ambrose had paid to the St. James Infirmary the night before. He recounted Congreve's conversation with the imprisoned elderly widow and explained Congreve's reaction upon discovering the Portuguese version of the novel.

"Giddy?" Hawke said, smiling.

"Your word, not mine. But, yeah, I'd say he was giddy over getting that book."

"Damn good work, you and Ambrose finding that woman. That book may yet help us stop this bastard."

"Well, all I can tell you, the man has been in his room ever since we got back just before dawn last night. Been holed up in there all day. Working on his code. Won't answer the phone, won't even come to the door. I sent him some room service and it sat outside the damn door so long they finally took it away."

"Got the bone in his teeth, all right. That's good. Let

him keep beavering away right up until it's time to shove off."

"What's so special about this book we got last night? It's a novel, isn't it? Fiction. We don't have a whole lot of time for fairy tales right now."

"The book was encoded. This woman's husband, Ambassador Zimmermann, was dirty. Mixed up with Hezbollah here in Brazil. And possibly the Mexican, Cuban, and Venezuelan governments as well. Remember what your friend from Caracas told us?"

"The Mambo King? Yeah, Colonel Monteras told us what we already knew. That *el Presidente* Chávez of Venezuela was determined to bring down the American government. And he was using his oil money, buying those Russian anti-ship missiles from Cuba to help make that happen. Sink tankers in the Gulf of Mexico. Start the war that way."

"Chávez has his own plans for dealing with America. I'll let the Yanks worry about those missiles for now. Top is the more imminent threat. We've got enough on our plate."

"But you think Top is in cahoots with Chávez?"

"Chávez may be bankrolling Top, Stoke. Based on what Harry Brock told me, Top's weapons development alone requires massive amounts of cash. And Chávez is rolling in the stuff right now. Chávez, Fidel, and Top all have the same objective. They're just coming at it from differing perspectives."

Half an hour later, Hawke straightened up and stretched his back muscles. He'd been bent over the bloody maps with Stokely for too long, and he hadn't had any exercise in forty-eight hours. He was tempted to go for a night swim in the river but there wasn't time.

"Now you know why they built their stronghold in this part of the jungle," Hawke said, looking at Stokely across the table. "No satellite imagery, no aerial recon photos, no thermals, nothing. Just a bloody map with a ton of green on it."

"It's a bitch all right. How do you find something that isn't on a map?"

"I think Harry Brock has at least gotten us within spitting distance. We'll see for ourselves shortly."

"So, when we do go in, this will be Brock's LZ here," Stokely said. "The strip where he saw the drones and the little remote control tanks."

Stoke was pointing to the small red grease mark Brock had placed on the laminated map of the target area. An inch away was a long yellow mark indicating the deep ravine that was believed to be the western perimeter of Top's compound.

"Yeah. Brock's land force goes in there, moves toward the river. We move west from the river and join them roughly here."

"Where exactly do we go in?"

"Good question. Captain Brownlow is plugging river waypoints into the GPS guidance and weapons systems now. Brock believes we'll find Top's central command approximately here. Somewhere along this stretch of water is a camouflaged bridge. Find that bridge and we've found Top."

Hawke used his index finger to trace his intended route on the map.

"The Black River?" Stoke said, looking through the large magnifying glass.

"Right. To get there, we execute a rapid backtrack east on the Amazon to the mouth of the Madeira River here. Then head due south along this large tributary. At this point, right here, the junction of the Aripuana and the Roosevelt, we—"

"Whoa. Roosevelt? That's the river's name? Down here?"

"Teddy Roosevelt. Back in 1908, he led an expedition looking for something called the River of Doubt. T.R. found it, everybody thinks anyway, and the Brazilians named it after him. Rio Roosevelt."

"You don't think he found it? The river?"

"There's still some doubt, pardon the pun, in London's geographic circles. There's another river. It's called the Igapó, or Black River. You can only see it with the glass. It's this tiny hairline tributary that disappears into the forest here. No one's ever found the source. Or, even where it ends. My friends back at the Geographical Society think it actually goes underground and resurfaces in a distant location still uncharted. I think this river might have been the one the great Bull Moose was actually looking for."

"So this river, the Igapó, is not really on any map. Even now, in the age of electronic miracles."

"Right."

"So, we're winging it."

"To some extent, yes, we are."

"Excuse me, Skipper?"

Brownlow was at the door.

"Yes, Cap'n?" Hawke said.

"Wanted to make sure everyone was aboard. We're topped off and ready to get under way."

"Is Chief Inspector Congreve aboard yet?"

"No, sir," Brownlow said. "Haven't seen him yet, sir."

Hawke looked at his black-faced wristwatch. It was almost one o'clock in the morning. Everyone was supposed to be aboard and prepared to shove off at midnight. "Well, we'll just have to go fetch him. Give us ten minutes, will you? We'll be back with him. He's the only one missing. Everyone else has gone ahead to the next rendezvous by air."

"Aye, aye, sir."

HAWKE AND STOKELY walked quickly through the deserted lobby, climbed three flights of stairs, and walked along the hallway until they came to Congreve's room. The hotel had gone to sleep, by and large, and the only room showing a light under the door was the one on the left, Room 307, belonging to Ambrose Congreve.

Hawke paused a moment, listening, then put his hand on the knob. The door swung inward.

"Holy Jesus," was all Stoke could say.

The room had been tossed. Not just tossed, heaved upside down and turned inside out. Every drawer had been pulled from desk and dresser, upended on the floor. The bed had been stripped of its bedclothes, the mattress had been pulled from the bed, sliced open and gutted, wads of stuffing everywhere.

"What the hell were they looking for?" Stoke asked.

Hawke's eyes were brimming with anger.

He said, "Last night, Stokely. Your visit to the St. James Infirmary. Was there any trouble?"

"We were in and out of there in fifteen minutes."

"It was Brock who told you she was there? And Brock who got you inside, too?"

"Right. Brock and five thousand U.S. dollars paid to a Major Rojales of the Military Police here in Manaus."

"No names, right? Tell me you two didn't use names last night."

Stokely thought about it. "Damn. Ambrose called himself 'Dr. Congreve' at Reception."

"Then it's the bloody letter they're after. The Zimmermann Code," Hawke said, barely keeping his anger out of his voice. How could Ambrose have been so bloody careless? A momentary lapse, probably because of his fixation with breaking that code book.

"We've got to help that poor woman," Stokely said. "God knows what they're doing to her out there."

"Whatever it is, they've most likely already done it. They extracted information about the letter and the fact that Ambrose had it. The Zimmermann woman is probably dead, I promise you. And she didn't die in her sleep."

"Look in the bathroom," Hawke said, furiously yanking open the closet door. His friend's expensive clothing was still on hangers, although all the pockets had been pulled out and many of the jacket linings had been slashed. The beautiful shoes, normally a neat file, were strewn about the room. He'd never had time to pack. His mind was racing, but one thought was winning. *What in God's name am I to tell Diana Mars?"*

"Alex. Come here."

Hawke went instantly to the bathroom door.

"Oh, shit," Stokely said.

"Where?"

"Come inside and close the door."

Hawke did so. On the white tiled floor and on the wall, a bright spatter of red blood.

Hawke stared at the pattern for a second, then looked at Stokely and said, "He didn't cut himself shaving."

"No."

"You didn't see him at all this morning?"

"Said goodnight outside that door last night around midnight. Didn't see or speak to him since."

"Look at this," Hawke said, holding up the black bowler hat he'd found in Congreve's closet.

"A hat with a hole in it. That's not Ambrose's style."

"It's a Voodoo calling card. From Papa Top, I'd guess. He's half-Haitian and they're big Voodoo worshippers."

"I got it now."

"Bastards have got my friend," Hawke said. "Let's go."

64

A nother ghost truck," Franklin said to Daisy, shaking his head.

"That's what I'm telling you, darlin'. Another ghost truck. Only this one, we got cornered."

"Who calls them ghost trucks?"

"Me and June. We got it from Homer."

Daisy was driving the pickup. She had just picked up her husband outside the American Airlines baggage claim at San Antonio Airport. All he had was a small duffel which he heaved in the back before he climbed in. She handed her ticket stub and five bucks to the hourly parking attendant and popped the clutch, not waiting for change.

"Daisy. Since I've been gone, you've gunned down an armed man in the street, you've—"

"Excuse me—that was June shot the Mexican looter. Not me."

"You were just driving the getaway truck."

"Correct. Trying to deliver your videotape like you asked us to do. And we did."

"And you did. I thank you for that."

"What are you so upset about?"

"Nothin'. I'm tired, honey."

Daisy reached over and took her husband's hand. "Didn't all those Washington people appreciate June's tape? Wasn't it what you needed down there at the conference?"

"It was. I think it's already on its way to the White House. The president might use it in his speech to the Congress tonight."

"Well, there you go."

"I'm sorry. I'm just whupped. I'm glad you're okay, that's all. I've been worried about you ever since I left."

"Well, I'm tired and worried too, Franklin. Haven't slept much in twenty hours. June and me grabbing alternating catnaps on the bench seat at a McDonald's is not my idea of beauty sleep. That's why I look so awful. Don't say anything sweet, either. Let's just drive and try to enjoy the scenery."

"Nice Wal-Mart," Franklin said, gazing out his window.

That quieted things down, all right.

They were driving into downtown San Antonio. Going back to the McDonald's on Commerce Street. When Daisy first picked up Franklin at the airport, she had told him they were driving directly downtown before heading home to Prairie. There was a suspicious vehicle she and June had staked out. June was there now, watching from their stake-out position across the street from the truck.

"Take me through all this, Daisy," Franklin said after

ten or so minutes. "From after you handed off the envelope and sent Buddy Shirley to Southwest Medical to see about his gunshot wounds."

"He's okay. I called his momma this morning. Already back at work."

"So then what happened? Where'd you manage to pick up all the bullet holes in your truck?"

"Well, like I told you *before,* we had just outrun the outlaw moving van when we saw a big fire burning over in Dolores. Those fires were started by a bunch of local Mexican druggies and teenage *banditos* calling themselves the *Reconquistas,* you see, and we chased 'em back south of the the the border."

"You and June?"

"Well, we helped. Mostly, it was a couple of bikers called Zorro and Hambone and their gang. Even the great *Re-Conqueros* didn't want to mess with those bad boys. So, it was a whole lot of bikers, plus a lot of folks from the neighboring towns, plus me and June who helped chase them home."

"I'm starting to see it."

"You know what they were yelling the whole time we were fighting with them? The *Reconquistas?*"

"Nope."

"'We didn't cross the border! The border crossed us!' That's the new Mexican anthem."

"Where's the burning and looting now?"

"Moving west on down the line for the moment. I hear it's pretty bad when you get past Laredo."

"Then you saw this truck."

"Yes, on the way back to Dolores, we had passed

Homer going the other way. He was following this convoy of tractor-trailer rigs headed north on 59."

"I got that part."

"You said from the beginning and—"

"Daisy."

"Sorry. Well, later, when we were headed back to Prairie, we came up behind another truck headed north. We figured it was a straggler from the convoy got left behind. Blacked-out windows and all, with a big fat orange painted on the back. Some citrus company called Big Orange Groves in Lakeland, Florida. Florida tags."

"Coals to Newcastle."

"Exactly. That is exactly what June said when she saw that truck. What the hell is a Florida trucker doing delivering oranges in Texas? That's what we wondered."

"So you two decided to follow him."

"We sure did. All the way north from Dolores up to San Antonio. Never went over fifty-five. Didn't take the Interstate, took the parallel state road. An hour later, he pulled over at a little rest stop just south of town. Remote, you know. So we just pulled in behind him. Only two vehicles in the parking lot since it was about two in the morning. Got out of the truck, both of us, and went around to the cab. June on the passenger side, me on the driver's side."

"Carrying the shotgun?"

"Damn straight. June says that Homer's got a weird feeling about these trucks. And I've seen enough and heard enough to share that feeling. I banged on the window with the muzzle of the gun. Nothing."

"Nothing."

"No one in the truck, far as we could tell. And then we climbed up on the running boards and tried to look in. The windows weren't just smoked, Franklin, they're really dark, like blacked out completely."

"Blacked-out windows are not a felony."

"Anyway, the damn ghost truck takes off with us still on the running board! I mean, come on! So I yelled at June and we both jumped off before he got rolling too good. She hurt her ankle anyway but she can still walk. I've got ice on it at McDonald's."

"So you jumped back in the pickup and followed him to San Antone."

"We did. And now, we've got him cornered. You know, Homer thinks these trucks are—"

"Speaking of Homer, where is he? I've been trying to reach him all day."

"Looking for you, too. He took the day off. Says he's got the flu. But we know different because we saw him. He finally called Wyatt. He's following that convoy headed north, is what he's doing."

"Wyatt's got an APB out on that van we caught looting and Wyatt's got the medical examiner's office trying to identify the men June shot. He's also covering Homer's butt on the J. T. Rawls shooting, not that it needs covering in my humble estimation."

"Wyatt's a fine peace officer."

"He's not you, but never mind that, here we are."

Daisy pulled into the parking lot on the backside of the old McDonald's on Commerce Street. There was one spot left in the shade of an oak and she took it. Even though it was January, it was a warm day.

"I don't see any truck," Franklin said, climbing out.

"Right around the front, parked in an alley off Commerce. Here, we can just use this back entrance."

They hurried inside and found June sitting on a banquette near the front. She seemed very upset and shook her head at the sight of the sheriff coming quickly toward her.

"Hey, June," Franklin said, smiling at her as he approached the table where she sat. "That videotape of yours is being looked at by the president of the United States this afternoon."

"It is?" she said. "That's great."

"How 'bout that, June? Isn't that fantastic? What's wrong?"

"Sorry, Daisy. Sorry, Sheriff. I lost the truck."

"Lost the truck? What?" Daisy said, running over to the window.

She looked back at June and her husband and said, "She's right. Shoot! The truck's gone!"

65

How in heck's name could you lose a truck, June?"

"I swear I was only gone three or four minutes," June said, "Damn it to hell!"

"Tell us what happened, June," Daisy said, calming down a little.

"Oh, the Secretariat Syndrome. You know."

"What's that?" Franklin asked.

"She had to pee," Daisy told her puzzled husband.

June said, "Yeah. Couldn't hold it another second. Went back to the ladies' room and, wham, he was gone when I came back."

Daisy already had one foot out the door. "We'll find him. Let's go, honey. He can't have gotten far."

"Sheriff?" June said, climbing to her feet, "Homer called my cell phone here maybe ten, fifteen minutes ago. Asked that you call him back. Sounded kinda urgent."

"Where's the phone?"

"Right here."

"Where is he?"

"Somewhere in Virginia. Some pretty little farm, he said. He's got it staked out but he needs to know what to do next."

She handed Franklin the phone.

"Now what?" he said, looking at it.

"Just hit star 69. It'll ring him automatically."

"Homer?" Franklin said, a few seconds later.

He'd walked with the phone and sat down at a table over by the window where nobody could hear his conversation. He'd sent Daisy and June out to look for the Big Orange rig. Seemed like a wild goose chase, but then, he'd been wrong before.

"Yessir. I'm glad you called," Homer said on the line.

"Tell me what's going on."

"You know I followed the trucks. You know I shot and killed J. T. Rawls."

"I do."

"You ain't mad?"

"Homer, I heard what happened in Gunbarrel from Wyatt. He says it was a clear case of self-defense. We don't have time for this now. Tell me where you are and what your situation is."

"Sheriff, I'm in a little farm town in Virginia. Somewhere south of Washington, D.C."

"All right. You know the name of the place?"

"Lee's Ferry. It's right on a river."

"What have you got?"

"Okay, the truck I followed all the way? We came up Route 1 north of Richmond. All the way to Fredericksburg. Then he cut east till he came to the river."

"Where's the truck now?"

"It's an old farm. Couple of hundred acres. Pretty place. The Yankee Slugger is tucked away under some trees by the river. Just setting there in the snow. Doesn't look like it's going anywhere. They came out and looked at it a few hours ago. Just walked around it a few times. Bent down and looked underneath. Then they all went back inside the house and pulled all the curtains shut."

"Who is 'they'?"

"Folks living here."

"Where are you calling from right now?"

"The kitchen."

"Their kitchen?"

"Yessir. There is a couple living here, like I said. And, Sheriff, these folks don't look like native Virginians to me. Arab, I think, if you'll excuse the racial profiling. A man and woman and a younger guy, I guess their son maybe. They got in a car and left here, oh, about half an hour ago. Driving a late-model Cadillac, maroon in color. Thought I'd have a look around inside the house while they were gone. Nice and warm in here. Fire going and all. That's when I called June to check in."

"Homer. They left the fire burning. That means they won't be gone long. Can you see or hear the owners approach? When they come back from wherever they went?"

"I can, yessir. House is on a hilltop. Long driveway down the hill. I can see the main road from this window I'm at right now. Called Old River Road and there's a white picket fence all along the property.

Plenty of time to slip out of the kitchen door and back into the woods where I'm staked out."

"Any idea yet what's in these trucks you followed?"

"Whatever it is, it ain't good, Sheriff. That's all I can tell you. I was thinking about taking a crowbar to the rear doors while nobody's here. But, I'll need some help, they come back and catch me breaking in their truck. Little nervous about calling in local lawmen in case it's all a bunch of nothing, though."

There was a long pause before the sheriff spoke.

"Listen, I'm going to get a taxi back to the airport. Is Lee's Ferry closer to Washington or Richmond?"

"Based on the mileage markers I saw, I'd have to say a lot closer to Washington. It's north of Fredericksburg. You can take Route 1 South and get off at state road 635 to Cherry Hill."

"Homer, sit tight, I'm taking the next flight out. I'll rent a car and find you. Is there a street address on River Road?"

"No, sir. But there's a sign at the end of the drive-way. 'Morning Glory Farm.' "

"I'll find it. Do not approach these people when they return. Do not go near the truck. Until I get there, you see something happening you don't like, you call it in to the locals. Let them handle it."

"It's starting to snow pretty hard now. Really coming down. Hope your flight gets in."

"I hope so, too. You get anything to eat?"

"Stole an apple from the bowl here. All right if I steal a little food from the pantry? I've been living on Twinkies and R.C. Colas for three whole states."

"Take something they won't miss from a high shelf and get out of that house, Homer. Now, git!"

"Sheriff?"

"Yep?"

"I might be wrong about all this. What these trucks mean, all of them headed north like they are. All along I've been thinking it was drugs. Now I'm not so sure."

"I hope you are wrong, Homer, but I'm not so sure anymore, either. I'll be there soon as I can."

66

"Focus. Concentrate. Look where you're going, not where you are," Hawke said. He was standing, feet planted wide apart to brace himself, at *Stiletto*'s helm. Stoke could only hear him because of the headphones he was wearing.

It was two in the morning. Having notified the police and searched the entire hotel and grounds for his missing friend, Hawke had decided he'd no choice but to press on without him. It had not been an easy decision to make. There was a big moon hiding behind swiftly moving clouds. Not much traffic at this hour, only the small double-decked ferries and few big cruise ships headed upriver to Manaus.

Hawke, outwardly calm but still angry, was driving the powerful offshore boat flat-out over the wide river, hurling masses of foaming white water out to either side of the razor-sharp hull. *Stiletto* was hammering east on the Amazon, backtracking down to the Madeira River before she'd make the turn south and head into the deep jungle of the Mato Grosso.

Hawke was in a hurry, running at the extreme edges of the powerful vessel's performance parameters. Stoke could see the digital speed readouts flickering red over Hawke's head well enough. They were doing nearly 100 knots. In the dark.

This would be pushing it in broad daylight. On the open sea, running in a flat calm. But at night? On a damn river? Stoke didn't even want to think about what would happen if they struck a submerged object at this speed. Radar only picked out what was on the water, not what was under it. At this speed, it was hard enough to avoid the lighted navigation buoys that were blurring by now and then, disappearing astern almost before you saw them coming.

"You want the helm, Stoke?" Hawke said, his eyes riveted on the onrushing river. All lights in the wheelhouse were extinguished. He was only a silhouette, standing at the wheel in the pale reddish light of the control fascia overhead. Everyone on the bridge deck was wearing headsets in order to hear. The noise of three 5,600-horsepower gas turbine engines at full bore, even muffled, was overwhelming.

"Like to watch you a little longer," Stokely said carefully, "then I'll take her."

In truth, he wasn't at all anxious to take the helm from Alex. He wanted Hawke's mind fixed on the boat and the river, not on what had happened to his friend Ambrose Congreve. And whatever was waiting for them in the jungle. The "Reckoning" as Ambrose said it was called in the code letter. Better to keep Hawke focused, concentrating on driving the boat as fast as it would go for long as he could. Stoke knew Hawke had to be thinking exactly what he was thinking.

Get there fast.

If Top had their friend, and there was not much doubt now that he did, *Las Medianoches* henchmen would soon be breaking that dear man into a million little pieces to find out what he knew. Congreve could not long survive the vicious blend of Voodoo tortures Top's terrorists practiced in the jungle.

The boat heeled sharply to starboard. A second later, she slammed hard to port. Hawke had just missed a low-lying barge, towed by a small tug plying her way downriver. Much as he wanted to, Stoke couldn't tell Alex Hawke to slow the boat down. Unless they found this damn River of Doubt, unless they found Muhammad Top, soon, the terrorists would have their Day of Reckoning. And Hawke's best friend Ambrose, the man who'd been a father to him since early childhood, would be gone the hard way.

In the end, Stoke knew, everybody talks anyway.

"Nav," Hawke said quietly into his lip mike. On the primary navigation monitor mounted above him, the image of the boat was rapidly moving easterly across the GPS map displaying the Amazon. They were quickly closing the distance to the mouth of the Madeira River.

"Navigation here, sir."

"Nav, when do we pass through zero-five-zero south, zero-fifty-five west?"

"Local time or Zulu time, sir?" Zulu was Coordinated Universal Time, which had replaced Greenwich Mean Time as the world's standard.

"Local."

"Zero-two-twenty, sir."

Hawke stole a glance at his watch and edged the throttle a notch forward. Except for the dull roar of the engines, it was deathly still on the bridge. Everyone strapped into his seat, keeping conversation to a minimum. All probably thinking the same thing. Hit a log or an oil drum at this insane speed and you're dead before you know it.

"Focus is the big one at this speed, right?" Stoke asked Alex, not wanting his friend's mind to wander down any bad roads even for one second.

Hawke was silent for a moment, his eyes scanning the river of blackness the boat was devouring at a staggering rate. He saw something ahead, a pinpoint of light, put the helm over a fraction and the boat heeled sharply, then corrected. On an even keel once more, *Stiletto* surged forward.

"Yes. Focus," Stoke heard Hawke say in his headset. The voice was calm, almost no emotion at all. "It's oddly cerebral. What you're thinking about determines what you tell the boat to do. What your inputs are. That's why you must always be thinking ahead of the boat. The further behind the boat you are mentally, the more forced and rougher your inputs are likely to be."

"Makes sense to me."

"The enemy of concentration is emotion," Hawke said, verifying Stoke's instinctive theory. "Or, exhaustion. Most high-speed accidents occur when the guy driving the boat becomes afraid he's in over his head, doesn't think he quite knows how to exit this turn.

Panic rules. Or, he's running on pure adrenaline. Can't do that, either. You have to quiet your mind enough to listen to the boat. Let it tell you what it wants you to do, and do it. This boat gives you a lot of feedback. But you've got to stay ahead of it. Ready to drive? I'd like to grab an hour or so of rack."

"Yeah. I'll take it. Just a sec."

Stoke had been watching Hawke carefully. He'd gone a little crazy with the local Military Police commander when nobody could help him find Ambrose. Realized, finally, they'd have to shove off without him. He seemed calmer now. Stoke thought Hawke could handle it now, do what he had to do in the next day or so. He'd already moved into his mission performance zone. He'd pushed emotion back in that dark closet where it rightly belonged. Still, he looked exhausted from pushing the boat hard all the way down from Key West, three days in open ocean. Stoke thought he'd soon be no good to anyone without some rest.

Stoke had unbuckled his restraining belts and now stood beside Hawke, moving his hands to the wheel as Hawke backed off the throttles momentarily.

"I got the helm, Alex."

"It's yours," Hawke said, only removing his hands when his own hands told him that Stokely had full control of the boat.

"Feels good," Stoke said, and he meant it. He saw how wide the river looked from here. He accelerated easily back up to one hundred knots. The sense of power was like nothing he'd felt before. Hawke stayed right by his side, his eyes ranging over the three dedicated groups of engine gauges and flat-screen navigation and weather monitors mounted above.

Hawke said, "You're good to go. Remember, Stoke, your hands are hardwired to your eyes. Look ahead; see where you want to be next. Don't look where you don't want to go. It's called 'target fixation.' Your eyes stray to a target you don't want to hit. Your hands will automatically take you there if you're not careful."

"Tunnel vision," Stoke said.

"Right. As you reach the limits of your ability to think ahead of the boat, your peripheral view narrows, and it's harder to see the next target. And let Brownlow or me know as soon as you're ready for a break."

"Go get some rack, boss," Stoke said, enjoying himself for the first time in a week.

"Yeah. Wake me in an hour if you don't see me back up here."

"Got it."

"We're going to find this bastard, you know. And kill him before he kills us. Any of us."

"I know that."

"I've seen this guy, you know. Had some quality time with him. You'll recognize Top when you see him, Stoke. Can't miss him."

"How's that?"

"His eyes."

"What about them?"

"Like two piss-holes in the snow."

HALF AN HOUR later, Stoke became aware of a small man standing just behind his right shoulder. He was using one of the handholds on the overhead to keep on his feet. There was light chop now, and the beginning of river traffic, and Stoke had wisely slowed the big boat to less than forty knots.

"*Mi scusi, Signore Jones,*" the man said.

It was Gianni Arcuri, the Italian engineer provided with the boat for the first three months of shakedown. He was a Neapolitan, and had a cherubic face, huge brown eyes, and a big black moustache under his generous nose.

"Hey, Gianni, what's up?"

"I'm so sorry, eh? But I've been down in the engine room. I don't like what I am seeing with Number Three engine. She's no acting so good."

"What is it, Gianni?"

"She's running a little hot. Manifold pressure is dropping a little bit. Nothing too serious, okay, but I'd like to shut her down for a while. We'll take a look, eh? Find the little problem and fix it before it becomes a big problem later."

"Should we reduce speed now?"

"Please. Twenty-five, thirty knots maximum. You'll be carrying the heavy extra load of the down engine so you'll have to trim, okay? I'll shut Three down now and fix it as fast as I can."

"You know we're in a big hurry tonight, Gianni."

"*Si, si.* Everyone knows that, Signore Jones. We do the best we can, eh? Give me twenty minutes, a half hour."

Stoke used the quiet time afforded by the slow speed to think. He'd studied the maps. He'd heard Brock's estimates of the enemy strengths and weaknesses. He and

Hawke had both gone over Harry's recon report enough times to memorize the thing. They both knew these would be suicide troops mainly, big-time Kool-Aid drinkers, jungle gangbangers ready to die for a one-way ticket to Paradise. And Caparina's report had talked about robotic tanks and unmanned drones with Hellfire missiles. There'd be mines in the river, too, as they got closer.

On the plus side, they had this damn kickass boat. The secret to successful riverine operations, as he'd learned the hard way in the Delta, was speed. *Stiletto* was insanely fast. She was heavily armed and armored. She had amazing navigation and missile warning systems. The deeper into Top's compound they could get *Stiletto,* the better chance they'd have.

The way Stoke saw this thing going down was pretty straightforward. He, Hawke, and the thirty badasses aboard this boat would mount a riverine operation against Top's compound; they would do as much damage as they could with *Stiletto*'s arsenal before going ashore. To that end, Hawke had ordered a PAM system installed on the stern. These Precision Attack Missiles weighed about 120 pounds each and had a range of 40 kilometers. They came in a container of 15 missiles, each with a 28-pound warhead. Once the container was plugged into the ship's wireless battlefield network, they were ready to fire at will. The black boxes Stoke had seen on the stern.

Brock's team would be composed of fifty or so Falcon spec ops guys, all of whom reported to Saladin. These were some serious anti-terrorist troops, all of them local boys with local knowledge. Saladin was even now briefing his men in the caverns he and Brock had discovered outside the town of Madre de Deus. Brock and Saladin's team would fly with Mick Hocking. Two flights. They would land at the LZ Brock had found near the compound. While Mick returned for the second batch, the first arrivals would start a rapid deployment east.

When ordered to do so, they would cross the deep ravine that formed the western border of Top's lair and advance toward the center, as the *Stiletto* force moved rapidly west, eventually creating a pincer movement.

Stoke and Hawke had debated and finally agreed to this strategy while calculating the forces available to them and studying the maps provided by Brock and Caparina. It was a basic element of military strategy used in nearly every war since people threw rocks. Even Hannibal used it against the Romans at Cannae, 216 B.C. Worked then, works now. The flanks of the opponent are attacked simultaneously in a pinching movement.

Draw the enemy in toward your base as you fake a retreat at the center, then, once they bite, move your outer flanks forward to encircle them. Then, everybody goes on offense. Trick was to get your flanks to fold at the exact same time so you don't give the bad guys even a single opportunity to retreat.

Hawke said he had one reservation about this strategy. He thought an enemy realizing it was completely surrounded would fight more fiercely than one still believing it had an escape route. Stoke agreed.

"Right, boss. Let's give 'em an escape route. Straight down to the river where we'll park *Stiletto*."

67

A Selva Negra

Good evening, Congreve," Papa Top said, entering the room where the Englishman was held captive. The big man was wearing his Voodoo regalia. An ill-fitting tailcoat, black striped pants, and his black bowler swinging from one hand. There were two stocky chaps in green fatigues on either side of the door. They stood stiffly, like mannequins. The room was round and sparsely furnished. There were arched windows, shuttered.

Congreve raised his head. The man they called Doctor was still there, off to one side, putting a hypodermic into a red leather case. The doctor had asked him a lot of questions. But, hadn't hurt him, oddly enough. He supposed that was coming now.

He'd been out, but now he returned to consciousness as easily and fully as if he'd been having a refreshing catnap. He tried to imagine what kind of amphetamine cocktail produced such startling clarity of thought? He was restrained to a kind of chaise-longue, made of bamboo but covered in some soft leather upholstery.

Top bent over him, looking into his eyes with a kindly solicitude that was mildly disconcerting.

"I've been reading your copy of the *Code*," Top said, pulling up a chair from somewhere. "Fascinating."

"Isn't it," Ambrose said, reclining his head and studying a piece of Brazilian folk art hanging on the wall. A face, with wildly distorted eyes. It was the only piece of art in the room.

"Dr. Khan says you're not being very cooperative."

"Where am I?"

"A reasonable question. You're in the Black Jungle."

"Those two by the door. Robots?"

"You've been reading too much science fiction, Inspector. Tell me. Where is Hawke now?"

"No idea."

"You know what this is?"

"Voodoo doll."

"Yes. But the needles don't go in the doll."

"Get that away from me."

"This will hurt."

"Good God."

A searing pain starting at his foot rose the length of his leg and caused his major muscles to spasm.

"Next question. We'll take it slowly, no more pinpricks or superficial burns. When you stole the book from the hospital, were you able to finish it? I promised your predecessor in this room, the late Madame Zimmermann, I'd ask."

"No."

"Safe answer. How far did you get in the book?"

"Far enough, you bloody maniac."

"Now, now. That's going to cost you. The doctor and I were happy to see you arrive. This way, we'll know who to expect and when. And, if we need to make any last-minute adjustments to our . . . plans. You see? Where is Hawke now? Where did he go after Key West?"

"Sod off."

"There's a special nerve here, just below the septum of the nose. Feel that?"

"Definitely."

"Hawke's vessel was picked up by our aerial drones patrolling off the north coast of Cuba. He outran two of our high-speed patrol boats. He was last seen headed south, southwest. I repeat the question, where is Hawke now?"

"Bugger yourself, Muhammad. That's your style, is it not?"

"Doctor? Sorry, would you bring your bag over here? Thank you. Doctor Khan is an engineer but he also dabbles in human anatomy. He is here to ensure that you undergo the worst possible pain, consistent with your remaining alive until your public execution at sundown tomorrow. It will be an interesting challenge to his skills . . . and your fortitude."

"There's really nothing else I can say."

"He's a brave one, isn't he, Doctor? A sip of whisky, Inspector? Here, hold your head up. That's it."

"Good stuff. Macallan, with a bit of an aftertaste. What'd you put in it?"

"I ask the questions. I'm sure you're accustomed to outwitting your opponents. That will not be the case tonight. I will ignore your promises as well as your pleas, so don't waste your breath or my time. Now. Once you acquired this book from the Germans, you acquired certain knowledge. How much of this did you impart to your friend Hawke before we had you arrested?"

"Ah. I told him enough."

"Doctor?"

"Oh, lord. Oh, God."

"Tell me. Now!"

"He's passed out," Khan said. "Let me revive him."

"Welcome back," Top said. "Let us continue. How much does Hawke know? Tell me now."

"We're losing him again. Hold this under his nose."

"There are twelve major bones in your body, Congreve. It will be a delicate task to break each one in ascending order of importance, starting with this one. Ready? You may begin, Doctor."

There was a loud crack and Congreve heaved upward, tearing at his restraints.

"Please, God . . ."

"Will you talk now?"

"Some kind of—some kind of attack on Washington . . ."

"Does Hawke know?"

"No."

"DOES HAWKE KNOW?"

"Y-yes. I mean, no. He doesn't. I—please, God."

"One more, if you please, Doctor? After the bones are broken, the doctor will inject you with a solution that will cause you to go into convulsions. It will be . . . difficult for you."

"NO! Please . . ."

"Does Alex Hawke know the primary target?"

"The . . . president."

"Who else?"

"Government."

"And when will this attack occur?"

"I don't know."

"I said *when*."

"The . . . pro—the procession to the Capitol."

"What about *Bedouin*?"

"Unmanned submarine. Inside the Tidal Basin."

"Weapon?"

"Small nuclear device. 150 kiloton."

Papa Top looked at Khan and nodded. The doctor lifted Congreve's right hand and bent the fingers backward at an acute angle.

"How much of this does Hawke know?"

"All of it. None of it. Choose."

"I repeat. How . . . much of this . . . does Hawke know? Hmm? How much?"

"Go fuck yourself."

"Very good, Inspector. I think that will be all for tonight, unless the doctor has any further questions? No? Good. We'll see you in the morning? Don't try to sleep by the way. It will be useless given what's in your veins."

"Wait!"

"There's more?"

"There's a woman. In England. I want to say goodbye. Please. Pen and paper. While I can still write . . ."

Top stared down at him for a few seconds, then looked at Doctor Khan before answering him.

"The doctor says 'no.' He doesn't believe you're telling the truth about Hawke. I will ask once more. Did you communicate with your friend Alex Hawke after you'd decoded the letter in its entirety?"

"No. Give me the bloody paper."

"I believe him," Top said to one of the guards, heading for the door. "For now. Give him what he wants. We begin again in the morning."

68

It was snowing, bad, just like Homer had said on the phone, coming down so hard Franklin could barely make out the shoulders of the road he was driving on. You could only see intermittently, through the fan-shaped area of glass left by the wiper. Every time it squeegeed a fresh coat of damp white stuff off the windshield, he leaned forward to see where he was. Wet snow mixed with sleet, heavy, about a foot of it already baked to a firm white cake on the hood of his car.

He was hardly doing twenty now, just blowing a thin layer of frosting off the cake. Up ahead he saw flashing yellow lights in the whirling snow, moving slow along the shoulder. The big plows were out, but clearly Route 1 South was not a priority. Not with a major corridor like I-95 just a mile away to the west. Even with the conditions, he was glad Homer had told him to take the old road south. Less traffic to deal with, and nobody was going anywhere fast to begin with.

He leaned forward over the wheel and squinted, trying to peer through the swirling stuff. This stretch of road he was on would be pretty near impassable to any-body not driving a big SUV. Or, a rented Jeep Cherokee 4x4, the last car left at the Hertz counter at Reagan Air-port. "It's red, is that all right?" the Hertz girl had asked him. He told her red was his favorite color.

A few miles back he'd seen the sugar-coated green signs for General Washington's home at Mt. Vernon, and then the town of Woodbridge, so he figured to be getting close. Route 1 was the old eastern seaboard road to the capital and time had passed it by. There were still places called the Three Oaks Motor Hotel, little log cabins built in the trees around a semicircular drive. There was maybe an hour of sun left in the sky. Then it would be dark and much harder to find Morning Glory Farm.

He hoped Homer was in his vehicle with the heat on. Temperature had been dropping since he'd landed. He reached over and turned the heater fan to high, wished he had his leather gloves. Glad he'd worn his duster.

Okay, there it is, he said to himself, seeing a frosted sign for River Road in the yellow cones of his head-lights. He took a left. Another sign said, Lee's Ferry, 1 mile. Good, we're in business. He slowed way down now, to a crawl. Big old trees, huge dark trunks, bare branches heavily laden with snow. And through them, the river. The farm should be coming up on his left pretty soon.

To his left, he saw, there was what had to be a split-rail fence under a mound of fresh snow and then a white wooden sign coming up that said Morning Glory Farm.

The drive came up fast and he braked too hard. The rear end fishtailed, caught up with the front end and then he was spinning, headed straight for the ditch. He eased his foot off the brake and slid around to a stop, the headlight beams aimed at a weird angle. Well. Bad start. He put the thing in low and gunned it. Tried reverse. The wheels just spun like he was on oily glass.

He cursed under his breath, shut the engine off, swung out of the car, and started climbing the hill on foot. Cowboy boots made the walking trickier than it had to be. No fresh tracks in the drive, but it was snowing so hard a car could have driven up this road twenty minutes ago and you wouldn't know it.

There was a long sloping white meadow to his left as he climbed. Up on the summit, a pretty two-story white farmhouse with dark shutters on all the windows. Nice views of the woods and town to the west and down to the river to the east. It would be pretty dark in the house now, sun was almost down behind him, but there were no lights in any of the windows. No movement around the house, no smoke coming from the two tall brick chimneys at either end of the roof peak.

There was a heavily wooded area to his right.

He figured Homer's vehicle to be parked deep in those woods, just over the ridge. Some kind of river access road maybe. A public boat launch? He angled off the drive into the woods as he got close to the top, moving slowly through the trees now, expecting to come upon Homer or his car at any moment. The footing here was more difficult, big drifts piled up beneath the trees, and by the time he'd reached the top of the hill he was breathing pretty hard.

He saw Homer's car.

It was parked in the trees down near the black, slow-moving river and covered with snow. He started down toward it, an unreasonable uneasiness suddenly pinging at his brain. He'd last spoken to the boy, what, five hours ago? Still, that was a long time to sit in your car, waiting, snow blanketing your windows.

Homer had the bone in his teeth now, and Franklin knew how it felt. You wanted to see how it ended. You wanted to end it. Still, the sight of that car made him uneasy. He quickened his pace, slipping and sliding, holding on to branches to stay on his feet.

Homer was not in the car. The driver's side door was hanging open. There was a lot of snow on the seat. On the dash and on the floor. Something was missing besides Homer. Yeah. The Mossburg shotgun was not in its mount under the dash.

Franklin stood up, breathing hard. There had been a small access road to the river, he'd crossed it coming down the hill. He started moving back up in that direction, the only one that made any sense, until he reached the road. The road angled through the woods down to the river. And there was the boat ramp. And there was the trailer truck they'd stopped that night outside of Prairie. Homer's ghost rider, the Yankee Slugger. The trailer was backed down the incline, the rear wheels a few feet from the water's edge. The tractor was facing this way, uphill, and the headlights were on. A few feet away, an idling forklift was parked on the slope.

On the ground in the pool of light was his deputy.

He was on his back, staring blindly up into the light from the truck's headlamps. The snow on the ground around him was soaked bright red. About a foot from his outreached hand, the Mossberg was almost buried but still visible. This had happened just before he'd pulled off the road. Within the last fifteen minutes or so. Maybe while he was spinning into the ditch.

Homer was still breathing.

Rapid, shallow breaths, but he was alive.

"Homer?" he knelt down and cradled the boy's head in his arms.

"You made it."

"Don't talk. We have to get you to a hospital."

"Too late for that, Sheriff. Don't worry about it."

"Who did this?"

"It was—the son. I was watching them unload the truck. Putting the thing in the river. Tried to stop them. The older one, on the forklift, saw me come out of the woods. He—he yelled something and the son just turned around and shot me. I shot back. I think I killed him. That's all there is to it."

Homer's eyes were going far away.

"You're going to be okay, Homer. You hold on, son."

"No, listen. You have to . . . wait. You have to hear about the thing they put in the river. It's—bad."

"What is it, Homer?"

"Some kind of—what. I don't know. A baby submarine. High tech. Nobody inside. Leastways nobody got in the damn thing. Just like the truck . . . remote control."

"Still there? The thing in the river?"

"Hell, no. Hit the water and started to submerge. Headed upriver. Going pretty fast, too, and it—it—"

"Which way? Which way was it headed?"

"North I think."

"Towards Washington?"

"I can't . . . I'm not . . ."

"Don't talk, Homer. Stay with it. Stay with me."

"Can't. I got to go."

"Homer?"

FRANKLIN SAT in the snow with the dead boy for a good five minutes. Just let the tears come since they wouldn't stop no matter how hard he tried. Teardrops and snowflakes fell on the boy's cheeks, still tinged pink with the icy cold. Then Dixon got to his feet and took his duster off. Covered his deputy with it. Watched the snow softly falling on the still form of his deputy for a minute or so. Bent down to grab a handful of the white stuff and rubbed it all over his face, knuckles digging into his eyes.

He stood and saw Homer's hand sticking out under the duster. Boy's pistol still in his hand. Franklin gently pried the gun from Homer's cold fingers and stuck it in the small of his back, inside his jeans. He stood for a second, breathing deep, put his head back, and looked straight up into the dark sky full of snow. There was maybe a half hour of daylight left.

After a minute, he picked up the Mossberg and walked around the truck to where a dead Arab kid lay-facedown in the snow. There was a wide pool of blood similar to the one spreading beneath Homer's body. Bright red, but that's where the similarities ended.

He jacked a fresh round into the shotgun's chamber and looked up at the farmhouse on the hill. He smelled smoke. They must have a fire going inside now. It was certainly cold enough outside.

69

RIVER OF DOUBT

Hawke stood alone at the stern, hands clasped behind his back. It was early afternoon, just half past one, local time, and the sun was blazing overhead. He gazed at the twisting wake trailing behind his stern, his feet planted wide against sudden yaw or pitch. He was thinking on how matters stood aboard his vessel. It was now twelve hours since they'd departed Manaus.

He'd managed a few hours sleep in his small cabin, then gone once more into the tiny and hastily organized "war room" to confer with Stokely, Girard Brownlow, and his fire control officer, a Welshman named Dylan Allegria. One problem, now remedied, had been the engines. Minor mechanical issue with one of the three, overheating, but troubling all the same. With two engines, the performance parameters of this boat went to hell.

The bloody River of Doubt was living up to, even beyond, expectations. The mood aboard *Stiletto* had degenerated from restless to apprehensive. Now, it was tense. They were late, that was part of it. Some aboard would argue privately they were lost as well. The sheer density of the forest and the endless uncharted tributaries spiking off the cocoa-colored river was creating confusion and sensory overload among his men.

This was certainly not abnormal for men going into battle. It was, Hawke knew, unusual for this handpicked group of warriors.

These men were, for the most part, seasoned fighters, battle-hardened veterans, recruited for their experience in modern guerrilla warfare. Many had been flown to Key West from Martinique, home of Thunder and Lightning, a mercenary outfit without parallel in modern jungle warfare. To them, this was just another opportunity to beat unbeatable odds and snag a hefty paycheck.

The ante was raised, however, when it suddenly became a hostage rescue operation to boot. And it was no secret to anyone aboard that the hostage needing rescue was the closest man on earth to Alexander Hawke.

Hawke had overheard bickering in the crew's mess. It wouldn't do. In an hour's time, he would gather them all in the wheelhouse. Show them his belief in them and this mission. His optimism. His absolute conviction that they could and would overcome every obstacle and succeed despite any difficulty. They would find Congreve alive and get him out. They would destroy Top. Put an end to his intentions, whatever the hell they were.

Nec aspera terrent, as the lads of the King's Regiment

have it. That's what he would tell them. Difficulties be Damned.

They'd been slowed by the bloody engine repair; but now they were slowed by the very river itself. Twisting, turning, endless. They'd been steaming nearly fourteen hours on the smaller rivers now, since they'd left the wide Amazon. Many hours on the much smaller Madeira, and now they were headed due south on the comparatively narrow Rio Roosevelt.

Many natives still called it by its original name, the River of Doubt. Now he could see why.

The wilderness had closed in on the crew of *Stiletto* just as the sea closes over a diver. Hawke and his men felt cut off from all they'd ever known; each man felt as if he were on a journey back to the beginning of time. They had entered a brooding world of plants, water, and, except for the deep rumble of the engines, silence. Everywhere you looked, a riot of vegetation. The big trees were kings of the earth this deep in the jungle. The forest air was thick and sluggish. The only sunshine was directly overhead and little comfort.

He'd forgotten, or erased, his well-stocked stores of bad memories of this hellish place.

All afternoon they'd been butting against shoals, trying to find the channel. Hawke had posted two men on the bow, looking for signs of hidden banks and sunken stones, some sharp, unseen edge that would rip the bottom out of this otherworldly craft and doom what was left of his hopes. To make matters worse, he heard the roll of drums inside the curtain of jungle now. And whether they represented war or peace or prayer he had no idea.

Xucuru scouts, maybe. Announcing his return.

Kill you, kill you.

Hawke tried to tell himself he was only imagining a vengeful aspect to nature here, but he couldn't do that either. Couldn't shake the notion that even bloody nature was deliberately conspiring against him. He'd felt this dreamy notion during his captivity. And, the deeper *Stiletto* traveled into the jungle, the more reality seemed to fade. He pressed his fingertips deeply into his eye sockets and willed himself to stop this foolishness. Only looking into Top's eyes would end this bloody nightmare. And that moment could not come soon enough.

Suddenly, Captain Girard Brownlow was standing beside him at the stern rail.

"Skipper, sorry to disturb you."

"Not at all, Brownie."

"At roughly 0330 we will be approaching a stretch of river where Brock has indicated submerged mines may be protecting the main enemy compound. I'm ordering the crew to deploy the mine probes in half an hour."

"Good. Take her speed down to fifteen as well, Captain. Mr. Brock has been known to be less than precise."

"Aye, sir. Anything I can do for you?"

"The PAM system," Hawke said, his eyes scanning the thick green vegetation, "Death from above. Missiles armed and ready?"

"Aye. Fire control officer Allegria confirms both PAM and LAM systems up and functioning normally, Skipper. We are currently mapping and tracking two targets."

"What targets?"

"Appear to be two small unmanned vehicles, sir. Couple of bots pulling guard duty, I'd say. Mr. Brock's recon report identifies these vehicles as Trolls. Mobile machine guns on tracks, really. Operating on either bank, parallel course, equidistant from the river, outbound range one mile. Our companions for the last ten minutes, sir, matching our speed and corrections. We did heat signatures on both vehicles. They definitely appear to be unmanned. Scouts, we think."

"So. The enemy already knows we're coming."

"That's accurate, sir."

"Tell Fire Control to monitor the scouts. As long as they're running parallel courses, leave them alone. They turn toward us, threaten the boat, take them out."

"Aye, aye, sir. I'll inform fire control officer Allegria immediately."

Brownlow saluted smartly, left the stern, and went forward to convey Hawke's orders. Hawke looked at the two ungainly black boxes mounted side-by-side on his stern. State of the art, Harry Brock had told him, missiles in a box. He just hoped the bloody things were all they were cracked up to be. Brock was convinced they'd need them where they were headed. And Brock had procured them.

Harry Brock, Hawke said privately, was a bit of a piss artist.

The two men had worked together a year ago in Oman. Hawke had rescued Harry from a Chinese steamer carrying the CIA officer back to prison in China. Then, to his credit, Brock returned the favor, getting Hawke alive out of the bloody jungle. That made them even, which is the way Hawke liked it. He had never liked the feeling of being beholden to anyone.

But now Hawke would have to rely on Brock's boots-on-the-ground intel about the enemy's exact location, defenses, and fortifications. Harry was coming aboard Hawke's boat for the final leg of the journey. *Stiletto* would make an unscheduled stop tonight, just after nightfall, at an abandoned river outpost called Tupo. With any luck, Brock would be there as planned.

Hawke had entered uncharted territory. He'd never ventured this far downriver during his captivity. Much as he hated to admit it, he needed Harry now. Navigation from this point onward would be exceedingly difficult without someone aboard who knew what physical landmarks to look for on the river. Maps were virtually useless. Because of flash flooding, the beds of rivers changed constantly. The rivers, forks, and tributaries had become indistinguishable. Some rivers were mined and some were not. Harry knew. It was Harry who'd told him about the armed drones and robotic weaponry. Harry who'd sold him the big black boxes on the stern.

PAMs were the fifteen Precision Attack Missiles mounted in a second 4x6x4-foot black container just aft of the wheelhouse. Fire and forget, meaning once a target was acquired, it was dead. Realizing that, in the jungle, there would be many targets the boat's myriad sensors wouldn't pick up, Hawke had also ordered a second NetFires missile system installed, the Loitering Attack Missile, or LAM.

These mini-cruise missiles were the same size and weight as a PAM missile. Unlike it, the LAM missile can fly around an assigned area for forty-five minutes looking for a target. If none is acquired, the missile simply crashes. If a target is detected by its built-in laser radar system, nicknamed Ladar, and the onboard software recognizes the target vehicle as an enemy one, the missile attacks from above. Its warhead is sufficient to take out all but the largest Main Battle Tanks of any known enemy force.

At that moment, a flying object struck the PAM box, hard, and fell to the deck at Hawke's feet. Hawke bent to pick it up. It was an arrow. A long one, maybe four feet, which meant the Xucuru warrior who'd fired it was not too deep inside the wall of jungle. Hawke leapt up into the protected .50-caliber machine gun turret just in time. The air around the boat was suddenly filled with poison-tipped arrows, a cloud of them, flying from both banks. Most bounced harmlessly off the carbon fiber hull or superstructure and sank. Still, it was unpleasant and there was always a chance someone could get hurt.

Hawke pulled the headset on and barked into the mouthpiece, "Nav! You have water under the keel?"

They could easily outrun this attack; it was simply a matter of not running hard aground or ripping the bottom out.

"Aye, Skipper. But not much. Shoals are—"

"Stand by, Helm." Hawke said, "I'll deal with it."

A burst of speed wasn't worth the risk to the boat. And besides, he owed these Xucuru chaps or their brothers-in-arms big time. Pity his old friend Wajari wasn't around to see this turn of events.

Hawke gripped the joystick that controlled his turret rotation, turned the bubble to starboard, and squeezed off a long burst. The noise of the twin .50-caliber guns ripped the silence. The hot rounds shredded the vegetation in a very satisfying manner. Another burst, then he swung the twin guns over to the portside banks and opened up once more. The guns' effect on the hidden Indians was instantly apparent. No more arrows from either side of the river. They were either all dead or had melted back into the forest.

The white devil had arrived.

"Heads up, Skipper, we've got a visitor," Brownlow's voice said in his earphones.

"What do you have now, Cap?" Hawke climbed down out of the enclosed gun mount and started moving quickly forward toward the wheelhouse.

"We've got a drone aircraft coming our way, sir. Flying straight toward us, nose-to-nose. Right down on the deck."

"Range?"

"Uh, he's a mile out now and closing. Altitude twenty-one feet. We should have visual contact any second now."

"I've got him," Hawke said, ducking inside the wheelhouse after spotting the drone's approach. He moved quickly to the helm and stood beside Brownlow, who was driving the boat. Both men were peering through the glass, watching the tiny speck a few feet above the water grow larger. Hawke grabbed the Zeiss binocs sitting atop the binnacle.

The drone looked like an upside-down spoon with wings. Made of lightweight metals and composite plastic, driven by a small, propeller-driven engine, the craft was painted a dull grey and had a top speed of only 150 mph.

Hawke said, "Definitely a drone recon. A UAV, streaming live video back to the command base, wherever that may be. It's armed. Two air-to-ground Hellfire-type missiles on the wingtips."

"Take him out, Skipper?" Allegria said.

"He's currently broadcasting our arrival. Let's give the folks crowded around the telly back home a great big bang."

"Roger, that's okay to launch."

"Affirmative," Hawke said. "Let's see if these bloody missiles-in-a-box really work."

A second later, a red-tipped PAM missile screamed out of its launch container, streaking skyward. At an altitude of one hundred feet, the slender projectile nosed over and dove straight down toward its locked-in prey. The men in *Stiletto*'s wheelhouse held their collective breath. This technology was so new it even *smelled* new.

Half a mile upriver, the air was split by a sharp crack as an intense ball of flame erupted about twenty feet above the river. The shockwave of the exploding warhead could be felt a second later by everyone aboard *Stiletto*. Spontaneous whoops of applause and high-fives erupted amongst the crew. The men aboard now knew that at least they had one effective weapons system aboard this as yet un-battle-tested warship.

"Nice shooting, Mr. Allegria," Hawke said.

"Ducks in a pond, sir," Allegria replied.

"That won't last long, Mr. Allegria. Stow that attitude."

"Aye, aye, sir."

70

There was smoke rising above the farmhouse. But it wasn't coming from the chimneys. Black smoke, thick and acrid, was pouring from the three dormer windows up on the second floor. Franklin could see licks of fire starting to race along up under the eaves, climbing up the shingled roof, pools of flame spreading rapidly up to the peak, like hot liquid running uphill, melting the snow.

Franklin slogged up the hill as fast as he could, the crusty snow up to his knees as he climbed. There was one entrance on this back side of the house. Looked to be the kitchen, a big bow window and one of those double Dutch doors. No lights on in the kitchen, even though it had suddenly gotten very dark on the hillside.

The sheriff paused at the top of the brick steps, listening for any sound from inside. All he could hear was the crackling noise of the shingled roof burning, snapping and popping, growing louder every second. The wooden farmhouse had to be almost two hundred years old. It would not take long to burn to the ground. Along with any contents that might prove useful. The inhabitants, he figured, were gone. Out the front door, maybe. A car hidden in the barn he'd seen on the way in?

Maybe not.

The door was slightly ajar.

Franklin kicked the door open wide, nearly taking it off the hinges. Adrenaline fueled his anger, still seeing Homer's pink cheeks with the snow on them. He went through the door in a blizzard of snow, the shotgun out in front of him, eyes scanning what looked to be a deserted room. Kitchen counters to his right, stovetops set in a bricked center island with a copper hood above it.

"Police, freeze," he said, putting his gun on a woman slumped over a kitchen table. She'd been sitting near the bow window. She was pitched forward, arms hanging at her sides, her head down on the table. Her shoulders were heaving, and he knew she was sobbing, even though he couldn't hear her. Strands of wild dark hair hid her face. Her hands were under the table. The right arm twitched.

"I need to see your hands, ma'am."

"You killed my son," she said, her head and twisted face slowly coming up from the table. "My son!" She stiffened in the chair, turning away from the window and the bloody scene below to stare at him. Hatred burning through the tears streaming from her eyes. Righteous fury.

Franklin steadied the gun on her. "Your son killed a

police officer. Get your hands up where I can see them. Now! Do it now!"

"You want to see my hands?" she said, her voice shaking.

She rose up suddenly, leaping up from the chair and overturning the heavy table, dishes and glassware crashing to the floor, the stubby 9mm machine pistol coming up with her body.

"Drop the weapon!" Franklin said, sidestepping to get nearer to the door.

"Allahu Akbar!" she shouted, her voice raw with grief and hate. "God is great!"

Mad despair in her black eyes as she pulled the trigger two, three times. Franklin was moving fast now and the shots were going wide and high but she was still staggering toward him, the gun extended at the end of her arm, firing blindly in his direction. She found the selector switch for full auto. He had no choice. Franklin dropped to one knee and shot the woman in the chest, killing her instantly. Her body was thrown backwards onto the floor, collapsing among the broken bits and pieces of china scattered there.

Franklin rose to his feet and left the kitchen, headed toward the front of the house. Where was the husband? Passing through the darkened dining room, he saw a litter of takeout food strewn across the pretty cherry table. The smoke in the house was strong now, burning his eyes. The fire had spread to the inner walls. He pumped a round into the chamber and raced into the living room.

The drapes on either side of the large picture window on the west-facing wall were aflame. Two large overstuffed chairs were also burning, and the hooked rug beneath them was steaming, primed to ignite.

And there was a roaring fire in the fireplace.

Not wooden logs, but masses of documents were burning there. Sheaves of paper, only recently thrown in by the looks of it. Most of the documents were already turning to ash, but not all. Also in the iron grate, three laptop computers hissed and melted, dripping molten black plastic that hit the hot stone hearth with a sizzle.

Franklin cleared the room of hostiles with his eyes before placing the Mossberg on the mantel. Then he quickly bent to retrieve what he could from the flames. He reached into the fire and managed to pull a handful of loose paper out, still burning his fingers and singeing all the hair off his forearm. He was reaching in again, realizing that his shirtsleeves were burning, when he saw the shoes, then the khaki legs of the man coming down the stairway leading to the second floor. Now his belt, now his torso . . .

No time to grab the shotgun.

He turned and faced him, letting the burning papers fall to the floor behind the sofa. He moved his right foot slowly, not lifting his heel, stamping out the papers with his boot, saving what he could.

The man in the red cardigan sweater was smiling as he came toward Franklin, kicking away furniture. The sheriff had seen the man's eyes light for a moment on the shotgun sitting atop the mantelpiece. He could have been a lawyer or a banker, a pediatrician come down from checking on the sick kids upstairs in their beds. But he wasn't. He had his finger on the trigger of the semiautomatic rifle in his hands, a 30-round banana clip waiting to be expended on a lone Texas sheriff.

In his other hand was a five-gallon plastic jerry can of gasoline. Gas was sloshing out of the can as the man descended the stairs and crossed the room.

"Put down the weapon, sir," Franklin said, moving behind the heavy sofa.

Red Sweater shouted something, a curse, in Arabic, and then heaved the half-empty can of gasoline toward the window with the burning draperies. The whole wall erupted into flames.

The sheriff used the moment to dive behind the large velvet sofa. The staccato sound of automatic fire filled the room. Franklin hit the wooden floor hard, using his shoulder to break the fall. He could hear and feel the thump of rounds slamming into the furniture as he rolled away, his right hand going behind his back, going for Homer's Glock, stuck inside his waistband. The man kept firing, short bursts, into the sofa. He felt the pistol stuck in his jeans and pulled it, got it out in front of him.

Gun in hand, he rolled onto his stomach and peered beneath the wide sofa.

Two feet in brown shoes, sagging orange socks, moving toward his end of the sofa.

Franklin put one round into each ankle.

The man screamed out his sudden agony as he came down hard before the stone hearth. Franklin was on his feet and moving around the end of the couch. The Arab was on his back, somehow grinning through all the pain as he moved the muzzle of his weapon toward Franklin. The two men locked eyes.

The Arab fired, point-blank range, the round grazing Dixon's forehead. It stung, dizzied him for an instant, but he stayed with it, stayed on his feet. Warm blood was running into his eyes, but he saw the man's finger tighten around the trigger.

The sheriff put one round in the center of the man's forehead.

Dixon stood there a second, woozy, his heart thudding in his chest. He looked around him. Fire was racing up the four walls now. The timbered ceiling above his head was steaming, the paint curling and peeling. It was seconds away from bursting into flames. Time to go. Franklin stuck the pistol back inside his waistband, then gathered up the shotgun and grabbed the smoldering papers he'd saved from the floor. Then he raced back into the kitchen. The fire had not yet reached this side of the house. At least not the ground-floor kitchen.

There was an old-fashioned black phone on the island. It was probably the one Homer had used eight hours ago, standing here, calmly eating an apple from the pantry, watching the gentle snowfall outside.

He put the papers down beside the phone. There were at least a dozen or more, some ruined completely, others intact. He scanned each one, his eyes running uselessly over the Arabic print mixed with unintelligible scraps of English. One of them, half-burned, caught his eye. It was a map of some kind with notations in red ink. He looked at it carefully, holding it up to his eyes, then picked up the phone and called information. He got a human for some reason. He asked for a number in Washington and got it.

He studied the exposed beam over his head while he waited. It looked hot.

"Federal Bureau of Investigation, how may I direct your call?"

He explained who he was and why he was calling to three people before getting put on hold a fourth time. Then he hung up and called the State Department and asked for Secretary de los Reyes, explaining that he was a law officer and personal friend, and that she would recognize the name from the Key West conference. And that this was an urgent emergency call involving national security.

"Sheriff Dixon, this is Consuelo de los Reyes," he heard her say after a minute or so. "Thank you for calling."

"Yes ma'am, thank you for taking my call. I can't talk long because the house I'm standing in is on fire."

"Sheriff, you've got to get out—"

"Please, ma'am, it's important, just let me talk here a second. I'm at a place called Morning Glory Farm. Lee's Ferry, Virginia. It's on the River Road north of Fredericksburg. I've got one dead—"

"What river are we talking about, Sheriff Dixon?"

"Uh, well, I'm not rightly sure. I guess the Potomac."

"The Potomac River, go ahead."

"Like I say, we need a coroner out here. EMS. I got a dead deputy. Two dead Arabs, maybe three. They put some kind of device in the river. Homer believed it to be an unmanned submarine."

"Homer?"

"My late deputy."

"Sheriff, hold on for one second please, I'm asking for some of my people here to pick up and listen in. Fire and EMS vehicles are already en route to your location. And state police."

"Yes, ma'am. Anyway, like I said, my deputy saw this high-tech submarine they carried in the truck. The wood crate it came out of, it's about the size of a small Volkswagen. One more thing, before I go. These people were burning documents and computers, but I saved what I could. I have one paper in my hand right now. Burned piece of a map of Washington with a squiggly red line on it, and the words, *parade route*."

"Parade route. Everyone get that?" de los Reyes asked her people listening in.

"And, trucks. There may be a lot of tractor-trailer trucks headed your way. No drivers, I don't think. I'm guessing they're remote-controlled too. I don't know what they're hauling, but it probably isn't good."

"Get out of that house, Sheriff. Local police and FBI agents from Quantico are en route to your location right now. Do not endanger yourself, but take every scrap of paper possible and give it to the FBI team. Tell them everything you know."

"Yes, ma'am. I've got to go. This beam here is about to give way on me."

"Go. Get out."

"These people killed a boy who was pretty near kin to me. I'd like to help out up there if I can."

"I'll make sure you get to Washington. We'll put you to work, don't worry. We're pretty busy around here because of the Inauguration."

"Inauguration. When is that exactly?"

"Day after tomorrow, Sheriff."

71

THE BLACK RIVER

I'd rather go down the river with seven studs than with a hundred shitheads."

The little Frenchman laughed. "*C'est geniale!* Brilliant!"

"I'm not making this stuff up, Froggy," Stoke said to his old war buddy. "You know who said that? The founder of fuckin' Delta Force, that's who. Charlie Beckwith."

"A tough guy, *non*? A legend, this man Beckwith. Even in France."

"Even in France," Stoke said looking at him in mock amazement. "Imagine that, will you? Hey, Frogman, listen to me," Stoke said, suddenly dead serious. "We still got a lot of shit to figure out, *mon ami*. We're going up against some true pencil-dick assholes in this frigging jungle. And we ain't got a whole lot of time left to screw around here."

Stoke had seen the worried look on Alex Hawke's face a few hours ago. The rivers weren't always where they were supposed to be. Every time it rained hard, the topography changed. The latest GPS positioning had the boat smack in the middle of a damn forest. So, he was feeling a little guilty, hanging out back here on the stern with Froggy, having fun.

The two men were sitting cross-legged on the deck in the cramped space between the PAM and LAM missile launching stations. A scattering of dog-eared playing cards lay face up on the deck between them; a game of Texas Hold 'Em had ended. For the last half hour they'd just been shooting the shit. That's how the little Frenchman put it, now that he'd learned another useful American expression.

It was late afternoon on the river, and the light was soft and gold. Cooler, too, and not too many mosquitoes at their current boat speed. Temperature dropping, somebody said, barometer dropping like a rock; you could feel the evil-looking cold front moving in over the jungle from the west. Heavy rain, high winds. For now, the palm fronds of trees along the bank drooped low, not a breath of air to sway them.

Captain Brownlow and Hawke remained on the bridge deck, taking turns driving the boat. Navigation at this point was a full-time obsession. And they were constantly talking tactics and adjusting strategies to changing conditions. The ability to arrive undetected on a hostile shore is essential. There was little hope of that now they'd been sighted by that drone they'd shot down.

Gunners were stationed in the turrets fore and aft. Every man aboard was armed and keeping a weather eye on the twin shorelines. For the last couple of hours they'd been lucky. No Indians, no drones, no nothing. *Stiletto* was bristling with firepower.

A young guy named Llwyd Ecclestone was manning the 20mm cannon up on the roof of the wheelhouse. Just a kid, Stoke thought, but the ex-Ranger came highly recommended by Froggy. "Hey," Stoke said when he'd met the kid in Key West and seen the name stencilled on his flak jacket, "your parents forget to put an *o* in your name?" Turned out Llwyd was Welsh, people who didn't go in for vowels much.

Froggy, barely five feet tall in combat boots, was one of the charter members of the infamous counterterrorist organization known as Thunder and Lightning. The former Foreign Legionnaire commanded the group of seven spec ops commandos who had come aboard at Key West. These warriors, all ex-Legionnaires, Gurkhas, and Rangers, were justly considered the best anti-terrorist combat team for hire. As an added bonus, Froggy and his squad were by far the most successful freelance hostage rescue team in the world.

Froggy, the HRT team's beloved squad leader, was dressed in his typical pre-combat uniform: khaki shorts, a faded blue and gold U.S. Navy SEAL T-shirt, and a sterling silver bo'sun's whistle hanging from the chain around his neck. He had his trademark white kepi perched atop his shaved head and his trademark cigarette dangling from his lower lip.

Froggy puffed out a cloud of pungent blue smoke and noisily spat the stinky Gauloise butt overboard.

"Dites-moi," he said, and then added in his heavy French accent, "Tell me about these assholes we're going to fight. Just don't speak so fucking fast."

"Okay. These people we're dealing with down here, been psyching themselves up about this for years. You'll hear all about it tonight from Harry Brock. What you've got down here is a lethal mix of guerrillas, okay? You got bikers and bangers, dopers and fanatic Voodoo jihadists. And old-style commies, too, all tied into one neat little bundle, right? Now, what does that tell you?"

"What?"

"They've all got one thing in common. What is it?"

"They suck?"

"Of course they suck. But, one other thing. They all hate America."

"Join zee fucking club, eh?"

"People like this, all these scumbags hating your ass so bad, that tells you something, right?"

"Tells me what?"

"America must be a pretty great fuckin' country."

"Pfft. If you like this kind of country, perhaps. America is no France."

"Thank God for small favors. Anyway, these crazy bastards hate our ass, Froggy. And, to make it worse, they're filthy rich. Twisted ideology is one thing. You back it up with oil money, drug money, illegal arms money, white slavery, it's something else. Brock says they've got robots. Drone aircraft, tanks. How do we kill robots?"

The demolitions expert grinned. "Anything can be blown up, *mon ami,* anything."

"Chrome don't bleed."

"*Mais non,* but it melts."

"I guess. Problem is, we got to get my man Ambrose Congreve out of there before we blow up one damn thing. I hope Brock's got a plan. I'm still not seeing exactly how that's going to happen."

"I've been talking to my squad about this subject all morning. We have an idea."

"Don't be shy. We ain't got a lot of time."

"We want you to offload us late tonight. A stealth insertion into the jungle. All eight of us. Upriver from the target compound. Four or five miles. I'll show you on the map, the precise spot I have chosen. We will hike to the target through the jungle. Standard Operating Procedures. Night-vision gear, hand signals. Locate the hostage. Rendezvous with the main force above the bridge. Deliver the hostage to the boat and get him out of the combat zone. Then destroy the enemy."

"Yeah. Sounds simple enough. How you plan to do all that shit, Froggy?"

"Take out the perimeter guards first, of course. Swift and silent. Infiltrate the village. Do a search. House-to-house. We'll find your friend Ambrose, I promise you. With or without Monsieur Brock."

"Brock's Brazilian girlfriend says the whole damn enemy village is built up in the damn trees. Like a goddamn Swiss Family Robinson."

"What goes up must come down, Stokely. Boom."

Stoke nodded in agreement. "Plant Semtex gift boxes at the base of all the trees. Bury the linked fuses between trees, all feeding one detonator."

"Boom, boom, boom."

"*Plastique, n'est-ce pas,* Froggy? Tim-berrrr! But look at these trees around here. They've got to be two hundred feet tall."

"So? Kiss-kiss-bang-bang. *Et voilà!* Victory is ours once more."

"Froggy, listen. This ain't going to be as easy as you seem to think. We've got to find out where they have Ambrose first, right? Let's assume he's up in one of the treehouses. We have to locate which one. Get him down safely and get him the hell out of there before the shooting starts and—What? Don't look at me like that."

"I am zee famous Froggy. Do not insult me."

"Chill. I'm just talking out loud. Hear how it sounds."

"If he can be found, we will find him."

"You sound like you don't think I'm coming with you."

"You want to come?"

"Is Paris a city? Two four-man squads. You take one, I'll take the other. Fan out, go in. Hop and pop, just like the good old days, *mi Corazon.*"

"We must talk now to Commander Hawke and tell him what we think."

"Yeah. Holy shit. What was that?"

Stiletto had shuddered to a halt, midriver.

"What is it? We run out of river?"

"Dead stop. Something's wrong. Let's get forward."

Hawke and Brownlow stood at the helm.

"Stoke," Hawke said as they entered, "take a look at this."

Stoke joined him. "Aw, shit. Blockade."

He was looking at the Indian war party two hundred yards farther downriver. A solid phalanx of war canoes was waiting for them. Had to be a hundred canoes, rafted up, row after row of them, twelve abreast, covering the entire width of the river at its narrowest point. Completely blocking the river.

Waves of canoes stretched back, maybe twenty, thirty rows deep. It was hard to see just how many were waiting in the evening light. The dugouts were decked out in all kind of exotic combat regalia, flaming torches hung at the bow and stern, each boat loaded to the gunnels with painted warriors ready to rumble in the jungle.

Right now they were just beating the drums. Soon, the whole concert would get under way. Seemed like they only knew one tune, stuck in a groove.

Kill you, kill you.

Hawke said, "What do you think, Stoke? We're already two hours late for our scheduled pickup of Brock. If he thinks we're not coming and bolts, we're finished."

"Slow down. But don't shoot."

"No? Why not?" Brownlow said. "We're being attacked. We could blow through those dugouts like a knife through butter."

"Not in these shoals, you can't. Besides, it's not necessary," Stoke said. "As long as everybody stays locked inside the boat, what can they do? Bounce spears and poison darts off the windows all night, that's about it. Let's just keep moving. Slow."

"He's right, Brownie," Hawke said. Then, into his mike, "Crew. Clear decks and batten her down. Everyone get below and stay there. Do not engage the enemy."

It took a minute or two to get everyone shut down inside.

"Not a lot of water under our keel, Skipper," Brownlow said, pointing at the monitor displaying a depth-sounder's 3-D depiction of the river bottom ahead. Ugly shoals filled the screen, a narrow channel snaked forward. It was barely wide enough to accommodate their slender beam.

"Look at those bloody shoals," Hawke said. "The Xucuru picked this location deliberately. We'll go through them dead slow."

"Yeah," Stoke said, "keep us moving, Brownie. Rule of tonnage. You fuck with a truck, you get run over, ke-mosabe. We just stay in the channel, let them do what they gotta do."

"One problem with that idea," Hawke said, eyes on the canoes a hundred yards ahead. "At this slow speed they'll board us. They'll be climbing all over the damn boat."

"I've got an idea," Stoke said. "Stop the boat."

"Spit it out," Hawke said, watching the Indians through the night vision binocs now. The sun went down in a hurry on the river. Stoke looked at him and smiled.

"First, we disable our deck guns, lock up the missile boxes. Not that these fellas could use them, but still."

"This plan sounds bad so far," Hawke said.

"Wait. Then, we break out the carpet tacks."

Brownlow said, "Did he just say, 'carpet tacks'?"

"He did," Hawke said, looking carefully at his friend.

"Secret weapon," Stoke said, "little low-tech trick I picked up on the dock in Manaus. Back in a flash."

Stoke left the bridge and disappeared below. While he was gone, *Stiletto* was locked down, all exterior weapons systems disabled, hatches closed and locked. A few minutes later Stoke reappeared on the bow, a heavy sack of carpet tacks on each shoulder. He was moving slowly, emptying the canvas sacks. He was laying down a thick carpet of tacks on the decks, all the way from bow to stern on the starboard side. Then he repeated the process on the port side, smiling through the window as he headed aft, spilling his tacks. When he was finished, he climbed the ladder and used the remaining tacks to cover the wheelhouse roof.

"That ought to do it," Stoke said, dropping down into the wheelhouse a minute later. "You may proceed whenever you're ready, Cap'n Brownlow."

"What the hell, Stoke?" Hawke asked and Stokely just smiled.

"Skipper?" Brownlow said. "Ready?"

"All ahead dead slow, Brownie," Hawke said. "Easy as she goes, no course deviation."

The waiting flotilla war party saw what *Stiletto* was doing. The otherworldly thing was advancing upon them, slowly, despite their blockade. Instantly, they unleashed the first wave of poison-tipped arrows toward the oncoming black boat. Those weapons expended, the archers gave way to a second force of warriors who stood and elevated their long blowguns.

Inside the wheelhouse, the noise was akin to being attacked by swarms of steel locusts, the incessant smacking noise of darts and arrows hitting carbon fiber. *Stiletto* had now sailed directly into the main force, encircled within the huge logjam of war canoes. The Xucuru were in full war cry, howling, giving vent to their frustration by banging with their fists on the sides of the sleek hull. Crude grappling lines made of twisted vines were thrown aboard the slowly moving powerboat. War canoes pulled alongside and warriors scrambled up the lines to the decks.

"They're boarding us, Skipper," Brownlow said under his breath. "Christ, they're all over the damn boat."

Screaming savages with torches appeared at the wheelhouse windows. But, the sounds coming from the howling Xucuru warriors were screams of anguish, not cries of war. The Xucuru appeared to be bouncing up and down beyond the windows; they hopped madly from one foot to the other on the carpet of tacks, grabbing their feet, howling and yipping in pain.

"Not staying long, I shouldn't think," Hawke said, grinning at Stokely.

"Look like they're hopping mad out there," Stoke said.

Most of the Xucuru, upon encountering Stoke's unpleasant surprise, leapt immediately back into the river. Those few who remained, faces illuminated by torches, were yelping and beating angrily on the wheelhouse windows. Hawke thumbed a switch overhead and all the interior lights were doused. The deck lights remained on. Now they could see the attackers clearly.

Brownlow said, grinning, "We've got a million dollars worth of high-tech weaponry on this boat. But that was one hell of an idea, Stoke."

"Best security system you can buy for four dollars a bag."

A few seconds later, all the Xucurus were abandoning ship. Ten, fifteen, twenty leapt from the decks of *Stiletto* and into the black river. No more boarded after that.

Brownlow looked at the surface of the river. The water was alive, frothing with darting and biting piranhas, swarms of them, lured by the sudden abundance of human blood in the water. The Xucuru, screaming, clawed the water, desperate to reach shore.

"Captain Brownlow, the river looks clear ahead," Hawke said. "Let's go get Mr. Brock. All ahead full."

"All ahead full."

Night had fallen in the jungle.

Soon, the torches of the war canoes and the cries of angry warriors were left astern, disappearing in the gloom.

Stiletto surged ahead, piercing the darkness, setting her course straight for the heart of the enemy.

72

A
ir Force One lands somewhere around here, doesn't it? I've seen that on the news a few times."

"Eighty-ninth Airlift Wing. Right over there, Sheriff," Consuelo de los Reyes said, pointing out a large hangar complex across the wide, snow-covered tarmac to their left.

The secretary of state and Sheriff Franklin W. Dixon were in the middle seat of the heavily armored black Chevy Suburban. There were two DSS agents from the Diplomatic Security Service up front and behind them three more. They were riding in one of six identical vehicles, their rooftops all bristling with antennas and sat dishes.

The convoy was just now exiting the main entry gate at Andrews Air Force Base in suburban Maryland. Consuelo de los Reyes had been one of the small group of people standing in the freezing cold on the tarmac when the FBI chopper transporting Sheriff Dixon had touched down at Andrews ten minutes earlier. She had greeted the sheriff warmly, and expressed her condolences about the death of his deputy, Homer Prudhomme, in the line of duty.

His death had not been in vain, she told Dixon, and indeed Deputy Prudhomme was most likely going to receive a posthumous citation for bravery. Sheriff Dixon had told de los Reyes he'd like to handle all the funeral arrangements, take the boy back home to Texas with him.

"I'll make arrangements for you and the deputy to fly home together, Sheriff."

"'Preciate it. What'd they do about that truck?" Dixon asked.

"They're putting it on a flatbed and taking it to Quantico. The technicians will take it apart bit by bit, see what makes it tick."

"Making it tick. I hope that's not a bomb."

"We all do, Sheriff."

As the convoy turned left and moved slowly through the small town of Morningside, heading northwest, Dixon was peering through the heavily tinted windows, trying to gather his thoughts and clear his head. The gunshot wound he'd received to the head had been purely superficial. A crease on his forehead. The EMS had stitched it up, splashed some brown stuff on it, and put a bandage over it. It still hurt pretty bad. More like a bad headache than a gunshot wound. He hadn't had much sleep, either.

And it didn't look like he was going to get much anytime soon.

"Where are we headed now?" he asked.

"There are some people at the White House who would like to speak to you."

"We're going to the White House?"

She nodded. "I've got a scheduled meeting there. They said you may as well come along. Tell me about that truck, Sheriff. How you came to find it."

"We pulled the first one about three weeks ago. Homer insisted on calling it the Ghost Rider because we couldn't find the driver anywhere. I thought he'd just run off into the desert. I'm afraid I didn't do too good a job of looking for him. That was the night we found the, uh, my posse."

"I know all about that, Sheriff. I'm terribly sorry about what happened to those brave boys. But I need to know everything you can tell me about those trucks before we go into this meeting with the president's security people."

"Homer stayed with it, no matter what I said. According to Wyatt Cooper, one of my deputies who talked to Homer, he followed one truck down to a town called Gunbarrel, right on the Rio Grande. That's where they were coming across the border. They'd built a huge tunnel underground, came up inside a deserted warehouse."

"They? Who built it?"

"Well, apparently, Mexicans, since that's where the tunnel is from. But there was a fella from Prairie who was in it with them on the American side. Local man named J. T. Rawls. He must have been the one ran the operation on this side of the border."

"What kind of operation? Had to be smuggling?"

"That's what Homer told my deputy. I think they were bringing drugs in originally. Drugs and illegals. Had to be a pretty big outfit too, all the money that must have been spent on that warehouse."

"And a tunnel that size. We don't understand the remote-controlled aspect of these trucks. Tell me about that."

"Heck, I don't understand it either. Doesn't make a lot of sense, the coyotes bringing in illegals that way. Or, drugs for that matter. Drivers and mules are dirt cheap down there. Expendable too."

"The one you found in Lee's Ferry. The deputy told you that a small submarine had been placed in the river."

"Yep. That's what he told me."

"He believed it to be an unmanned craft?"

"Yes he did. Said it took off with no one inside."

"How'd you come to be there? At the farm."

"Homer called me from the house where the terrorists were living. Right after I'd got back from your conference. My wife picked me up in San Antonio. She'd followed another truck herself up there. To San Antonio. Same black windows."

"Where is that truck now?"

"I reckon she's still looking for it. I haven't had a chance to call her. Or, even Wyatt to tell him about Homer."

"How do we get in touch with Mr. Cooper? We'll do that for you. We'd like to speak with him as well."

He gave her the Sheriff's Office number at the Court House. The Secretary leaned forward and whispered to an agent in the front seat. Then she turned back to him.

"Homer told you there were a lot of trucks headed north?"

"Yes, ma'am. He said he'd followed about a dozen trucks out of Gunbarrel, moving in a convoy, all headed the same direction. They split up along the way. Taking different routes. He finally picked one and followed it to Virginia."

"Northeast? All the trucks were headed that way? No one going south. Or, west?"

"He said north, ma'am."

"The people living in the farmhouse. The doctor and his family. Tell me about them."

"He was a doctor?"

"A pediatrician. Iranian. They'd been living in that house for four years. The son was in law school."

"Well. A doctor. That's something. You never know, I guess."

"Don't worry. We deeded the farm all the way back to a German ambassador and a small holding company in Dubai. This Iranian family, they were sleepers, all right. What your deputy did was the right thing. You, too."

"You find that sub?"

"Not yet. We've got divers and salvage operations out from Fredericksburg all the way north to D.C."

"It's bad, isn't it?"

"It's always bad. Especially now that we've got the Inauguration coming up. Everybody's a little tense. I've got to make a few phone calls, Sheriff. You put your head back and take it easy. We should be there in half an hour."

73

S now day, huh?" Metro Patrolman Joe Pastore said. "Remember snow days?"

"The best, Joey," his partner, Tom Darius said. "Man. I loved snow days. More than life."

Joe said, "Snow forts. Snow wars. Your kids' school close down, too?"

"It was on the radio at six or something, just as I was leaving the house. I think every school in D.C. is closed. Look at this shit coming down. Has to be a couple of feet already, right?"

"I hope it keeps snowing. Right through the frigging Inauguration. That way people will stay home and watch it on TV. Make our lives a whole lot easier, right? Hey! Watch out for that truck! You see that guy?"

"Is this fruit nuts?" D.C. uniformed Patrolman Tommy Darius said to his partner, Pastore, who was driving the cruiser. A huge tractor-trailer truck had suddenly appeared out of nowhere, turning into the road right in front of them, barely visible in the swirling snow.

Joey laughed and hit the brakes, nodding his head. *Is*

this fruit nuts? You have to ride around in a car all day, it better be with someone funny. Like Tommy. The two of them had been together ever since the academy, hell, every since grade school in Silver Spring. Inseparable, even back in the day. Next-door neighbors. Spitshooters. Hellraisers. Crimebusters. Partners to the end. Close, that's what they always said. Like wallpaper to a wall.

Their D.C. squad car, a white Crown Vic, followed the big tractor-trailer along a winding wooded road in the middle of Rock Creek Park. There were few people using the vast park today, because of the snowfall. They'd seen a few hikers, a couple of hardy folks on horseback, riding through the huge mounds of snow drifted up under the trees.

Darius and Pastore began following the truck on North Waterside Drive, headed southeast, the only two vehicles on the road. They'd only passed one other vehicle, a big Lexus SUV, going the other way. Not only were trucks not allowed in the park, ever, they especially weren't allowed on Waterside. That's because the damn drive was closed, all the way from Massachusetts Avenue to Rock Creek Parkway. Clearly marked "Closed," and here was this guy.

Now the guy braked and hung a right on Beach Drive, going wide, and headed toward the Riley Spring Bridge.

"Hit the lights, Tommy," Pastore said. "I've had enough of this dickhead."

"Yeah, let's pull him," Darius said, firing up the light bar and red flashers. "Then we'll go get some supper."

The driver of this rig, who was apparently hauling

frozen seafood from Louisiana, was either lost or smoked up or both. "Crawdaddy & Co.," that's what it said on the truck. Big pink crawfish or something painted on the back and sides. Didn't look all that tasty. Looked more like big bugs.

The guy was crawling through the park, ten miles an hour, pausing to stop at every intersection and then proceeding through it, moving along as if he owned the road. The truck being from way down south in Louisiana, Darius and Pastore assumed nobody'd told this ragin' Cajun that this was a national park, run by the Department of the Interior, and trucks weren't welcome.

"He's not stopping, Joey. What do you want me to do?"

"I'll pull along side this asshole. Roll your window down and flag him over to the shoulder."

"It's fuckin' freezing out there, Joe."

"Just do it."

"He won't stop. Look at those tints. Thinks he's a movie star. We ought to bust him for those limo windows, too."

"He stops at stop signs but he won't stop for us. Jesus."

"Hey! Watch it! You trying to kill me?"

Joey had pulled one car length ahead of the truck's cab, then put the wheel hard over, jumping in front of the truck and then getting on the brakes, slowing to five miles an hour.

"Is he slowing down?" Joey asked, looking in the

rearview. You could hardly see because of the snow and fog.

"Yeah. I think."

"All right, that's it, I'm stopping."

"He ain't," Darius said, turning around in the seat and peering through the frosted rear window. The red and blue flashers lit up the snow-covered cab. "Jesus, he's pushing us off the road."

"He skidded. That's all. He's stopped now. Okay. Let's go introduce ourselves, make this cracker feel at home here in our nation's capital."

They both got out of the car and went back to the truck cab. Big Peterbilt, bright red. The windshield so dark you couldn't see a thing inside. Tommy stepped up onto the running board and rapped on the driver's window with his flashlight.

"What's this guy, playing possum or something?"

"Bang harder. Break the fuckin' thing."

"Police!" Tommy said, rapping harder. "Open your window!"

"This guy's unbelievable. I'm going to get the ram out of the trunk. We'll bust his window for him he doesn't open up."

Joey jumped down from the truck and came back with the light-weight metal ram they used for taking doors down in a hurry. Tommy looked at him, then jumped down from the running board, shaking his head.

"Still nothing?"

"Maybe he's dead."

"Fuck it. I'm freezing my nuts off out here."

Joey climbed up and used the ram on the driver's side window. The glass was unbelievably thick. It took three tries. On the third, the window imploded inward in a shower of Saf-T-Glass. A weird smell came from the cab. Not sour sweat stink and tobacco like Joey and Tommy were accustomed to, stopping these rigs. Nothing like that. More like machinery and hydraulic fluid.

Tommy aimed his Mag-Lite inside.

"Holy shit."

"What?"

"Nobody in here. Get up and take a look. Fucking Buck Rogers."

Joey climbed up and peered through the window. "What the hell is all that stuff?"

"Some kind of remote-control driving thing. I don't know. Weird shit, huh? Listen, it's beeping."

"I don't like beeping," Joey said.

Tommy played his light across the polished stainless steel steering mechanism; saw that there was more elaborate machinery mounted on the floorboard where the pedals and transmission normally were. A split-screen monitor on the console showed four live views: front and rear, and on both sides. The two police officers stared at the screen for a moment, transfixed.

"Is that TV snow? Or, real snow?" Tommy said.

"Can't tell. Should we call it in?" Joey said, staring at the little red light that was blinking rapidly.

"You see any cameras? You think we're on *Candid Camera*?"

"Off the air. Reruns only. We gotta call this in. I don't like it."

"Let's go see what's in the back first. Must be some freaking high-tech seafood, man." Tommy jumped down into the snowbank and ran toward the rear. He was pumped about the robot truck. It was bad. But it was cool, too.

"I'm calling it in first," Joey said, running back to his squad car.

It was a Rol-R-Door, which meant it rolled up from the bottom like a garage door. Slid up into the roof. There was a big steel padlock securing the door to the truck frame. Tommy used the ram on the lock, basically just took out the bottom third of the door. Joey was back.

"Call this thing in?"

"They think I'm crazy, but, yeah, I did."

"They sending back up anyway?"

"Beats me."

Patrolman Darius nodded and stuck his flashlight inside the opening. He leaned forward and peered into the dark body of the trailer.

"What's in there? Baby robot Lobsters?"

"I dunno, but it ain't seafood. Something big. Black and shiny. Two of them. Heavy plastic sheeting covering them up, whatever the hell it is."

"Rip it off. The plastic. You want my knife? Here."

"Thanks . . . hard to get my arm far enough inside to—".

The horrific explosion killed the two young police officers instantly, vaporizing them. It blew down every tree within a radius of a hundred yards and created a black hole in the frozen ground fifteen feet across. The blast completely destroyed the truck from Louisiana and its contents, as well as the Crown Victoria cruiser parked in front of it on the shoulder. Automobile alarms a quarter of a mile away were activated. Windows rattled at Walter Reed Hospital.

No one seeing the black hole gouged in the earth could quite believe it. A lot of neighborhood kids came out to see it. It looked like a flaming meteor had hit. Debris was scattered in the snow as far as you could see.

It was January 17.

The Day of Reckoning was near.

74

THE BLACK JUNGLE

Deep below ground, in A Selva Negra's heavily fortified underground communications bunker, Muhammad Top and Dr. Khan were silent eyewitnesses to history. Neither said a word. It was cold in the Tomb, but the subterranean crypt was the safest place in the jungle. The walls were steel-reinforced concrete, six feet thick. Hardened steel blast doors could be found on both the dormitory level and the one above it, where the electronic heart of Top's world buzzed day and night. A massive antenna tower, disguised down to its rough bark and air roots as a tree, rose directly above the compound. It was, Top thought, a brilliant work of sculptural art.

The two men, bathed in soft blue light, stared with greedy eyes. They embraced the vision displayed on the monitors: a humbled America, blown apart at the heart. There, on multiple screens mounted around a curving, twenty-foot wall, were images of violence, hatred, and destruction. A hot wind was blowing through America. Few realized yet that it was coming up from the south.

The bunker building had been designed by Khan. It was the only below-ground structure in the village. Khan had deemed it necessary, despite the frequent floods. It was airtight, watertight, and equipped with heavy-duty direct bunker-buster hit pumps in the event of a cracking of the outer shell.

Men manning the five rows of individual monitor stations were facing northeast toward Mecca. Before dawn, each man in the room had washed himself according to ritual, then knelt and bent his head to the floor, praying for martydom. An attack could come at any time. They were ready.

It was succeeding. Top knew, because the hand of Allah was cradling him, lifting him toward the sun. Top had seen the future. All was going according to Destiny. His Destiny. His alone.

Various monitors depicted American National Guard units now manning the borderlines of Arizona, California, New Mexico, and Texas. Too little, too late, in the eyes of Top and Khan, this vain effort to suppress the violent eruptions along those fragile 2,000 miles.

It was only a feint, at any rate. Khan had predicted a full-blown war with Mexico over the border. For all they knew, it still might happen. Two nations, one border. Always an opportunity. For two years, Khan had held secret meetings with the Mexicans. These had been arranged with the help of a certain German ambassador, a man named Zimmermann. Zimmermann, accompanied by certain high-ranking members of the government in Mexico City, had traveled to São Paulo and brokered a deal with Khan.

The Mexicans' motives were clear. It wasn't the spread of Islam that ignited them. Or drew them into Khan's coterie. With the exception of the German, it wasn't even money. It was the chance to avenge the abuse and perfidy suffered at the hands of their northern neighbor. And to reclaim precious northern territories seized by the Yankees in the bitter U.S.-Mexican War of 1848.

The movement of the few remaining American reserves to hotspots along the southern border meant major cities, including Washington, D.C., were woefully exposed to the impending attack. When the time came for the second wave of his planned attacks, there would be plenty of fireworks in Chicago, New York, Boston. But the Big Bang, as Top gleefully dubbed his first strike, was reserved for the sacred capital.

The only real misfortune thus far was the loss of the Muammar Massaouri family, three of the faithful, devoted sleeper comrades, who seemed to have been sacrificed at the farm in Virginia. The Massaouris had missed a scheduled sat com call with the UCB. This was to be an Internet data burst, subsequent to the successful launch of the unmanned vehicle. The message never came. All attempts to contact them had failed. It was assumed Dr. Massaouri and his family had been killed.

To their everlasting glory, the Massaouris had successfully launched the unmanned underwater weapon.

Even now, *Bedouin* was en route to the target thirty miles north of Morning Glory Farm. The video images streaming from the submarine's nose camera were murky and dark but of no crucial importance.

The sophisticated UUV, an unmanned underwater vehicle developed over the years by Dr. Khan for littoral area incursions, was transporting the 150-kiloton nuclear weapon. After undergoing months of successful sea trials here on the Igapó River, *Bedouin* had been preprogrammed with GPS waypoints for navigating the Potomac en route to her destination in Washington. Every hour, a needle-thin antenna broke the surface for a data burst to the com sat traveling far overhead.

So far, God willing, the little torpedo-shaped craft was performing perfectly.

She weighed just less than two tons. She was powered by a large bank of lithium batteries, quiet and undetectable. In the busy river, the noise of *Bedouin*'s propulsion system would also be unnoticeable. The underwater robot's forward-looking radar allowed it to make constant course corrections to avoid obstacles or other craft in its path. At its current speed, twenty-two knots, it would reach the Tidal Basin in Washington, D.C., well ahead of schedule. The thick lead shield inside the hull would prevent its detection by any nuclear-sensitive probes along the way.

Once inside the basin, *Bedouin* would remain there, inert and immobile, buried in the mud a few thousand yards from the White House until the appointed hour.

The Appointed Hour. It was drawing nigh. Top sighed, and gazed at the oversized digital clock above the monitor bank. It continued to roll down inexorably to the zero hour, now a thousand minutes away. He was thinking in minutes now. Even seconds. And every one counted.

"Where is Hawke?" Top shouted to one of the technicians manning the perimeter defense system. "Get the map up on the screen."

"The blinking orange dot is Hawke's vessel," Dr. Khan pointed out.

"I don't want a fucking dot, I want a live picture."

Khan looked at him, but held his tongue. They had come a long way together. It was no time to let the man's intemperate behavior distract him from his destiny. Any blasphemy could be tolerated now. In a few hours, it would be his finger on the button.

A technician said, "We have no drone on him at this moment, sir."

"Why not?"

"The enemy shot it down, sir. A missile."

Silence, save the electronic hum of the equipment, settled over the room.

"He has missiles on this fucking speedboat? Why was I not informed?" Top asked, trying to keep his voice low and controlled.

The short technician with the bushy beard was visibly trembling now. "It only just happened, sir. A few minutes ago. I thought you'd been told."

Top waved him away. "Assuming the vessel maintains current speed, when does the enemy enter the mined portion of the river?"

"Two hours, perhaps less."

"Track his speed. Any change, let me know."

Suddenly, Khan's hand was on his shoulder and his lips were close to his ear. "I think you should take him out with attack drones," Khan said softly, eyes up on the screen. "Take him out now, my brother, and be done with him."

Top's eyes flashed. "Did you not hear what this man just said? He's got a missile defense system! The acoustic mines will protect us from this mosquito. Nothing could survive that stretch of water."

"With all due respect, my dear brother, I imagine we have more drones than he has missiles. His is not a warship, after all."

"You imagine! What if you're wrong? What then? I'm left defenseless."

"Muhammad, calm yourself. We've been at this too long without sleep. I'm going to rest in my quarters until the final hour approaches. Please let me know should anything develop that requires my immediate attention."

Without another word, the robed man strode toward the elevator at the back of the darkened room. Top watched him leave with some satisfaction. He had no need of him now. Destiny was in his hands alone.

"Any word from the Xucurus?" Top asked the room.

"Nothing yet," a controller murmured, afraid to look up.

Before reaching the small elevator, Khan paused at the last row of monitor workstations. Each workstation was a semi-enclosed pod and comprised a small, virtual-reality environment for the controllers. The key components were screens displaying live streaming video from the armada of trailer trucks en route to Washington.

Once the trucks had resurfaced inside the cartel-owned garage at Gunbarrel, Texas, they had been driven northeast by diverse routes to the American capital. Live video superimposed upon 3-D situation maps using satellite photos made the controllers' work possible. GPS coordinates and a multidirectional live video feed from each vehicle were fed to a COMS satellite positioned over the East Coast of the North American continent.

Inside each monitor pod sat a controller and a sensor operator. The man on the left actually drove the vehicle, while the other monitored every kind of road, traffic, and weather condition. He ensured all traffic laws were strictly obeyed. In combat, he would also provide constant battleground feedback, giving second-by-second direction to the controller. These were the men who actually operated the remote machines, using a large joystick resembling something in an arcade.

"I'd mind your trucks if I were you, Muhammad," Khan said, just loud enough to be heard by everyone in the room. "One of them appears to be lost."

"What?"

"See for yourself, my brother," Khan said, tapping the monitor in question. "This one appears to be lost in the snow."

Khan stepped aside for Top, who peered intently at the image. There was so much snow whirling around the camera lens that it was difficult to see what was being broadcast. "You're lost?" he said to the young curly-haired controller, whose name was Yashim.

"Only momentarily, God willing," Yashim said.

"Shit. Police. Two of them. How did this happen?"

He leaned in to scrutinize the scene. Two uniformed officers could now clearly be seen standing at the rear of the truck. Both were looking up at the rear door. One appeared to have some sort of battering ram in his hands.

Khan said, "The truck was stopped by police? Why? And you alerted no one?"

Yashim trembled visibly and said, "I am most sorry, sir. In the storm, we lost the route through the park. A wrong turn perhaps. The snow. I thought I could find the way out again. But, then I—"

"Where is the truck located?" Top shouted, "Now! Put up the GPS map! Show me!"

"Here, sir. In Rock Creek Park," the sensor operator said, his voice shaky. "About three miles from its rendezvous point in this heavily wooded area."

"What's this large building? The one here?"

"Walter Reed Hospital. Veterans' facility."

"Blow up the truck," Top said evenly. "Use the anti-tampering explosive device in the trailer."

Each truck was equipped with an anti-tampering system that could be triggered remotely. Or, in the event that the primary contents of the truck were in any way disturbed, the explosive package would destroy both the vehicle and its contents automatically. So far, the police had only broken a window in the cab. It had not been enough to trigger the automatic explosion.

"Now?" Yashim asked.

"You'd like to wait for the two policemen to discover the contents and alert their superiors? Yes, now. Do it!"

The controller pushed a button marked FIRE and the resulting violent explosion instantly caused the screen to go black.

"Your mission is complete," Top said to the man seated before him. He put the muzzle of his pistol to the back of the controller's head and fired one round into his brain. The sensor operator seated next to him screamed and shoved his chair back, struggling to get to his feet.

"Yours, too," he said to the second man before he killed him, putting the muzzle to his chest and pulling the trigger.

Top made his way to the front of the room, every eye glued to him.

"That was unfortunate. But, necessary. Victory is near. I assume there will be no further trucks lost in the snow. Correct?"

"God willing!" the controllers all shouted in unison. It was standard Arabic courtesy to give God the benefit of the doubt.

"God willing you will all be alive to share the fruits of our victory in a few hours. Now, get back to work. All trucks should be at their designated rendezvous locations and unloading their precious cargo in the next hour. Does anyone in this room see a problem with that? Tell me now."

Silence.

"Good. Let it be."

"A thousand pardons, sir," a technician in the front row said, breaking the silence.

"Yes?"

"Hawke's vessel has stopped. Here. At an abandoned village called Tupo."

"How long has he been there?"

"Just pulled in. There's a dock. Could be loading or unloading."

"Tanks nearby?"

"One, sir."

"Send it to the location. And order four drones up. Attack drones. Perhaps Dr. Khan is right. Nevertheless. I want to sink that sitting duck. Now."

Khan smiled and slipped quietly from the room.

An old song popped into his head and he sang a lyric softly as he entered the elevator.

Send in the drones . . .

75

THE BLACK RIVER

Brock was late for his scheduled river rendezvous with Alex Hawke. He'd been making his way through the jungle to the outpost at Tupo when he got into a life-or-death race with some tanks. He'd accidentally tripped a sensor and a whole squadron of Trolls had been sent out to find him. He seemed to have confused most of the joystick jockeys when he'd crossed a wide ravine, deftly tightrope-walking a fallen tree to the other side. Now he realized another of the little bastards was still on his butt.

Before he'd found the ravine, this last group almost got him. He'd carved one out of the pack and tried to climb aboard and bull-ride the damn thing like he and Saladin had perfected. The smartass controller had applied full throttle forward to one track, full reverse to the other. The Troll spun like a goddamn top on its axis and flung him off into the bushes.

High fives in the control room, oh yeah.

This new guy was seriously spitting lead. The air was

full of tracer rounds too, the shrubbery getting chewed to pieces all around him as the sensor operator tried to find his range. Head down, pumping his knees high, bobbing and weaving, Harry ran for his life. He was seeing sunlight ahead now. The river was close. There was the dock through the trees. He could make out a boat, a crazy-looking black boat, had to be a hundred feet long, waiting at the end.

Had to be Hawke. Nobody else he knew would have a boat like that. He'd almost missed his ride. Fucking Troll remote operators had gotten their shit together, all right. All that practice with Harry and Saladin had made them a lot better at this game. Harry ran for daylight.

He tripped over a big root, cursed as he went down. Now he was up and running for his life again. The tank was still on his ass, spitting lead at him. He dodged and feinted, using the thick undergrowth as cover. He was almost to the clearing.

Now he had to sprint across open ground. There was a dilapidated shed at the foot of the dock, about a hundred yards away. As he got closer, he saw machine gun turrets on Hawke's boat. Shoot back, you assholes! Get this tank off my ass! Fifty cals on the bow and stern. Christ, there was even a 7.2mm cannon up on top of the wheelhouse! What the hell was going on? Were they all asleep?

No, they were just busy.

Unseen by Harry Brock, armed drones were approaching the black gunship moored at the end of the dock. Hawke was up on top of the wheelhouse with

Ecclestone who was manning the 7.2mm cannon. Both men were keenly focused on enemy craft approaching from every compass point. Hawke had his glasses on the tiny black specks dead ahead, another drone flying low over the water toward his bow. Hawke was straining his eyes, trying to determine if there were missiles on the wingtips or if these were just more recon flights. He'd no intention of wasting another PAM on a mere recon.

"Radar showing four small drone aircraft approaching out of the west-southwest, sir, altitude two hundred feet, speed fifty-five knots," he heard fire control officer Allegria say in his headphones. "Range one mile and closing."

"Four bogies?" Hawke said.

"Four, roger. Three bogies are breaking formation. Climbing. Looks like they intend to circle around behind us, sir. The lead one, too, seems to be climbing. Appears to be circling. Looks like a holding pattern."

Why send four when one would do? Hawke wondered.

"Awaiting further orders, I expect. Keep an eye on them, Allegria," he told the fire control officer.

Then he heard rapid machine-gun fire from the bank and saw Harry Brock emerge from the jungle. He'd been waiting nearly an hour and was about to give orders to shove off. He'd no desire to remain a sitting duck any longer than he had to. But, here Harry came, running flat out toward the clearing. Somebody was shooting at him, but who, or, what?

A tank. Small, but fast and firing twin machine guns

at his friend Harry. One of the two robots that had been shadowing them no doubt.

"Ecclestone," Hawke said to the gunner seated inside the heavily armored Plexiglas turret.

"Sir!"

"Do you think you can take out that little tank without killing Mr. Brock?"

"Aye, aye, sir. I think I've got a shot."

The turret instantly rotated ninety degrees west and the GUN DISH got a lock on the approaching robot Troll. Hawke felt the deck shudder beneath him as Ecclestone squeezed off a burst from the cannon. The muzzle flashed, spouting flame as recoiled. Hawke saw the small tank lifted up high in the air by the exploding rounds, disintegrating in a perfectly symmetrical ball of fire and flaming debris.

Harry kept running down the long dock.

"Come along, Harry," Hawke shouted through cupped hands from the roof. "We're about to shove off without you!"

"You can't leave me! I'm your ticket to Paradise, Hawke," Harry said, pounding down the rotting boards of the sharply canted structure.

"Let's get out of here!" Hawke shouted, his focus back on the rapidly approaching drones. "Cast off all lines!"

The crew hastily cast off the bow, stern, and spring lines made fast to the dock pilings. Harry Brock, seeing the water opening up between himself and Hawke's boat, had to leap for it. He made it, arms pinwheeling, and a waiting crewman wrestled him safely aboard.

"Hello, Hawkeye," he smiled up at Alex, who was standing on the cabin top looking down at him. "Permission to come aboard, sir?"

"Hello, Harry. Permission granted."

A nearby explosion rocked the boat on its beam and a geyser of water shot fifty feet in the air. The dock where Harry had been standing seconds ago, was no more. Harry and the crew stowing lines on the starboard side were knocked to their knees and had to scramble to stay aboard.

"I should have mentioned we're under attack. You might want to get inside where it's nice and safe, Harry."

"Is there no peace?" Brock muttered, getting to his feet.

"We've got four confirmed armed drones, Skipper," Allegria said in the phones. "Fore and aft, and two more on our stern quarters, sir. Closing at eighty knots. Armed with Hellfire-type missiles. Request permission for immediate launch PAM weapons system, sir."

"Denied. These things are slow moving. Ecclestone and the fore and aft turrets should be sufficient. Save PAM for when we really need it. Fire when ready. I'm going to the bridge."

Hawke stepped on to the top rung, lightly gripped the stainless ladder rails, and slid down onto the bridge deck. Brownlow was at the wheel, Harry and Stokely were embracing just aft of him, pounding each other on the shoulders.

"Break it up," Hawke said, clapping Harry on the back. Despite his misgivings about the American, he was very glad to see him. Brock stuck out his hand and Hawke shook it. "Been a while, Harry. Good to see you."

"Likewise. I didn't think—"

Harry's sentence was interrupted by the muffled but still loud chatter of both fore and aft twin fifty calibers opening up at the same time, a metallic cacophony enhanced by the heavy thudding of the cannon directly overhead.

"Incoming!" Brownlow shouted. "Hit the—"

Hawke saw the missile streaking directly for the wheelhouse. A second later an explosion directly overhead rocked the boat, sending all three men inside the wheelhouse to the deck. Hawke scrambled over to the ladder and climbed topside. The cannon turret had taken a nearly direct hit and Ecclestone was slumped forward over his weapon, blood pouring from a deep gash in his forehead. Hawke pulled the man from his station and saw that he was wounded in several places but still very much alive.

"Get below," he said to the dazed man, helping him to the ladder. Off to his left he saw one drone explode, brought down by fire from the stern gunner, whose turret was now rotating clockwise to take out the drone on their aft starboard quarter.

"Can't walk too well, sir," Ecclestone said. Then Stokely emerged at the top of the ladder, lending a hand.

"I'll take him to sickbay, boss," he said, and Hawke steered the wounded man to his waiting arms. He heard a nearby explosion as another drone was blown out of the sky by the *Stiletto* stern gunners. The boat was moving rapidly through the water now, thirty knots perhaps, making her harder to hit. The one remaining drone, the one that had fired the initial missile, had circled back again and was now on another approach coming directly at them low out of the sun.

"Let's see if this damn thing still works," Hawke said, slipping into the seat inside the damaged turret of the cannon. The weapon was equipped with its own GUN DISH radar, capable of acquiring, tracking, and engaging low-flying aircraft, like the drone now attacking *Stiletto*. It fired full auto, but Hawke had ordered the gun set at bursts of two to three rounds to conserve precious ammunition. No time to change that now.

He squinted his eyes, trying to use the conventional optical sight, aided by the GUN DISH. The sun was fierce and blinding, but he thought he had the little bugger. A sharp beeping tone agreed. He had target acquistion. He had the bastard in his sights now, centering it in the red crosshairs, seeing the one missile remaining on the port wing, knowing it would be fired at any second . . . and squeezing both triggers simultaneously, he blew the drone out of the sky.

HALF AN HOUR later, Hawke, Stokely, the Frogman, and Brock were huddled in the boat's tiny war room, deep into refining their plans with the aid of Brock's much-needed information. It had already been decided that, instead going in with two squads,

Stoke and Froggy would mount a combined operation.

Best of all, Brock had even created a rough but reasonable facsimile of the compound itself, rendered in black pencil on the back of a map of the Amazon Basin's Mato Grosso region. Because of the canopy, Mick Hocking had been unable to get any aerial recon photos. Now, at least, the team could visualize the objective.

"A large force here to the north?" Hawke asked, studying the crude map.

"Saladin has his scouts tracking the main body of Top's troops. He has begun moving them out."

"I'D SAY THE TROOPS remaining inside the compound number about a hundred right now," Brock said. "The hardcore Imperial Guards, let's call them. The vast majority of troops have moved north and west, using these jerry-built highways you helped build in the jungle. I saw three armored divisions pull out late last night."

"Headed where?"

"Central America is all I know. All the way to Mexico, maybe, join up with forces in the mountains up there. The idea is, once they take the Great Satan out, that's the signal. Then the troops fan out into the countryside, get the populations to rise up, and they all march together on the cities. Knock them down one by one. Take the capitals."

"They all want to be the next Bolívar," Hawke said, rubbing his chin.

"These guys want it all. And they think now's the time to go for it. Who's going to stop them?"

"You got inside," Hawke said, smiling. "Good work, Harry."

"I've still got someone inside. A woman named Caparina. She could probably take Top down all by herself."

Hawke looked at Brock's baggy pajamalike fatigues. "Disguised like that?"

"Exactly. Except she's wearing a fatigue hat pulled down over her ears. And these green camo pajamas like all of Top's grunts in there. She'd be hard to spot. We all look equally bad."

"You don't know where they're keeping Ambrose Congreve, do you, Harry?"

"Hard to say."

"Christ, Harry, what's this woman doing in there?"

Harry spun the hand-rendered chart of the compound around on the table so that it was facing him. He knew this was Hawke's primary objective now. "Hold your horses. Let me look at this thing a second."

"Talk to me."

"All right. Based on Caparina's last radio transmission, I'd say there is a good chance they might stow any hostages right here."

His finger was pointing to a cluster of tree houses at the edge of the compound, hard by the main bridge.

"Why there?"

"Caparina managed to get herself assigned to some scutwork on the bridge. Raking debris from all this rain. She said she heard a lot of very unpleasant noises coming from the three houses by the river."

"When was this?"

"Eleven hundred hours. She's got a radio stashed somewhere."

"Ambrose was still alive at eleven hundred hours," Hawke said, looking at Stokely and then at his watch.

"We'll get him out," Stoke said to Alex. "Don't worry."

Hawke said, "Any tomb will do. Where is Saladin now?"

"Moving his squad through the jungle toward this location here. Airstrip I found two miles from the west perimeter. He'll wait there for our signal before moving into the compound to rendezvous."

"Rendezvous point?"

"Right here. I told Saladin we'd hook up a half mile above the bridge connecting the two sectors."

"No river mines there?"

"None. The mines are all here."

"Where we're headed now."

"Exactly."

"Christ."

Froggy said, "Now that we have an *idée* where Congreve might be, his rescue is perhaps not impossible."

For the first time since Ambrose had been kidnapped, Hawke felt a surge of hope.

It had started to rain. Hard. A heavy drumming on
the cabin top over his head. Maybe it was a good
sign.

God knew he could use one.

76

The phone rang. Dixon reached over and grabbed it before it could ring again, looking at his glow-in-the-dark watch as he did so. Almost eleven. He'd been sleeping for an hour. Couldn't even stay awake long enough to tell Daisy about meeting the president of the United States; even if he only stuck his head into a meeting to say hello. He'd told her about Homer. That was about all he could manage. Out the window, he could see the vapor lights of the hotel parking lot. It had stopped snowing.

"Hello?"

"Sheriff Dixon?"

"Speaking."

"Sheriff, this is Secret Service Special Agent Rocky Hernandez, assigned to the president's detail. I was with the team that greeted you and Secretary de los Reyes at the White House earlier this evening?"

"Yes, sir. I remember you. One of the K-9 fellows."

"Right. Sorry to disturb you, but my boss just asked

me to call. He said to tell you there's just been an explosion in Rock Creek Park."

"I thought I heard something. About fifteen minutes ago? Woke me up. I thought it was normal."

"No, sir. Not normal. It was a huge explosion. People are very jumpy around here tonight because of the Inauguration tomorrow. Threat level high, Internet chatter over at NSA is going through the roof. Police are headed to the scene. I was off duty and headed home to Maryland when I got the call from the White House."

"How can I help you, Agent Hernandez?"

"Call me Rocky. I'm turned around on the Beltway and headed back to the White House. Your hotel is on my way. Agent-in-charge was wondering if I could come by and pick you up? There was apparently a big semi truck involved in the explosion and he thought maybe you and I could swing through the Park over there and—"

"How long?"

"Two minutes."

"I'll be out front."

The Secret Service agent's car pulled up in front of the Doubletree lobby and Dixon climbed inside. It was a Jeep Cherokee with a wire cage in the rear and a dog back there.

"I appreciate this, Sheriff," Hernandez said, pulling out of the lot.

"No problem at all. What kind of explosion was it?"

"That's what we want to find out. Looks like a tractor-trailer rig and a D.C. squad car were involved. A collision, is what they're thinking so far."

"Pretty big collision to make a bang like that."

"That's what we think, too."

"That your dog back there? Or, an official one?"

"That's Dutch. Mandatory retirement after eleven years' service. He's got one year to go."

"Dutch, huh? Good name."

"Named after my first boss, President Reagan."

"Dutch still goes to work?"

"All the K-9 dogs get to go home every night with their handlers. Part of my family, Sheriff."

"What is he? Looks a lot like a German shepherd."

"He's a Belgian Malinois. That's all we use now. Trained to detect drugs, explosives, firearms."

"Explosives, huh?"

"Yeah, that's what I was thinking, too."

"Great minds think alike," Dixon said, and, looking out the window at Washington in the snow, he added, "And so do ours."

There had to be twenty squad cars and emergency vehicles already at the scene. Tape was up, surrounding a big black hole in the ground. The surrounding snow-covered trees were lit up with flashing blue and red lights. Dixon noticed two vehicles marked BOMB DISPOSAL parked near the blackened center of the explosion. On the far side, a large FBI crime scene van was a hive of activity.

He and Hernandez climbed out of the car and fetched Dutch out of the back. Once he was on his lead, they went up to an officer standing inside the tape and showed their shields.

"White House dog?" the D.C. uniform asked Hernandez, rubbing Dutch's coat.

"Yes, he is."

"Glad to have him at the scene. You gentlemen let me know if you need anything."

"Two vehicles involved, officer?" Dixon asked the uniform before he could turn to go.

"Correct. We've got tracks of only two vehicles leading to the scene. Most likely a D.C. Metro cruiser and an eighteen-wheeler. Not much left of either one as you can see. I suppose the gas tanks on both vehicles blew when they collided."

"Collided," Dixon said, pushing his short brim back on his forehead and looking at the hole.

"That's what it looks like."

Dixon said, "Anything else you can tell us?"

"Well, this doesn't make a whole lot of sense, but an Officer Darius called in with something about a remote-controlled vehicle here in the park. What's that all about? Some kid flying a toy plane? Nobody knew what the hell to make of it. A couple of minutes later, boom."

"Have you heard from Officer Darius?"

"No, sir."

Dixon and Hernandez looked at each other, thanked the officer, and walked away. There was a small group of uniformed officers and others who stood looking down into the hole. Three men in HAZMAT suits were down at the bottom taking soil samples or whatever it was they did. Dixon looked around. A bomb disposal technician was playing with a little robot back in the trees where the road had been cordoned off to protect any tire tracks in the snow.

The hole was nearly fifteen feet across and ten feet deep. Hernandez released Dutch and the dog took off at a trot, circling the crater and the dirty black snow all around the edge, all fired up.

"How good is he?" Dixon asked, watching with admiration as the dog worked.

"They learn to detect almost nineteen thousand individual scents. After twenty-six weeks of training, Dutch scored 650 out of a possible 700 points. He's good."

"I think I'll stroll back down that road a ways. Take a look around. Let Dutch here do his job in peace."

"I'll be right here, Sheriff."

The scene had been carefully protected for about five hundred yards. The two-lane road curved back and disappeared into some trees. There were still two sets of tire tracks in the snow, lightly covered with fresh snow but you could still make out two distinct tread patterns. Dixon bent down and looked at a point of intersection between the two. He got his pocketknife out and stuck the blade into the snow. He'd seen something while staring at the treads. He pried it out and picked it up with his handkerchief. It was shiny, maybe some kind of glass.

Black glass.

"What have you got, there?" the bomb technician said, walking over with his robot in tow.

"Piece of glass."

"Lots of that around. A lot of this black shiny stuff.

Kinda weird, isn't it? Here, hold your piece up to my flashlight. See that? Something inside, like another layer or something."

"Yep. I do. It's mirror."

"Mirror. That's what I thought too. Now, what do you suppose that is all about?"

"Excuse me, will you please?"

Dixon turned and hurried back through the deep snow to the crater. Hernandez was still there, working the dog.

"Could you take a walk with me over here a little ways? The trees over yonder."

"Sure." Hernandez followed the sheriff to a nearby tree, away from the crowd. "What have you got?"

"Got your flashlight?"

"Right here."

Dixon showed him the piece of glass he'd found, turning it over in his hand so it caught the light. Hernandez said, "You're seeing something here, Sheriff. I'm not."

"That truck Homer and I stopped that first night? The Yankee Slugger. Had heavily tinted windows. Blackouts with a layer of mirror in the middle. I tried to see inside that truck's windshield, with my light right up against the glass just like this. Couldn't see through the stuff. Just like this piece right here."

"You check the truck in Virginia?"

"Identical glass in the cab. That bomb technician over there says this glass is all over the place. Lots of it."

"So, you think this truck was one of the remote-controllers?"

"I'd bet on it."

"Keep an eye on Dutch for me? I'm headed to my car to get the boss on the radio. Tell him what you've found. See what he wants us to do about it."

Dixon nodded, "Won't let him out of my sight. Borrow your flashlight while you're gone?"

Dixon took the Superlight and walked back to the crater. He watched Dutch working something on the far side of the crater. Nobody in the crowd was paying any attention but he was on to something, all right. Dixon wasn't a trained dog handler. But you didn't need to be. You could see the whole thing in Dutch's body language. He was all over something or other.

"Hey, Dutch," Dixon said, rubbing his ears, "what have you got, boy? Huh?"

There was a jagged piece of blackened metal lying between the dog's feet. Dutch was guarding it, but decided to let Franklin look at it. Dixon took out his hanky again and held the thing up to the light. Twisted metal, burned, but you could make out some letters stamped into it.

R-O-L-E.

"The dog found this," he said to the FBI man standing in the open door of the van.

"Who are you, sir?" the skinny man with the thin black tie asked. Franklin told him as he flashed his shield, climbed up a step to hand the piece of steel to him. "Where'd he find it, Sheriff?"

"Near the crater. He's a White House K-9 dog, name of Dutch. That sticky stuff on the other side there's probably bomb residue, way he's acting. I'd take him seriously if I were you. He's pretty good."

"We'll add it to the pile. Check it out when we can. Thank you, Sheriff."

"I was thinking. Those letters? R-O-L-E? Could be the middle of a word. Chevrolet."

"Chevrolet. Well, that's an interesting idea. But hardly likely. There were two vehicles involved in this explosion. We've seen the tread marks. A Ford Crown Victoria and a Peterbilt tractor trailer rig riding on Goodyear. That's confimed all the way to the top."

"Well, you may be right."

"Thanks again."

The man turned to go back inside the crime van.

"There could have been a vehicle inside the truck," Dixon said to his narrow white back.

"What'd you say?"

"I say there could have been another vehicle inside the truck. Truck that big, could have been two vehicles inside of the trailer. Two Chevrolets."

"Two Chevrolets."

"I rode in one just this evening. Over to the White House to meet with the president. Big black Chevy Suburban belonging to the Secret Service. You know the ones I'm talking about?"

"I know the ones."

"I've been seeing a lot of them since I got up here to Washington. All over town. I guess for the Inauguration?"

"I guess."

"All with blacked-out windows."

"Right."

"A lot of busted black glass on the ground over there. I found this piece down the road a ways." Franklin handed him the piece of glass he found.

"Will you look at that? Huh."

"Well. It's just an idea. Add it to the pile."

Dixon turned and headed back to the crater to find Agent Rocky Hernandez, Dutch trotting happily along right beside him.

Good dog.

77

THE BLACK JUNGLE

Stokley Jones stuck the flat of his hand in the air. His patrol froze at the signal. Ten minutes had elapsed since the squad's insertion into extremely dense terrain. Two-hundred-foot trees loomed above their heads; he'd never seen anything like it. The squad was moving out carefully in patrol formation. They were moving much too slowly for Stoke, but there wasn't much he could do about that.

It was raining up there somewhere. The water streaming down from above made the jungle floor a boggy mess. And there were tripwires everywhere.

Stoke was acting as point man, followed by Froggy, who'd been designated patrol leader. Right behind them was the radioman/grenadier, now using a back-up PRC 117 emergency VHF radio providing instant communications with the boat; he was giving *Stiletto*'s fire control officer the exact coordinates of the squad's location. He could call for fire support if needed, but he didn't want shells landing in his own backyard.

Behind the radioman was the first of three heavily laden M-60 machine gunners whose job it was to lay down a base of fire if the squad got hit. His objective was to use the heavy machine gun to keep the bad guys with their heads down until the squad either flanked the enemy or got the hell out of there. Bringing up the rear was another M-60 man and a second point man covering the squad's six. Should they need to reverse direction, he automatically became the new point.

It was rough going, wet and muddy, but Stoke felt good. If there was a tougher, better trained, meaner Hostage Rescue Team on earth, Stokely had yet to hear of those lying sons of bitches.

Stoke had a CAR-15 with an M-203 grenade launcher slung over his shoulder. He was also carrying a Mossberg shotgun loaded with buckshot. It would give him a broader kill zone in the tight confines of jungle combat. The shotgun could also come in handy clearing foliage in the event of a firefight. Each man also carried a machete to hack through the dense undergrowth. All were wearing identical woodland cammies, jungle boots, and floppy bush hats.

"Tripwire," Stoke said softly into his lipmike. It was the fifth one he'd seen in the last ten minutes. They were all over the place, slowing them way down. Some of them were even strung with little Voodoo dolls and spooky artifacts so you couldn't miss them. Keep the natives from bothering Papa Top, he figured. Problem was, some of these little trinket clotheslines were real live wires. Blow your bottom half off. Some were not. So you had to take them all very seriously.

Froggy, the designated PL, was maybe 20 or 30 yards behind him. He was carrying a GPS handheld as backup navigation; his job right now was to keep them moving in the right direction. The Frogman also had a CAR-15 with grenade launcher. Like every man, he was carrying an NVD or Night Vision Device. As the PL on this mission, he was trying to use it sparingly so as to give his eyes time to maintain his natural night sight.

Stoke was the true eyes and ears of the squad. It was up to him to alert the squad of impending danger. Not that he could see much of anything in this shit. The combination of rain, fog, and foliage made it so you couldn't see your nose in front of your goddamn face.

"Alors," he heard Froggy say in his headphones, *"Merde* and *merde encore!"*

Well said, Froggy. Shit and double shit.

It was a good thing he'd stopped the squad in their tracks. He heard something mechanical, caught a glimpse of a foot patrol of heavily armed guards approaching at double time along a narrow trail just below the ridge that the squad was descending. Looked like maybe an eight-man squad. They were preceded on the trail by two of the weirdest-looking war machines Stoke had ever seen. Had to be the Trolls, remote-controlled tanks Brock had told them about. Moving slowly, just in front of the enemy patrol. Out looking for his squad probably.

Stoke made a slashing motion across his throat and

stepped lightly as he could over the tripwire. The men behind him carefully did the same and began moving down the hillside sloping to the twisting trail. The darkness, foggy rain, and thick vegetation provided all the cover they needed. Stoke's flat hand shot into the air again when they reached a spot twenty yards above the muddy trail.

"Get down," he said, dropping to one knee and pulling two grenades from his belt. He set the timers on sixty seconds, checked his sweep second hand, and heaved the grenades underhanded. Plop-plop, into the muddy center of the trail. The two robot vehicles and the goon squad were still double-timing toward them. Using hand signals, Stoke directed his guys to move into ambush formation.

Thirty seconds remained on his dive watch. The Troll tanks were advancing rapidly now, the barrels of the twin machine guns up front swiveling toward the incline where Stoke and his men waited, low in the undergrowth. Had they been seen? Sensors, maybe, on the jungle floor. Stoke moved the selector on his assault rifle to full auto and waited. He saw the first tank come around the bend, treads slogging through the thick brownish mud.

C'mon, c'mon.

Stoke's two grenades exploded almost simultaneously. The two tanks were blown off their treads and over-turned. The enemy patrol scattered, diving into the thick underbrush on either side of the trail.

"Boomer! Bassman!" Stoke shouted to the two machine gunners. "Move up!"

The M-60 is a very heavy weapon and each man carried nearly a thousand rounds of linked 7.62 ammunition adding to his burden. Normally, they don't move too quickly because of that load. This time they did. Boomer and Bassman, both seasoned veterans and ex-Navy SEALs, raced to the position indicated by Stokely and laid down a murderous wall of fire on both sides of the trail. There was no possibility that anything had survived. The vegetation, shredded and smoking, showed no signs of life.

"Move out," Stoke said when he was satisfied no further threat existed. The squad moved down the hill and onto the muddy trail where the enemy had just died.

Froggy, paused at Stoke's side, looked at his compass and GPS handheld.

"Allons vite, mes enfants, allons vite!" Froggy said, "Quickly, children, quickly!"

"ALL BACK ONE THIRD," Brownlow said, eyes on the narrowed river ahead. It was raining so hard it was difficult to make out the vine-shrouded banks on either side. Only radar kept him on course. His depth-sounder depicted nearly impassable shoals and less than ten feet of water beneath his keel. *Stiletto* slowed to idle speed, barely moving, churning muddy black water at her stern. Any advantage afforded by the boat's power and speed was long over.

The twisting stretch of river that lay just beyond these shoals was mined. If they could even reach that stretch of water. Any time now, they'd be deploying the two minesweeper probes. According to Brock's chart, the heavily mined portion of the Black River lay only two miles distant.

These small minesweeper sensors had been developed by the Royal Navy's Admiralty Mining Establishment, a quaint name for one of the most technically advanced mine countermeasures departments on earth. MCM had developed the two probes now aboard *Stiletto*. Mounted at the bow, launched underwater much like a torpedo, the probe raced ahead of the boat and sent back a detailed visualization of the minefield. The drone's electro-optic system provided very high resolution 3-D images for positive mine identification and location.

On paper, AME had shown a vessel could successfully navigate a minefield, even in littoral zones, confined straits, or choke points. But that was on paper. It had never been attempted in the field or under combat conditions. Hawke had readily agreed to be the guinea pig when C had suggested he try the damn things out.

Hawke and Brock appeared moments after the boat slowed, both men outfitted for night jungle operations.

"Talk to us, Cap," Hawke said. "Are you ready to deploy the probes?"

"We've got another problem, sir. We've run out of water." Brownlow tapped his index finger on the 3-D depiction of the river bottom.

"Christ," Brock muttered.

Hawke leaned over Brownlow's shoulder and studied the monitor.

"I see what you mean."

"Whitewater rapids ahead, sir. Judging by the bottom, this is going to get a lot worse before it gets better. I'd say we're looking at maybe a mile of very rocky whitewater before it opens up again."

"Any ideas, Harry?" Hawke said.

"Keeps raining like this, the river keeps rising at this rate, we just might be able to get through."

"Praying for rain is not an option. We'll take the bloody canoes."

"What? And leave all these expensive weapons systems behind?" Brock grinned and cocked an eye.

"We've got no choice. Skipper, all stop."

"Aye, sir. All stop." Brownlow hauled back the throttles and *Stiletto* ghosted to a stop.

"Mr. Brock, tell the crew on deck to launch all four canoes. Then go forward and inform our team to check their weapons. We shove off in fifteen minutes."

Hawke headed below to his tiny cabin to retrieve his weapons and ammunition.

"Sir?" the radioman said, sticking his head out into the companionway just after Hawke passed.

"What is it, Sparks?"

"Call for you, sir. On the scrambled line."

"Who?"

"Washington, sir. State Department. Urgent."

"Put it through to my quarters," Hawke said and went two doors down into his cabin.

"Alex?"

"Hello, Conch."

"Alex, listen carefully. This is the deep shit call. Where are you now?"

"Still on the bloody river. It's impossible to go further. We're launching canoes for the final leg. Weather is socked in. Good, because it keeps the drones from pestering us. Bad, because you can't see a bloody thing. And how are you doing on this lovely January evening?"

"Insane. The president walks down the steps of the Capitol to be sworn in at noon, less than twelve hours from now. Rumors of some kind of attack are flying so fast you can't keep track. The Secret Service's Joint Operations Command has assigned a threat level of most serious and credible. Your idea is only one of many we are running down right now."

"My idea."

"A feint on the Mexican border. Originating in the Amazon. An attack on a major city. Washington."

"Washington? How do you know that?"

"Think about it, Alex."

"The Inauguration. Christ, Conch, of course. That has to be it."

"It gets worse. Six hours ago that nice sheriff from Texas called me. His deputy followed a convoy of remote-controlled trucks to Virginia. In one truck was some kind of remote-controlled sub. It was placed in the Potomac. We've been dragging the river from Fredericksburg to the Pentagon Yacht Basin. Divers are down everywhere. We haven't found it yet."

"What about the airborne minesweepers? Those new helos that laser scan from above?"

"Nothing. There is a move afoot to evacuate key government officials from the city. One more thing. I just got a call from FBI Chief Mike Reiter. He says the explosion in Rock Creek Park turns out to have involved at least one Chevrolet Suburban packed with Semtex explosives. Secret Service vehicle, Alex."

"You've got assassins inside the Secret Service?"

"That's certainly one possiblility, however remote. The other is, someone went to a whole lot of trouble to duplicate a government Suburban. We even found pieces of light bars, the same heavy door armor the Service uses. Before the bomb went off, this Chevy was being transported in a remote-controlled tractor-trailer rig. Just like the one that ferried the sub to Virginia."

"You said 'convoy.' How many of these big rigs, Conch?"

"According to Sheriff Dixon, maybe a dozen remote-controlled trailer trucks are known to be headed to the northeast from Texas."

"All going to Washington?"

"I hope not. But we have no way of knowing that. I wish to God we did. We have no idea what we're looking at here. It's too bizarre for even me."

Alex was silent for a long moment and then he said, "Conch, this jungle compound I'm about to take out. It is mecca for combat droids. Armed drones, tanks, you name it."

"I know. I just read Harry Brock's report. That's why I'm calling you, Alex. I think there is at least the ghost of a chance that these remote-controlled trucks are a Muhammad Top operation. Perhaps even controlled from his jungle complex."

"That could well be it. Brock says there is a heavily fortified command-and-control bunker. Twenty-feet down. Two-hundred-foot antenna disguised as a tree."

"A tree?"

"Don't ask."

"Theoretically, I've got a dozen or more phony Secret Service vehicles driving around, each identical to the real thing. And possibly packed with high explosives. Could be plastique, Semtex, could be nuclear for all we know. Perfect bombs, Alex, hiding in plain sight. Movable. And, another weapon, possibly nuclear, may be buried in the muck in the Potomac River. I've got to run along now."

"Conch? One thing. They've got Ambrose. When they took him, he was deciphering a code log that could make a difference. The man who wrote the code was trying to stop these people."

"Oh, God, Alex. Poor Ambrose."

"If he's still alive, we've got a chance."

"In eleven hours and change, the president puts his hand on that Bible and takes the oath of office. That moment in time is the single most vulnerable few seconds this country faces every four years. The vice president, Congress, hell, the entire government is out there on the street standing with him. Tens of thousands of schoolchildren and—oh, Holy God."

"Conch, listen to me. Can't you get the president to postpone the ceremony? Move it?"

"Since General George Washington took the oath in 1789, the swearing-in ceremony has only been moved once. Bad weather and Andrew Jackson was ill. You think Jack McAtee is going down in history as the guy who called off his own inauguration at the last minute? What's your next idea?"

"I see what you mean."

"With or without that code, Alex. Take out Muhammad Top. I wish to God I could do it for you. But I can't."

78

J ust before dawn, Agent Rocky Hernandez swung
the old Cherokee into the parking lot of an all-night
diner. Across the street, the Annapolis harbor looked
quiet, sailboats riding at their moorings, peace and tran-
quility disturbed only by the sound of halyards flapping
against aluminum masts in the gusty wind.

The two men climbing out of the car looked frus-
trated, haggard, and worn. The excitement over
Dixon's breakthrough discovery in Rock Creek Park
was long faded. Time was running out. They had spent
the last five hours combing the countryside, coming up
empty. There was hardly a park, isolated farm, or
stretch of rolling Virginia or Maryland woodland
within thirty miles of the capital that they had not yet
searched.

"Ten-minute break," Hernandez said. "You go ahead
inside. I'll call in, see what's going on. Please order me a
black coffee and a couple of doughnuts. Maybe they'll
give you some water for Dutch too."

Dixon entered the empty diner and took a stool at

the counter. He ordered coffee and doughnuts and a bowl of water for the dog. Abigail, a perky high school senior, brought him the food and drink. "What kind of dog is it?" She stood on tiptoes with the bowl in her hands, looking out the window.

"He's a hero," Dixon said, managing a smile.

"Can I take the water out to him?"

"I guess. Truck's open. He's in the back. His handler's out there making a call."

"Dutch says thanks, he was thirsty," Hernandez said, taking a seat a few minutes later. He took two gulps of coffee and bit into his doughnut.

"How is it back in Washington, Rocky?"

The agent looked over at Dixon, his eyes red with strain. "It's bad," he said.

"I figured."

"Chaos. A lot of pressure from the First Lady and others in the Service to evacuate, postpone, or at least move the swearing-in ceremony. Take the whole show inside. Some secret location they're working on. Outside of Washington. My guys are going crazy right now. The media smells blood and they're hounding the White House every step of the way. It's a lose-lose situation."

"What do you mean?"

"We postpone, we move, we evacuate? And nothing happens, we're idiots. Don't evacuate, don't postpone, and something happens, we're idiots."

"How do you feel about that?"

"Doesn't matter how I feel. I know how the president feels. In five hours, he's going to walk down those

Capitol steps in the sunshine and put his hand on that Bible. Period. End of report. I know that man better than I know my own soul."

"I guess we were wrong about wooded areas," Dixon said, taking a sip.

"We'll keep looking, that's all. The Virginia truck, the Rock Creek truck. Both wooded areas. Secluded. Where the hell else are you going to secretly unload something as big as a Suburban?"

Franklin stared down at his cup in silence.

"A garage," he said quietly.

"What?"

Dixon, looked at him, his tired eyes alight. "Rocky, how long you figure it takes to run a cross-check on every garage and body repair shop in Washington? Cross-check the ownership? Match the owners against all the names on the D.C. counterterrorist watch list?"

The agent slammed his fist on the countertop. "A garage. Jesus. Why didn't I think of that? Let's get started."

Franklin put five dollars on the counter and headed for the door.

HALF AN HOUR later, they were on their third garage. The first two had been small one-man body shop operations, no way to back an eighteen-wheeler inside. The one they were headed for now was off Massachusetts Avenue, near Union Station. It was called the Teapot Dome Body Shop.

"This one feels good," Rocky said as they cruised by

the place and pulled around the corner to park. "I don't know why, but it does."

They got Dutch out of the back and sprinted around the corner to the entrance. They were moving fast, Dutch racing ahead as if he knew the schedule was tight. They had eleven more garages on their A list, six more on the B list. It was seven-thirty a.m. on what promised to be a snowy Inauguration Day. The president's address was now less than five hours away.

A tiny bell above the door tinkled when they pushed it open. The office reeked of sweat and oil. Old-fashioned nudie calendars hung on the walls. A fat dark-haired man in filthy white mechanic's coveralls sat behind a battered wooden desk that was littered with invoices, catalogs, and greasy automobile parts. He had an Arabic newspaper spread across his lap and looked up from it slowly.

"Help you?" he said, a smile spreading across his moon face.

"Secret Service," Hernandez said, flipping open his badge. "Special Agent Hernandez."

Franklin tipped his hat. "Dixon. Prairie County Sheriff."

"Yeah. So. What can I do for you two?"

Dutch had something. Inside the desk. On the man. And behind a door on the right. He went for the door.

"Where's the garage?" Franklin asked the man, moving quickly toward the closed door just right of the desk. "Through here?"

"Private property, cowboy. You got a warrant?"

Franklin ignored that, put his hand on the knob, and

turned it. Dutch bolted ahead of him through the narrow crack.

"Hey! I said, this is private—" The fat man was coming out of his chair.

"Gun!" Hernandez shouted. "Gun! Get down!"

Franklin shoved through the door and dove to the cement floor. He rolled twice, heard two loud shots explode inside the office, and pulled his weapon. Through the door he saw the gun still in the mechanic's hand, his arm coming up, even though the upper part of his coveralls were soaked with blood.

Franklin shot the fat man in the head.

He looked through the doorway at Agent Hernandez. On the floor behind the desk, but he was getting to his feet.

"You hurt?" Dixon said.

"Not bad. Grazed my shoulder. What have you got in there, Dutch? It better be good."

"You won't believe it."

"The Teapot is the jackpot," Hernandez said, smiling at Dixon and moving quickly past him to catch up with his dog.

The garage was cavernous. You'd never know it from the facade on the street outside. Inside, it looked like two or three old warehouses had been combined into one. You could easily get twenty tractor-trailer rigs inside.

It was now empty except for the three black Chevy Suburbans with blacked-out windows parked along one wall. Dutch was running back and forth alongside all three vans. They were sheathed in clear thick plastic covers. Hernandez crossed the greasy floor and approached the first one, running his hand along the smooth black fender where the plastic had been partially peeled away.

"Dutch! Come!" Dixon said. He'd found something interesting on the far side of the garage. The dog started pawing through the stuff in the corner.

"Will you look at this?" Rocky said, ripping back the torn plastic covering one of the big vans, his voice a mix of admiration and dread. "These things are perfect! Light bars, antennas, running boards, grab handles, the whole nine yards right down to the five-star U.S.S.S. decals on the doors."

"Stay away from that stuff, Rocky!" Dixon said, keeping his distance. "Don't touch it!"

"Why?"

"Two cops already died finding out. Come here and see what Dutch has got. Huge pile of plastic wrappers over here in the corner. Maybe a dozen of them. That means the rest of the vehicles are already on the streets."

"Yeah . . ."

"Don't do that!"

"Aw, c'mon, Sheriff, we've got to find out what's inside these things, don't we? I mean—"

The explosion was blinding.

79

THE BLACK JUNGLE

Top was ecstatic as he left the prisoner alone in his room overlooking the river that morning. He and Khan had just pushed the man to the edge of endurance and beyond. The Englishman was near death now and would probably expire before his scheduled beheading at sundown. Pity. Still, both Top and the doctor were now fully convinced the English detective had not communicated anything to this man Hawke; nor to anyone else.

Their plans thus intact, with no need of dangerous last-minute alterations, he and the doctor rushed across the rope bridge leading to the subterranean bunker.

The rain was heavy.

His drones, sadly, were grounded. Even the patrol tanks were having a rough go of it in the deepening mud that carpeted the jungle floor. The river was rising. It was possible an early flash flood might occur. This was of no concern. His watertight bunker was secure and his fortress built in trees for just this kind of situa-

tion. He who has the high ground, reigns, Top reminded himself, even if he must reign from below."

The hour was at hand. He was surprised to find that
he was wholly at peace. Unconcerned with trivialities
or small setbacks such as had occurred on the farm in
Virginia and in Rock Creek Park. It was too late for the
Americans. They just didn't know it yet. Nothing could
stop him now. He had built his fortress well. Nothing
could stop his machines.

There had been scattered reports of incursions along
the northern perimeter. There had been probes along
the western front as well. Let them probe. His men
were ready. His remaining guards would fight to the
death. He was also unconcerned about an attack by this
nobody named Hawke. His vessel was now stopped,
stymied by the rapids just as Top had expected it would
be. He'd seen her size on the live feed from the aerial
drones. There was no way a boat that size could navigate this stretch of the Black River.

Hawke was nothing but a runaway slave and when
he was found, he would be dealt with in a manner be-
fitting his station and his sins.

Four entire divisions had moved out from this camp
as well as the satellite camps in the jungle. His soldiers,
wearing the new red patches proclaiming them *Bolívaristas,* were on their way north, en route to Colombia.
There, in the jungles outside the city of Medellín, his
forces would join a large battalion of FARC guerrillas
and launch their assault on the first stepping stone in
Central America, Panama. After the fall of Panama City,

the unstoppable *Bolívaristas* would advance into Costa Rica and Nicaragua where they would be joined with yet more of their brethren.

And then into El Salvador they would march, gathering strength as they moved into Guatemala for the final surge before joining their comrades in the mountains of Mexico. The final push would, of course, be north across that beleaguered borderline, north, always north, until the lost territories of his friends in Mexico City were at long last recovered.

What Simon Bolívar had begun in 1820, Muhammad Top would finish. A united continent, brothers-in-arms, true believers all, faithful soldiers of Allah.

Now, to the matters at hand.

He and Khan entered a short tunnel, brilliantly disguised inside a large flowering fern, and came to the blast door that protected the elevator.

Seconds later they were inside and descending to the bunker.

Khan and Top entered the Tomb. They could hardly contain their joy at the images on the multiple screens. His black Chevrolet war wagons were circling the American Capitol. Their cameras were sending back pictures of a cloudy January morning in Washington. A holiday. Parade marshals were directing traffic around the Capitol building itself. High school marching bands gathering on side streets, tubby children tooting their tubas. Even now, joyful Americans were lining up three deep behind the ropes that lined the parade route from the White House.

Top looked up at the digital clock he'd positioned so carefully where all eyes could read it.

9:59 a.m.

In two hours, the president of the United States would place his hand on the Bible and swear to uphold the Constitution and defend his country. At that exact moment, America, its entire government decapitated, would go crashing to the ground with a sound that would be heard around the world.

The Bible was a nice touch, Top thought. One of Khan's better ideas.

"IT'S TIME," Saladin said, handing the field radio back to his radioman. He'd just talked to Brock. The canoes were on the river, headed for Top's compound three miles distant. Saladin moved his men quickly east through the jungle. The rain was heavy, but they'd trained in worse. At his hand signal, the men halted just inside the tree-line. The wide ravine lay ahead. And the great rope bridge.

Thanks to Caparina, who had shaved her head and disguised herself as a lowly foot soldier inside the compound, he now knew this was the weak link. It was the back door of Top's compound. A lot of troops had moved out, and were marching north. His scouts had pinpointed the position of the main enemy force and communicated the troop's position to Fire Control aboard *Stiletto*.

The compound would be primarily guarded by Trolls now. But he and his demo experts had figured out a way to reduce the Troll population of the Black Jungle.

Now, Saladin ran from man to man, making sure the main body of his squad was well situated within the tree line and knew their orders. Then he looked at the two young Brazilian spec ops guys who would accompany him across the bridge. They had volunteered for the most dangerous part of this mission. "Ready?" he whispered.

They nodded, their faces smeared with camo paint.

Into the jaws of death, Saladin thought, but he kept those dark words to himself.

"We go."

Saladin and his two volunteers sprinted across the open ground and raced out onto the swaying bridge. He'd left the main body of his squad inside the trees, weapons ready. When it was time, they would strike. At the far end of the bridge, they could see the enemy forces aligned, waiting for them. Each of his two comrades had been told to hold his fire until his signal. They would get as close to the far side as they could before engaging. That was the plan.

Halfway across, running hard, they could see the robot tanks forming up to defend the western perimeter. Saladin and his men kept running, weapons at the ready. A hundred yards, now, fifty . . . still, no one fired. The burned-out bunker had not been returned to action. But there were more enemy troops moving up through the trees. Why didn't they shoot? He and his two men kept running toward them, weapons poised, fingers itching on the triggers.

Twenty yards from the end of the bridge, Saladin raised his hand and signaled for the two men with him to halt. They each dropped to one knee, covering him. He ran ahead alone across the bridge. He was firing his weapon, spraying the oncoming tanks now streaming toward the bridge. The tanks returned fire, troops moving in behind their advance.

Saladin went down. As the tanks advanced, his two comrades raced forward and grabbed their leader under each arm, retreating back across the bridge on the run, firing as furiously over their shoulders as they were able, knees pumping, running hard for the safety of the jungle where their squad was waiting. The tank controllers, seeing all this disarray, would be filled with glee. And speed men and machines across the bridge for the kill.

Saladin craned his head around, looking back over his shoulder. The tanks were rolling onto the bridge in high-speed pursuit of the enemy.

"Excellent!" Saladin shouted, as they dove, pulling him headfirst into the foliage. Everyone had played his part perfectly. They now turned and watched the enemy tanks and men behind them streaming across the bridge toward them. The suspension bridge was sagging under weight it was not designed to hold. But it *would* hold, the engineer in Saladin told him. That was the idea.

"Ready, sir?"

"Five seconds, Sergeant," Saladin said. "Wait for those last three tanks to roll on—okay—now!"

The young soldier pushed the old-fashioned plunger.

The charges his team had so carefully placed beneath the bridge blew in perfect sequence. Three massive charges exploded: one at either end of the bridge, and finally one in the exact center. The explosions tore the heavy rope bridge to pieces, sending at least fifteen Trolls and thirty of the enemy guards plummeting into the deep ravine below.

Saladin allowed himself a grim feeling of satisfaction. He had just struck a serious blow against his enemy. *Bolívaristas,* my ass. It was a narco-criminal terrorist army, financed and led by foreigners with no interests beyond their own benighted religious fantasies of a humbled America.

Now, Saladin's squad would all descend into the ravine, cross the river, and begin the tough climb up the other side. Such a climb under fire would be hell. But this recent action, and the one that would surely follow it, had drawn resources from the center to the western perimeter. And destroyed them. The first blow against Top had been struck.

Saladin believed his actions now would give Hawke and the men on the river a fighting chance later.

80

P resident is waiting in the Oval," Betsey Hall said. Jack McAtee's pretty ash-blond secretary was standing just outside the office. She was frowning at her watch as the chairman of the Joint Chiefs approached. General Moore, a lean six-footer in his dress blues, did not look happy. In fact, nobody looked very happy on this Inauguration Day morning.

"Sorry," Moore said. "We couldn't get here any faster."

"You're all right. He just got back from across the street. Morning worship service at St. John's. He's only been in there ten minutes."

"How is he?" Moore asked her, pausing before he went in.

"In a word?"

"Yeah."

"Pissed. At everybody."

"He's not postponing?"

"He's not postponing and he's not canceling and that's that. You talk to him. He listens to you."

"What did you tell him to do, Betsey?"

"I'm not in the habit of telling the president what to do."

"Right," Moore said, smiling and squeezing her shoulder. He snapped off a salute at the two Marines standing guard at the door and went inside.

The president stood by the windows with his back to the door, looking out into the snow-covered Rose Garden. "Hello, Charley," he said without turning around.

"Morning, Mr. President. I got here as quickly as I could."

"Town's a mess. Another Inauguration Day, you know. What will they think of next?"

Moore laughed. "We're lucky to be here, sir. It could easily have been the other guy."

"Not that easily," McAtee huffed. "Take a seat, General." He walked around his desk and collapsed into the upholstered sofa by the fireplace. Moore sat opposite him and picked up a silver urn.

"Coffee?"

The president waved the question away and Moore filled his own cup. "Mr. President, what do you intend to do?"

"You're the tenth person to ask me that question in the last goddamn hour."

"Sorry, sir."

"Charley, I like you. Always have. You were the guy I most looked up to at Annapolis. Hell, I still look up to you and I'm the damn president. A lot is riding on this decision. If I run, everybody runs. Park Police estimate there are already half a million people out there on the parade route. The media is already going apeshit. Positively salivating at the chance to see me slip out the back door. What the hell would you do? You going to rain on my parade too?"

"What are the options, sir?"

"Marine One is warming up its engines out on the lawn. Ready to fly me to Site R in Raven Rock Mountain. There are also two identical Secret Service motorcades waiting for me. One of them is going to Camp David. The one at the North Portico will take me to the Capitol steps where I will be duly sworn in for my second term. Pick one."

"Intel right now points to a possible WMD in that Potomac unmanned sub."

"What sub? Nobody's seen it. We've got sensors on every bridge. The most advanced electronic countermeasures on earth can't find a radiation signature! Nobody can even guarantee me the damn thing exists. I'm going to cancel because some kid lawman from Texas told some sheriff he saw some bad guys put something in the river? C'mon, Charley, you know me better than that."

"What about Rock Creek Park?"

"What about it? Somebody trucked a couple of Suburbans packed with conventional explosives into the park and blew them up. Rattled some windows at Walter Reed. BFD."

"The Suburbans were designed to exactly replicate Secret Service vehicles. Very sophisticated plan of attack, I'd say. Hide your bombs in plain sight."

"Everybody's all over that, Charley. Media says I

shouldn't have sent all those troops to the border. Left the capital unprotected. Unprotected from what? So far, nobody's been able to find a single heavily armored black Chevy Suburban in this town that does *not* belong to the Secret Service."

"I still don't like it. One of those look-alike machines could roll right up alongside a bunch of Iowa cheerleaders and no one would think anything of it."

"Hell, I don't like it either! But I'll be damned if I'll run based on any of this airy-fairy crap I'm hearing from the boys at Langley."

"What's the First Lady say?"

"Aw, you know Lynn, Charley. She only wants to protect me."

"So do I."

"I know that. So, what the hell do I do? No, I've got a better question. What the hell would *you* do?"

General Moore took a long time to answer. He'd known he'd be asked this question. It was the reason he'd been called to the White House. One of those pivotal moments history is so fond of throwing our way. The president's safety versus the country's need to see presidential resolve and courage in the face of adversity. By chance, Moore's gaze fell upon the small bust of Churchill standing at one end of the great Lincoln Desk. The set of his shoulders, that bulldog expression. He looked at his old friend of thirty years.

"Grab your hat, Mr. President. We're going to the Capitol."

"Thank you, Charley. Either way."

"I hope and pray it's the right answer, sir."

The president stood and straightened his tie. "Want a ride? I've got plenty of room in the limo. No former presidents full of phony platitudes this time."

Moore smiled and said, "One call, Mr. President. I'll be right behind you."

McAtee strode from the Oval Office. Betsey Hall and Scott McComsey, the White House press secretary, were waiting to hear what they would now tell the world. Moore reached over and picked up the phone from the coffee table. He speed-dialed the president's direct line to the JCS office at the Pentagon.

"This is General Moore. Belay my previous orders. The president has decided not to go to Zone R. The swearing-in will take place as scheduled on the Capitol steps. No delays. I want a combat air patrol scrambled and over the city. I want the surface-to-air-missile batteries at both the Capitol and the Pentagon activated. And I want to expand the no-fly zone around the city. Take it out to sixty miles. Anybody find that goddamn sub? Harbor Police? No? Good God, somebody better start praying."

Moore stood, and spent a minute gazing around the Oval Office, remembering happier times in this room.

What is happening to our country? the general thought, and headed for the door.

"YOU FEELING okay, now, sir?" the blond kid said to him. He looked around. Dixon didn't feel too good. His head hurt, for one thing. He reached up to rub his forehead and felt something wrapped around it. Bandage of some kind.

He was half-sitting, half-lying in the street, his legs straight out in front of him. Bloody. There was a line of vehicles in the street. A motorcade of Black Suburbans. Lights flashing. Men were standing at all four corners of each vehicle with guns drawn, pistols and submachine guns. Big men, all wearing some kind of black jumpsuits and body armor.

"Who are they?" Dixon asked the blond kid.

"CAT, sir. Counterassault team. Secret Service."

"Where's Agent Hernandez?"

"He didn't make it, sir. I'm sorry. You want to try and stand up again? You tell me."

"Hernandez is gone?"

"Yes, sir. I'm afraid so."

The door to the vehicle right next to him was open and he could hear scratchy voices on the radio. "Roger, Rawhide is rolling. Repeat, Rawhide is on the move. Rolling to the Punch Bowl."

"Everybody copy that?" the blond kid said into his sleeve. "Rawhide is rolling. Looks like it's going to be showtime after all."

"Who are you?"

"Agent-in-charge, sir. Andy Hecht. We've been ordered to move you to a secure location, sir."

"You've got to look inside that building first. I've got to show you something."

"What building, sir? It's gone."

Dixon craned his head around and looked over his shoulder. Half of the building where he'd last remembered being had collapsed to the ground. There was a smoking pile of rubble two stories high. The site was crawling with men wielding axes and picks, digging through what was left of the garage. He must have been out for quite a while.

"You want me to get in that truck?"

"Yes, sir, I'd appreciate it. We're going to get you further medical attention." Hecht helped the sheriff get to his feet. Dixon swayed a bit, then steadied himself and looked back at where he'd been when the truck exploded.

"Inside that building were three vehicles exactly like this one. Except they weren't. They were remote-controlled bombs. And I found evidence in there of a lot more. If you keep digging, you'll find it."

"We believe you, sir. We're looking for those trucks right now. Step this way, sir. Take it easy."

It was a struggle just to stay on his feet. Dixon was determined to climb up into the back seat under his own steam. He had a lot of work to do yet, finding those things. He was the only one left who really knew what to look for.

"What will you do if you *do* find more of these things?" Dixon asked.

"I'm not at liberty to discuss that. I'm going to close the door now, sir. Agent Ross is going to take care of you from here on in. Good luck, sir."

Hecht went to close the door but Dixon put out a hand and stopped it midway. He leaned halfway out, his red-rimmed eyes searching the rubble across the street. Then he looked down at his boots and his whole body seemed to sag.

Dixon said, "I'm sorry."

"Something wrong, sir?"

"Where's the dog?"

"Dog?"

"Dutch? Did he make it?"

"Sheriff, maybe you better lay back down for a little—"

"Hernandez had a dog, son. His name was Dutch."

"Oh, okay, hold on a second," Hecht said and spoke into his sleeve once more. "This is Agent Hecht. Anybody at the scene find a K-9 dog? Answers to the name of Dutch? What? Repeat, I didn't copy that . . . yeah, got it."

He looked at Dixon, shaking his head.

"Gone?" Dixon said.

"Wait a minute . . . no. I believe that might be him over there, sir. Some of my men were patching him up and getting him some chow."

Dixon swung his boots out of the back seat and looked back down the street.

Dutch was trotting slowly toward him. He was bandaged up pretty well, and he was limping a little bit, sure, but he looked darn good, all things considered. At least his tail was still wagging.

"Good boy," the sheriff said, bending down to hug the dog around the neck. "Good boy, Dutch."

81

Hawke's radio squawked.

It was bloody tough going on the river. Driving rain, icy cold. The four canoes kept getting pinned against boulders by the raging torrents. Hawke pulled his paddle from the turbulent water and picked up the field radio lying between his feet. It was Saladin, reporting in, to Hawke's great relief.

"Hawke? Do you copy? Is that you?"

"Go ahead, Saladin," Hawke replied. "I told you I'd come back. Glad you're still with us. I was beginning to worry. What's your current position?"

"We just blew that primary west bridge. A lot of armor and troops went into the drink."

"Well done!" It was the first good news in a long time. "Casualties, Saladin?"

"Minimal, but that could change rapidly. We are going up the side of the ravine en route to our scheduled rendezvous with Froggy. We are taking heavy fire now, but we should be there in twenty minutes. Some of us, anyway."

"I look forward to our reunion."

"One more thing. My forward scouts report heavy troop movement north of the camp. It's Top's main force, Alex. They're moving out."

"Give me that position, Saladin. I'll take care of it."

Saladin gave Hawke a description of Top's main body of forces and the GPS coordinates. Hawke jotted down the fresh intel in a soggy notebook and jumped back on the radio. His canoe was about to smash into a large boulder and he shouted a warning to his crew. They managed to avoid the thing, barely.

"*Stiletto,* heads up, Fire Control, this is Hawke. We have heavy enemy troop movement headed north. Approximately six miles northwest of my current location on the river."

He gave Dylan the exact GPS coordinates.

"Roger that, Skipper, target description, sir?"

"Ground troops, Dylan, the main body is on the jungle road north. The force consists of various types of armored robotic vehicles, and hundreds of five-ton troop transports holding twenty soldiers each. We can't stop them, but we can slow them down a bit. Acquire targets and launch LAM missiles now."

"Affirmative, sir."

"One more thing. This road the troops are taking. It's limestone and I can personally vouch for the shoddy construction. Launch PAM missiles. Try and take out the highway two miles north of the troops. Destroy it, and we could halt their progress for at least a week."

"Roger that, Skipper, acquiring and launching as ordered." Hawke picked up his paddle and started digging with new resolve. He could hear dull thuds to the north. He took grim satisfaction from the fact that the road he and others like him had slaved on was now being destroyed. The PAM missiles would slow the troop advance for a while. Conch could figure out what she wanted to do about that later.

Meanwhile, *Stiletto*'s Loitering Attack Missiles would remain airborne above the enemy troops for forty-five minutes searching for moving targets. When a LAM acquired a tank or an armored troop carrier, it would automatically nose over and destroy it.

Death from above.

And from the river, if they could stay afloat.

"Watch out!" Hawke cried.

Hawke and his crew dug their paddles deep into the roiling river, paddling furiously. It was too late.

The roaring currents of vicious rapids had finally pinned their canoe hard up against two huge boulders. The power of the water was so strong, it was all Hawke and the four others could do to keep the canoe from overturning and spilling them out. Had the five men been in a wooden dugout, and not the sleek carbon fiber craft, the hull would have been shattered to splinters long ago.

He gritted his teeth and plunged his paddle again and again into the roiling water. The sudden surge of energy he felt was frightening in its intensity. He worried it might be another feverish illusion, but he'd kept the fear that the fever might be spiking again to himself. Hawke had said nothing these last days, but the first signs of returning malaria had appeared.

Of the four five-man canoes launched, only three had successfully been run through the rapids. Harry Brock, in the lead, was now navigating his own and two other canoes through the mined stretch of river guarding Top's lair. Harry's charts told him they were less than three miles away. Mercifully, the weather was so atrocious, that drones, either from above or along the shore, were not hounding them.

Hawke, trapped near the bank, saw only one escape. Trees bent low over the water, strangled with twisting vines as thick as cables. If he could reach one of the looping vines, called bejucas, he might be able to pull the canoe off the rocks and get the prow headed back into the channel Brock had found and successfully navigated. But he'd need to get out of the boat to do it.

He informed the crew of his plan and swung himself over the gunwale and into the river. He found his footing and saw that the water was up to his armpits. Somehow, he had to dislodge the canoe without overturning it or having it catapult downriver and smash on the jutting rocks twenty yards further ahead. He could see Brock's channel now. It was narrow, but if he could get them properly aligned, they might make it.

Keeping a firm grip on the canoe, he started to make his way toward the thick vine hanging over the river. It was hard sledding against the current, his feet slipping over the moss-covered rocks, and he stumbled twice on the sharply uneven river bed. But he managed to grab the vine with his free hand. Now that he had leverage, he started pulling the canoe toward the bank. The men saw what he was attempting and started paddling with a will.

The current that had pinned them to the rocks was now in their favor. The canoe was moving slowly but surely toward him.

"That's it!" Hawke cried to the men. "You can do it, lads!"

Yes. Pull the canoe straight for the bank, keep the bow pointed into the current as much as possible, let the bloody river swing the stern around until the canoe was parallel to the bank and pointed in the right direction. Now! The men were holding her fast to the bank, and Hawke swung himself back aboard.

This time, they managed to stay within the narrow confines of the channel. Hawke's watch put them at maybe twenty minutes behind Brock's group. The fact that they'd heard no mines exploding downriver was a great comfort.

Hawke could no longer tell if the water in his eyes was rain or fever sweat. But he paddled harder and so, too, did his crew. Stoke and Froggy had to be getting close to Top's compound now. They might have already found Congreve. He shook his head, trying to rid himself of the unbidden words:

"Hang on, Ambrose," Hawke muttered.

Hang bloody on.

82

THE BLACK JUNGLE

Stoke caught Frogman's eye and raised one hand into the air, palm flat. Then he clenched his fist. Enemy ahead. Nobody move. The two *jihadistas* were one hundred yards away. Smoking cigarettes, their hands cupped over the butts, talking to each other at the base of the enormous tree. Standing sentry, it looked like, in their dark green camo fatigues under ponchos. The wide black river was just to the right. Ambrose's hut was supposed to be by the river. The tree looked good. The sentries guarding it made it look even better.

A great bridge arched over the river. A real bridge, not one of the typical wood and rope one-day wonders you saw everywhere in this jungle. Not much traffic. A platoon of guards marching double-time, couple of soldiers on bicycles, two or three of the little robot tanks Brock called Trolls. There were pickets out, and probably electronic sensors in the jungle. But nobody on the bridge seemed to be aware that not only had their perimeter been breached, some bona fide badasses were on the prowl inside the hen-house.

Probably because all the pickets were currently dead.

Froggy and his guys were crouching in the heavy bush fifty yards to his left. For an hour, they had moved swiftly and silently through the jungle, taking advantage of the plentiful natural ground cover, moving from tree to tree. They had left in the bloody wake behind them a large number of seriously dead individuals, scouts and pickets who'd gotten in the squad's way as they advanced deeper inside Top's jungle fortress. They'd used assault knives to cut the wire fences and silence the enemy. And silenced CAR-15 submachine guns, the selector set to 3-round bursts, when they couldn't get close enough for the knives.

Stoke and Froggy still had all their guys, and all their guys still had all their fingers and toes. So far it was Good Guys 17, Top 0. He'd heard Brock's guy Saladin talking on the squad radio. He was moving in from the west and sweeping up any bad guys who got between them and their rendezvous point just a mile north above the bridge.

Stoke looked up at the underside of the dripping canopy. Treehouses, if you could believe that. A whole damn village up in the trees. It was weird. But, Stoke had to admit, strangely beautiful. Magical, like that movie he'd seen as a kid. *Swiss Family Robinson,* that was it. Name a kid who ever saw that movie and didn't want to live in a treehouse. Maybe Ambrose Congreve, but that was about it.

Stoke was ready to take the tree. He looked at his

feet. He was standing in ooze that covered his boots, felt like it was sucking him down. They were on high ground now. In some places, the water was already up to your knees. The rain still came and the river was rising rapidly. In many places, camp was already flooded. That's why the treehouses, dummy, Stoke said to himself, looking over at Froggy.

He caught his eye and then pointed at the two tangos smoking at the base of the tree. They still had their backs to Froggy. Stoke gave his patented hand signal, pointing his index finger at the side of his own skull and lowering his thumb hammer twice. Froggy nodded. Understood. Two headshots.

The Frogman rose up to his full height of five-foot-five and raised the CAR-15, sighting, and, almost instantaneously, firing. *Pfft-pfft*. The two guards crumpled to the ground, dead before they hit the mud. Good guns, these Colts. Now. When Stoke first used this weapon in the Delta, it had been too loud. Guys went deaf firing that gun. And the muzzle flash was too bright, blinding his guys at night and giving away their position to the enemy. They'd fixed all that, now. Had a longer flash suppressor that actually worked.

Stoke moved quickly to the tree, his eyes scanning the trunk, looking for the thin slash mark that would tell him he'd found the right tree. He did a three-sixty around the base. Nothing at eye level. Wait a minute. That was his eye-level. Harry's girl, Caparina, who'd cut the bark for them, would have a lot lower eye-level, wouldn't she? Unless she, too, was six-six. He doubted it. He'd heard she was a total babe.

He bent down and went round again, running his index finger lightly over the bark as he circled, a foot lower this time.

There. A thin diagonal slash, fresh greenish white wood showing.

He took a deep breath. Ambrose Congreve was at the top of this tree. Whether he was dead or alive was the question. Stoke waved Froggy and the squad in closer, circling the wagons with his index finger. There was heavy ground cover and good scrub not ten feet from the tree. Froggy could lay low there, cover his butt for at least the ten minutes this might take. He was going up the tree alone.

There was a funky hand-operated elevator. Basically, you just stepped onto a four-by-four-foot metal platform, grabbed the handrail, and pushed the red button on the controller hanging from the rail. Zip, you were airborne.

He looked up as he rose from the ground, his weapon at the ready. The treehouse was a round structure, supported by trusses underneath. The thing was built right around the trunk. Another house, slightly larger and a few feet higher up, was connected to this one by a small ropewalk. The houses had corrugated metal roofs, raised up to let the air flow in this tropical heat. There were narrow verandas that went all the way around.

He saw a head bending out over the rail, looking

straight down at him, the guy obviously wanting to say something to whichever of his buddies was on the way up.

"How you doing?" Stoke said.

He saw the guy's eyes go wide, looking straight down into the muzzle of a light alloy CAR-15 commando rifle that must have been growing bigger and blacker by the second.

Stoke squeezed off a shot, hoping the guy would not tumble forward and fall from the railing. He didn't. He collapsed halfway over the rail and stayed there.

Stoke stepped off the platform onto the circular porch. All clear so far. The door to the house was a quarter of the way around. He moved that way in a semi-crouch, gun out front. The dead guard was hanging there, blood dripping from what was left of his head. The sliding metal door was closed. To the right was a window. There was a light inside, but curtains blocked the view.

Stoke did a three-sixty around the veranda, not taking any chances. He moved in fractions of inches, trying not to make any noise, and then edged back around to the door. He looked at the steel window again, trying to peer beyond the edges of the blackout curtain. Couldn't see diddly.

He put his hand on the door, pausing to control his breathing. Slowed the system way down, just the way he'd been trained to do at Heat & Skeet, down in the Keys.

Then he slid the door along the track. Slowly. One inch at a time until he could get a look-see.

No bad guys inside. Only a room with no furniture except a picture hung on the wall. There was a hospital gurney on the far side of the little round room. A pool of light from a lamp on a steel table lit the whole room. There were surgical instruments in a tray on the table. And a man was lying on the narrow gurney, his hands and legs shackled to the frame. An intravenous tube ran down to his arm from a bag of liquid hung on the trolley. Stoke's heart beat a little faster.

From a distance he looked a whole lot like Ambrose might look, if he hadn't eaten in a week. Stoke moved quickly to the gurney and looked down at the grey face of the man on the gurney.

It was Ambrose Congreve, all right.

He looked a whole lot dead.

A voice behind him caused him to spin around and tighten his trigger finger at the sight of the soldier. Not squeeze it, which was good, because this soldier was wearing a long white coat over jungle camos. The figure framed in the doorway yanked off a floppy hat revealing a recently shaved head. It belonged to a beautiful woman. She was carrying an armful of medical supplies instead of a gun.

"Stokely Jones?" she said.

"Yeah?"

"Caparina. Harry Brock's friend."

"Is he dead?" Stoke said, looking at Ambrose.

"Not yet."

"You think you can do anything for him, Caparina?"

"I'm going to try."

Stoke pulled out the small handheld radio and hit speaker.

"Hawke, Hawke, copy?"

"Stoke, where are you?"

"He's alive, boss. I'm with him now."

"Hurt?"

"Yeah. He needs an exfil, pronto. We've got to get him to sickbay."

"Your job is to keep Ambrose alive, Stoke. Whatever it takes. Can you stay in position? I'm on the river. The canoes are ten minutes away. Has Brock made the rendezvous?"

"Negative. Haven't seen him."

"He's upriver, ahead of me. Should reach you any minute."

"Where's *Stiletto*?"

"Navigating the minefield with the probes. She's maybe twenty minutes out, depending on how bad it is. I'm assuming there's enough water to get there."

"We'll do what we can for Ambrose till you get here. Meanwhile, I got another report of troop movement from Saladin's guys. They're all headed north."

"*Stiletto*'s got them dialed in. Saladin's scouts radioed the position. Fire Control is launching everything we can spare. Take care of him, Stoke. Keep him breathing."

"You heard the man," Stoke said to the woman bending over her gravely injured patient.

"What's his name?" she asked, resting a cool hand on his forehead.

"That's Ambrose Congreve of Scotland Yard. He's the only man on the planet who might know how to keep Papa Top from pulling the big trigger."

83

Franklin zipped up his last pair of clean blue jeans and pulled the T-shirt and sweater over his head. It was a tight squeeze with the bandages and all. His only clean clothes he had left in the bag he'd taken to Key West. He put on his boots. He was ready to go home, soon as this mess was over.

The State Department had been kind enough to invite him to attend the Inauguration ceremony. He'd said he'd rather help than watch but they said no, somebody would pick him up. After that, they'd take him to Reagan Airport for the flight back home.

He sat down on the edge of the hotel bed and reached for the phone. Right now, all he could think about was talking to Daisy. Hearing that sweet voice on the phone. A song where the music was more important than the lyrics.

"Hello?"

"Hey. It's me."

"Oh, my lord! Franklin! Where are you, baby? Still

in Washington? June and I got the TV on. They showed your picture this morning! I can't believe what all they're saying."

"You never should."

"Are you all right?"

"I'll tell you later. You got my messages about staying away from those trucks? I left three or four there for you on the machine."

"I got them, Franklin."

"Tell me you and June stayed away from that one in San Antone. I've been so worried about that."

"We found that sucker, honey. Big Orange."

"I was afraid of that. Is everybody okay? June? What happened?"

"Franklin, we found that damn Big Orange truck! Can you believe it, the thing was parked right outside of the Alamo. Isn't that perfect? The Mexicans blowing up the Alamo? June said, 'Shoot, why didn't we think of that?' "

"You didn't go near it?"

"After what you said? Heck, no! June called the San Antone PD on her cell. They told us to go straight inside the Alamo to warn all the tourists to get out of there. And you'll never guess what happened."

"Tell me," Dixon said, lying back on the bed, cradling the phone to his ear. Now that he knew she was all right, he just wanted to listen to the words.

"We went straight to the souvenir shop, of course, because that's where all the tourists head first anyway, right? So, we go over to the counter and there's this really beautiful cashier girl, a dead-ringer for that June Carter actress, Reese Witherspoon, and you will never believe who she was talking to!"

"Davy Crockett?"

"No! She was talking to the Big Orange himself! A really cute blond guy with a Big Orange logo on his shirt! He was the Big Orange driver himself, all the way from Lakeland, Florida!"

"What was he doing in Texas?"

"Took a detour to see his best girl who worked at the Alamo Gift Shoppe! Isn't that the funniest thing you ever heard in your life?"

"What about his truck?"

"Regular old truck. Blacked-out windows, but not the mirrored kind. My mistake, Franklin."

"I love you, Daisy."

"Well, I love you too! When are you coming home?"

"I've been invited by this nice lady at the State Department to attend the Inauguration. She's swinging by here to pick me up in a few minutes. Then I'm headed to the airport."

"How exciting! June and I'll be looking for you on the television. We heard they might call it off and then it was back on again. All right, I can tell you want to get off the phone. One more thing, did you hear what they found in that underground garage down in Gunbarrel?"

"Nope."

"Homer opened a can of worms. It was an old Chevy dealership. Owned and operated by Mr. J. T. Rawls. Selling SUVs to the Federales last couple of years. Had a tunnel. Had a shop, too, and he was customizing those SUVs to make them look like official cars. He was in cahoots with the Mexicans the whole time! Isn't that something?"

"Homer would have been a fine lawman."

"He already was, Franklin. You know that."

FRANKLIN got picked up out front of the Doubletree ten minutes later. It was a State Department sedan with a driver who looked like she just got out of college. Her name was Holly Rattigan and she was from Seattle. Said she worked in the Secretary's office but had the day off for the Inaugural Parade and had volunteered to drive the sheriff around.

"I'm honored to meet you, Sheriff Dixon," she said, checking traffic and then pulling out into it. "Everybody's talking about you. Call me Holly."

"'Preciate that, Holly."

They drove in silence, headed for the Capitol building. Downtown Washington was fortresslike. Ten-foot-high barriers lined the park in front of the White House. Security and bomb removal vehicles were everywhere. A hundred city blocks were closed. Franklin imagined there was a lot more security you could not see. He knew surveillance cameras were everywhere, sending pictures to a joint command center at a secret location in Virginia. Forty agencies there were monitoring sensors testing for chemical, nuclear, or biological agents.

Holly's official sedan and credentials got them through the checkpoints and roadblocks easily enough. A D.C. Metro policeman waved them into a special lane on Constitution Avenue. They drove toward 1st Street to a lot where they had special parking for government employees.

"Isn't it exciting?" Holly said. "They're expecting eleven thousand people to march in the parade down Pennsylvania Avenue to the White House."

"It's exciting, all right," Franklin said as Holly pulled into an empty parking space. He checked his watch as he climbed out of the car. The president would be sworn in in twenty minutes.

Their seats were in a roped-off section in a small park near the U.S. Grant Memorial. Seemed like all of Washington had showed up. Security here on the west side of the Capitol was everywhere you looked. All the roads were blocked off with huge concrete barricades. Everyone approaching the site of the president's speech was subjected to metal detector screening and inspection by security personnel.

It was January 20. The weather forecast for the president's inaugural speech was thirty degrees, cloudy, and light snow flurries. Franklin stood there beside Holly, listening to the beautiful music and admiring the beauty of the west steps of the Capitol, hung with red, white, and blue bunting. The State Department folks had provided pretty good seats. Still, you couldn't see much from this distance. Holly and Franklin excused themselves, and started moving through the crowd, trying to get closer to the podium.

Franklin was glad he'd come. It was festive and grand, and he liked seeing the mounted Park Police and their beautiful horses, moving slowly through the crowds keeping an eye on everything. One mounted patrolman had paused under a tree where Franklin was standing.

"Is that the president?" Franklin asked the officer, when he heard someone speaking solemnly over the public address.

"No, sir, that's the vice president. He goes first."

Franklin looked at his watch. It was a quarter to twelve. At noon, the president would take the oath.

"Oh my God," Holly said, grabbing his arm. "What's going on back there?"

Franklin turned to see. The crowd was surging forward around him. You could hear cries of panic coming from the direction of the Grant Memorial, a few hundred yards behind where he and Holly were now standing. There was a small reflecting pool behind the monument, and parked alongside the pool were four black Suburbans belonging to the Secret Service.

A fifth Suburban had pulled away from the curb and was moving slowly across 1st Street at a weird angle. It wasn't speeding, but people were shouting warnings and jumping out of its path. The black truck plowed ahead, gaining a little speed. It appeared to be headed right toward the wooded park area directly in front of the Inaugural stand. People were running, panic-stricken, scattering in all directions now.

The police and security people Dixon could see seemed to be momentarily frozen in place.

He instantly understood their reaction. Maybe that rogue van held a truckload of agents racing toward the podium on orders from the Secret Service com center.

Maybe someone inside that van had spotted a bomb or an armed man in the crowd. It was an impossible situation. No one knew what was going on. How could they?

You couldn't distinguish the legitimate vehicles from the remote-controlled version. Perhaps this Suburban rolling across the grass really had been ordered into the crowd. It was going to check out a threatening individual. Or perhaps it had been ordered to disarm a madman and shield the president? It was impossible to be certain.

At that exact moment, the sun came out from behind a snow-filled cloud. Brilliant beams lit up the Capitol building. In that instant Franklin knew for sure.

He'd seen the sun hit the black Suburban's mirrored windshield. He was the only man alive in Washington who had seen these windows close up. This one didn't look right.

The crowd had parted now, leaving a clear path for the vehicle now picking up speed and headed right toward him.

"Officer," Dixon said to the mounted policeman, "You've got to stop that vehicle. Now!"

"Me? I've go no authority to—"

"It's packed with explosives. It's headed for the Inaugural stand. They mean to kill the president and the whole damn government."

"Who the hell are you?" the mounted cop shouted at him. He was in high panic, half-listening, half-talking into his radio, trying to make sense of this craziness. He was looking to find somebody with the authority to tell him what to do in this bizarre situation.

Franklin grabbed the horse's reins and managed to hold on to the man's gaze an extra second. "I'm nobody. A Texas county sheriff. But I'm telling you the truth, officer. You've got to stop that thing right now!"

"How the hell am I supposed to do that?"

"I guess I'd better do it," Franklin said.

In a second, he'd reached up and grabbed the man's arm and hauled him down out of the saddle. The surprised cop was on the ground, going for his weapon but suddenly Holly was on top of him, knees on his chest, flashing her State Department ID right in his face. Franklin heaved himself up into the saddle, reining in the frightened horse and turning him around.

"Giddyup," Franklin said, clicking his tongue and touching his boots to the horse's flanks.

There was open ground between him and the Suburban. Franklin galloped straight toward the oncoming truck. He swerved out of its way at the last moment, then reined the horse sharply left and circled back. The horse was fast enough, and the sheriff caught up with the truck in a hurry. He matched the vehicle's speed and got the horse right alongside the right hand side of the damn thing.

"One shot at this," he told his horse.

He swung his right leg up and over and jumped.

It was an English saddle, which made getting off a lot easier. He'd timed it pretty good, got one boot down on the running board, and grabbed the handrail on the roof. He could see the mirror inside the glass and knew at least he'd not made a complete fool of himself. He hauled himself up onto the roof and rolled flat onto his stomach. He grabbed one of the satellite dishes and pulled himself forward.

On the truck he'd seen in the garage, he'd noticed the middle light on the light bar was black instead of red like it was supposed to be. That had to be the camera lens.

He grabbed the light bar with his left hand and held on tight. The truck was veering right to left, trying to throw him off maybe. He whipped off his short brim with his right hand and inched forward a little more so that he could do what he had to do. There were agents running alongside him now, guns drawn, all shouting at him and threatening to shoot him, he guessed.

But he had an idea and figured, at this point, it was worth trying.

He held on with his left hand, grabbed his cowboy hat in his right and reached all the way forward. He was just close enough to cover the lens. He stretched all the way forward and slapped his hat in place over the camera.

The damn truck kept going a second, then slowed way down. It made a wobbly left-hand turn, plowing up grass, then a right. Finally it just rolled to a dead stop. Franklin stayed put, keeping the lens covered with his Stetson, blinding whoever it was who wanted to kill his president.

He saw the familiar face of Agent Hecht standing there on the ground with all the other agents, every one of them looking up at him and shaking their heads, all with a big smiles on their faces.

"That's Sheriff Franklin W. Dixon of Prairie, Texas,"

Hecht said to his men. "He's the one who first found these damn things."

"Howdy," Franklin said to them.

"BLOW IT!" Top screamed at the top of his lungs. The Washington controllers staring at their suddenly black screens just looked at him. "Blow that fucking truck up now!"

"There's no provision for that, sir. We are no longer able to perform that function. All of the modified Chevrolet trucks have been keyed to the main timing device."

"What?" Top screamed, his face turning bright red. "Who authorized that?"

"Dr. Khan, sir."

"Why? Why did he do that?" Top was breathing hard, trying to control his raging emotions.

"He said he wanted to eliminate any possibility of human error, sir."

"Khan did that?"

"Yes, sir."

Top drew his sidearm and pointed it at the nearest controller. "Put it back. Go to manual override."

"I'm sorry. I cannot do that, sir."

He blew the man's head off.

"Next?" he said, looking around wildly.

84

"Merde! Merde! Merde!"

Froggy felt no need to translate: Shit was shit in any language. His squad had been flanked. Somehow, the bastards had gotten behind them. He couldn't see them yet, but they were coming. He could hear those fucking mini-tank engines revving as they approached, crashing through the underbrush. And the war cries of Xucuru Indians.

Indians? He thought *Stiletto's* firepower had killed most of them upriver. They were determined bastards, he'd grant them that much. They were either on Top's payroll or simply offended at the idea of uninvited guests in their pristine jungle. He hand-signaled Bass-man and Boomer to spread out and get turned around; they needed to get the heavy M-60 machine guns into position for an attack from their rear.

"Hold your fire until my signal," Froggy said into his lipmike when the squad was set.

It had all started when an arrow, five feet long and, no doubt poison-tipped, had thunked into a tree a foot above Froggy's head. He'd just looked down at his map. Now, he had seconds to reposition and fight a rear-guard action. And he needed to warn Stokely, who was up in a treehouse a hundred feet above his head.

"Stoke, this is Frogman."

"*Parlez,* Froggy."

"You have the hostage?"

"I've got him. He's alive, barely. Not mobile. I'm going to try and bring him down. We need to evac him to *Stiletto* pronto."

"Negative! Negative! We've got tangos down here, approaching from the rear. Tanks and Indians."

"Tanks and Indians?" Stoke said.

"You heard me, goddamn it!"

He let that go, thinking he'd misunderstood, and said, "Hawke's ten minutes out, Froggy. Brock should be even closer. We need to get a perimeter around this tree and hold it until they get here. I'm coming down alone."

Froggy waved his men to him with a circular hand signal, and they rapidly formed up around the fifteen-foot wide base of the tree. By the time Stokely stepped onto the platform and began his descent, the first wave of painted warriors was almost upon them in the heavy green stuff.

Froggy's guys still hadn't opened up.

Arrows whistled through the air, many of them aimed at Stokely. He was in plain sight on the slowly descending lift. He also had a perfect field of fire spread out below. He raised his CAR-15 and mowed down eight or nine war-painted archers who were stepping forward out of the thick green wall of undergrowth to launch their arrows.

"Fuck it, fire!" Froggy said, seeing Stokely's predicament. The M-60s erupted in heavy, thumping fire. Now the indiscriminate barrage of lead ripped up vegetation and flesh with equal ferocity. Backs to the river, every man was unloading ammo on the enemy. But still the warriors came out of the jungle. And now the Trolls approached, four of the lead tanks spitting lead from their rapid-fire machine guns. One of Froggy's men screamed and went down, cut in half by the vicious fire.

Stoke was halfway down the tree. He still had a good angle on the Trolls. He attached the grenade launcher and aimed at the nearest tank. Fired. Whoosh. A long trail of white smoke and the tank disintegrated in a massive ball of flame. Stoke fixed another RPG on his weapon's muzzle and took out a second tank. He was down to his last grenade. He heard fire from the river and looked over to see three canoes bearing Harry Brock and his squad of fourteen commandoes. They were firing their weapons at the tangos they could see in the jungle.

"*Merde diabolique!*" he heard Froggy cry in his headphones. "Unholy shit!"

"Froggy?" Stoke said. "What's up?"

"Zee fucking bridge, *mon ami*! Look over there!"

Armed troops poured out of the jungle compound barracks on the far side of the river. They formed up in a long column, ready to cross the bridge. In front of the troops, advancing slowly toward the bridge was a clanking monstrosity. It was a mechanized vehicle unlike anything Stoke had ever seen outside of a movie theater.

It was a tank, all right, a ridiculously oversized main battle tank, like an Abrams on major steroids, with what looked like two 120mm cannons. Eight-inch-diameter gun barrels were protruding from two turrets mounted on either side of an upright superstructure bolted to the chassis.

Stoke kept firing with his left hand, got his radio to his ear with his right. "*Stiletto! Stiletto!* Do you have GPS coordinates on the main bridge here at LZ Alpha? Copy?"

"Affirmative," Fire Control Officer Dylan Allegria responded.

"I need a missile locked on that target now, copy?"

"Uh, roger that, sir. We, uh, yes. PAM missile is locked on."

"Don't fire . . . I want this thing on the bridge when we blow it."

"What is the target, sir?"

"*War of the Worlds,* Dylan. I wish you could see this mechanical monster before you destroy it . . . ready . . . Fire now!"

Stoke held his breath. The mammoth war machine was halfway across the bridge now. There were maybe twenty tangos trotting right behind it and more right behind them.

The PAM missile's laser targeting device kept it on track after firing. It nosed over and hurtled toward the target. It struck a second later and the tank exploded violently. Through the black smoke and flame, Stoke could see the thing was not destroyed but certainly disabled. The men nearby on the bridge had been killed. Others retreated back down the road or faded into the jungle on the far side. Stoke didn't wait for the platform, he jumped the last few feet.

He opened up on the few remaining jungle warriors who'd managed to survive the withering fire laid down by the two M-60 machine guns. Most of the Xucurus and uniformed troops had fled back into the jungle. Regrouping. They'd be back as soon as they got their shit together for another attack.

"*Blue Goose, Blue Goose,* where the hell are you, Mick?" Stoke said into his radio.

"*Blue Goose,* Stokely. What can I do for you, mate?"

"Mick. I'm in a hot LZ with a critically injured hostage. I need to exfil him *now* and *Stiletto* is not an option. What's your location?"

"Five miles due east of the LZ. I can see smoke rising from the bridge."

"Mick, I know the river here is too narrow for your wingspan. It widens out upriver. But Ambrose won't survive a jungle trek to the plane."

"Ambrose is the hostage?"

"Affirmative."

"Who says it's too narrow, mate?"

"I do. Can't you see it? There's no way, Mick."

"I'll do a flyby and take a look."

"Watch out for bullets."

"HOLD YOUR FIRE!" Froggy yelled.

At that moment, Stoke saw Alex Hawke swimming rapidly toward shore, then clawing his way up the riverbank. His canoe had been blown into pieces by fire from the opposite shore. The remains now lay floating on the top of the water, drifting with the current downriver. Two of Hawke's four crewmen were swimming toward shore. Two other men were floating facedown.

"Stoke!" Hawke cried, running toward the little band at the base of the tree. "Where is he? Where the hell is Ambrose?"

"Up there," Stoke said. "Climb aboard the magic carpet and watch your step."

They swiftly rose to the top, Stokely pointing out all the scenic attractions of Top's jungle compound. Hawke jumped off and raced inside to find his friend.

"Ambrose, it's me," Hawke said leaning over him, his face grave and full of worry.

"I'm sorry," the girl named Caparina said. Her face was lovely in the dim light.

"Has he spoken?" Stokely asked her.

"You have to give him a minute," Caparina said. "He's coming around."

She was holding Ambrose's hand to her bosom, gazing at the old fellow. "I gave him something to counteract the truth drugs. Ten minutes ago. It should be—"

"Are you a doctor?" Hawke asked her.

"Just a night nurse from Manaus."

"Will he be in much pain?"

"I'm afraid he will."

"Alex," Ambrose said, his eyelids fluttering.

"I'm here. Come to take you home."

"Home," he sighed. His eyelids closed again.

"Ambrose. Please. You have to stay awake for a few minutes."

"So tired."

"The code, Ambrose. Remember the code. When and where?"

"Top's attack."

"Yes. Where is Top going to attack?"

"Washington."

"When?"

"The president. All of them. The government."

"When, Ambrose?"

"January the . . . twentieth."

"That's today," the beautiful girl said. "Holy Mother of Mary."

"Ambrose, listen carefully," Hawke said. "What time is the attack? Do you know?"

"Swear on the Bible. Don't let him," Ambrose croaked.

Hawke looked at Stokely and said, "Swear on a Bible? The Inauguration. They're going to attack the Amercian government on the steps of the Capitol. What time is it?"

"Almost noon, boss. I don't know how much time we've got."

Hawke shook his head and put a gentle hand on Congreve's shoulder. "Ambrose. The code, what is it?"

"The code."

"Yes. What is the code? Those numbers we worked so hard on? That bloody book?"

Ambrose smiled weakly, "The da Zimmermann code?"

"Yes, Ambrose. That's it."

"Numbers make letters, Alex. Will of Allah. Da Vinci."

"What?" Hawke said, his mind racing, looking at Stoke for help.

"Will of Allah," Stoke said. "That sounds like a password. So what's Da Vinci got to do with it?"

Ambrose nodded.

"He shouldn't talk anymore," Caparina said, looking at Hawke.

Stoke grabbed Hawke's arm. "We got to go, boss. Caparina will take good care of him till we get back. Let's go."

"I want him out of here. Now. *Stiletto*'s not even close! Where the hell is that seaplane?"

Stoke shook his head and handed Hawke his radio.

"Mick! It's Hawke. Copy?"

"Copy, Hawke."

"Can you land that bloody thing? Here? Now? I'm about to lose him!"

"No worries, sir. I'll splash sideways."

"Sideways?"

"Little trick I learned in the bush. I'm coming in now."

Hawke looked at Caparina. "You stay with him. Someone's coming."

HAWKE AND STOKELY stepped onto the platform and began their descent. For the moment, Froggy's men seemed to have stanched the flow of troops. A few were still using the bridge, climbing over the blown tank. There'd been a brief effort to maneuver sponson pontoons across the river, but the M-60s were discouraging a lot of that kind of activity.

They heard a loud engine roar to the right, just above the bridge. The *Blue Goose* swept in low through the thick black smoke, just a few feet above the smoldering tank hulk on the bridge. Mick Hocking's wingtips were catching clumps of foliage on either side of the river. For a moment, both men thought he'd surely catch a wing and go down.

He managed to keep the the *Goose* on course, God alone knew how, and flared up for a landing. At the last possible moment, Mick lowered one flap and spun the big plane a few degrees on its axis. The slight angle was enough to clear the heavily wooded banks. The *Blue Goose* splashed down on the river.

It came to a very quick stop. Mick opened the door and climbed down onto the float, a machine gun cradled in one arm. He swung an anchor, heaving the anchor line into the trees, and started hauling the airplane close to the bank.

"Cover that seaplane!" Stoke shouted in his radio. "Form up! Don't let anyone near it." Hawke was reassured by the sight of two men with M-60 heavy machine guns racing along the bank, headed for the waiting seaplane. There was sporadic gunfire from the bridge and the M-60s opened up, silencing it.

Froggy was at the bottom of the tree, waiting for them.

"Froggy," Hawke said to the little Frenchman, as he and Stoke stepped off the platform.

"Mon ami," Froggy said to Hawke, bowing from the

waist. Hawke smiled and squeezed his old comrade's shoulder.

"Froggy, get two men up there immediately. Ambrose is badly hurt. Tell your men to be very careful bringing him down. Soon as he's safely loaded inside the plane, tell Hocking to fly back downriver to *Stiletto* and get him to sick bay."

"It is done, Monsieur Hawke," Froggy said, already on the radio to two of the biggest guys he had.

"Let me borrow that satphone, Froggy," Hawke said when he signed off. "We might need it."

The Frenchman handed it over.

"We've got ten minutes, Stoke," Hawke said. "Which one of those trees is the antenna?"

"That one there," Froggy said. "Come along, *mes amis,* we're going to blow it."

"Timber," Hawke said with a wry smile, racing toward the fake tree.

85

Jack McAtee was ready. The day was cloudy and cold. This was an historic occasion and the president revered history. The Chief Justice was already in place standing beside the George Washington Inaugural Bible. In a few moments, McAtee would place his left hand on it, exactly where Washington had placed his, and be sworn in. It was the moment he most cherished. It was living history, McAtee thought, looking out over the throngs who gathered under the trees.

On April 30, 1789, General George Washington arrived at Federal Hall in lower Manhattan for the very first presidential inauguration. He discovered that there was no Bible present. Someone recalled seeing a suitable Bible at St. John's Lodge, a few hundred feet down the road, and went in search of it. Returning, he placed the Masonic Bible on a red velvet cushion. The book was opened to the pages between Genesis 49 and 50. Washington placed his left hand upon the Bible and the first oath of office was administered.

Washington had added the words, "So help me

God," and then bent and kissed the book. Shortly afterward, a silk page was placed inside to mark the precise location where Washington had rested his hand. An engraved portrait of Washington was added, facing the existing one of King George II. And, since the Bible was from a fraternal lodge and not one of New York's twenty-two churches, it was decided the book would be used for all future inaugurations. Washington liked the fact that no specific church was being endorsed.

The two-hundred-year-old Washington Inaugural Bible was still used every four years. When not in use, the historic volume was kept under lock and key right where Washington's men had found it. No one was allowed to touch it without wearing gloves. It sat in an undistinguished room at the back of St. John's Lodge in lower Manhattan.

THE PRESIDENT was waiting at the top of the Capitol steps. The Chief Justice of the United States, Howard L. Clark, stood at the bottom beside the opened Washington Bible. The First Lady, McAtee's wife, Lynn, was standing at his side, greeting old friends with a warm smile and trying to hide the fact that she would rather be anywhere else on earth than the Inaugural platform. Her hands were trembling so badly, she could hardly hold on to the small red leather family Bible she always brought along when they flew or on important occasions.

Secret Service agents were everywhere, eyes darting from side to side. Amored vehicles and bomb disposal trucks had tried, unsuccessfully, to park unnoticed at the foot of the podium. She still believed her husband was in imminent danger. She saw Secretary de los Reyes, who smiled at her, knowing the First Lady was just as concerned about the events of the day as she was herself.

Even now, she saw with mounting anxiety, there was some kind of skirmish going on over by the Grant Memorial. Protesters were scattering, being moved along by the Secret Service Suburban moving slowly through the crowd. At least, she hoped it was something as benign as unruly protesters. And not the thing she most feared on this grey and threatening day.

"HOW THE HELL did you find this bloody thing?" Hawke asked Froggy, who was busily wiring satchels of Semtex to the base of one of countless and indistinguishable two-hundred-foot-high behemoths. The phony tree was twenty feet in diameter at the base. Cables, disguised as roots, ran underground in every direction. Hawke had to concede that there was a bit of genius about the thing.

"Frogs always see the trees, not the forest, *monsieur,*" Froggy said.

"Which way will it fall?" Stoke asked.

"Toward the river," the Frogman said, twisting the timer. "Okay, charges set! One minute! Clear! Clear!"

Everyone ran like hell for the safety of the surrounding trees.

"YOU IDIOT!" Top screamed at the only controller he had not yet shot. He was plainly enraged now. Most of his assets had been compromised by the Secret Service. One of his few remaining options was the explosive-packed Chevrolet War Wagon he'd sent plowing through the crowd toward the Inaugural stand.

But Top watched in disbelief as, at the last minute, a man had leaped aboard the Suburban and blinded the camera lens. Despite the controller's efforts to shake the man off with violent maneuvers, he was still there.

With the help of a pistol to the temple, he'd just convinced Khan to at least put his one remaining controllable asset back under manual control. If he could move the Suburban only a thousand yards nearer to the presidential podium, there was still hope. Thousands would die in the initial blast, even at this distance. But if he could get closer, the government of the United States would cease to exist.

"Just go east," Khan said quietly, punching in the manual override code. Top pushed the controller aside and grabbed the joystick.

"I can't see a thing!" Top cried. Whoever was atop the truck still had the lens covered.

"It doesn't matter," Khan said. "The further east you can move the asset, the better chance you have of killing the president and everyone on the podium."

The clock above them continued to roll down inexorably toward noon.

They had less than ten minutes.

"East, you idiot!" Khan screamed in Top's ear. "Go east!"

Top nudged the joystick and the Suburban started moving again, blind. He had retained a mental image of the truck's location relative to the podium. Still, it seemed impossible.

But Top was a master at this. He summoned all of his skills, moving the blinded asset on instinct alone. There had been human error, but it had not been his. His impossible dream could still come true.

Under my thumb, he thought, power singing along with the Stones in his brain as he moved the joystick.

THE PRESIDENT and Mrs. McAtee were ready to begin their descent of the Capitol steps. At the bottom, Chief Justice Howard Clark was waiting, his long black robes whipping about in the stiff breeze. There was a roar from the crowd as the president turned and waved at the mass of people come to witness this historic event. The Marine Band played the first notes of a stirring martial tune. The president put his arm around his wife. It was almost time. The U.S. Marine Band, called the President's Own, in their scarlet jackets, played on, a rousing Sousa march that McAtee loved.

So far, so good, the president thought.

It looked like he'd made the right decision after all. History would record that Jack McAtee had stood his ground.

86

The tree rose up from the ground, rising like an Atlas rocket from the pad, majestic, slowly gathering momentum. The blast had lifted it upward, intact, straight up for what felt like a long second, and then it pitched forward, falling in slow motion toward the river and landing with a resounding crash on the jungle floor.

"Allez-oop!" someone shouted joyfully from behind the trees. It had to be Froggy.

Thick, acrid smoke and sharp licks of fire poured forth from the fresh wound in the ground. Hawke and Stokely edged forward to inspect the damage. Exposed cables sizzled and snapped, still carrying electricity. There was a twisted spaghetti of wire and thick conduit still running from the hollow of the fallen tree and disappearing down inside the six-foot hole left by the blast.

"Shit," Stoke said. "We flattened their antenna, but I'm guessing they're still up and running down there."

Hawke was on the radio, looking down into the

hole. He heard shouts and some small-arms fire below. At least a few people in the Tomb were still alive.

"*Stiletto,* this is Hawke. I need a PAM missile at my location. Now. You have my GPS coordinates?"

"Aye, sir, uh . . ." the fire control officer responded nervously. "Uh, you say you want this one at your exact GPS location?"

"Affirmative. I say again, right on top of my bleeding head," Hawke said, "Fire it now, Dylan!"

"That's affirmative. Launching PAM now, sir."

"Get back! On the ground!" Stoke shouted. "Incoming!"

"Fire in the hole!" Froggy shouted, diving for cover.

THE PRESIDENT AND the First Lady, arm in arm, began their slow and careful descent of the steps leading down to the podium. Their smiles were radiant. Cheers and applause erupted from those nearby and from the thousands gathered on the west side of the Capitol. Not a few among them were holding their breath. Everyone pressed forward, hoping for a better view.

THE GROUND SHOOK from the explosion of the PAM missile deep in Top's underground bunker. After the blinding white flash, Hawke and Stokely again ran toward the hole. It was bigger now, maybe eight feet in diameter. Smoke was pouring out, but there was light down there. Electric light.

"Emergency generators," Hawke said, slinging a machine gun over his shoulder. "Froggy, pick two men and come with us. We're going down."

Stoke had secured a line to a nearby tree. He dropped the bitter end into the smoke-filled hole.

"Me first," Hawke said, and before anyone could say anything, he disappeared, grasping the line. Stokely followed, then Froggy, then the two machine gunners, Bassman and Boomer.

Hawke's feet hit the floor and he rolled left. He leapt to his feet and secured the room with his eyes. He saw Stoke land and go right. Then Froggy and the two gunners. There were still some tangos alive, getting to their feet amidst the smoke and rubble. Froggy and his two gunners dispatched them before they could get a shot off.

The bunker communications room was devastated. Broken bodies lay slumped over what had been control consoles. Small electrical fires were still burning everywhere and there was the familiar roast pork stench of burned flesh in everyone's nostrils.

A small, bespectacled man in charred robes came out of the smoke, a curved knife raised above his head. Hawke had seen enough pictures to recognize Abu Khan. But the man was headed for Stokely.

Stoke raised his hand to ward off the man's blow, but the tip of the blade sliced Stoke's forearm.

"This is sacred ground, infidel," Khan said, shrinking back but raising his blade again. "We are divine martyrs!"

Stoke looked at him and smiled. "Warm up the virgins," he said.

Hawke came at Khan from behind, got one arm around his throat, and jammed the muzzle of his weapon to the man's temple.

"Welcome to paradise, Khan," Hawke said. "Drop the knife. You have five seconds to tell me what I need to know."

"I don't know what you—don't kill me!"

"Hawke, over there!" Stoke shouted. "There's a monitor still up and running! Washington! Shit, that's the Inauguration!"

Hawke looked over at the only working monitor. A perfect digital live feed of the ceremony now taking place on the podium. Chief Justice Clark stood waiting for the president.

The president and his wife were descending the steps.

"Tell me Dr. Khan," Hawke said quietly in the man's ear, "how terror feels at the wrong end of the gun."

The man refused to speak.

Hawke stared at the monitor. There was something he wasn't seeing. Something he was missing. What? What the bloody hell was it? Something Ambrose had said . . . *Swear on the Bible . . . don't let him.*

"Tell me what you did to the Bible!" Hawke screamed at Khan. "Or die now!"

Khan moaned, "A paper-thin sheet of high explosive. Heat and pressure sensitive. When he places his left hand on it . . ."

"Fuck!" Stoke shouted. "Where's Top? We gotta do something!" Stoke had searched the room for the giant, but he was nowhere to be found. Dead most likely, Stoke thought, buried under all the rubble.

Hawke was already on the sat phone, punching in Conch's secure number. He kept his left hand around

Kahn's throat, increasing pressure every time the man moved.

"Conch," he said when he heard her voice. "Don't let the president touch the Bible!"

On the monitor, Alex Hawke could actually see Secretary de los Reyes's face change as she listened to what he told her. A fleeting look of horror crossed it, and then she was smiling again, talking to the handsome young Marine sentry standing right besider her.

The Marine moved quickly.

"PLEASE RAISE YOUR right hand and repeat after me . . ." the Chief Justice said. The president raised his right hand and reached out to place his left hand on the Washington Bible.

Suddenly, a young Marine appeared at his side, putting a firm white gloved hand on the president's forearm. It happened very quickly. The Marine deftly lifted the old Bible from the bookstand and handed it to a burly Secret Service agent standing just behind him. The agent handed the Marine another Bible, a small red leather one just passed to him by the First Lady, and the Marine placed her Bible upon the bookstand.

Hawke was so transfixed by the scene on the monitor that he was barely aware of his fingers tightening around Khan's scrawny neck. At the edge of the frame, he saw one of the president's men hand the Inaugural Bible to another man waiting beneath the podium. The man was standing atop the roof of a bomb disposal truck . . . Hawke looked down, surprised to see Khan dead at his feet.

"Mr. President, are you ready to take the oath?" the Chief Justice asked, as Hawke's eyes returned to the screen.

"I am," the president responded.

The president placed his left hand on the small Bible, which had now been opened to Genesis, and raised his right hand. He was smiling at his wife, whispering something to her.

"I, John J. McAtee, do solemnly swear . . ." Clark began, leading the president through the oath.

"I, John J. Mc Atee, do solemnly swear . . ."

The smoke had now cleared somewhat and Hawke was startled to see the shadowy figure of a man in a perforated bowler hat seated before the only remaining live control monitor. He was maniacally manipulating the joystick. On his screen, the president was visible on the platform. He seemed to be looking off to his right. Something was going on. Agents were moving quickly toward the president. Hawke had dared to breathe a sigh of relief, but now he saw that something was still terribly wrong.

"Top!" Hawke cried, but the man did not turn around. He had his right hand on a joystick, twisting it right and left while he tapped at a keyboard with his left. Below the podium, the crowd parted as if a knife were slicing it in two. Something, Hawke could not see what, was causing a panic; people were running for their lives.

Hawke raced toward the giant, hairless creature who had abused Congreve so viciously. Hawke could still remember the pain the man had inflicted on his own body. But it was nothing compared to the hurt and pain

he'd seen in Ambrose Congreve's eyes. That, he would
never forget.

"Top," Hawke said again, stepping directly behind
the terrorist who had tortured them both so mercilessly.
He bent and whispered in the man's ear.

"I'm back."

"Lord Hawke," Top said evenly, his eyes riveted on
the screen above. The digital clock read 11:57. Three
minutes left. "You are just in time to witness America's
death throes. The Bible was just an hors d'oeuvre. Take
a seat for the main course, Lord Hawke."

THE PRESIDENT'S WORDS were echoing in the
small room, coming through the remaining speakers
above the control panel.

"That I will faithfully execute the office of president
of the United States . . . and will to the best of my ability . . ." the president said.

He paused, seeing some movement out of the corner
of his eye. The Secret Service agents on the platform
were speaking into their sleeves, edging toward him . . .

HAWKE HEARD CONCH'S tinny voice coming
from the sat phone. He wanted to say something to her.
Anything. But there was no time. And he really had no
idea what to tell her.

HAWKE'S LEFT HAND grabbed the lank ponytail
and tore the man's head back. With his right, he put the
naked blade of his assault knife up under Top's chin.

"You know what I think, Muhammad?" Hawke said,

piercing the fleshy skin round the neck. "I think you are a coward. I saw it in your eyes that night. You like to inflict pain, but you cannot endure it. Am I right?"

"Too late for this," Top said through gritted teeth. "The blow for Allah is about to be struck. No one can stop it now."

"Wrong answer!" Hawke screamed, inserting the point of the blade inside the man's nostril.

"I have the termination code," Hawke said. "I want you to enter it now!"

Top laughed out loud.

Hawke tightened his left-hand grip, feeling the tendons compress and the voice box start to collapse. He added pressure with the knife, and blood started to trickle from the man's nose.

"I've got two whole bloody minutes left," Hawke said, withdrawing the knife from the nostril. He put the point beside the bridge of the man's nose, inserting the point into the corner of his right eye. Blood spurted onto the control desk.

"No!" Top screamed, clenching the joystick.

"First the right eye, then the left," Hawke said. "You won't even see the second one land in your lap.

"*Allahu Akbar!*" Top shouted. "I'm ready to die."

"Good. We'll start the process here . . ."

"God! No! Stop!"

"I will. Just enter your bloody password. Now!"

Top's trembling left hand typed out the phrase "*Save the fire.*" And the words "Access granted" appeared on the screen.

"Good," Hawke said. "Now we'll enter the code."

"You don't have the fucking code."

"Trust me. Will of Allah. Type!"

Hawke watched as the man's trembling fingers began to enter the letters as he spoke them aloud.

"Access denied" appeared.

"Any other ideas?" Top croaked, a sick smile on his compressed lips. The clock had scrolled down to 11:58.

Hawke looked at him for a second and said, "Backwards. Enter the fucking thing backwards."

"H-A-L-L-A-F-O-L-L-I-W," Top entered.

"Access granted."

Will of Allah. Backwards. Da Vinci, Hawke had remembered, wrote backwards so that his words could only be read by looking at them in a mirror. Ambrose had given him what he needed. All he had to do was use it.

"Now shut this fucking thing down," Hawke said, his voice low and full of menace.

Top moved his bloody finger across the keyboard, punching in a sequence of letters and numbers.

"TERMINATION. TERMINATION."

Those two words appeared on the control screen in a continuous scroll.

The numbers on the clock had stopped at 11:59. The weapons that had been recently moved into the American capital were instantly rendered inert and useless. Even the unmanned submarine now circling in the Tidal Basin, under the watchful eye of Thomas Jefferson, shut itself down. It rolled over once, belly-up, and then banked swiftly into the muck below.

Hawke raised his eyes once more to the monitor.

The president stood his ground as the agents moved in to surround him at the podium. He had the look of a man who wasn't going anywhere.

"AND WILL, to the best of my ability," the president said, concluding the oath of office, "Preserve, protect, and defend the Constitution of the United States . . . So help me God."

THE MARINE BAND struck up "Hail to the Chief" as the cannons out on the lawn commenced firing the twenty-one-gun salute.

Hawke, his eyes on the scene being played out in Washington, held the man's head still as he drove his blade swiftly and deep into his brain.

"This is for Ambrose Congreve," Hawke said.

Allah's will was done.

EPILOGUE

W hile England slept, a soft blanket of snow had covered the countryside. The unexpected snowfall had continued all the next day. Surprise made it all the more beautiful. For a few brief moments, the sun came out from behind a cloud. It was low in the sky, about to slip behind the far western hills. Sunlight painted the gently rolling hills in shades of rosy gold and pink. The twisting road ahead was black and glistening.

It was pleasantly warm in the old Locomotive, and Conch was curled against the Bentley's worn leather front seat, drowsy from her hectic schedule and the long-delayed flight from Houston. Hawke reached over and switched on the dashboard radio. The dial began to glow, and a song was playing, sweet and slow, faint in memory.

"It's so lovely, Alex," Conch sighed, her eyes half opened. "I've never seen the countryside like this."

"England hasn't had snow like this in decades."

"So kind of Ambrose and Diana to invite me to their party. And of you to come pick me up at the plane."

"Well, I was in the neighborhood," Hawke said, smiling.

"How is he doing, Alex? Ambrose?"

"It's been a painful recovery. But he's walking again. He uses a cane now. Terribly embarrassed about it, but I keep telling him the swagger stick looks dashing."

She smiled.

He looked over at her. "I'm glad to see you, kid."

"Me, too. Thanks."

"Do you want to sleep? We've got an hour or so before we arrive at Brixden House."

"I want to talk, Alex. Shh—stop. Don't worry, it's not about us. I want to tell you about the funeral down in Texas."

"Homer's funeral."

"Yes, I'm glad I went. It was small, just local people, and very . . . moving. Homer was a much-loved soul in that little town. Sheriff Dixon said a few words before I spoke. You remember—that wonderful man you met in Key West."

"Kind of man who makes you believe in cowboys again."

"That's him. He talked about the law, mostly. How sacred it was in his life; how deeply he believed in it. How people have to respect it. He said Homer had given his life for something far more noble than a line drawn in the sand."

"Yes. How is it down there now, on the border?"

"Better, I guess. Having the Guard so visible has helped a lot. The Mexican government is finally making an effort."

"Arresting terrorists, so I hear."

"It's a start. The Texas Sheriffs Association has asked Dixon to head up a new joint border security unit. He'll be good at it."

"I still find it absolutely terrifying, Conch, that somehow, in parts of America, borders have become politically incorrect," Hawke said.

"I'm afraid you're right."

"I just don't understand it, Conch. Without borders, we've got nothing."

"Nothing but chaos."

"Whatever happened to simply defending your homeland? Whatever happened to, 'We shall fight on the beaches . . . we shall fight in the hills'? "

"It's frightening. I feel like America's on the verge of losing it, Alex."

"I hope Jack McAtee doesn't share that view."

"No, he's boundlessly optimistic. Full of confidence that we will ride out the storm. And so am I. Except when I spend time on that border . . ."

"What we just had was a close call. But I hope there was also a big wake-up call here, Conch. You had a chance to have an entire continent as your ally. But you either neglected them or meddled dangerously in their internal affairs. By not treating them as equals, you frittered away a lot of enormously valuable friendships and—"

Hawke glanced sideways at her. Her head resting against the seat, she was sound asleep.

So much for his speech-making ability.

HALF AN HOUR later, Hawke had his headlamps on as he turned off the Taplow Common Road and drove through the gates of Brixden House. He slowed, idling along the broad curving drive, while Conch did something to her makeup in the lighted vanity mirror.

There were untold acres of formal parkland, bare orchards, and evergreen gardens, all now covered with soft, wet snow. The house, when they finally caught sight of it in the distance, was imposing. The classic Italianate mansion stood atop great chalk cliffs overlooking a bend in the Thames below. It looked as though the entire house was alight, every room, and there was a hazy orange glow from every window.

As he pulled up to the porte cochere, he saw the government cars that had been following at a discreet distance pull into the car park. Agents hopped out and began talking into their sleeves the way they do. A valet took the Bentley at the covered entrance, and they made their way into the Great Hall. A fire was roaring at the far end of the room and to the left of the fireplace hung the famous John Singer Sargent painting of Lady Diana Mars's great-grandmother.

There was a festive mood in the room and it continued throughout the house as they went in search of the host and hostess. Ambrose had been very excited about this soiree when he'd followed up Hawke's engraved invitation with a telephone call. Hawke had a pretty good idea of what Ambrose Congreve was up to, but he didn't share any of that with Conch. He didn't want her disappointed in the event he was mistaken.

Hawke took two flutes of champagne from a liveried footman and asked where he could find Chief Inspector Congreve.

"He and Lady Mars are in the library, sir," the man said. "I believe there's going to be music in a few moments."

"Yes, sorry. Our plane was late," Hawke said.

Hawke and Conch made their way through the glittering crowd and saw Ambrose and Diana standing by the far windows overlooking the garden. A small string quartet was tuning up, and the host was beaming at all and sundry, now crowding round the happy couple. Alex caught Ambrose's eye and each man raised a glass to the other.

It was too crowded to get any closer to the hosts, so Alex took Conch's arm and steered her toward a deserted nook, a bay window. Beyond the windows, snow had started falling again. Alex took Conch's hand as Ambrose moved in front of the seated musicians.

"My dear friends," Ambrose said, taking the microphone handed him by one of the orchestra, "Diana and I are so glad that you could all be with us tonight. Sorry about the dreadful weather, but isn't it marvelous?"

There was laughter and much applause.

"I've asked our wonderful orchestra to play a very special song for you tonight, by the French composer, Hector Berlioz. It's my favorite piece and, not surprisingly, it has an intriguing story behind it. A love story, in fact.

"Our story takes place in Paris in 1832. Berlioz is despondent. He has fallen madly in love with Harriet Smithson, a beautiful English actress playing Ophelia in a local production of *Hamlet*. Berlioz has sent her dozens of love letters and countless proposals of marriage, but Harriet leaves Paris without responding.

"On the verge of madness, Berlioz composes a symphony inspired by his love for the actress. As it happens, on the night of the premiere, Harriet Smithson has just returned from London to Paris. Berlioz has a friend persuade her to attend. Just as the orchestra is about to play, the composer takes the stage and announces that his new symphony was written as a proposal of marriage. And, that his intended was seated in the first row center. The orchestra then played the *Symphonie Fantastique*. You will now hear the Berlioz symphony, played by our splendid musicians. Gentlemen? If you please?"

Congreve stepped aside, and the strings began to play the beautiful first movement of the symphony, the strings soaring with emotion toward the end. When they finished, everyone in the library fell silent, waiting for Ambrose Congreve to speak.

When he moved in front of the musicians again, his eyes were glistening. Hawke, too, was full of emotion, watching his oldest and dearest friend gathering himself, with some difficulty, to speak.

"Some of you may be curious about Miss Smithson's response to Hector Berlioz's symphonic proposal. Well, I am very happy to tell you all that Harriet Smithson said yes."

The audience clapped loudly.

"I think Monsieur Berlioz was on to something, don't you all agree?" Ambrose said, his voice breaking and his eyes alight.

The guests exploded. Everyone in the room, especially Alex Hawke, began looking from Ambrose to Diana with faces full of expectant delight.

Ambrose looked at Diana across the small dance floor, saw her eyes shining, and went toward her, moving a little slowly because of his cane.

When he was at last facing her, he reached out and took her hand. Then he bowed his head near hers and they whispered something into each other's ear.

Ambrose Congreve turned and faced all of his old friends. They were all clapping and cheering loudly now, and Congreve's face was shining with tears.

"She said . . . *yes*!"